CRITICAL PRAISE FOR LYNDA CURNYN'S DEBUT NOVEL, *CONFESSIONS OF AN EX-GIRLFRIEND*:

"First-time novelist Curnyn pens an easy, breezy first novel that's part *Sex and the City* with more heart and part Bridget Jones with less booze."

—*Publishers Weekly*

"A diverse cast of engaging, occasionally offbeat characters, the hilarious sayings attributed to them, and a fast-paced style facilitated by Emma's pithy sound-bite 'confessions' add to the fun in a lively Manhattan-set story..."

—*Library Journal*

"Readers will eagerly turn the pages..."

—*Booklist*

"Fabulous fun. The perfect antidote for the break-up blues."
—Sarah Mlynowski, author of *Milkrun*

"...absolutely hilarious secondary characters. They alone are worth the cover price."

—*Romantic Times*

"Lynda Curnyn has written a novel featuring a heroine that most people will enjoy reading about and even sympathize with her intense angst. *Confessions of an Ex-Girlfriend* is part comedy, but mostly a serious, delightful look at people at a painful point in their lives."

—Bookbrowser.com

"Well written, with catchy dialogue and heartfelt sincerity."
—*Rendezvous*

For Alexandra and Samantha

Dream big, little girls!

Engaging Men

Lynda Curnyn

**RED
DRESS
I N K**™

First edition May 2003

ENGAGING MEN

A Red Dress Ink novel

ISBN 0-373-25028-2

© 2003 by Lynda Curnyn.

Visit Red Dress Ink at www.reddressink.com

Printed in U.S.A.

ACKNOWLEDGMENTS

A *big* thank-you to all who inspired and supported me
during the writing of this book:

My family, especially my wise and beautiful mother,
who always knows what to say, just when I need to hear it.

My wonderful editor, Joan Marlow Golan,
for her insightful editorial expertise,
her amazing support and most of all, her TLC.

All the talented people behind Red Dress Ink,
especially Margaret Marbury, senior editor extraordinaire
and dear friend. Laura Morris, Margie Miller, Tara Kelly
and RDI's own engaging man, Craig Swinwood.

All my wonderful friends, especially Linda Guidi,
for *always* listening (even when I don't...).
Stacey Kamel, for bringing on the laughter.
Julie Ann Coney, for that fab photo of me and the facts on
adoptive search. Anne Canadeo, for the Tight-Lid Theory
that inspired this book, and her sage writing advice.
Jennifer Bernstein, Lisa Sklar and Farrin Jacobs, for keeping
me from wigging out. Sarah Mlynowski, for always telling
me how fabulous I am and for, umm, lending me her
boyfriend (it's not what you think...).

Elizabeth Irene, who told me just what it takes to make it
as an actor in this town. Michael Scotto di Carlo
(aka Motorcycle) and Katrina Lorne for the cool Web site.
Pam Spengler-Jaffee, for sharing her PR savvy, as well as
margaritas and the post-book Elton and Billy serenade.

And let us not forget all the ex-boyfriends
(you know who you are...) who inadvertently inspired me
to write this book, by sheer virtue of the fact that
none of them ever actually got around to proposing.

1

Tight lids and other theories of male behavior.

It started with a message on my answering machine.

"Guess who's getting married?" came a voice I knew all too well.

It was Josh. My ex-boyfriend. Turned someone else's fiancé. Not that I'd ever wanted to marry Josh, who suffered from an aversion to dental floss. "Did prehistoric man floss?" he would argue. "Is prehistoric man still around?" I argued back. We lasted only six months, then I told him I couldn't see myself at sixty-five, making sure he took his teeth out at bedtime every night. "Okay, okay. I'll *floss,*" he'd replied. But it was too late. The romance was gone.

Now he was getting married. To someone he'd met not three months after we had broken up four years ago. And he wasn't the first ex-boyfriend to go this route. Randy, the boyfriend before Josh, was whistling "The Wedding March" a mere six *weeks* after we had tearfully said our goodbyes. Then there was Vincent, my first love—he'd been married for nearly a *decade.* According to my mother—who lived within shouting distance of his mother in Marine Park, Brooklyn, and never failed to keep me updated—Vincent and his wife were already on their *third* kid.

One ex gets married, a girl can laugh it off. Two begins a nervous twitter. But three? *Three?*

A girl starts to take it personally. I mean, what was it about me that didn't incite men to plunk down large sums of money in the name of eternal love?

"It's the tight-lid dilemma," my friend Michelle said when I expressed my despair at sending another man to the altar without me.

"Tight lid?" I asked, awaiting some pearl of wisdom that might turn my world upright again. After all, in the time it had taken me to get a four-year degree in business administration that I no longer made use of, Michelle, who'd grown up three blocks away from me in Marine Park, had gotten a husband, a house and a diamond the size of New Jersey.

"You know the scenario," she continued. "You struggle for a good while trying to open a jar and the lid won't budge. But sure enough, the next person you hand that jar to pops the lid off, no problem. I mean, you don't really think Jennifer Aniston, cute haircut aside, would have landed Brad Pitt without the Gwyneth factor, do you? Then there's me and Frankie, of course," she continued, referring to her husband of seven years, whom she had snagged soon after his devastating breakup with Rosanna Cuzio, the prom queen of our high school.

I couldn't deny the pattern, once Michelle had laid it out so neatly before me. Clearly I had been instrumental in warming Josh, Randy and Vincent up for the next girl to come along and slap with a wedding vow. Gosh, I should have at least been maid of honor for my efforts.

Instead, I was nothing but the ex-girlfriend who might or might not get invited to the wedding, depending on how secure the bride felt about her future husband.

Suddenly I looked at Kirk, my current boyfriend, with new eyes. We had been together a year and eight months, by far the record for me since my three-year stint with Randy. We had become quite a cozy little couple, Kirk and I. I even got party invitations addressed to both of us—that's how serious everyone thought we were. The question was: Would Kirk be inviting me to his wedding someday or...?

"Kirk...sweetie," I said, as we lay in bed together that night, a flickering blue screen before us and the prospect of sex lingering like an unasked question in the air.

"Uh-huh," he said, not removing his gaze from the cop show that apparently had him enraptured.

"Your last girlfriend...Susan?"

"Yeah?" he said, glancing at me with trepidation. Clearly he saw in the making one of those "relationship talks" men dread.

"You guys went out a long time, right? What was it, two years?"

"Three and a half," he said with a shudder that made me swallow with fear. Apparently I was heading for rough waters.

Still I plunged on. "And you guys never talked, um, about...marriage?"

He laughed. "Are you kidding me? That's what broke us up. She gave me the old ultimatum—we get married or we're through." He snorted. "Needless to say, I chose door number two."

Aha. Relief filled me and I snuggled closer to Kirk, allowing him to sink back into his vegetative state as the cops on TV slapped cuffs on some unsuspecting first offender.

If Susan was the lid loosener, that could mean only one thing: I could pop this guy wide open. Hell, I could be married within the year.

The next day, I met my best friend, Grace, for a celebratory lunch, which was always an event as Grace, with her high-powered career and high-maintenance boyfriend, barely had time to get together at all anymore. As a concession to her hectic lifestyle, we met at a restaurant two blocks from her office on E. 54th Street and Park Avenue. Of course, Grace didn't know I was celebrating until I clinked my water glass into hers and said, "Congratulate me. I'm getting married."

"What?" Grace said, her blue-gray eyes bulging in disbelief. Her gaze immediately fell to the ring finger of my left hand, which, naturally, was bare.

"Not *now.* But someday."

She rolled her eyes, sniffed and said with her usual irony, "Congratulations."

Leave it to Grace to laugh in the face of being thirty-three without a wedding band on her finger. She is the strongest, most independent person I know. Not only does she always manage to keep a killer boyfriend on hand, she has a killer job as a product manager for Roxanne Dubrow Cosmetics. Yes, *that* Roxanne Dubrow. The one you have to hike all the way to Saks Fifth Avenue for. Grace briefly dated my brother Sonny when we were in junior high, but we didn't really bond until she saved my life on the playground of Marine Park Junior High. I was about to get my head slammed into the concrete by some giant bully of a girl named Nancy, who seemed determined to hurt me just because I was a good fifty pounds lighter than she was. Grace stepped in, tall and blond and strong, and told Nancy to take a hike. Everyone, even Nancy, was afraid of Grace. I was in awe of her. Even more so when she adopted me as her new best friend, despite the fact that I was in eighth grade and she in ninth. Her posse of ninth-grade girlfriends was not happy to have me tagging along. But Grace wouldn't have it otherwise.

And here we were, still friends. The only two from the old neighborhood who had escaped unscathed, without marrying some thick-necked thug named Sal and popping out babies on an annual basis. Of course, Grace's parents had dragged her away from the neighborhood to Long Island when she turned sixteen, hoping suburbia would save her from the cigarettes and boys and bad behavior to which she had taken and in which I couldn't wait to indulge, myself. But we still spent our summers together. In fact, I felt a bit like a Fresh Air Fund kid, the way my parents shipped me off come June. Then Grace moved into the city right after college, and I followed a year later. She was the sister I'd never had, and my mother had even dubbed her an honorary member of our family.

"Don't you ever worry, Grace? That you'll wind up alone?" I asked now, searching her face for some sign of vulnerability.

She shrugged. "A woman in this city can have everything she wants. If she plays her cards right."

Easy for Grace to say. Tall, voluptuous, with chin-length, tousled blond hair and perfectly sculpted features, she was beautiful. While I...I had always been "little Angie DiFranco"—and still was—five foot four with a head of wavy black hair that defied all styling products, and thighs that threatened to turn into my mother's any day now. I sighed. It suddenly occurred to me that if I didn't marry Kirk, I didn't know what would become of me.

"What about you and Drew?" I asked now, wondering if Grace had been contemplating her current beau as a future husband. "Do you ever think about...you know?"

"Of course," Grace said. "Every girl thinks about it."

I felt relieved. At least I wasn't the only thirtysomething unmarried hysteric. And Grace and Drew had been dating barely a year—at least eight months *less* than Kirk and I.

"But it's not everything," she said with a shrug.

Grace was right, I realized the next day as I headed for work. Marriage wasn't everything. I had so much going on right now, it was practically a nonissue. I was an actor, and at the moment a working actor, which was really something. Granted my steady gig was *Rise and Shine,* a children's exercise program on cable access, but it was good experience in front of a camera, at least according to an agent I had spoken to, who refused to take me on until I had experience outside of the numerous off-off Broadway shows I'd done.

But as I slid into the yellow leotard and baby-blue tights that were my lot as the show's co-host, I wondered, for about the hundredth time, what, exactly, my résumé would say about me, now that I had spent six months leaping and stretching with a group of six-year-olds.

"Hey, Colin," I called out to my co-host once I entered the studio, cup of coffee firmly in grasp. One downside of this job was that it meant getting up at five in the morning to make the show's six o'clock taping. Apparently, it was the only time the station had allotted studio space for the program, which had a solid, albeit small, audience of upper-middle-class parents and the children they hoped to mold, literally.

Colin looked up from the book he was reading, startled, before he broke out in his usual smile. Colin was the only person I knew who could smile at six in the morning. It was his nature to be cheerful, which was why he was such a fabulous host for *Rise and Shine*. The kids loved him, and in the six months that I had gotten to know him, I loved him, too. He was warm, generous, loving, good with children. Not to mention gorgeous, with softly chiseled features, blue eyes surrounded by thick lashes and short dark hair always cut in the most up-to-date style. Everything a woman could want in a prospective husband. In fact, I might have dated him until he married someone else—if he weren't gay, that is.

"Whatcha reading?" I said, bending over to see the title of his book.

"Oh, this." He smiled, looking somewhat embarrassed as he held up a well-thumbed volume of *The Challenges of Child-Rearing*. "Figured it might help, you know. With the show."

I laughed at this. "Colin, we just have to keep them fit, not raise them."

He chuckled. "I know, I know. But you've seen how rambunctious they can get."

I smiled. Colin really took this job on *Rise and Shine* very seriously.

"You ready?" he said now.

I sighed. "Ready as I'll ever be."

It still amazed me that I had even landed this gig—up until my audition, I hadn't exercised a day in my life. Yet, there I was, every weekday morning, cheerfully urging a group of ten sleepy-eyed kids to stretch, jump, run and tone. Lucky for me, my baby-blue tights were thick enough to hide cellulite.

"Positions, everyone," Rena Jones, our producer, called out with a glare in Colin's and my direction. Well, mostly my direction. She adored Colin. And tolerated me. Mostly because she was a stickler for timeliness, while I…wasn't.

Once Colin and I had positioned ourselves in front of the cameras, I put on my required happy face and chimed in with Colin as we gave a three-minute intro designed to inspire a demographic with probably the lowest body-fat ratio of any age group to jump, leap and stretch, in the name of good health. "Good health is all about *habits*," Rena would say, whenever anyone—mostly me—alluded to the fact that most six-year-olds weren't in need of cardiovascular training.

Still, I took a certain satisfaction in the routine, assured that once the music—a strange mixture of circus rhythms and a singer who sounded like the love child of Barney the Dinosaur and Britney Spears—began, my feet would move into the steps of the opening warm-up dance right along with Colin's. That when we progressed into the series of stretches, squats and leg lifts, my body was not only limber enough to make all the maneuvers, but could jog, jump and shimmer across the floor while I shouted out inspiring words to the ten little tumblers before us. Children, I might add, clearly struggling to keep up under the eye of their parents, who sat on the sidelines, their faces a mixture of parental pride and paralyzing anxiety that their kid would stumble, fall and be torn too early from the six-week segment they had lobbied long and hard to get said child on.

There was also the reassurance that when the clock against the back wall hit the thirty-minute mark, I would be able to heave a silent sigh of relief (which I disguised as a healthy exhale for the sake of my tiny followers), and bow down into a final stretch before leading the happy munchkins in the applause that ended the show.

"Hanging out with Kirk tonight?" Colin asked as we headed to the small dressing area at the back of the studio. I could tell by the way he always asked that question lately that he took a certain satisfaction in the progress of my relationship. His breakup with Tom two months earlier had been hard—Colin was clearly a one-man man—but he evidently took comfort in the fact that there were others in the world out there who were living monogamously-ever-after.

"Of course," I replied, with all the confidence a girlfriend should have at the stage Kirk and I were at in our relationship.

Later that very night, however, I realized that Kirk was at a different stage.

I was spending the evening at his place, where I spent most nights during the week. Not only because he lived on E. 27th and Third, which was somewhat closer to the studio on W. 54th than my East Village apartment was, but because we liked to spend our every waking moment together—and every sleeping moment, which was often the case, as Kirk had a tendency to nod off early.

Besides, Kirk's doorman-building one-bedroom was a welcome respite from the cluttered two-bedroom walk-up I shared with Justin, my roommate and other best friend beside Grace. Kirk's place was an oasis of order, his closet filled with rows of well-pressed button-downs and movie posters lining the walls with precision (yes, we both loved movies, though Kirk had an unsettling predilection for horror flicks while I liked the classics and anything with Mel Gibson). Even his medicine cabinet was a sight to behold, I thought as I scrubbed my teeth before bed that night. The toothpaste was curled up neatly next to a shiny cup containing his brush; his shaving kit (a gift from the ex that I once tried to replace with a packet of Gillettes, but to no avail) nestled sweetly next to a bottle of Chanel for men (from me, thank you very much, which he only spritzed himself with under serious duress). I also kept an antihistamine there—I had a tendency toward congestion at the slightest provocation: pollen, dust mites, mold. With a contented sigh I spit my mouthful of paste—and water—into the shiny white sink, carefully rinsing out the suds to return it to its porcelain perfection, before I returned to the bedroom, where Kirk sprawled on the bed, laptop in hand, studying the screen intently.

"Time to play," I said, bounding onto the bed in a pair of boxers and a T-shirt (pirated from his bottom left drawer).

"Just give me a minute, sweetie," he said, glancing up from the screen briefly to flash me a small smile of acknowledgment.

I settled in beside him, sparing a glance at the screen, which was covered in a series of incomprehensible codes, and picked up the book I kept on Kirk's bedside table, Antonin Artaud's *The Theatre and Its Double*. Turning to page five, the precise place I had been the last six times I had attempted to immerse myself, I started to read. Well, not exactly *read,*—my gaze was too busy roaming over to Kirk's profile.

He had the most beautiful brow line I had ever seen. Almost jet-black against creamy skin and normally smooth, though right now it was furrowed over his gray eyes as they studied the screen, almost without blinking. One of the things I had admired from the start about Kirk was his ability to concentrate against any odds. I didn't really understand it, frankly, since I inevitably threw away any thoughts of intelligent life the minute

I found myself faced with the prospect of sex. In fact, it was Kirk's seeming lack of awareness of the opposite sex that, oddly enough, had tantalized me from the first.

We met at my "day job," or second shift, at Lee and Laurie Catalog, where I was a part-time customer service rep to make up for all the money I didn't get paid as an actor. At the time, Kirk had been working for Lanix, which happened to be the software that Lee and Laurie thrived on, and had come to update our systems. From the moment I saw him, studiously occupied at one of the many terminals that littered the landscape of Lee and Laurie, I was intrigued. Not only was he good-looking, with dark brown hair, intelligent gray eyes, full lips and a strong jaw, he was smart. So smart, in fact, he didn't seem to notice anyone or anything except the scramble of codes he typed into each terminal as he bounded from cubicle to cubicle. Which was probably why I succumbed to him so quickly, at least according to Grace, whom I called repeatedly to report to on how my every effort at flirtation fell completely flat. Still, I couldn't stop conjuring up reasons to lure Kirk to my workstation—a lazy mouse, a jammed keyboard (sesame seeds from lunch, but at least I got a smile out of him) and a surprising lack of understanding of the new software updates he'd just installed. And as he patiently wiggled my mouse, dusted my keyboard and explained the new procedures yet again, I made goofy-but-good-natured jokes, standing close enough to "accidentally" brush his arm (delightfully solid) or smile winningly up at his smooth and seemingly unruffled features.

"I'm obsessed with him," I told Grace during the second week of failed innuendos.

"It's the challenge," she replied. "You can't resist it."

She was right, I realized later, when I finally gave in to her advice to "just ask him out, for chrissakes," and he, to my surprise, said yes. But I was hooked good from date one. Kirk was so different from all the men who had come before. For one thing, he made enough money to actually pay for dinner. And I couldn't help but admire his ambition when he told me his dreams of running his own software company…or his well-toned physique, when things got to that level between us, honed from four times a week at the gym.

Now, as the warmth of that lean, muscled body seeped into my consciousness, I snuggled closer, eyes intent on my book, until I felt his weight shift as he closed the computer shut and reached over to rest it on the night table.

Closing the book with a joyful snap, I thrilled to the feeling of triumph that winged through me, as it never failed to do, even almost two years into the relationship. Call me competitive, call me a nymphomaniac, I don't give a damn—there was nothing, to me, like the sight of Kirk smiling down at me, a predatory gleam in his eye.

"Come here, you," he said in a husky voice, as if *I* were the one who'd been resisting all this time.

Without hesitation, I straddled him, reveling in the discovery that he had gone from software to hardware in seconds flat, even though you could barely tell I was female beneath the roomy T-shirt I was wearing. Still, his big hands unerringly worked their way under my tee, found the somewhat meager mounds there and stroked.

I sighed, knowing what was coming. Because if there was one thing Kirk and I had down pat by now, it was sex. Like the scientist that he was, he had experimented endlessly on me to discover just what buttons to push to get me where I wanted to go. And it was never boring, despite this precision on his part, I thought, as he rolled me beneath him, did away with both of our boxers, then rested back on his heels momentarily to cover himself in latex procured from its ever-ready place in the nightstand.

I would have hated myself for being such putty in his hands, if it weren't for the heat that inevitably overcame me as he slid inside me. My only complaint might have been that Kirk wasn't much of a kisser during sex. In fact, he rarely brought his mouth to mine once we were joined. But that was okay, I thought, gazing up at his flushed features, his dark lashes against his cheeks, his full mouth. The view was pretty damn good from here.

Rather than revel in the view as I usually did, I closed my eyes. And just as I was settling into the rhythm, a sudden—and unexpected—image filled my mind of Kirk peeling away my clothes, lifting me into his arms and depositing me on a canopied bed I had never seen before in my life. And when, in my mind's eye, I turned to look at the heap of cloth that had pooled at my feet as Kirk freed the last button on my— T-shirt?—I saw, to my horrified surprise, swaths and swaths of white silk. What looked to be, in my heated imagination a wedding gown?

Oh, God, I thought, as my body contracted—almost unwillingly, for it seemed *way* too soon—and I felt the biggest climax of my life shudder through me. My eyes flew open as the foreign sound of an earth-shattering moan left my mouth. I might even have thought it was Kirk who had cried out so freely because, unlike me, he made no bones about noisily expressing his pleasure, if I hadn't found myself looking straight into his surprised gaze. Moments later, I felt and heard his own satisfied shudder as his body went lax on mine.

"Wow," he said, when he lifted his head and met my gaze once more. "That was something," he continued, a smile lighting his features as he bent to graze my surprised mouth with a kiss.

"Yeah," I said breathlessly, studying his expression. It *was* something, I thought, hope beating in my breast. But did it *mean* something? I wondered, remembering the image of that dress in all its surprising detail. Well, clearly it did mean something, as sex between Kirk and me had always been a revelation. But this felt like a revelation of a very different kind. For me, at least, I thought, gazing into his eyes and seeking out the foreign emotions that I felt racking my own heart and mind.

I did see something shining in Kirk's eyes, but what it was had yet to be determined. Until I heard his next words.

"I never felt you so…strongly. That must have been a big O, huh?" he said with a laugh, then leaned back with a look that told me exactly what *he* was feeling. Pride. The garden-variety male smugness over a sexual performance well done.

As if to punctuate my realization, he went into scientist mode once more. "What do you think it was? I mean, it was the fucking missionary position, for chrissakes. Nothing special there." He pulled his hand away from my waist, where it had been gently massaging me, and thumped the bed. "Maybe it was this new mattress? God, had I known, I would have tipped that salesman at Sleepy's."

Oh brother.

I might have been thoroughly disgusted at this point, if Kirk hadn't rolled onto his back, bringing me with him, and pulled me into that solid body of his. Maybe it was the feel of his muscled chest beneath me. Or the tenderness in his hands as they slid over my back. Maybe I just wanted to believe that, though Kirk was a guy and thus given to fits of euphoria over the technicalities of sex, he did feel something more—something he couldn't possibly express—that made me relent, pressing my body into his in an attempt to hold on to whatever that feeling was. At least until reality set in. And it soon did.

Glancing at the clock, Kirk sat up, suddenly disentangling himself from my limbs. "Is it ten already? I gotta pack."

"Pack?" I asked, cool air crawling over me as he leaped from the bed, pulled on a pair of boxers and headed for the closet.

"Damn, did I forget to tell you?" He turned to look at me, his expression baffled, as if he were mentally going over one of his meticulous to-do lists and realizing he'd forgotten one of the most important items on it: me.

Assuming he was going away to meet a client, I prepared to launch into a speech about how nice it would be to know these things in advance. Then I heard his next words.

"I'm going home this weekend."

That stopped me short. Kirk was going home to Newton, Massachusetts. To visit his parents. Parents, I might add, I had yet to lay eyes on myself.

"When did you decide this?" I asked, a vague panic beginning to invade my rattled senses.

"Mmm…last week? Anyway, I just booked the ticket this morning. I was going to tell you…."

His voice faded away as my mind skittered over the facts: Kirk was going home for one of his semiannual trips, and he hadn't invited me. Again. The memory of Josh's taunting voice on my answering machine ran through my frazzled brain. While I was orgasming over wedding dresses, Kirk was planning a pilgrimage to the parental abode without me. Clearly I was *not* the woman who was about to pull the lid off this thing with Kirk. In fact, given that I was oh-for-three when you tallied up the number of times Kirk had gone home in the past year and a half and not invited me, it might even seem like his lid was still airtight.

Since I didn't know how to broach the subject of a meet-the-parents visit, I addressed the more immediate problem: "I wish you'd told me sooner…" *So I might have had a chance to rally for position of serious girlfriend,* I thought but didn't say.

"I'm sorry, Noodles," he replied, contrite. "You know how busy I've been with this new client. Did I tell you that I'm designing a program for Norwood Investments? They have offices all over the country. If I land Norwood, I could have work lined up for the next few years…."

His words silenced me for the moment. Maybe it was the injection of the nickname he had given me during the early days of our relationship, when I had ventured to cook him pasta, which, all-American boy that he is, he referred to as noodles and sauce. After I had teasingly told him that my Italian mother would toss him out on his ear if he ever referred to her pasta as "noodles," he had affectionately given me the name instead. But his warm little endearment wasn't the only thing that shut me up. There was also his subtle reminder that he was a software designer on the rise. That the program he had created six months earlier to automate office space was the only thing on his mind, now that prestigious financial companies like Norwood Investments had taken notice. In the face of all this ambition, I somehow felt powerless to express my desire to be considered parent-worthy in Kirk's mind.

"Hey, Noodles?" Kirk said now, pulling a pair of jeans over his boxers and donning a T-shirt. "I'm gonna run down to Duane Reade and pick up a few things for my trip. Need anything?"

Yeah, I thought: my head examined. "Um, no, I'm all right," I replied cautiously.

"Okay, I'll be back in fifteen, then." He gave me a perfunctory kiss on the forehead before making his way out the front door.

The minute I heard the door slam behind him, I picked up the phone. I needed another perspective. Specifically: an ex-boyfriend's perspective. And since pride prevented me from calling back the newly engaged Josh just yet, I dialed up Randy, whose number I still had safely tucked in my memory banks. After all, not marrying the men in your life did have its advantages. I had managed to turn at least two of my ex-boyfriends into friends.

"I didn't think you were into all that," Randy said, after we'd exchanged greetings and I'd inquired about why the marriage issue had never come up for us.

"Into all *what*?" I asked.

"You know, marriage, kids. Hey, did I tell you Cheryl and I are working on our first?"

"That's wonderful," I said in a daze. "What exactly do you mean I'm not into marriage, kids?"

Randy chuckled. "C'mon, Ange, you know as well as I do that your career came first. You always wanted to be the big movie star."

"Actor. I am an actor."

"Whatever."

When I hung up a short while later, I began to wonder if maybe I was projecting the wrong image. True, I had long been harboring the dream of making a career of the acting talent I had been lavishly praised for all through high school and college. And though I hadn't exactly landed my dream role in the four years since I had left a steady job in sales to pursue acting, *Rise and Shine* counted for something, didn't it?

Suddenly I had to start getting realistic, if I hoped to ever get a grip on this particular lid. I was thirty-one years old. I wasn't getting any younger, as my mother lost no opportunity of reminding me. I needed to start looking like a wife.

2

I'm not really
a wife, but I play one on TV.

When I arrived home after the show the next morning and discovered Justin trying to tug a sofa through the narrow entrance foyer of our apartment, I realized that even if I didn't look like a wife, I was quite capable of sounding like one. Big time.

"What on earth are you doing?" I cried, though I knew exactly what he was up to. Collecting other people's castoffs. For as lovable as Justin was, he had the single worst trait you could have in a roommate: He was a pack rat.

"Hey," he said, glancing up at me from where he stood, bent over his latest find: a turquoise-green sofa that had clearly seen better days. "Can you believe someone left this for garbage?"

Uh, yeah, I thought, studying the yellow floral trim and sunken seat cushions with renewed horror.

"It was right out front, too."

I felt a groan rising up. A threadbare couch, circa 1975, right in front of the building. Clearly there was no way Justin could have resisted. "Justin, we already have two couches." One of which he had promised to get rid of after he dragged home his last couch acquisition. I realized once again why inheriting your Aunt Eleanor's spacious, rent-stabilized two-bedroom could be a curse, at least in Justin's case. In addition to the assorted furnishings Aunt Eleanor had left behind for her favorite nephew, Justin had acquired, among other things, four television sets, three VCRs, six file cabinets and a Weber outdoor grill that I assumed he was saving for some suppressed suburban dreamhouse with a garage big enough to store Yankee Stadium, should any future mayor carry out Rudy Giuliani's threat to tear down the current home of the Bronx Bombers. For surely if that day ever did come, Justin would feel compelled to save some part of it. In his warped little mind, Justin didn't think he was collecting junk so much as rescuing it.

"Ange, you think you could give me a hand with this?" he said.

I sighed, realizing I would have to give in for the moment, trapped as I was in the hallway until my roommate's monstrous new acquisition was moved.

"How did you get this up here anyway?" I asked. Though Justin was well muscled for a lanky guy, I somehow couldn't picture him maneuvering a three-hundred-pound sofa up the two long flights to our apartment.

"David in three-B gave me a hand. And he said he had some old lamps if we were interested—"

Ack! "Justin, honey, we need to talk…." I began gently, trying to not completely douse the delighted gleam in his eyes. But just as I was about to launch into a speech about the dangers of recycling, the phone rang.

"Can you…?" I asked, gesturing toward the couch that stood between me and the rest of the apartment.

I slumped against the doorway as Justin grabbed the receiver. "Hello," he sang into the phone, in his usual chipper voice. "Hey, Mrs. Di, how are you?"

My mother. I sat down on the edge of the sofa and waited while Justin practiced his usual charm on her. I sometimes think she called to talk to him, judging by the giddiness that was ever present in her voice whenever Justin finally handed over the phone. That was just Justin's way, I supposed. Even I had been charmed by him from the moment we had met in an improv class four years earlier. At the time, we were both just starting out in acting, Justin having given up a career behind the camera when the feature-length film he'd directed won a lot of buzz on the festival circuit and a prestigious award but ultimately no distributor. He claimed that he wanted to expand his horizons now that he had realized just how hard it was to get a movie out there. I wondered at that, since it seemed to me that it was just as hard to get yourself out there as an actor. But Justin seemed happy enough to take a union job as a grip for a production company based out of Long Island City, which gave him the kind of flexibility he needed to pursue acting.

Our improv teacher had paired us together, me being the only student without a partner when Justin straggled in, even later to class than I had been. I was a bit scared of working with Justin, who, with his dark blond hair, green eyes and tall good looks, was just the kind of babe I avoided. After all, a good-looking man—and an actor to boot—was bound to be cocky. So you can just imagine how I felt when the instructor led us in our first theater game, which required me to stand with my back to Justin and allow myself to fall straight back into his arms. "To build trust," the instructor had explained. And build trust it did. From the moment I felt Justin's firm grip beneath me after those first spine-tingling moments in midair, I knew instinctively he would always be there for me. In the years that followed, he had been. Like when my old roommate threw me out of our apartment two years ago to make room for her new live-in boyfriend. Justin had opened his two-bedroom to me without batting an eye, though my mother had batted hers a bit about my having a male roommate. She got over that right after I dragged Justin home for dinner and he easily won her over. Justin and I have been living together ever since.

"This Sunday?" I heard Justin say now, "Oh, Mrs. Di, you're torturing me. You know I'd never turn down your manicotti, but Lauren's coming to town."

Lauren was Justin's girlfriend, of the past three years, though their cumulative time spent together was probably more like three months. Lauren was a stage actress who always found herself in some leading role or another, but, somehow, never in

New York. Currently she was doing Ibsen in, of all places, South Florida.

"Yep, gotta do the girlfriend thing this weekend," Justin continued with a chuckle. "But Angela's not doing anything, as far as I know. Hang on a second, sweetie, I'll let you talk to her. You take care, Mrs. Di," he finished cheerfully, handing me the receiver now that he'd managed to sew up my Sunday plans.

"Hi, Ma," I said, sliding awkwardly from the arm of the sofa onto the seat cushion and sending a poof of dust into the air.

"Angela!" my mother shouted in my ear, as if surprised to hear my voice. I honestly believe she thought it was a miracle I wasn't gunned down on a daily basis, living as I did off of Avenue A. The only thing Ma knew about Alphabet City was the bloody battles featured in the movie of the same name, which my brother Sonny had deemed it necessary to show her, just days after I had moved in with Justin.

"What's up, Ma? How's Nonnie?" Nonnie is my grandmother, who lives on the lower level of my mother's house in Brooklyn, which is as good as living with my mother, judging by the amount of time she spends in my mother's kitchen.

"Nonnie's fine. In fact, she's looking forward to seeing you this Sunday for dinner. Sonny and Vanessa are going to be there!" my mother informed me, as if my arrogant brother Sonny and his obscenely pregnant wife were some kind of enticement.

I gave a silent inner groan. Once Ma got it in her head that her family was coming together for Sunday dinner, there was no excuse, short of emergency brain surgery, that could get me out of going. "Family comes first," she was fond of saying to me and my brothers. And I knew she was right. Only it made it difficult sometimes to compete in New York City, where it often seemed as if no one had parents at all.

"You're bringing Kirk, right?"

"Um, he's going out of town for the weekend," I said.

"Oh, yeah?"

I could tell by the impressed tone of her voice that she assumed it was on business. And since Kirk did make semifrequent trips to see clients, I decided not to burst her bubble just yet.

After all, Kirk had met my family before. Hell, he was practically an honorary member. The creep.

"Listen, Ma, I gotta go. Justin brought home this...couch," I said, glancing down at the worn fabric once more, "and we need to move it out of the hall."

"A couch? I thought you just got a couch."

"We did. Justin is starting a collection."

She laughed, as if anything Justin did was perfectly delightful. And as I clicked off the phone and glanced over at the cradle across the room, which there was no way in hell I could reach with this monstrosity in the way, I decided to summon my perfectly delightful roommate, who had since disappeared into his bedroom, probably to watch the Yankees game.

"JUSTIN!" I bellowed loud enough for the whole floor to hear.

"What's up?" he said, popping his head out of the bedroom, a puzzled frown on his face. As if *I* were disturbing *him*.

"What do you mean, what's up?" I said, slapping my hand on the couch and sending another load of dust into the air.

"Sheesh, I didn't realize that couch was so dirty," he said to my chorus of sneezes.

"Apparently there are a lot of things you don't realize," I said in frustration. "Like that we already have two couches. Like that I have to schlep out to Brooklyn Sunday night and still be up at five on Monday—"

"But you never go to bed any earlier than midnight. Even when you're home."

"That's not the point!" I shouted.

Startled, Justin simply stared at me. "What is the point, then?"

"The point is...the point is..." My throat seized, and suddenly I burst out with, "Kirk is going to see his family this weekend."

"So why didn't you tell your mother that you're going with him?"

"Because I'm not going with him."

"Oh," he replied, and I could tell by his confused expression that he still wasn't getting it.

"He didn't ask me to go."

"Oh," he said, his tone implying that it all made sense to him now.

"Shouldn't he have asked me to go?" I asked, clutching the phone receiver in my lap.

Justin seemed to consider this for a moment. "Did you want to go?"

I sighed. "That's not the point." Maybe men were thicker than I realized. "The point is, we have been dating almost two years and I have yet to meet his parents, despite the fact that he has been to my mother's house in Brooklyn more times than I can count."

"Brooklyn is a lot closer than—where's he from again? Brookline?"

I sighed. "Newton. But the point is, he doesn't take me seriously. Not seriously enough to introduce me to his parents. Or to…to marry me."

Justin visibly blanched at this. "Marry you?" he said, as if the word caused a bitter taste in his mouth. What is it with men and the *M* word anyway?

"Yes, *marry me,*" I replied. "Why is it so hard to believe that Kirk would want to marry me? After all, I've been sleeping with him, eating with him, sharing some of my most intimate thoughts with him, for a year and eight months. Don't you think it's time we made some kind of commitment?"

"We eat and sleep together," Justin said, a smile tugging at his lips, "and we're not getting married." Then he paused, glancing over at me with a glint of amusement in his eye. "Are we?"

"Forget it," I said, realizing that as lovable as Justin was, he would never understand. He was, after all, a guy. And I knew about guys. I had grown up in a family full of them. "Let's just find a place for this couch," I said, wondering where we were going to put it until I convinced Justin of its utter worthlessness. Then I thought of Kirk's clutter-free one-bedroom and realized there were other reasons to get married besides love. Like real estate.

I decided to take my problem to the Committee. The Committee, so named because of their unfailing ability to have an opinion about everything and everyone, consisted of the three women who filled out the other three corners of the office cubicle I shared four times a week, answering the demands of the discerning customers who shopped the Lee and Laurie, a catalog company claiming to be the purveyor of effortlessly casual style. Though I was grateful to Michelle for hooking me up with the job when I decided to give up my nine-to-five gig as a sales rep in the garment district for the actor's life, I had learned in my short career at Lee and Laurie that there is nothing casual— to me, anyway—about paying seventy-five dollars for a T-shirt designed to look unassuming enough to, say, take out the garbage in. Still, it was a job that suited my actor's lifestyle, with convenient three-to-ten-o'clock shifts and, believe it or not, health insurance. Lots of it. It was the just the kind of thing a girl with dreams and chronic postnasal drip craves.

It was also the mecca for the wife, judging by the number of Comfortably Marrieds who flocked to Lee and Laurie's employ, hoping to earn some extra income once their kids were old enough to become latch-key.

Hence my decision to go to the Committee, which was composed of Michelle Delgrosso, who seemingly only worked at Lee and Laurie to be able to indulge herself in the expensive lip gloss and overpriced trims designed to keep her dark, layered shoulder-length hair smooth, shiny and enviable; Roberta Simmons, a forty-something married mother of two perfect children, and Doreen Sikorsky, who was a bit of a wild card, with an alleged divorce in her past and enough conspiracy theories to make me wary of most of the things she said.

"Hey," I said in greeting as I approached our four-seater cubicle, which was currently occupied only by Michelle and Doreen. And since Doreen was on a call, I was glad to have Michelle's ear. After all, Michelle was the epitome of everything my mother deemed good in this world. Brooklyn born. Married at twenty-three years old. And the owner of a three-bedroom house in Marine Park.

"Where's Roberta?" I asked, realizing I might need a better balance of opinion. Roberta's life was a little closer to what I aspired to, if only because she lived in Manhattan.

"She's in the can, as usual," Michelle said with a small smile. "I swear I don't know what that woman eats."

"We can't all be bulimic, Michelle," Doreen said, having finished her call just in time to tune in to the conversation. "Hey, DiFranco, how's it hanging?"

I sighed. These were the kind of people you worked with when you accepted $15.50 an hour as your starting salary. Maybe I should just keep my dilemma to myself....

But then Roberta showed up, looking like her usual sane and steadying self. Maybe it was the short haircut—women with short hair always seemed smart and responsible—that framed her soft, elfin features and wide blue eyes. Or maybe it was the expensive camel trousers and well-cut black tee, compliments of the employee discount Lee and Laurie gave its devoted staff. "Hey, Angie," she said, sitting herself down and putting her headset back on.

"Hey, Roberta," I said, adjusting my own headset over my ears. But just as I was about to launch into my dilemma, the familiar long beep sounded in my ear, indicating that my first phone call was coming over the line. Suppressing a sigh, I launched into the introductory script that had been drilled into us during training, "Thank you for calling Lee and Laurie Catalog, where casual comes easy. This is Angela. How can I help you today?"

Fortunately, I had a quick and easy call from a woman who thought the new boat-neck tee looked so clean and comfortable on the blond goddess who modeled it on page 74 that she deemed it necessary to order it in every color. Once I had inputted all the information into my computer, thanked her for her order and hit the call end button on my phone set, I swiveled around to face my cube-mates once more.

"So listen to this," I said, as Roberta and Michelle fixed their gazes on me and Doreen rushed her customer off the phone.

"Kirk is going home to see his parents this weekend," I continued, studying the expressions of all three women expectantly, "without me."

"Have you ever met his parents before?" Michelle asked.

"No," I replied, noting that Roberta's brow had furrowed at my response.

"Break up with him," Doreen said succinctly. I glanced toward Roberta frantically, but she had already launched into a call.

"Don't listen to her," Michelle said, waving a hand in Doreen's direction dismissively before focusing her dark brown eyes on me. "Let me ask you something, Angie. How long have you two been together?"

"A year and eight months."

"That long, huh? Hmm…" Michelle's well-penciled eyes grew pensive and her glossy lips pursed.

"You don't want to marry this guy. Or any guy, for that matter, trust me on this," Doreen chimed in again. I glanced once again over at Roberta, but she was still on her phone call and would be for some time, judging by the way she was typing furiously into her keyboard. "A man like that will never give you anything you need," Doreen continued.

"Well, that all depends on what Angie wants," Michelle said, her face brightening as she looked at me hopefully. "What do you want from him, Angie?"

For some reason, her question filled me with a flutter of confusion. What *did* I want from Kirk? Looking into her face, I saw all the hopes and dreams the Comfortably Marrieds of the world felt for the Anxiously Single. Then I remembered that wedding gown—and my amazing climax. Clearly, marriage was something I had been craving. And why wouldn't I want it? I loved the idea of coming home to someone night after night, someone I knew would be there for me during the rough patches. I wanted to share my life with a man, not just some two-to-four-year interval we would later laugh about over drinks, as I often found myself doing with Josh and even Randy.

And as my eyes roamed over Michelle's well-groomed coif and expensive jeans, I realized I wanted something else: a dual income. Could you blame me? Living in New York City was no cakewalk on the measly salary I gleaned from a part-time job and my illustrious role at *Rise and Shine*. This is not to say I didn't love Kirk. I did. All the more reason for us to combine incomes, phone bills and, even more important, rent, I thought, remembering the sofa-laden flat I shared with Justin.

"I want to marry him, of course," I said, as if the answer were self-evident.

And to Michelle, who had, from age eighteen, plotted and planned her wedding to Frankie Delgrosso, co-owner (with his dad, course) of Kings County Cadillac in Brooklyn, this was not only self-evident but cause for celebration. "Angela is getting married!" she practically shouted before moving seamlessly into "Thank you for calling Lee and Laurie Catalog, where casual comes easy…."

"Married?" Roberta said, now done with her call and swiveling to confront me. "To Kirk?"

"Of course to Kirk!" I replied with a laugh. "Who else?" *Beep.* "Thank you for calling Lee and Laurie Catalog, where casual comes easy. This is Angela. How may I help you today?"

Turning away from Roberta's somewhat confused expression, I attempted to focus on the customer's question, which had to do with sizing on the slim-cut trousers we'd just debuted in our fall collection. But as I tried to guide the poor woman toward pants that would accommodate the somewhat peculiar proportions she described, I couldn't help but wonder what had struck Roberta as so odd about the notion of Kirk and me getting married. Frustrated after a solid four minutes of flipping through catalog pages while the customer rejected my every recommendation, I barked somewhat irritably into the phone, "Have you ever considered something with an adjustable waist?" The woman made some equally irritated reply and huffed off the phone. With a quick prayer that no one in the quality assurance department was monitoring *that* call, I turned to Roberta once more.

"What's wrong with Kirk?" I asked, studying Roberta's expression. After all, she had gotten to know Kirk somewhat during his brief time servicing Lee and Laurie. She had witnessed the flirtation between us, had seen the first fluttering of romance as we began dating, watched as we eased into coupledom. If she had an issue, I needed to know.

"Nothing's wrong with Kirk," she said. "In fact, I like Kirk very much."

"So?"

"I'm just surprised, that's all. I didn't think you two were moving in that direction."

"That's just the problem," I said. "Kirk isn't moving in that direction."

"Some men need a little nudge," Michelle said, turning to face us once more. "A little lid loosening," she continued, reminding me of her tight-lid theory. "You know, Frankie wasn't even thinking marriage when I started leading him into jewelry stores to look at rings. I think he had his credit card out before he even knew what hit him," she added with a gleeful little giggle.

"Oh, brother," Doreen said, with a roll of the eyes.

"What's got you moving in that direction?" Roberta asked now.

Her question filled my face with heat. I couldn't even confess my wedding-fantasy orgasm to Grace, much less to these women. "I'm thirty-one years old—shouldn't I at least be thinking about it?"

"Ah," Roberta said with a knowing smile. "It's the old biological clock, isn't it? I guess that makes sense. When I turned thirty, all I could think about was having my first child."

Oh, God. Who said anything about kids? I mean, they're cute and all, but one thing at a time…. "It's not that, really. I just want to be taken seriously," I said, realizing that Roberta wasn't listening as she launched into a story she'd already told us countless times, about her struggle to potty-train her daughter, who had just now turned thirteen and I'm sure wouldn't appreciate the fact that her mother still dwelled on this part of her history. Fortunately, another call came in just before Roberta got into the particulars. Clearly she was going to be no help, I realized, as Michelle clicked off her call and faced me once more.

"You want to be taken seriously?" she asked. "I'll tell you how." Then she leaned in low, and whispered, "Go on break."

"I just got here. I can't go on break," I whispered back.

"The call volume is pretty slow," Michelle said. "Go on break." Then she leaned back in her chair. "Gee, Roberta, all that time you spend in the can is putting ideas in my head. Now

I have to go to the bathroom." She put her phone on standby and took off her headset, giving me a meaningful look.

I clicked my phone onto standby mode. "I have to go, too," I said, sliding off my own handset.

"You can't both go on break!" Doreen began to protest before her cries were cut off by her own rather curt "Thank you for calling Lee and Laurie Catalog…"

Though I felt guilty leaving Doreen and Roberta to juggle all the calls that came into the phone cue for our unit, I was desperate for help. And I was sure Michelle was going to be able to provide it, judging by the confident sway of her Calvin Kleins as she headed through the office, out the double doors which closed off customer service from the rest of the world that was Lee and Laurie Catalog and to the elevator bank.

"Let's go outside a minute. So I can smoke a butt."

I sighed. Clearly I was at Michelle's mercy now, I thought, feeling even more guilty as we got on the elevator and headed down eleven floors and outside into the cloying summer heat.

The moment we stepped onto the concrete out in front of the building, Michelle had already lit up a Virginia Slims and was puffing steadily. "Want one?" she asked, holding out the pack with one well-manicured hand.

"All right," I said, taking a cigarette though I had given up the habit, for the most part, shortly after my father died from cancer four years ago. Some things, however, still required nicotine.

After she had lit me up and I had taken one heady drag, Michelle started in. "Getting married is a game. You want to do it, you gotta play the fucking game."

"Game?" I said, grimacing at the all-too-frequent swearwords that flew out of Michelle's mouth, especially when she was on her favorite subject: men.

"You know, getting the lid loose. It doesn't happen overnight—"

"This tight-lid theory is bullshit," I said, taking another acrid puff of the cigarette before I dropped it to the ground.

"Bullshit? I'll give you bullshit. You remember who Frankie was dating before I hooked up with him, don't you?"

"Yeah, yeah. Rosanna Cuzio. But that was high school. No one marries their high school sweetheart anymore—"

"But Rosanna Cuzio was the prom queen. The fucking *prom queen,* Angie. She and Frankie went out for *four fucking years.* Then, just about the time she's picking out china patterns, he dumps her. Dumps her!" Her eyebrows shot up and she took another drag of her cigarette. "So a few months later, Frankie and I start going out. Within two years, whammo," she said, holding up her left hand, which was covered in gold rings, one of which sported a one-and-a-half carat emerald-cut.

I have to say, the sight of that ring was about to convert me once more. Until I remembered Susan, Kirk's ex. No, she wasn't the prom queen, but with a degree in engineering from MIT, she was a pretty strong contender for a lid-loosener of the very best kind. "Kirk's last girlfriend gave him the old ultimatum. But I don't see him shopping for rings with me anytime soon. He didn't even invite me to meet his parents, for chrissakes. Does that indicate a man who is about to pop the question?"

Michelle shook her head, blowing out another blast of smoke. "You're not fucking getting it," she said. "The lid is loose, but it's not off. You have to apply a little pressure. You have to play the game. In fact, it's really only a matter of three steps."

"Steps?"

"Yeah, to get him to pop the fucking question. The first one is deprivation."

I didn't like the sound of that. "And what, exactly, does that entail?"

"Just don't be so available. When he calls up to make plans, tell him you're busy."

Maybe that was what I was doing wrong, I thought, remembering the look of pure longing I'd seen in Justin's eyes at the thought of Lauren coming home after three months. Hmm...

"And whatever you do, *do not* have sex with him."

"What?" This particular step would be a lot harder on me.

After all, sex was one of the best things in Kirk's and my relationship.

"I know it sounds crazy, but all that shit about getting the milk for free is true," she said, blowing out a last puff of smoke and crushing the butt beneath one three-inch heel.

"I don't know, Michelle, it sounds kind of…manipulative." I wanted a proposal that was genuine—that came from Kirk and Kirk alone. "That's just not me," I continued. "I'm not a game player."

"Okay," she said, waving that weighty engagement ring in the air as she pulled open the door and headed inside once more. "But, remember, you got to be in it to win it."

3

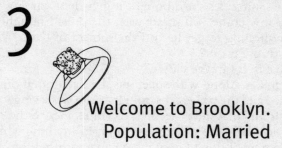

Welcome to Brooklyn.
Population: Married

"I don't like that, Angela," my mother said, standing over a sizzling pan of eggplant on the stove. It was Sunday, and after an
utterly uneventful weekend spent mostly alone (Justin and Lauren had disappeared to the Hamptons on Saturday, thank God,
to celebrate their happy reunion), I had gone to my mother's
house early, ostensibly to help her cook, and was now being sub-
jected to the third degree while chopping garlic. It was my own
fault, really, for admitting that Kirk had gone home to see his
parents. And for saying it with a less-than-cheerful expression.

"How many times has he been here?" Ma said now, flipping
the eggplants with barely contained indignation. "It's not right."

For once I had to agree with her. She was from the old
school, where a man treated a woman with the utmost defer-
ence. My father was one of those men. It seemed when I was
growing up, there was never a moment when he didn't put my
mother's concerns above his own. Even up until the moment
he died, as he lay on his sickbed, where my mother had per-
manently stationed herself, he begged her to go to sleep, knowing he would be up and in pain for the rest of the night. Of

course, my mother didn't dare close her eyes during those last few days. In fact, she still blames herself for succumbing to exhaustion the night he passed away. "I closed my eyes for one minute, and he was gone!" she laments, as if the fact that she couldn't stay awake had ultimately done him in. Even four years later, she still wore mourning clothes, and judging from the way her knit skirt was starting to fray around the edges, they were the same ones she'd bought in her first year as a widow.

"Ma, how come you never wear the dress I bought you?" I said now, hoping to get her off the subject of Kirk. "What did you do, throw it out?"

"I have it. It's in the closet."

I bet it was. Along with sheet sets she had gotten on sale and never used and the tablecloths from Italy she was saving for a "special occasion" that never seemed to come. Hence the one flaw in the Old World ways: You never enjoyed anything while it was fresh and new. "I don't know what you're waiting for," I said.

"Don't worry about me. Worry about yourself," she said, starting to pull the eggplants out of the pan and placing them on a plate.

"Who's worried about Angela?" Nonnie said, coming through the kitchen door from her apartment downstairs.

"Hey, Nonnie," I said, jumping up to enfold her in my arms. I breathed in her flowery scent and leaned back to gaze at her soft, smiling features with relief. Cheerfully attired in a bright red blouse and a pair of polyester capris—like most of her peers in the eighty and over set, she couldn't resist synthetic fabrics— my grandmother was a breath of fresh air in the gloom that permeated my mother whenever she thought one of her children was in danger of unhappiness. Since I was the one who usually fell into that category, I had come to rely on Nonnie to keep things on an even keel.

"You gonna cook in that?" my mother said, turning from the sauce she stirred momentarily to take in my grandmother's festive outfit and made-up face.

"I sure am," Nonnie said, then defiantly grabbed a bowl of chopped meat off the counter. After dumping in the garlic I had just finished dicing along with breadcrumbs and myriad other ingredients so secret she claimed she was taking their names to her grave, Nonnie reached into the bowl of red meat and spices and, rings and all, began to mix the ingredients by hand.

"So what's your mother worried about now?" Nonnie asked, addressing me as if Ma weren't standing two feet behind her at the stove.

"Oh, you know. The usual. Me and Kirk."

"Hey, that's right," my grandmother said, as if it just occurred to her I was without my other half. "Where is the Skinny Guinea?" she asked, using her nickname for Kirk. It was Nonnie's way of accepting Kirk as a permanent fixture in my life despite the fact that he had no relatives whatsoever who hailed from the boot of Europe. She believed that all the meals he had eaten in our home qualified him as an honorary Italian, albeit a thin one. "I don't know where he puts it!" she would say after he cleaned a plate heaping with pasta and red meat.

"He went home," I admitted now, watching her face carefully as she grabbed up a clump of meat and began rolling it into a meatball.

"Oh, yeah?" she said, plopping the meatball into the pan my mother had laid out on the table and grabbing up another clump of meat. "Too bad. He loves your mother's eggplant. He's gonna miss out, huh?" she said with a wink as she finished up another meatball.

I smiled. Leave it to Nonnie to turn things around and make it seem as if Kirk were the one missing out on something. Reaching into the bowl before her, I started to roll meatballs right along with her.

"You don't think that's wrong?" my mother chimed in, giving the sauce one last stir before she joined us at the table. "He's been to this house I don't know how many times, and he doesn't invite Angela into his own home? To meet his parents?"

Nonnie shrugged, grabbed up some more chopped meat, rolled. "Don't his parents live in, whatsit—Massachusetts?" she said. The way she said Massachusetts made it clear that this wasn't as desirable a location as, say, Brooklyn. Because in Nonnie's world, there really weren't too many places outside of Brooklyn she felt it necessary to be. Her own mother had moved here from Naples as a teen, and Nonnie had grown up right on Delancey, at the foot of the Brooklyn Bridge. In all these years, she'd never really seen any reason to go anywhere else. According to her, Brooklyn had everything a person could need: Al's Butcher had the best Italian sausage, and there really wasn't a better bagel to be had anywhere in New York than at Brooklyn Bagelry, never mind the rest of the country. And with Kings Plaza a short walk away and packed to the brim with shops that kept her in polyester and high-heeled Cubby Cobblers, what more did a woman need?

"He's not serious about her. And I don't like that," my mother said, putting up the water for the pasta.

"Serious. Who needs serious? There's plenty of time for that," Nonnie said with a wave of one ringed hand.

She was right, I realized. Why was I in such a hurry, anyway? Kirk and I hadn't even been together two years yet. Getting all worked up about marriage seemed a bit…premature. Didn't it?

Returning to the table and grabbing a hunk of chopped meat, my mother eyed me and Nonnie with a shake of the head. "Did you bring up the sausage from your freezer?" she asked my grandmother.

"No, I didn't have any," Nonnie said lightly. "But don't worry. I asked Artie to bring it."

"Artie?" my mother said, "Gloria Matarrazzo's husband?"

"Gloria's dead," Nonnie said, rolling the meat between her hands. "Has been for a good year now, God rest her soul. You should know that, Maria. You went to the funeral."

"So why's he coming here?" Ma asked.

"I invited him," Nonnie replied, as if this should come as no surprise to anyone.

"You *what?*" my mother said, pausing midroll.

"What?" my grandmother replied, eyes wide with innocence. "We're friends. We've been playing poker together on Friday nights for fifteen years now. I can't invite the man to my home for dinner?"

But as Nonnie turned her attention to the meat once more, I could swear her cheeks were slightly flushed.

"What are you up to?" Ma demanded, putting words to the suspicion that lurked in my own mind.

But before she got her answer, the doorbell rang. "I'll get it!" my grandmother announced, rushing to the sink to rinse her hands. Then, checking her reflection in the microwave door, she gave her curls a quick pat and headed to the living room and the front door, leaving my mother and me staring after her in surprise.

"Artie! Glad you could make it," we heard her exclaim from the next room. And within moments, she was leading Artie Matarrazzo into our kitchen. "Look who's here!" Nonnie announced, gripping his hand. "You remember my daughter, Maria, and my granddaughter, Angela?" she said to Artie, who looked somewhat unsure how he had wound up in our kitchen, much less by my grandmother's side. I might even have thought he'd stumbled to our house by accident, judging by his somewhat rumpled attire and bewildered brown eyes beneath bushy gray brows, if it weren't for the sausage he pulled out of the shopping bag he carried.

"Oh, Artie, you remembered," Nonnie gushed, gazing at the package as if it were a dozen roses, and leaning over to kiss his fleshy cheek.

Oh, my, I thought, exchanging a look with my mother.

Nonnie had a beau. And if the size of that sausage he was sporting was any indication, it was *serious.*

No less than an hour later, my brother Sonny arrived, with his wife, Vanessa. Of course, dinner was pretty much done by this point, and even the table had been set, leaving Sonny and Vanessa with nothing more to do than stand in the middle of the living room, while both my mother and my grandmother oohed and aahed over Vanessa. Or more specifically, Vanessa's abdomen, which was round and bursting with her and Sonny's first child. My mother's first grandchild. "First grandchild from *birth,*" my mother would always clarify. My brother Joey had fraternal twins that came with his fiancée, Miranda, and once my mother had accepted the fact that her oldest son was not likely to give her any grandkids unless he married Miranda, she embraced little Tracy and Timmy as her own.

"There is nothing like it when *your own son* is having a baby," she declared now, as she often exclaimed when Joey and Miranda weren't around.

Vanessa, of course, ate it up. Standing before my mother, she ran one well-ringed hand over her abdomen, pressing the fabric of the pink maternity top against the swell, as if to show it off, as she said, "I can't believe how big I am—and I'm only in my fifth month!"

It was true that Vanessa was huge, but I don't think it was all baby. At five-nine, with a mane of blond hair sprayed so high it practically hit the woodwork on the way in the door, she still wore her trademark four-inch heels. Huge hunks of gold jewelry dangled from her ears, neck and arms, which somehow added to her girth in an oddly glamorous way. Her overwhelming size made her pregnant state seem all the more glorious. When Vanessa was in the room, she literally took it over. You couldn't *not* talk about her.

"How are you feeling? Still getting that morning sickness?" Ma asked. Then, "You really should sit down. Especially in this heat. Summer's barely begun and already the humidity is unbearable. Angela, get Vanessa one of those nice armchairs from the dining room."

There really was no escaping Vanessa's reign over a room, I thought, heading to the dining room for an extra chair as I heard Sonny begin to regale Nonnie and my mother with story of Vanessa's latest sonogram. "I saw something on that screen. I *swear* it's gonna be a boy…."

There was only one thing that could dispel the Vanessa obsession. Well, actually two things. Tracy and Timmy, the Twin Terrors, who had just now exploded through the front door and into the living room, practically barreling Vanessa down in their six-year-old exuberance.

"Hey, hey, hey," Joey called out in admonishment, as he came through the door, his hand firmly around Miranda's tiny waist.

It still amazed me to see Joey in "dad mode," as he'd taken on the role rather abruptly when he met Miranda a year earlier. Up till then, he had devoted all his time and energy to running the auto-parts empire my father had left to him. And whatever spare time he'd had was spent waxing and detailing the '67 Cadillac that was his pride and joy. Now, suddenly, Tracy and Timmy were his pride and joy. Miranda, his raison d'être.

My mother should have been satisfied with this turn of

events. For years, she worried Joey wouldn't lift his head up from the Caddy long enough to settle down and give her the grand-kids she craved. But somehow she couldn't swallow down the idea of Miranda. It was as if she saw Miranda only as some des-titute single mother scheming to get her hands on the dough from our family's business.

Fortunately, Miranda didn't notice—or at least acted as if she didn't. "Hi, Mrs. Di," she said, leaning in to embrace my mother. I saw my mother's arms go around Miranda's petite frame, though I could tell she refrained from her requisite squeeze until she moved on to Joey, whom she not only hugged but gave a firm swat on the butt. "He gets better looking every time I see him!" she said to Nonnie, a wistfulness in her voice that indi-cated to the more astute observer, like myself, that she felt all that magnificence was somehow being wasted on Miranda.

"He's all right," Nonnie responded, with a wink that said Joey was more than all right in her eyes, as she engulfed him in a hug that practically swallowed his six-foot frame. "You re-member Artie Matarrazzo, right, Joey?" Nonnie said, dragging Joey to Artie, who sat obediently on the couch. "Hey, Mr. Matarrazzo," Joey said, shaking the older man's hand with the same surprise my brother Sonny had displayed at the sight of my grandmother, flushed and beaming over a man other than Grandpa, who had been dead a good ten years now.

But no one had too much time to wonder over Artie, now that Tracy and Timmy had launched a full attack on the living room. They had already pulled all the cushions off the couch and were about to proceed with a pillow fight when my mother swooped down to hug them and shower them with the gifts she kept hand-ily beside the sofa they had all but destroyed. It was as if she would gladly have taken on Tracy and Timmy, who with their big blue eyes and curly brown locks were irresistible, and put Miranda, who stood by gazing on the scene with love, out to pasture.

But whatever lingering animosity there was, it was immedi-ately dispelled when, moments after Nonnie went into the kitchen to check on the sauce, she returned and announced, "Dinner's ready. Let's eat!"

Once we were all settled around the table, with me sitting between Tracy and Timmy to keep them from tearing at each other's hair while we were eating, it suddenly occurred to Sonny that my other half was missing.

"Hey, where's Kirk?" he said, between mouthfuls of eggplant and linguine.

"Who's Kirk?" Tracy asked, completely forgetting the guy who had kept her giggling all afternoon with his silly little jokes the last time we were here.

"You idiot," Timmy declared. "Kirk is Angela's *boyfriend*."

"I'm not an idiot, *you're* an idiot," she said, reaching behind me to yank her brother's hair and sending my head jutting out neatly over my plate, giving my mother an easy aim as she set about taking it off.

"He went home to see his parents," my mother supplied, eyebrows raised as if inviting speculation about Kirk's intentions.

"Oh, yeah?" Sonny said. "I didn't think that guy had a home, judging by how often he eats with us."

"Doesn't his family live in Massachusetts somewhere?" Vanessa said, clearly proud of herself for remembering the details of my boyfriend's life. For whatever you wanted to say about Vanessa, she really did make an effort when it came to family.

"Newton, Massachusetts," I replied, leaning back and neatly frustrating Tracy's effort to get a grip on her brother's head in turn. With a glance at my mother, I continued in what I hoped was a matter-of-fact voice, "It's about six hours by train." Not that Kirk ever took the train. He had so many frequent flier miles, he could probably take us *both* on the shuttle out of La-Guardia without making a dent in his considerable savings account. The jerk. Still, I had an argument to win here. "So it's not exactly a hop, skip and a jump from New York."

"I didn't say anything!" my mother protested, completely denying the subtext her raised eyebrows were sending everyone at the table.

And just in case anyone missed the subtext, Miranda innocently laid it out for all to see. "Have you ever met Kirk's parents?"

As I stumbled toward an answer, my mother declared, "No, she hasn't. Don't you think that's wrong?"

"Wrong?" Joey said, as if he weren't following.

"I just think that if a man is serious about a girl…" my mother began.

"What? You thinking of marrying this guy?" Sonny said, as if marriage for his baby sister was an option he had yet to think of.

"I don't know what I'm—" I began.

"Why shouldn't she be thinking of it?" my mother chimed in. "She's thirty-one years old."

"Believe me, you're better off waiting," Miranda said. "I married Fred when I was twenty-five, and look where that got me," she continued with the habitual roll of the eyes she made whenever she referred to her ex-husband.

My mother's mouth dropped open, then she shut it soundly. But her expression, as it roamed over her prized firstborn son sitting next to his bride-to-be, said that she didn't think Miranda had done too badly in the long run.

"Hey, Vanessa was only twenty-five when she married me. And you're happy, baby, aren't you?" Sonny said, turning to his wife, who scrunched up her nose and rubbed it against his, as her hand roamed over her ever-present abdomen. Somehow the sight of them made me feel…wistful. But only for a moment.

"Well, I was a young bride, too," Nonnie said, "and all that made me was a young widow," she continued, giving Artie a significant look. "But things are different today. Women today like to date around. Test-drive a man before they take him home for good."

"What? I was wrong to marry my husband at twenty-two?" my mother said defensively. "We were in love. We *wanted* to be together."

And there, I thought, lay the thing that stabbed most about Kirk's weekend away. Did he even want to be with me? *Really* be with me?

"Tell you the truth," Sonny said now, "I always liked that first guy you went out with. Vincent Salerno. Whatever happened to him?"

"Married," my mother said, as if whatever point she was trying to make was already proved. "For over nine years now."

"Whoa-ho," Sonny said with a barely contained laugh. "Another one bites the dust. And didn't you recently go to the wedding of that guy you went out with in college? What was his name? Randy?"

"That was five years ago already," my mother said. Clearly she was a stickler for details tonight.

Oh, God, please don't let them ask about Josh next....

But Sonny didn't even need to ask about Josh to make his point. "Hey, you wait any longer, Ange, and all of the good ones will be taken," he said.

"Not all of them," Nonnie said, giving Artie a look that stopped his fork midway to his mouth.

Even my own grandmother was going to beat me to the altar, I realized now, judging by the blush that was crawling up Artie's neck.

"Angela's different," Vanessa said in my defense. "She's *artistic*," she declared, her thick Brooklyn accent making the word sound more like "autistic."

"Hey, Angela, can you do that headstand for us again?" Tracy asked, remembering a *Rise and Shine* routine I once demonstrated for her in my mother's living room.

"No headstands," Joey said as Tracy began to scoot out of her chair. "You gotta eat first. Then Angela will do her tricks for you."

Tricks? *Oh, brother.*

When had I gone from "artistic" to circus sideshow freak?

I sighed. Maybe there really was something wrong with me.

4

I just called...
to SCREAM...I LOVE YOU!

There is only one thing worse than returning to an empty apartment on a Sunday night—that's returning to an empty apartment littered with the remains of someone else's good time. Specifically, Justin's and—judging by the two wineglasses nestled cozily together on the dining room table—Lauren's. Apparently they'd come home early from the Hamptons. Candles littered the windowsill; the smell of burning wax was still in the air. A note left by the answering machine indicated in Justin's loopy scrawl that he had taken Lauren to the airport. Which meant, since Justin didn't have a car, that he was taking an expensive round-trip cab to LaGuardia, just so he could spend an extra hour with the woman he once described to me as "the best thing that ever happened" to him.

I sighed. When was *I* going to be anyone's best thing?

As I headed into the living room and saw that sofa #3 had been maneuvered from its position in the middle of the room to a less prominent place in front of sofa #2, I realized I did have something to be thankful for. At least Lauren had used her considerable influence over Justin to persuade him that his most recent sofa acquisition was atrocious enough to warrant a slip-cover, which Lauren had no doubt created from one of Justin's bedsheets, I deduced from the pale blue covering that now disguised sofa #3's threadbare expanse. Since the two sofas faced the largest of our four TVs, their positioning created a movie-theater effect that satisfied my inner actor on some levels, despite the sacrifice of a good three feet of living space. I plopped down in the front row, grabbed the remote from the marble-topped coffee table (all the French provincial castoffs were Aunt Eleanor's) and clicked on the TV, my eyes roaming to the clock on the far wall. Seven o'clock. Kirk's flight landed at 7:50 (I saw the ticket on his dresser—not that I was checking). No luggage (Kirk always carried on), so he'd head straight for Ground Transportation. Give him five minutes to land a cab. Twenty minutes to the Midtown Tunnel. Ten minutes through the tunnel (after all, it *was* Sunday night, there was bound to be traffic). Kirk lived six minutes from the tunnel (he actually timed it once). That would put him in front of his building at precisely 8:31 p.m. Two minutes up the stairs, twenty minutes settle-in time (Kirk couldn't relax until his bag was unpacked and his toiletries safely tucked away in his medicine cabinet once more. I found it cute at first. Annoying later, when I was waiting to hear from him after one of his frequent weekends away.) That took us to 8:53. By nine o'clock he would be on the phone, proclaiming how much he had missed me.

I only had to wait two hours for a reminder of why I had been in the relationship with Kirk for twenty months despite the fact that he hadn't felt it necessary to bring me home with him. We loved each other, dammit. Had declared it so in month three. Reveled in it until month eight. Settled into things at the year mark. And now…now we sometimes took it (love, that is) and each other for granted. So what that he hadn't asked me to come with him? It didn't really mean anything in the face of all we had. Why, I bet if I just opened my mouth (because Grace always told me I was guilty of not communicating what I wanted) and told him how much it would mean to me to go home with him next time around, he'd happily invite me along. In fact, he might regret he hadn't brought me along this time.

He might even want to schedule a trip home within weeks just to make up for it!

And so, with this soothing thought I settled in to watch a round of mindless TV, starting with a rerun of *Friends,* which seemed to be on six times a day now that it had gone into syndication. I studied Jennifer Aniston with renewed interest, imagining this cheerful blond goddess settling in at home with her golden-blond god, Brad. Surely there was something to Michelle's tight-lid theory if this woman who had had trouble attracting the attention of David Schwimmer in her fictional life had landed Brad Pitt in reality.

So much for my reality, I mused, quickly changing channels once Rachel et al's coffee-shop existence was wrapped up with a rousing laugh track. One hour to go, I thought, with another glance at the clock. I spent it watching a news program on the deadly bacteria that resides in common household objects. And just as I was absorbing the fact that I had greater things to worry about than whether or not I will one day marry (like that I will certainly one day die), I realized it was just about nine and anticipation warmed me, reminding me that I was at the moment very, very much alive.

I jumped off the couch and headed for my bedroom to throw on a pair of boxers and a tee. Might as well get comfortable, I thought, with a vision of myself curled up cozily with the phone while Kirk whispered how much he'd missed me. Admittedly, he wasn't usually so demonstrative, but I had begun to look forward to a certain heightened display of intimacy whenever he returned from one of his business trips. Once I even lay in wait at his apartment, wearing a black lacy bra and thong. You can imagine what kind of amazing sex we had that night.

With a glance at the clock, I realized it was 9:10 already—so where was my phone call? My hey-baby-missed-you-so-much-I-could-die speech? Maybe there were delays at the airport....

I heard a key slide in the door. Or maybe he decided to drop by!

"Hey," came the sound of Justin's voice in the hall. What was

I thinking? Dropping by wasn't the kind of thing Kirk did, after all. It wasn't that he was unromantic, just…orderly.

"Hey," I said, joining Justin in the living room, where he was toeing off his sneakers and settling in on sofa #3. "Lauren get off the ground okay?" I asked, my face a mask of concern. The subtext of my question was: Any delays at the airport that I should know about?

"Without a hitch," he replied, his gaze falling on the dining room table with the two wineglasses. "God, I hated seeing her go."

My stomach plummeted at his forlorn expression, and I remembered suddenly what it was like to really miss someone. The look on Justin's face was the kind every girl pines for.

But it was only momentary, that look. For, suddenly, Justin glanced at the clock and snapped to attention. "Hey, mind if I put on the game? I just heard in the cab that the Yankees are up by three against the Red Sox." He grabbed the remote.

I had my answer. The Yankees were playing the Red Sox. Kirk was a Red Sox fan. Was it possible he got home and immediately flipped on the TV to catch the rest of the game?

I glanced over at Justin as he pounded a fist in the air. "Yea!" he roared along with the crowd on TV.

Oh, yeah. It was not only possible, it was probable.

Despite the fact that I was annoyed at being beat out by baseball, I joined Justin on the couch, never mind that I was a Mets fan, mostly by birth rather than from any true allegiance to game watching. Yeah, I could sympathize. I had watched the subway series with great trepidation. But it wasn't something I worked up a sweat about on a regular basis. Wasn't something I ignored friends, families and people I allegedly loved for.

The clock ticked on. Justin became more jubilant with every pitch. The Yankees were up by five now. By the time I did talk to Kirk, he wasn't exactly going to be Mr. Happy. I thought about calling him during the game, but didn't want him if his attention was going to be divided. I decided to wait until the seventh-inning stretch.

When the seventh inning finally arrived and a Yankee win was all but secured, Justin decided this called for an all-out celebration. "I'm going down for beer and chicken wings. Want anything?"

"No, no. I'm good," I said, making my way casually over to my bedroom, where I hoped to make my long-awaited phone call with Kirk in privacy. I was so high-strung at this point, I feared I might do something I'd later regret—like yell.

Kirk picked up on the second ring. "Hey, Noodles, I was just about to call you...."

Ah, if I could only have waited thirty more seconds, I would have had the upper hand. Still, I was glad to hear his voice. I missed him. "The lure of baseball was too great, huh?" I joked.

"You kidding? I couldn't bear to watch that travesty once I saw the score. I shut it right off."

Oh, brother. Then, as if to answer my unasked question—What exactly *have* you been doing in the one hour and fifteen minutes you've been home and not calling me?—he said, "I've just been settling in, unpacking."

Uh-huh. "Did you have a good weekend?" I asked, trying to rise above it all.

"Great," he said, his voice perking up. Then he proceeded to tell me, in lavish detail, all about it. Playing touch football with his cousins in the legendary acre lot his parents lived on (legendary to me, who had never actually seen it); holding his sister Kate's baby; meeting his other sister Kayla's boyfriend. All the children in Kirk's family had first names beginning with *K*. His mother's idea, according to Kirk. I wonder if she realized that she had created KKK with her alliteratively named progeny? The funny thing was, Kate had married a guy named Kenneth, and their new baby's name was—guess what?—Kimberly. I wondered now if the other sister had managed to line up a K-man with this new boyfriend. Hey, wait a second. *New* boyfriend? Kayla's *new* boyfriend was there?

"Um...how long has your sister been seeing this guy?" I asked, hoping "new" boyfriend meant new to Kirk but practically married to Kayla. After all, that was the only reason I could drum up why Karl, Kasper, Kirby, or whatever the hell his name was, had been invited and I hadn't.

"I dunno. Couple of months?"

Couple of months? Remain cool, remain calm.

"Seems like a nice enough guy, but who knows? Kayla goes through guys like they're going out of style."

Remain cool, remain calm. Get the facts. "So, um, does anyone ever ask about your girlfriend, sweetie?" I knew it sounded like I was fishing, but there was no other way to do this. I had to know.

"Oh, yeah. My mother's always harping on that subject, ever since Susan and I broke up. She always liked Susan…."

Liked Susan…

"But I learned my lesson that time around. Telling my family about stuff like that is like feeding hungry piranhas. They don't let up."

"Stuff like what?"

"You know, who I'm dating, whatever."

Whatever. "Kirk, do you mean to tell me that after almost two years, your parents don't know I *exist?*"

"Oh, they know I'm dating someone. But that's all their getting outta me. Besides, they know I'm intent on getting my business off the ground…."

"Excuse me, Kirk. Someone? You're dating *someone?*"

Silence on the other end. The dumb lug probably just realized he'd stepped on a land mine with his blithe comments.

Finally he said, "You know what I mean, Ange. Didn't you tell me the less your mother knew about your daily life, the better?"

"I was talking about stuff like what I ate, how late I stayed out. Not the person I'm contemplating marrying!"

A new silence descended, this one a bit more harrowing. But no worse than the sigh that finally emerged, the words that followed. "Ange, you know how I feel about that…."

I did?

"My whole focus now is on building my business. I thought you understood. I thought…"

But I was no longer listening. I was tired of what he thought. It was just so…unromantic. I wanted to be caught up in a passion. I wanted a man to want me so badly it hurt to imagine life without me. And I wanted it with Kirk. Was that so much to ask for?

That's how it happened. I suddenly found myself putting step one of Michelle's engagement scheme into action. I don't know why I succumbed. Maybe it was the fact of my absence (both literal and figurative) from Kirk's big family weekend. Maybe it was the blasé tone Kirk used when he said before hanging up, "Hey, when you come over tomorrow night, could you bring my U2 CD?"

See? This is where we're at. We don't even ask each other out anymore. It's all assumed.

Naturally, I had to start shaking up some of those assumptions. "Uh…actually, tomorrow night I'm meeting up with Grace." There! Take that!

"Oh. Okay. Where're you going?"

Wouldn't you like to know, I thought, feeling a tad triumphant. Until I remembered *I* didn't know where I was going with Grace, who didn't yet know we were going anywhere. "Shopping."

"Have fun," he said, as if I'd said I was having my body dipped in hot wax. Kirk was not a shopper, unless we were in say, CompUSA. "You could come by after, if you felt like it…." he offered.

"Oh, well, I'll probably be too tired. You know shopping wears me out."

"Okay. I guess it's just as well. I've got a lot of catch-up to do with work—I could stand to put in a little overtime. In fact, I'm gonna hit the sack now. I got a big day ahead of me tomorrow."

"Yeah, me, too," I said and, after a muttered goodbye, I hung up the phone, dissatisfied. This lid might need the rubber glove treatment. Or maybe even a sledgehammer.

"Just sit tight," Michelle advised at work the following Tuesday, when I informed her that I had put step one of her plan in action. "Give it a few days."

"A few days?" I didn't think I'd last that long. As it turned out, Grace had had plans with Drew last night and couldn't be lured to Bloomingdale's even to make an honest woman out of me. And since tonight she was attending some work-related cocktail party, I was faced with going straight home from Lee and Laurie to another fun evening at home.

So I sat tight. After all, I had plenty of couches to choose from.

Thank God for our large-screen TV, a hand-me-down from Justin's friend C.J., who had married his long-time girlfriend, Danielle, and moved on to Westchester and a forty-two-inch. The only thing on, of course, was *Friends,* and, somehow, tonight I just couldn't deal with it.

Deprivation was going to be a lot harder on me than on Kirk, I could tell.

Because the truth of the matter was, I had done that shameful thing that most women do when they get too cozy in a relationship. I had thrown over my own life for the sake of our life together. Take an average week in my life:

Monday: *Rise and Shine,* which I only get through at six o'clock on a Monday morning by telling myself that I am going to buy *Backstage* this week and begin to search for that great film or TV role I plan to land now that I have TV experience on my résumé and union cards from both AFTRA (for TV—see what a few leaps in front of a camera can get you?) and the Screen Actor's Guild. But what usually happens is, I bypass the newsstand on the way home from the studio and pay a surprise visit to Kirk at his home office, where we eat bagels and lox until Kirk realizes he has too much work to do to sit around all day eating bagels and lox and sends me on my way.

Tuesday: *Rise and Shine.* Maybe breakfast with Colin. Maybe I buy *Backstage* today, but usually just go home to watch a movie (we have a hell of collection, mostly due to Justin) or read the complete plays of August Strindberg (if I really want to depress myself) until I realize it's 2:10 and I'm never going to make it to Lee and Laurie on time for my three-to-ten shift. Rush to shower and change, arrive at Lee and Laurie at three-fifteen. Leave work at ten, take the crosstown bus to Kirk's (thus securing myself sex and saving myself a transfer to the Second Avenue bus, which *never* comes every ten minutes like it says it will on the schedule posted at the bus stop).

Wednesday: *Rise and Shine.* Sometimes Rena wants to have a planning meeting, and then Colin and I have to sit and listen to her drone on and on about her dream plans for *Rise and Shine.* Go to lunch with Colin, complain about Rena (whom Colin defends), until it's time for Lee and Laurie. Get off at ten, go to Kirk's.

Thursday: *Rise and Shine.* Maybe breakfast with Colin, after which I decide that that the edition of *Backstage* on the stands is too old and not worth spending the cash on. Sometimes I go home to clean my apartment (a fruitless endeavor with Justin as a roommate, but I can't seem to stop myself), or sometimes I find myself lured in to some treacherous sample sale, where I spend the afternoon trying to convince myself of the utter necessity of owning yet another stretchy black shirt. If I've dawdled in midtown long enough, I usually just go straight to Lee and Laurie. Sometimes I'm even on time! And guess where I head afterward? Kirk's, of course.

Friday: *Rise and Shine.* And since I have no shift at Lee and Laurie and no desire to start any self-actualizing project, I find some way to waste the entire day. Like renting the complete movies of Bette Davis. Or giving myself a pedicure. Until Kirk and I go out for dinner, or simply sit around the apartment like the old married couple we are (not that *he* realizes that).

Saturday: The dreaded ten-to-four shift at Lee and Laurie. After a day like this, can you blame me for going straight to Kirk's, where we order takeout and while the evening away in front of the TV or at the movies?

Sunday: Day of rest. Except when my mother manages to convince me of the utter necessity of my coming down to Marine Park for family dinner. Kirk comes, of course. After all, he loves my mother's cooking. Kirk never says no to a Sunday in Brooklyn.

Now do you understand how I've gotten so wrapped up in being wrapped up every day of the week? Kirk and I might as well get married at this point. What would be the difference, anyway?

"The ring," Michelle explained somewhat impatiently when I complained the next day about how much I am suffering and wondering, really, what it's all going to get me.

"When a guy buys you a ring, it means something."

So I sat tight for yet another night, telling Kirk I had a monologue I was working on. "Oh yeah?" he said with surprise.

Of course he was surprised. I hadn't done any auditioning since *Rise and Shine* became a cable-access phenomenon. Why should I? I was on the road to superstardom in a yellow leotard.

But suddenly there I was, reverting to my former self. The actor who had played Fefu in *Fefu and Her Friends.* (Don't let the name fool you—this was a *serious* role.) The woman who had once wowed crowds at the Classic Stage Company with my powerful rendition of Miss Julie. In case you were wondering, I was once a force to be reckoned with. But an actor has to earn a living....

"What are you doing home?" Justin asked, loping in from God knows where. He'd turned down the last production gig he'd been offered, so I knew he hadn't been working on the set all day. In fact, he seemed to be working less and less ever since he had landed a few commercial spots for a long-distance telephone service a year ago, which I thought was pretty ironic, considering the number of long-distance relationships Justin had been in (yes, Lauren wasn't the only one. Denise, his previous girlfriend, was from Oak Park, Illinois, Justin's hometown—a place Justin hadn't lived in himself since he was twelve, although his romance with Denise had begun on a visit to relatives one summer when he was in college). The commercial, which featured Justin looking frazzled and gorgeous as he ran across a campus and up the dormitory stairs, all in time to pick up a long-distance call from his mom, was so well received that they made two more. One in which Justin leaped across buildings to pick up a call, and another where he hijacked a campus security cart. His success had mostly to do with that utterly beatific smile on his face as he picked up the receiver and said, "Hi, Mom." Ironic, too, since both of Justin's parents had been killed in an auto accident, leaving him an orphan at the tender age of twelve, shipped off to live in New York with his aging Aunt Eleanor and Uncle Burt, who were now gone a good nine years themselves. Maybe there was something of the yearning I knew he still felt for his parents injected in the smile he projected from the small screen once he picked up that telephone. Whatever it was, the commercial ran so often—it even made Superbowl Sunday slots—that Justin was still coasting on the pile of residuals money he'd racked up. Perhaps that was making it harder and harder for him to get out of bed for the odd production job that came his way.

"What does it look like I'm doing?" I replied, defensive. Sometimes the ease of Justin's life annoyed me, I have to admit.

He ignored my irritated reply, plopping down next to me on the couch.

"Where's Kirk?" he asked. Even Justin realized my life was so intimately entwined with Kirk's that my being home on a weeknight meant something.

"Don't know. Home, I guess," I said, picking up the remote and surfing through, hoping my expression showed my indifference. I didn't really want anyone to know what I was up to, especially not Justin. It was downright...humiliating. But utterly necessary.

Then the phone rang and I was completely unmasked. "If it's Kirk, I'm, I'm...not home," I blurted as Justin reached for the receiver.

He turned to look at me, one eyebrow raised, as he spoke into the phone. "Hello? Hey, Kirk, my man, what's up?" he continued, his voice belying the suspicion in his eyes as he gazed at me. "Angie? Naw, she's not home. But then I didn't check under the rug...."

I glared at him, despite my humiliation.

"Okay, I'll tell her you called," he said. "Take it easy." After he hung up, he turned to stare at me full in the face.

I ignored him, lost in my own quagmire. "What the hell is he calling me for anyway? I told him I was busy."

Justin's eyes widened. "What are you up to?"

"Nothing!"

"God, Ange, don't tell me you're playing games," he said. "I didn't think you were like that...."

"I'm not!" I insisted. But suddenly it seemed glaringly apparent that I was one of those women I despised.

5

A rose by any other name...might still do the trick.

I would have despised myself even more for shamelessly avoiding Kirk if I didn't come off the Saturday shift at Lee and Laurie to find him waiting out in front of the building for me.

"Hey," he said, a smile lighting up his features as I came out the front doors.

"Kirk!" I said, surprised, realizing that he hadn't done anything so spontaneous, so...romantic, since the early days of our relationship. "What are you doing here?"

"Looking for you, stranger," he said, putting his arms around me and tugging me close. "I missed you." Then he kissed me so tenderly I felt a rush of warmth toward him.

Now I ask you, can you blame me for playing these stupid games? Especially when Kirk led me back to his apartment and made love to me like it was our last night on earth together.

Two simultaneous orgasms later, I was a goner.

Which is probably why I found myself sitting across from Michelle at a tiny table in the back of a bar by our office on Tuesday night, plying her with drinks while I smoked cigarette after cigarette from her pack, reveling in my relationship revival and anxiously awaiting advice on my next maneuver.

Hanging out with Michelle after hours was a peculiar enough event as it was, because we hadn't really been social since high school—specifically, since just after Grace moved to Long Island and I had moved on to my first serious boyfriend, Vincent. At the time, Michelle had been dating Vincent's cousin Eddie, and we bonded simply because it was always useful to have a girlfriend around all those nights we roamed the streets with the guys, restlessly searching for adventure and usually winding up at a diner or the movies, blowing what little money we had. Though Michelle was a bit of a fair-weather friend (or a fair-man friend—we parted ways when she moved on to Frankie, who ran with a different crowd), at least for a while I had someone around to tell me whether I had lipstick on my teeth or if some cheerleader had been spotted at school that day flirting a little too hard with Vincent. In truth, Michelle and I wouldn't even be friends now, except that when I gave up my job in the garment district four years ago, my mother had told the whole neighborhood (including Michelle's mother, whom she'd run into at the supermarket) that I was jobless, penniless and about to pursue a career with no pension plan. Mrs. Delgrosso had happily told my mother about her daughter's illustrious career and flexible hours at Lee and Laurie and put me in contact.

But despite all my doubts, I couldn't help turning to Michelle now that step one had succeeded in at least a quarter turn on Kirk's lid. Suddenly I was ready to be persuaded that the art of persuasion was my only resource when it came to Kirk.

"Make him jealous," Michelle said with a definitive crack of her gum.

"Jealous?"

"Yeah, that's your next step," she continued. "You need to convince Kirk that he's not the only man who's pining for you."

This was not as easy as it sounds. Kirk was just not the jealous type. In fact, during the first months of our relationship, when we were caught up in the throes of new passion, I was suddenly the object of every man's desire. So much so that one overzealous suitor even followed me home from Lee and Lau-

rie one night, trying to get my phone number. Kirk, who had
been waiting out on the stoop for me (yes, there was a time
when he did that), had found the whole thing quite amusing.

"That's because he didn't see the guy as a serious threat," Michelle advised. "You need to bring on the heavy artillery."

I looked at her. "Heavy artillery?"

"Yeah. You need to show him some other guy is serious about
you," she said, her eyes narrowing speculatively. Then, realization lit her face. "Flowers," she said. "You need to get flowers
from another guy."

"What other guy is going to send me flowers?" I said, going
through my catalog of men and coming up short. The only man
who'd ever bought me flowers was Randy, romantic that he was.
But Randy had been married for five years, and was not inclined
to buy me anything nowadays except the odd drink whenever
we happened to get together.

"That's the beauty of this plan," Michelle said. "You don't
need another guy. You can send the flowers yourself."

"Myself?" This plan was starting to seem ridiculous. And expensive. "Do I sign the card from myself, too?" I asked.

"No, no," she said, shaking her head at me as if I were the
insane one. Then her dark eyes lit up, as if my faux Prince
Charming had just stepped into the bar. I even turned my head
to see if, in fact, there was some bouquet-wielding charmer
waiting in the doorway. Then swung it back just as quickly
when I heard her say, "Jerry Landry."

"Jerry Landry?" I asked, incredulous. Jerry was our boss
and—at least according to his calculation—the Office Stud.
He made a point of hitting on every available woman—and
even some of the unavailable ones, depending on how short
they happened to wear their skirts—who worked for Lee and
Laurie Catalog. It was rumored that he slept with at least fifty
percent of the incoming trainees, but I had a feeling Jerry himself started these rumors. Because although we all laughed at
his stupid jokes and even batted our lashes playfully at his off-
the-mark flirtations (after all, he *was* the man monitoring both
our phone calls *and* our break times), I seriously doubted any
woman in her right mind would find him attractive. Maybe
it was the amount of Brylcreem he used to get his suspiciously

dark hair (suspicious for a forty-two-year old with *gray* chest hairs peeking out beneath his oft unbuttoned collars) slicked back, guido-style (hello? The eighties are *over*, Jerry). Whatever it was, something made Jerry utterly unappealing to most of the female population. Men, however, thought he was the greatest. Probably because he was the one buying the rounds during those rare after-office outings. And because the guys actually believed all those conquest stories he told. Even Kirk had, during his short stint at Lee and Laurie. So much so that, on more than one occasion, he had sidled possessively toward my cubicle when Jerry was leaning over me, giving me his usual schtick while trying to look down my shirt. Hmm, maybe Michelle wasn't so far off in this far-off scheme of hers....

Then I remembered that it wouldn't be Jerry's credit card that took the hit. "How do you propose I *pay* for these flowers?"

"Look," she said, "do you want to land this guy or what?"

Apparently, I did. Because suddenly I was willing to forgo that seventy-eight-dollar pair of pants I had been coveting in the Lee and Laurie Catalog (that was the other problem with this job—it fed my shopping disease) for the sake of my future.

That's when I got caught. No, not by Kirk. By Justin. Which seemed worse, somehow.

I was on the phone ordering flowers for myself. I know, I know. Stupid, right? On my budget I was the last person who should've been dialing up for a dozen long-stems, but I was a different woman. I didn't even recognize me. The thing is, I had invited Kirk over to my place for our usual Friday night together and, according to Michelle, I had to undo some of the damage I had done by sleeping with him with a quick follow-up maneuver.

So, I'm on the phone, ordering up flowers from Murray's 24-Hour Florist—New York City is probably the only place in the world where you can get anything delivered at just about any time. It's this type of convenience that makes a girl capable of anything, right? And I wouldn't have felt so bad about my behavior if Justin hadn't strolled through the door just after I had handed over my credit card number.

"…if you could deliver those flowers promptly, I would appreciate it. Thanks."

"Who died?" Justin asked, heading for sofa #3 (he always developed an especial fondness for the newest sofa as if to prove to me, and the rest of the world, the worthiness of salvaging it) and picking up the remote.

"Died?" I asked, puzzled, as I hung up the phone.

"Didn't I just hear you ordering flowers?" he said, his gaze seeming somewhat speculative despite the way he was already cruising through the TV channels.

Humiliation shot through me. Then panic. Justin wasn't supposed to be home tonight. Fridays he often frequented the open-mike night at the Back Fence, watching musicians try out their material and, I imagined, gathering the courage to get up there himself. Or something. Because ever since he had left film, and then acting, ostensibly to pursue music, he seemed to have lost his energy to do anything but strum a few chords on his guitar now and then as he gazed dreamily at his assorted artifacts around the apartment. The only reason I knew he was still pursuing anything was his vigilant attendance of Friday night's open mike. It was one of the reasons I had picked tonight for this wretched little plot. I didn't even want to bear witness to what I was about to do, and I certainly didn't want one of my best friends to. "Aren't you going to the Back Fence tonight?" I inquired, ignoring the fact that he had settled on a program and sunk deeper into the sofa.

"Nah. I'm beat," Justin said. After a few moments, he finally looked up at me, probably because I was hovering over him, anxiously trying to figure out a way to get him out of the apartment. It wasn't so much the fact that Kirk was coming over. After all, Kirk had accepted Justin's presence in my life, albeit grudgingly. It was just that I was absolutely appalled at the idea of Justin discovering my plot to win Kirk's pledge of undying love.

"What's up?" he asked, studying me with concern.

"Nothing!" I protested, completely blowing my cover. Then I glanced up at him from where I had begun to pick at a nonexistent piece of lint on the sofa. "It's just that…Kirk's coming over."

"Oh yeah?" he replied with some measure of surprise. It

wasn't that Kirk never came over, it was just that we spent more time at his place. Probably because of my roommate factor, but I feared mostly because of my (or should I say "our," meaning Justin's and my) clutter factor. Kirk had a decided distaste for the disorder Justin and I so willingly chose to live in, and when he was here, he couldn't help but point out the problems that resulted from irregular removal of recyclables (I had an increasingly bad habit of saving all the newspapers, magazines and trade papers I never seemed to get around to, in the hope that I would, one day, get around to them) and accumulation of other people's irretrievables (You-know-who was responsible for that). I couldn't help but agree with Kirk. There *was* something wrong with living with six lamps, three sofas and a stack of newspapers and magazines that rivaled the periodical room of the New York Public Library.

"Anyway, I was gonna cook him dinner."

This got a raised eyebrow.

"What?" I said.

"Nothing," he replied, turning his attention back to the TV. But I knew he was thinking of the time I threw a dinner party for all our friends, which was nothing short of disaster. Thank God, Justin had come to the rescue and pulled together a quick pasta fagioli. For a guy from the Midwest who was a mixture of every ethnicity except Italian—English, French and even a dash of some sort of Scandinavian—he certainly had a way with Italian cuisine. It was as if he had inherited the Italian gene that I hadn't. "You need help?" he asked as I continued to stand there looking at him uncertainly.

"Not exactly…" I began, not sure how to tell him that I simply needed him to go away. "What's C.J. up to tonight? You haven't seen him in a while," I hedged. C.J. was Justin's best male friend, who somehow managed to be married, successful, and yet still one of the coolest people I knew. He was vice-president of an independent record label that had found phenomenal mainstream success and yet still managed to maintain its indie roots. Though C.J. lived in Westchester now, he often came in on weekends when one of his bands was scheduled to play. "Maybe he's in town tonight. Isn't that new band he signed supposed to play CBGB's?"

Finally Justin got it. "Oh, I see," he said, his gaze falling on the table, where the candles from his weekend with Lauren were still strewn. "You want to be alone...with Smirk." "Smirk" was what Justin called Kirk when Kirk wasn't around. It wasn't that Justin didn't get along with Kirk. He just despised everything Kirk stood for: material success, technological innovation. The future. I had to forgive Justin for it—being an East Villager before the dot.com gentrification, I was on the same wavelength. Sort of.

"Do you mind?" I said, hoping he would suddenly find some other venue for his slacker revue tonight.

"Nah." He shrugged. "I'll just watch the game in my room."

So much for getting him out of the apartment. I had forgotten about the Yankee game. There was no way I could hide my embarrassing little ploy now, I thought, heading for the kitchen to tackle my next project: domestication. It wasn't that I couldn't cook at all—I make a mean marinara—it's just that I stuck pretty much to those things which wouldn't kill anyone if I messed them up. But if I was going to make Kirk pine for the woman he could possibly lose, I had to tackle something a guy like Kirk could understand: meat.

I headed for the fridge, where I had stacked a package of perfectly cut—or so said the butcher at Lenny's Meats—perfectly thick and perfectly frightening sirloin steaks. I wasn't a veggie or anything, I just was a little afraid of foods that had the capability to inadvertently poison me if undercooked. I put the steaks carefully on the counter, wondering just how long I had to grill them on the George Foreman (a Christmas present from Sonny that I had yet to take out of its original packaging) to destroy any of that malicious bacteria I seemed to know way too much about for a woman with such limited culinary experience. Fortunately, my mentor in man-catching, Michelle, had loaned me her copy of *Cooking With Style,* which, despite the suspiciously bright platter of vegetables that graced the cover, had a section on grilling.

Flipping the book open, I was amazed at how easy it all seemed. Six minutes for each side? No problem. Knowing that timing was everything, I set the asparagus to steaming and tossed the potatoes in the microwave. This was easy, I thought, laying the steaks on the hot grill just as the buzzer rang.

"I'll get it!" I yelled, running for the intercom, though Justin hadn't budged from the couch.

"Hey, it's me," came Kirk's voice as I pushed the listen button. I depressed the door buzzer with something like dread. Then I immediately went to the front door and waited, as if by greeting him at the door I could protect him from my own madness—or Justin's all-knowing gaze. When I heard him ascend the third flight, I stepped into the hall.

"Hey," I said, as he approached.

"Hey, Noodles," he said, his face creasing into a smile that made me feel guiltier and guiltier. Clearly I wasn't cut out for this level of subterfuge.

He kissed me, his eyes roaming over my face as if he could see the deceit there. And there must have been something in my expression because he asked, "What's wrong?"

"Nothing!" I said quickly, turning and leading him down the narrow hall toward the living room.

"Hey, Captain Kirk, what's up, man?" Justin said with a wide grin from his—semipermanent, I hoped—position on the couch.

I felt Kirk stiffen with tension beside me. Though Kirk had been forced to accept the fact of Justin's presence in my life from day one, it was clear he didn't always approve of Justin's seemingly carefree lifestyle. Justin must have sensed this, as he seemed to revel in his slacker ways in Kirk's presence. But Justin *did* make some attempts to bond, I suppose. Like the whole Trekkie thing. When Justin discovered Kirk was a fellow *Star Trek* fan, he took great delight in rehashing the finer plot points of what he considered the Great Episodes, while Kirk couldn't get past the way Justin took the good captain's name in vain every time Justin greeted him.

"Justin," he said with a curt nod. And while I was pointedly rolling my eyes toward Justin's room in a silent message that I hoped said, *Time for you to go,* Justin was gazing happily at Kirk as if he was his new best friend.

And apparently he was, judging by the way Kirk's own eyes lit up when he spied the television screen. "Is that the Yankee–Red Sox game?" he said, swiftly leaving my side and planting himself cozily beside Justin on the couch.

Oh, brother. *Now* how was I going to get Justin the hell out of here?

I decided that the best I could do at the moment was hit the kitchen. After all, I had bigger things to tackle at the moment. Like meat.

I headed for the kitchen, where those bloody red steaks still sizzled. Thank God I had asked the butcher to cut an extra steak. It looked like I would be cooking for three.

I can do this, I thought, when I had flipped all the nicely browned steaks and began placing the freshly steamed asparagus on a serving platter and pulling the baked potatoes out of the microwave. Studying my handiwork, I realized I was practically a Domestic Goddess.

Once the six minutes designated for side two were up, I pulled one of the steaks off the grill and cut into the middle, just to make sure they were good and cooked and I wasn't about to poison myself, my best friend and my, um, future husband. Red juice rushed out, sending a shiver through me. There was no way we could eat these like this, I thought, my head filled with visions of dancing microbes. That cookbook couldn't have been right....

I threw the steak back on and closed the lid on the George Foreman, just as the intercom buzzed.

"I'll get it!" I said, rushing for the intercom with an anxious glance at the sofa. Kirk continued to stare at the TV, unfazed. Justin, on the other hand, looked over at me, his eyes narrowed.

Hands trembling, I pushed the talk button, praying my beloved roommate wouldn't betray me now. "Yes?"

"Flower delivery," said a voice with a thick Spanish accent. I glanced over at the couch. Now I had Kirk's attention, I realized. But the thrill of victory was quickly squashed by the look on Justin's face as he sat back, folding his arms across his chest. He knew what I was up to. With a quick don't-you-dare-say-a-word glare that I hoped Kirk didn't pick up on, I headed for the door and swung it open.

Only to discover the deliveryman holding what looked like some sort of flower bush. A very large flower bush. "What the—" I stopped myself, glancing back into the living room, where Kirk and Justin looked on. *Where are my roses?* I wanted to scream but couldn't for obvious reasons.

"Flowers for Miss—" the man began, studying the order slip he clutched in his free hand. "DiFranci?"

I sighed. A florist who couldn't even get a name as easy as DiFranco right obviously hadn't been the best choice for this ridiculous plan of mine. Correction, Michelle's. Why had I listened to her anyway?

As I stared at that large pink bush, I realized this screwup by Murray's had left me with a way out of this ridiculous scheme. "There must be some kind of mistake," I began. "I didn't order a…a…plant." That was the truth, right? I *had* ordered roses. One dozen long-stemmed ones. At $54.95.

A frown creased the man's features. Lifting the order slip closer to his face, he squinted at it. "Miss, the order here says I am to deliver these flowers to Miss Angela DiFranci?"

"I'm sorry but, I can't accept—" I glanced back when I realized that Kirk now stood at the end of the hall. Of course, Justin stood just behind him, the smirk on his face even more pronounced now.

"What's going on?" Kirk asked. "Is there a problem?"

"Mmm, nothing. Just go back to your game. I think they have the wrong apartment."

"No, miss. It says right here that I'm to deliver these flowers to Miss Angela DiFranci, three-forty-seven East Ninth Street, apartment three-B." Then, squinting at the slip, he said, "The order was placed by—"

"Okay, okay," I said, grabbing the offending plant and pulling some cash out of the pocket of my jeans to silence my plant-wielding nemesis.

God knows how many singles I handed the guy, because with a wink and a smile, he disappeared before I could even ask for pruning directions. I only prayed that this bush I was now the proud owner of wasn't any more expensive than the roses I had ordered. And that Kirk would at least get some of the secret romance they had been intended to invoke.

"Hey, is that an azalea?" Justin said as I walked toward them, wondering how I was going to carry on in the face of this…madness. "I love azaleas. My mom used to grow them back in Oak Park when I was kid."

So much for romance.

"What's the card say?" Kirk asked as I set the offending plant carefully on the coffee table.

"Yeah, what does it say?" Justin said, clearly curious as to what my little game was.

Curious myself, I opened the card. At the words printed there, I felt my perfectly ridiculous plan take a turn for the worse. "Best wishes for a speedy recovery. Love, Sam and Stella."

"Who're Sam and Stella?" Kirk asked.

Wouldn't I like to know.

As it turned out, I made an (almost) complete recovery from the azalea fiasco. After dining on asparagus, potatoes and roast chicken (ordered up from BBQ when the meat had been rendered inedible by excessive overcooking), Kirk and I retreated to my room, leaving Justin to the azalea, which he was so taken with, he even moved some of the heaps of books he kept on the windowsill to make room for the latest addition to our happy little home. And while Kirk and I were languishing in bed, cozily watching a rerun of *Seinfeld,* the phone rang.

Kirk immediately looked at me, his brow creased. "Who the hell is *that?*"

Shrugging, I reached for the receiver. Late-night calls were not uncommon for me, though Kirk didn't know that. After all, he didn't spend enough time at my place to know my habits.

"Hello?" I said tentatively.

"Were you *never* going to call me back?"

"Josh!" I exclaimed. "I'm sorry, I've been, uh, busy," I said. "So, uh, how are you?" I asked, not daring to look over at Kirk, who was probably wondering why Josh was calling me at— quick glance at the clock—11:47 p.m. But Josh's and my friendship was such that we could call each other at any hour of the day for a consult on anything from the dangers of medical mismanagement (Josh was in insurance, now that he had given up his acting career) to the pitfalls of auditioning (because somehow Josh still had *lots* of career advice on the career he had himself given up). Though the late-night calls had all but ended since he'd moved in with Emily, he still sometimes resorted to them when he couldn't get in touch with me otherwise.

"Didn't you get my messages?" he asked.

"Yes, yes. I did. That's, uh, wonderful news."

"Yeah, well, it's not every day a man finds the woman he wants to spend the rest of his life with," he said smugly. Then, as if to console me that *I* hadn't been that woman, he continued, "But I want you to know, you're the first person I told—after Emily's family, of course."

Some consolation. Who else would Josh have told? He didn't speak to his parents anymore (years of therapy had shown him that they had not only damaged him in the past, but would prove even more damaging to his future), and I was probably one of the few friends Josh had left now that he had thrown his whole life over for Emily.

"So what do you say to a little celebratory dinner Monday night?"

"Monday night?" I replied, realizing that, as usual, I had nothing planned other than the usual takeout-and-a-rental with Kirk. "What time?"

"Around eight?"

"That's fine," I said, resigned to my fate.

"Looking forward to it, Ange."

"Yeah, uh, me, too," I replied, hanging up the phone feeling something like dread.

But a quick glance at Kirk's expression revived me immediately. Judging by the scowl that now creased his handsome brow, he was jealous. Jealous!

"What the hell was that about?"

Very jealous, obviously.

"Oh, nothing." I waved a hand nonchalantly and burrowed in beside him again to watch TV. "That was Josh. You remember Josh, right?"

They had met over a year ago. I had been playing Miss Julie in an off-off-Broadway production of the play of the same name, back in the days when I believed playing obscure characters in even more obscure venues would actually get me somewhere. Though by that time Josh had given up all pretensions of having an acting career himself, he still came to see me whenever I managed to land something juicier than, say, a crowd scene in a Christmas show. Josh had been dating Emily at the time, though he hadn't brought her for one reason or another—I suspected because it had been too soon in their budding relationship to introduce her to the ex-girlfriend. I had introduced him to Kirk as merely "a friend," though months later, during one of those relationship talks in which you 'fess up to your past, I did let it drop that Josh and I had dated. At the time, Kirk took it in stride, but now that my ex-boyfriend had given me a midnight call, it seemed the playing field had changed....

"What did he want?"

"Oh, he wants to have dinner Monday night." See? Not a lie.

"Don't *we* usually hang out on Monday?"

"Oh, did we have plans?" I asked innocently.

That was the crux of the problem with relationships. Those presumed dates. Just because I often hung out with Kirk on Monday night, I suppose he had the right to assume I would continue to do so without any sort of prior confirmation. But, if I was practically living at Kirk's place four out of seven days a week, didn't *I* have a right to presume we would one day make that seven out of seven days? No, I was not allowed that presumption. And, therefore, Kirk would no longer be allowed his.

"So you're going out to dinner with your ex-boyfriend," Kirk said, his gray eyes wide with disbelief.

"Oh, I don't think of Josh that way," I said. "We're just friends," I added. "Very close friends."

And then, before a smile of satisfaction threatened to blow my cover, I rested my cheek on Kirk's bare chest, presumably to settle in to television once more.

But who was I kidding? My heart was racing out of my chest with the thrill of victory. Kirk was jealous! That had to mean something, didn't it?

6

Love means never having to pack an overnight bag.

What it ultimately meant was that I had to suffer through an evening with Josh. Not that he wasn't a good friend—he was. Or he used to be, pre-Emily. I just preferred him over the phone or via e-mail. I think it was because I could…manage him better.

"Hey, Angie, how are you?" he said as I approached him where he stood outside of Holy Basil, a Thai restaurant in the East Village we had agreed upon after much debate. Josh always tried to coerce me to go the Upper East Side, where he now co-habitated with Emily. But, truthfully, the only time I ventured higher than midtown was to see Grace, who lived on the Upper West Side.

Despite what I knew about his flossing habits, Josh looked spectacularly well-groomed in a navy pinstripe suit, hot-pink tie (this, I suppose, was his attempt to show that despite his dreary nine-to-five life, he still had a wild side) and wire-rimmed glasses.

We hugged hello. Actually, Josh hugged, while I went for a quick kiss on the cheek. The end result was that I wound up kissing his neck. I stifled a groan. Somehow, no matter how hard I tried to avoid it, I always did something to convince Josh I still "wanted" him. This was what happened when you broke up with a guy before he got a chance to break up with you, even though it was evident to both of you the relationship was over.

When he leaned back from the embrace, Josh stood staring at me in a pose that looked surprisingly like his head shot: chin down (drawing attention to his dimpled cleft), blue eyes forward, a slight smile lingering on his well-shaped mouth. Yes, Josh was a good-looking guy. The problem was, he seemed to need constant affirmation of that fact—especially now that he wasn't acting anymore and having agents and directors tell him that he had the kind of look that could sell anything from toothpaste to hair-replacement products (did I mention that thick mass of dark, wavy hair?). Hence, the reason he had always gotten great commercial work. He had the kind of face that made him just good-looking enough to make you covet whatever skin-care system or toothpaste he was touting, and unassuming enough for you to believe he actually used it.

I decided to throw him a bone. After all, we were friends. And I understood that particular anxiety (heightened in actors, who base their work on their looks) that drove lesser people to face tucks and chin lifts.

"You look great," I said, smiling up at him and, I'll admit, waiting for some confirmation that I, too, was flourishing enough to consider giving up my day job.

"You let your hair go curly," he said, his eyes roaming over my hair, which I suddenly realized was sticking to the back of my neck in the heat. This was not a compliment from Josh, who used to tell me (with great regularity) during our grand-albeit-brief romance that I should have my hair straightened.

"Yeah, well. Summer. Humidity. Can't fight nature forever," I said, smoothing my hands over one of the shorter layers that usually framed my face but were now, I was sure, flying frightfully away from it.

Once we were settled at a cozy little table for two in the dimly lit restaurant, Josh became Josh again. The goofy little numbers cruncher who was trying so hard to seem like he was anything but the insurance actuary he was.

"So Emily and I went to see *The Yearning* Saturday night," Josh began, naming a play I had seen over a year ago, back in the days when it was playing at an avant-garde theater and people like Emily Fairbanks didn't know of its existence. After all, what interest would Emily Fairbanks, prep school girl from Connecticut, have in Lower East Side residents battling AIDS (because that's what *The Yearning* was about), unless she was paying eighty-five dollars a ticket? I guess at those prices, even Emily could afford to be sympathetic.

"Whose idea was that?" I asked, suspicious. In fact, I had been suspicious of Josh from the moment I had seen him in front of the restaurant, wearing what looked like a Brooks Brothers suit. This from the man who could never justify buying popcorn at the movies, no matter how tempting the smell ("Five dollars for *corn?*") Invariably, I would buy my own, which he would guiltily eat. At the time, I accepted his frugality. Even admired it. We were both actors then, and of the mind-set that we could do without expensive frivolities for the sake of art. But ever since Josh had gotten a day job—and a princess, because that was what Emily appeared to be—he'd changed.

"Emily got comp tickets from her boss," he replied with a certain smugness, as if his future wife's skill at attaining freebies was to be admired. Apparently, Emily didn't even have to pay for her kinder, gentler feelings.

"Yeah, well, I saw it already at LaMama," I said, battling back with my superior I knew-it-was-great-art-even-then attitude.

But this didn't faze Josh, who had an uncanny ability to lay me bare and bleeding with one well-put question. "So how's the auditioning going?"

And there it was, the truth of just how far I *wasn't* from Josh's own bourgeois world. I hadn't auditioned in months. Six, to be precise. Ever since I had landed my gig as exercise guru to the six-year-old set. But in the face of Josh's inquiry, my career at *Rise and Shine* took on epic proportions. "Haven't really had a chance," I began, "what with the show being so successful and all. My producer has us rehearsing new routines already, so we can start up the new season as soon as the old one ends. And then there's work and Kirk…."

He bobbed his head, as if this answer made sense to him. Then, with the apparent wisdom of a man who had spent all of one year pursuing his alleged lifelong dream, he said, "Yeah, I remember that life well. Always running around. Never sure where your next paycheck or your next meal was coming from. You know, I just read a report the other day that something like sixty-nine percent of all people working in creative fields die of causes that could have been treated during routine health-care…."

And there you had it: my "attraction" for Josh. We had met over an antihistamine on the Great Lawn of Central Park while playing disinterested bystanders in a student film that we hoped might make it to Sundance, but that ultimately wound up on the cutting-room floor. After six hours of waiting for the two leads to get through a breakup scene on the blanket before us, my allergies had gone into overdrive. Josh, a fellow sufferer, had recognized the symptoms right away, and during the break slipped me a Claritin. Afterward we had shared coffee and the kind of conversation that could convince a woman she had found her destiny, or at least a man she could fearlessly fall apart in front of. We had a lot in common: the same allergies (pollen, dust mites, cats and certain varieties of nuts); the same neuroses (death, poverty and the imminent collapse of the retaining wall that kept the Hudson from flooding the F train) and the same fear that all our waiting around at open calls and suffering through rejection would ultimately result in nothing.

You would think that since he'd given up the precarious life of an actor for the relative safety of life insurance, he would have calmed down, but no. Now that he had succumbed to a career of creating tables designed to measure such things as death due to, say, consumption of common household products, Josh was a font of horrifying statistics. And though I knew better, I could not, somehow, keep from waiting with rapt attention for some morbid little tidbit to drop from his lips. It was as if I needed him around to remind me that even if there were things in life I couldn't be sure of (my acting career, Kirk, the number of sofas in my apartment at any given time), I could be sure of one thing: the fact that I would die.

"So, you folks ready to order?"

"I am," said Josh, glancing up at me in question.

"Uh, yeah. You order first," I said, burying myself in the menu, my appetite gone. How was it that Josh always had a knack for making me realize the pure insanity of my life?

"I'll have the Pad Thai," I said finally, ordering the same thing I always ordered whenever I ate Thai. Boring, yes, but at least I knew what I was getting. And I liked to be sure of *something* in life. Besides, I was allergic to so many things, it saved me from having to interrogate the waiter about hidden ingredients that could potentially kill me in the other entrée choices.

"So let me tell you how I did it," Josh said, and I knew, without any further clarification, what "it" was. The proposal. I sipped my water, pasted on a smile and listened while Josh proceeded to tell me all about the glorious evening he asked Emily Fairbanks to be his wife. Josh prided himself on being a romantic. In fact, he still gets on my case that I didn't appreciate all his valiant attempts to woo me (okay, forgive me if I didn't find rowing across the lake out front of his parents' family cabin in the Poconos on the hottest day of the year romantic). But as he told me about the carriage ride across Central Park (a bit clichéd, but we'll give him points for big spending), how the moon hung low in the sky and the only sound was the gentle clip-clop of the horse's hooves (I'm sure there was traffic. There's always traffic. But never mind…). How Emily's eyes lit up when he turned to her in the cozy little seat, took her hand in his and said those words he had never uttered to another woman before.

I have to say, I got a little choked up there. Especially when I saw shining in Josh's eyes what looked like the real thing. Love. For Emily Fairbanks, whose most notable quality (in my mind, anyway) was a certain nobility of brow and good skin.

I smiled, the lump thickening in my throat. I was happy for him. Really, truly happy. Because if Josh, with whom I shared not only the same allergy prescription but the same paralyzing anxieties, could get married, then, hell, I would be just fine.

"So let me know when I have to get my tux," I said, referring to our old joke that I would have to be Josh's "best man," since I was (at least according to him) his closest friend.

And then Josh ducked his head and actually *blushed*.

"Okay, okay," I continued to banter, unaware of the source of his discomfort, "I'll wear a dress if I have to. But no taffeta!"

But when Josh continued to avert his gaze, I realized our old joke was no longer funny. And I suspected I knew why.

"I *am* coming to the wedding, aren't I?"

Finally he looked up, his gaze hesitant. "Actually, Emily and I…well, we were just talking about, well, you…and she doesn't really feel, uh, comfortable with, uh, inviting…that is to say, uh—" he ducked his head once more "—you."

My mouth opened to speak, but not a word was forthcoming. After all, though we didn't hang out much anymore, Josh and I were friends. And though we hadn't fared well as a couple, we had come to depend on each other in some ways. At least until Emily had entered the picture.

"C'mon, Ange," Josh said now. "You have to understand how Emily must feel. I mean, you *are* my ex-girlfriend."

And, apparently, I thought as I scanned his embarrassed features for some sign of the man I thought was one of my closest friends, that's all I would ever be.

But I didn't have time to ponder my flagging relationship with Josh. Because suddenly my relationship with Kirk took a turn for the better.

When I came home from dinner that night, there was a message blinking on my answering machine. "Call me when you get in," came Kirk's voice over the machine (rather insistently, I might add).

I opted not to call.

What? It was *late*. I didn't want to wake him up.

Besides, I didn't want to do anything to break my feeling of sheer power. A power that only grew when, while I was sitting at my desk at Lee and Laurie the next day, Jerry Landry leaned over my cube, eyes gleaming as if he were going to tell me some dirty secret, and said, "You got a call at the control station from Kirk. You want me to transfer him?"

"Sure," I said, my insides shimmering with an excitement I had not felt since the early days of Kirk's and my relationship. I glanced at Michelle, who raised an eyebrow at me. Kirk never called at the office. Not only was it near impossible to get through during the day, he never really had a need to. Until now.

"Thank you for calling Lee and Laurie Catalog, where casual comes easy," I answered as I was supposed to, praying Kirk's call had gotten to me before a customer's.

"Hey," Kirk said, "what's going on?"

"Hey," I replied, as calmly as I could.

"Why didn't you call me back last night?" he demanded. I almost felt a pinch of guilt at the hurt in his tone.

"I'm sorry, sweetie," I said, rushing to make amends as was my nature (despite what you might think of me, I really am no good at this game-playing stuff). "It was just so late when I got home and I figured you were tired, and—"

"What the hell time did you get home?"

Wow, he was mad. "Uh, eleven-thirty." I neglected to explain it was because I had spent a major part of the evening letting Josh know just what I thought about the fact that he felt it necessary to exclude me from the most important day of his life. An utterly fruitless endeavor, as I discovered that not only did I not understand Emily Fairbanks, I understood Josh even less.

"What the hell were you doing?" Kirk barked. "Oh, never mind. You coming over later?"

"Later?" I glanced at Michelle, who was nodding her head in the affirmative. "Uh, okay."

"Good, because we need to talk.... See you around ten-thirty."

"Okay," I said, clicking off the line and turning to face Michelle. "He wants to talk...."

"Bingo!" she proclaimed, clapping her hands together.

My eyes widened. My God. It was working....

I showed up at Kirk's place around quarter to eleven. I don't know what I was expecting, but it wasn't Kirk standing in the doorway of his apartment, waiting for me.

"Hey," I said, approaching cautiously.

He didn't answer, only pulled me into his arms and proceeded to kiss me in a way he never had before. A bit roughly. Not that I minded. In fact, I liked it very much.

I linked my arms around his neck, pressed my body into his, looked up into those gray eyes I thought I knew so well and saw something unfamiliar stirring there. I would have called it anger, if not for the kisses he kept feathering over my mouth, my chin.

And here I thought I was going to get a speech about Josh.

Kirk broke the kiss, but only long enough to lead me down the long hall to his bedroom, where he pulled me down to the bed and proceeded to molest me.

In the best way, of course.

Better. Because I had never seen Kirk in such a…fever. He was always so in control (not that that was a bad thing—it accounted for his longevity in the sack). Now he was like a man driven by demons, tearing at my clothes (well, not exactly tearing—he did have a certain respect for fashion and knew what these little Lycra numbers went for), running his hands over my body as if committing it to memory.

Once he was inside, I nearly came when he gazed down at me, a look of pure possessiveness in his eyes.

You can just imagine what effect that had on me. And this time, Kirk didn't even attribute it to the mattress.

Now, as we lay curled into each other, I felt a ribbon of pleasure move through me. For no matter what manipulative devices had brought Kirk to this point, I couldn't deny that what had just happened between us was very, very real.

"That was nice," Kirk said, nuzzling my face with his and causing another flutter to rush through my satiated body.

"Yeah, it was nice," I said, gazing up into his eyes, which had now gone soft and were looking at me in a kind of wonder.

I came home the next day after an evening during which Kirk had made love to me no less than three times. It was if he were trying to drive home (literally) the fact that I was his and no one else's. A pretty heady experience, as you can imagine. Not even the rigorous morning I had spent at *Rise and Shine* could dispel the glow I was feeling.

As I rode the bus home from the studio, I realized how foolish I had been to spend money I didn't have on azalea plants I didn't want and steaks I would inevitably render inedible. Kirk loved me. Really loved me. I felt like an idiot for going to such lengths to prove something to myself that I should have already known. And since I knew I'd feel like an even bigger idiot when my Visa bill came, I had resolved to undo some of the damage I had inflicted on myself by returning the azalea. After all, I *hadn't* ordered it. I *could* march it right back to Murray the florist, play the disgruntled consumer and get my money back. It was a simple plan.

Only I hadn't counted on the Justin factor.

"What the hell have you done!" I yelled when I strolled through the living room, carefully dodging the flowerpots and bags of potting soil that littered the floor only to discover that lovely little azalea on the windowsill now sported a brand-spanking-new flower box in which to spend the rest of its happy little plant life.

Justin poked his head out from the kitchen, where he was apparently creating some other sort of mess, judging by the sound of pots clanging. "Hey, Ange. What's up?" he said, oblivious to the cause of my distress.

"What's up?" I asked, gesturing to the brightly colored bush. "You repotted my plant?"

"I think it's actually a tree, though you could categorize it as a bush. Azalea," he said, stepping into the living room and gazing fondly at it.

"Why would you *do* something like that?"

"Why?" He shook his head at me as if I were the clueless one. "Did you see the size of that pot it came in? Poor thing needed room to breathe, to grow. In fact, when I went back down to Murray's to explain the problem, he gave me this great flower box for free. He's a pretty nice guy, that Murray."

My anger exploded. "But I was going to return it to…to *Murray!*"

"Return it?" he said. "Why the hell would you return such a beautiful—" He stopped then, as if suddenly remembering the circumstances of how this beautiful azalea had come into our lives. His gaze narrowed. "Oh, I get it. Now that this innocent azalea has served as your little...*ploy*—" and he said "ploy" with such disgust, I admit, even I cringed "—you just want to send it back, is that it?"

"It wasn't a ploy. It was a...a mistake."

"Why?" he demanded. "Because you didn't get what you wanted? No pledge of undying love—" then, grabbing my hand with a fury I found surprising for Justin "—no ring?"

"I don't expect you to understand, Justin."

"You're right. I don't understand," he said. "I don't get this sudden desire to be married. I thought you wanted to be an actor."

"Since when is it against the law for actors to get married?"

He thought about that for a moment. "I dunno. Getting married seems kind of...time-consuming."

Suddenly the memory of my brother Sonny's wedding leaped to mind. I remember his then-fiancée, Vanessa, and how she somehow managed to fill her days, her mind, her whole entire life, with choosing everything from the perfect dress to the perfect finger food to serve during the cocktail hour. Hmm....

Then I snapped to my senses. "You don't have to make the wedding a three-ring circus," I said. "Besides, I'm...I'm ready to get married. I've got a good gig at the moment and—"

"*Rise and Shine?*" Justin said, eyes bulging.

"It's *TV,* isn't it? Who knows where it could lead to?"

"Maybe a jail term for child abuse. I was looking over those tapes you brought home. Some of the yoga poses you did on that one episode looked...lethal. You sure kids are supposed to bend like that?"

"Okay, smarty-pants, I'd like to see you take your career beyond the odd open mike now and again. Have you even been performing on any of those nights you've been spending at the Back Fence? Ever since you left acting, I haven't seen you do anything to pursue this...this music thing." I couldn't call it a dream. I knew Justin's dream was film—a dream he'd reduced to the somewhat menial job of a grip. And he barely even did *that* anymore.

When I saw the worried frown descend over Justin's features,

I immediately regretted that last statement. I didn't know what had been holding him back lately, but now that he was finally doing *something,* I didn't want to quash whatever creative impulses he had left. "I'm sorry, Justin. You know I want to support you in whatever you do. I just wish you would support me…in this thing with Kirk."

"This 'thing'? Meaning marriage?"

"Yeah," I said uncertainly, as his eyes narrowed on me. "Or…whatever."

"Okay," he said, "but it's your funeral."

In the end, I couldn't stay mad at Justin, especially after he cooked me an omelette so amazing I felt almost guilty for trying to take the azalea away. I couldn't believe how attached he'd grown to the bush in such a short time. But then, Justin did seem to form attachments to things the way I formed them to men. Besides, I knew he had a point. Now that I was assured of Kirk's affections, I felt no pressing need to push the marriage plan any further. I sensed that good things would happen for me in due time, if I just let them.

Michelle, of course, had other ideas.

"You're going to lose ground if you don't move on this," she warned.

I wanted to resist her. I really did. And I would have, if it hadn't been for the late-night chat Grace and I had on the phone that evening.

"Drew wants me to come look at houses in Westport," she said when I idly asked what she was doing over the weekend, thinking that I might round her and Drew up for dinner with me and Kirk. I knew that Kirk liked Drew from the rare time when our schedules meshed and we managed to meet up for drinks or a movie. And I figured it wouldn't hurt to remind Kirk that there were other upwardly mobile men who were not afraid to make some sort of commitment. Because Drew had "marriage and kids" stamped all over him, despite Grace's protests that it wasn't happening anytime soon. But I hadn't realized how soon.

"Westport, Connecticut?" I asked, astonished.

"Yeah," she replied blandly. "His boss just bought a three-bedroom and has convinced Drew that the burbs is the place to be. To be honest, I think he's just looking for a golf partner, but now Drew is suddenly hellbent on finding a house."

"Grace, you realize what this means, don't you?"

"Well, for one thing, Drew's gonna get a nice little tax write-off next year."

For such a smart woman, she was incredibly dense sometimes. "He's *nesting,* Grace. And he's taking you right with him!"

"Oh, c'mon, Ange, we've been together barely a year."

But I was sure that Grace was simply ignoring the facts. I wouldn't be surprised if she was engaged by Christmas and living in Westport by next spring! The thought filled me with sadness. Grace was going to leave me alone and single in New York City.

I had to get Kirk on board—and fast.

And so I sat listening raptly the next day during a break at Lee and Laurie while Michelle informed me of the third and final step. "Assume the position."

What this meant, of course, was that I needed to become such an intricate part of Kirk's life that he didn't know where his life ended and mine began. Essentially, I needed to become his wife…in every way.

I started spending even more time at Kirk's place. Even went as far as surprising him with dinner when he came home from work. Granted it was linguine marinara (I wasn't risking anything after the meat fiasco), but he seemed quite happy to come home and find me and a hot meal waiting.

Still, I knew there was only one way for a woman to gain true intimacy with a man in New York City. And that was by sharing the one thing that came at a premium in this fine metropolis: closet space.

It's true I had already made some gains in this area. An antihistamine in the medicine cabinet, a bottle of spray gel on the toilet tank. A travel-size box of tampons tucked into the carryall basket kept beneath the sink. I even had some workout clothes lingering in the depths of one of Kirk's drawers, for those rare occasions when I felt a need to leave his apartment for a jog. But I had yet to traverse the Great Divide and gain a drawer in the neat little bureau in his bedroom or, even more important, a permanent place in his orderly closet. It wasn't for lack of effort, either. I had been known, in the almost two years we'd been together, to leave behind the occasional bra in the bed, jeans on floor or dress on the back of the door, mostly due to my own disorganization rather than any concerted design. But every time my clothes started to accumulate in his apartment, Kirk would gather them together, and at fairly regular intervals I would be confronted with a tidy bundle to take home. Not that I had minded, really. In fact, there was nothing more irritating to me than to be home dressing for a night out with friends or even an audition (not that I'd been on any of those lately), only to discover that that black stretchy tank I had my heart set on wearing was at least four stops away on the M15 bus.

But now I had more important considerations than what I would be wearing that night. Like where I would be spending the rest of my life. Or, more specifically, with whom.

I started out slowly, so as not to raise any suspicion: a pair of jeans here, a T-shirt there. Even managed to slip a pair of slides onto the shoe tree on the floor of his closet. And when, after a few weeks during which I had managed to accumulate a verifiable wardrobe at Kirk's place, I was confronted with the inevitable shopping bag—from Banana Republic, the only clothing store Kirk ever seemed to venture into—I stood ready to stake my claim.

"Uh, do you think maybe I could leave some of this stuff…here? You know, for when I stay over," I said as Kirk tried to press said shopping bag into my hand one afternoon when I had dropped by in the hopes of scoring some quality time (read: sex) between jobs (cut me some slack, okay? I was stressed out about this game playing. I needed some kind of…*release*).

I nearly lost heart at the sight of what I perceived to be abject fear crossing Kirk's face.

After a few horrifying moments of pensive silence, he said carefully, "I suppose we could do that…."

I practically skipped all the way to the wall-to-wall closet behind Kirk, where he had wandered, seemingly in a daze.

Sliding open the door, he stood, arms folded, contemplating the space I was about to invade.

I'll admit, the sight of all that closet room filled my heart with greed. Especially since my own meager closet was crammed full of God-knows-what (when it came to clothes, I was just like Justin—unable to part with anything, right down to the bridesmaid dress I had worn in my brother Sonny's wedding, six years ago). As I stood beside Kirk, visions of all that outerwear I never had a place for in the summer months filling in all the gaps between the line of button-downs and Dockers that barely filled that expansive space (I mean, leaving *that* much room between hangers was practically a *crime* in a city this cramped), I must have been holding my breath in sheer anticipation, because I suddenly felt it burst out of my mouth when I heard Kirk's next words.

"Maybe a pair of jeans. There really isn't much room...."

"A pair of jeans? A *pair* of *jeans?*" I asked, incredulous.

"Well, gosh, Noodles, it's not like you're moving in...."

That's when I let him have it. I couldn't help myself. "Maybe you haven't noticed," I said, "but I practically *live* here during the week. And every day I'm packing a bag, wondering do I need a sweater tomorrow or will a tank be fine? Can I stick with sandals or is it going to rain? Thank *God* for the weatherman. At least Al Roker cares whether or not I'm going to spend my day shivering and wet. It's a good thing we never actually go out anywhere, because deciding on a daily basis on a change of clothes that will take me from day to evening might just...just kill me!"

Now, admittedly, I was exaggerating. Though it's true that I'm an anxious packer. Don't ask me why limiting myself to whatever I could put into a knapsack sent me into the kind of tizzy that most people reserved for the bigger questions of life—like what to name their first child, or which mutual fund to dump their life savings into. Maybe that was my problem. Maybe I needed to get a life. A real life.

"We go out...." he said finally, avoiding the real issue.

"That's not the point," I said. "The point is, I need a real place—" in your life I wanted to say, but prudently refrained from doing so "—in your closet."

"I'm sorry, Noodles. I suppose it isn't fair to ask you to lug all that stuff back and forth...."

And so that's how I gained a whole foot and a half of hanger space in Kirk's wall-to-wall. Because if nothing else, Kirk was all about being fair. And even if I had been hoping to appeal to something other than his innate sense of justice, a girl had to take her gains where she could, right?

7

All a girl needs is a little courage—and a hefty credit line.

There were other gains as well. Immeasurable things, like the way Kirk consulted me on the choice of a new shower curtain or how he linked his arm protectively around me when a ranting homeless man lumbered too close one night as Kirk walked me home. He even starting talking about a vacation together in the winter.

"...someplace romantic, like the Bahamas," he said one dreamy night as we lay in his bed curled together under the covers. This was big—in my mind, anyway. Up until then, we had only done spontaneous weekends away whenever Kirk found a lull in his workload—out to the vineyards on the North Fork of Long Island, or to the mountains of Upstate New York. I couldn't attribute this new development entirely to my Calvins in Kirk's closet. Or the fact that he'd even gone so far as to give me a drawer in his triple dresser (significant, considering it was the only dresser in his apartment). It was as if the fact of my very real existence in his life had sunk in.

It hadn't sunk in for my mother, however. "You're bringing *him?*" she asked after browbeating me into a Sunday dinner in

Brooklyn. I was long overdue for a visit—probably because I was anxious about the damage my sometimes overbearing mother might do to my relationship during this delicate lid-loosening process. I discovered I had reason to worry.

"Of course," I replied, suddenly realizing that while my relationship with Kirk had moved to a new level, Kirk's relationship with my family had sunk to an all-time low.

"Humph" was all she said to that. "Well, at this point I wouldn't care if you brought Jack the Ripper. Do you know it's been over a month since you even set foot in Brooklyn? I'm not getting any younger, Angela. And neither is your grandmother. Though judging from the way she's running around with that Artie Matarrazzo, you'd think she was sixteen."

"Is that still going on?" I asked, incredulous.

"Going on?" she replied. "He comes over here three, four times a week now. Taking her to the park, food shopping. Do you know, the other day I came home and found him in her apartment, setting her hair? And she's sitting there, her shirt damp from shampooing in the sink, or God knows what, and you can see right through it from here to…to Christmas!"

Oh my. Clearly Nonnie was getting in…deep.

"And I'm standing there, feeling like some kind of damn fool for interrupting. Me! Last time I checked, *I* was the one setting her hair on Monday nights…."

Now we had gotten to the heart of the matter. My mother, left without Nonnie to care for, didn't feel needed anymore.

"Ma, maybe now that Nonnie is busy with…with someone, maybe you need to find some other way to spend your time. Maybe take up a hobby…."

"A hobby? What do I need with a hobby? I have your father's tomato plants."

That, precisely, was the problem. They were my father's tomato plants. Ma never really had anything of her own, and now that my father was gone, she seemed to be devoting the rest of her life to keeping alive whatever remained from his.

"Ma, I'm talking about something *you* need."

"I have my family," she replied simply. "What more do I need?"

Obviously nothing else, I thought when I arrived at the

house on Sunday with Kirk in tow. I should have been worried at the way my mother's eyes narrowed at Kirk. Should have realized that she had taken his absence last time—and the reason for it—as some kind of betrayal, on my behalf. But I could hardly explain to her the new strides I had made, relationship-wise. My mother would take the fact that I was practically living at Kirk's as some kind of cardinal sin rather than the leap forward I knew it to be.

But there was no time to consider these matters, not with Vanessa and Sonny at center stage, Vanessa aglow while Sonny went on and on and on about how he felt the baby kicking up a storm the night before. "He's gonna be a fighter, this little guy." I watched sullenly while Joey, Miranda, Tracy, Timmy and even Kirk took turns touching Vanessa's rounded abdomen. I felt a frisson that felt decidedly like fear when I saw Kirk slide his own wide palm over that smooth expanse, a smile turning his handsome features boyish, as the baby, apparently, responded with a firm kick.

Eesh. I didn't even want to touch it. All I could think about was the suffering that would have to be endured to bring that baby into the world. The blood…

"Where's Nonnie?" Joey asked now.

"God only knows," Ma began. "She left the house hours ago with that Artie Matarrazzo to do a little shopping, and I haven't heard a word! She was supposed to pick me up some garlic for the stuffed mushrooms. How are we gonna eat stuffed mushrooms with no garlic?"

"Oh, Mrs. DiFranco, stuffed mushrooms? You shouldn't have," Kirk said, acknowledging, as he usually did, his lust for my mother's cuisine.

"Well, I might not be," she replied, sparing him a glance that said (to me, anyway) that garlic had nothing to do with why she might withhold her famous stuffed mushrooms.

Fortunately, Kirk didn't notice, because just then the door opened and a flushed Nonnie stepped into the room, trailed by an even redder-faced Artie Matarrazzo, who was carrying more shopping bags than an eighty-six-year-old man technically should.

"Well, everyone's here!" Nonnie said breathlessly. "Hello,

hello!" Then she hurried about the room dispensing kisses and hugs and, in the case of Joey, Sonny and even Kirk, swats on the rear end. Apparently Nonnie wasn't bearing a grudge the way my mother was.

"Did you bring the garlic?" Ma asked, grabbing the two Waldbaum's bags Artie held.

"Of course," Nonnie said, turning as she pulled from her head the scarf she had worn to protect her hair. Hair, it should be noted, that looked even fuller and more lush than usual. Apparently Artie was a man of many talents.

"Artie, honey, the garlic?" Nonnie said, holding out one well-manicured hand while Artie fished around in his trouser pocket.

"Ma, you better have paid for that garlic," my mother warned when Artie finally retrieved a cluster of cloves from his right-hand pocket.

"Who pays for garlic?" Nonnie said, taking the cloves and giving Artie a pat on the cheek. He didn't even blush this time. Only smiled like a man who had found his partner in crime. Obviously Artie shared not only a mutual affection with Nonnie, but also her staunch belief that garlic was the food of the people and should be given—or taken, as the case might be— freely.

"Impossible!" Ma said, snatching the garlic from Nonnie and heading into the kitchen in a huff.

"What's eating her?" Nonnie inquired. Then she shrugged, as if my mother's ire was not her concern. And it wasn't, I supposed. It was mine. Or more specifically, Kirk's, I discovered once we were seated around the dinner table.

"So, Kirk," Ma began, when everyone else was immersed in eating. "Angela tells me you went home recently, to see your family?"

Uh-oh. I knew exactly where this conversation was going.

"Yeah. Had to make the rounds, especially now that I'm an uncle," Kirk said proudly.

"Is that right?" Ma said, looking at me as if I had withheld some crucial information. "Girl? Boy?"

"Oh, a girl. Kimberly. And she's a cutie."

"How old?" Vanessa asked.

"Ten months." Kirk replied.

"Well, that must be hard," Ma chimed in. "What with your family living so far away and all. You probably hardly get to see her."

"Yeah. But I'll be seeing her soon. In fact her christening is Labor Day weekend—and that's only a month and a half away. My sister Kate just called and asked me to be the godfather," he said, beaming at us all.

I tried to smile back. I really did. But suddenly one of those stuffed mushrooms had lodged in my throat, right there beside the realization that Kirk was going home without me again. And how come he hadn't mentioned to me before that he'd been invited to be a godfather?

But if my mother picked up on this, she didn't show it. "Ten months and they're just having the christening *now?*" she exclaimed, not even trying to disguise her horror at the idea of letting a baby go unblessed for so long.

"Well, that was my mother's idea actually." Kirk chuckled ruefully. "She seems to have it in her head that the act of baptism might be a bit traumatic for an infant."

"Traumatic?" Ma replied, her eyes wide. "I should think it would be more traumatic if—God forbid—something should happen to the baby before the baby was recognized by God!"

"Ma!" Sonny interjected now, clearly sensing my mother was on the verge of offending my future husband.

"Things are different today," Vanessa said, adding an extra syllable to the word "different," which somehow undercut her claim, in my mind anyway.

"I suppose you're right," Ma said, then she looked me right in the eye, taking in the way I struggled to get down that mushroom. "Things *are* different today. Having children. Getting married. I mean, in my day, we married once and we made it work," she said, shooting a glance in Miranda's direction, which (thank God) Miranda missed. "Even dating has changed," she said, her eyes roaming back to Kirk before focusing on me. "Do you know that your father introduced me to his mother on our second date? Our *second date.*"

There was no way anyone at the table could have missed my mother's intentions that time. Least of all, Kirk, who suddenly had a hard time swallowing the mouthful of linguine he had just heaped into his mouth. As I watched him slowly chew, eyes averted, I felt a wave of protectiveness for him. And a mixture of sadness and anger I was powerless to articulate.

Fortunately, Nonnie piped up, "As I recall, his mother showed up at the party he took you to that night. Something about wanting to make sure that the kids weren't drinking beer, but we all knew what she was up to, nosy body that she was."

"She was wrong to care what her son was up to?" my mother protested.

But her point was lost as Nonnie went on to regale us all with tales of how Grandma Anna notoriously used to butt into her son's life. "Do you know she tried to go with them on the honeymoon? The honeymoon! You're lucky your mother chose to live in my house, or you kids might never have been born!" Then she chuckled and winked at Artie.

I, however, could not forget my mother's point. Instead, I carried the weight of it with me on the Avenue U bus, which we boarded a few hours later on the way home. And I discovered, in the silence that thickened between us as we sat side by side, that Kirk was carrying it, too. At first, I wondered at his sullen silence, until he gripped my hand almost painfully and pulled it into his lap.

Gazing at me steadily, he said, "Look, I want…that is, I think…do you want to come with me to the christening, Angie?"

Joy shot through me. Followed by dismay. "Look, just because my mother—"

"No, no, it's not that. I should have brought you home sooner. I know that. It's just that my family…" He paused, scrambling for words. "Well, let's just say that they aren't at *all* like your family."

"Thank God for *that*," I replied with a nervous chuckle.

"Are you kidding me?" he said, turning in his seat to look at me. "Your family is great. I mean, Nonnie is so warm and sweet. And funny! Sonny and Joe are like the brothers I never had. And your mother!" He chuckled. "Look, the worst that woman could do to me is overfeed me."

He didn't know the half of it.

"On the other hand, my family…" He seemed to struggle for words. "Well, they're lovable once you get to know them, but they're a bit…odd."

"Isn't that adorable?" I said to Grace that night on the phone. "All this time I'm worried he's afraid his parents won't like me. And now I find out he's worried *I* won't like *them.*"

"Adorable."

"Grace, what is wrong with you? I thought you'd be happy for me."

"I am happy for you. If this is what you want."

"Of course it's what I want. Isn't it what we all want?"

Silence reigned for a few minutes. A very pregnant silence.

"Grace, is everything okay?" I asked.

"Oh, everything's fine," she said eventually. "I'm just distracted. Drew has this work-dinner thing he wants me to come to this weekend and I…I don't know what the hell I'm going to wear." I heard the rustle of hangers in the background and knew she was standing in front of her enormous closet faced with a range of fashion possibilities that most women would kill for.

I felt the chasm between us open wider. It was so easy to be Grace, I thought, when the biggest thing you had to worry about was whether the Calvin Klein or the Donna Karan was more appropriate for a "work-dinner thing." What could my minuscule gains matter to her when she had not only met Drew's parents but had gone on vacation with them?

"I'll let you go," I said.

"Hmm? Yeah, okay. I'll call you tomorrow…."

But I knew I wouldn't hear from her tomorrow. Tomorrow night she'd probably be with Drew. The day after that, she'd probably be wining and dining with some of her colleagues, who could better afford to eat at the five-star restaurants Grace frequented than I could. I guess that's just what happened when you grew up and got a life. With a sigh, I hung up the phone, taking comfort in the fact that I would at least see Grace at the wedding. Either hers or mine, I thought with a shimmer of something that felt like…fear.

But if I was having doubts, they were dissipated by the time I walked into Lee and Laurie the next afternoon. On the *Rise and Shine* set that morning, Colin had been ecstatic when I'd told him the news, even joking that he wanted to be my maid of honor. And I expected no less enthusiasm from Michelle.

"Well, I'm going to Newton," I said, dropping my bag on my desk along with the stack of magazines I planned on grazing through to pass the hours.

"Kirk's parents?" Michelle said, glancing up from the copy of *In Style* she was perusing.

When I nodded, she pounded her fist into the air. "Yessss!" she hissed. "Didn't I tell you? Didn't I?"

"Tell her what?" Doreen said, swinging around in her chair with her usual wiry violence.

Knowing better than to let the Conspiracy Theory Queen in on my own personal little plot, I quickly answered, "Oh, I'm going home with Kirk for a christening."

"A christening?" Roberta chimed in as she came off a call. "Oh, Angie, who had a baby?"

"Kirk's sister, Kate."

"Girl or boy?" she asked, eyes gleaming with excitement.

"Uh, a girl. Kimberly," I said, wondering what relevance this had to anything. Then I remembered whom I was dealing with. Roberta Simmons, Mother of all Mothers.

"So you're going to meet the parents," Doreen said.

"Uh-huh," I replied, sitting down and pulling my headset out of the drawer.

Doreen barked out an abrupt chuckle. "Well, I'll tell ya. You never *really* know a man until you meet his parents. Did I ever tell you my ex's father was a prison guard at Riker's Island? Whoo-hoo. That explained a lot. Up until then, I thought the handcuffs were just a harmless sexual perversion."

"You're a fucking weirdo, Sikorsky," Michelle said with disgust.

Doreen simply smiled, then smoothly moved into a call.

"I remember when I met Lawrence's parents," Roberta said dreamily. "Do you know, I think I had a little crush on my father-in-law when I first met him?"

"Me, too!" Michelle exclaimed.

I stared at her. "A crush on Mr. Delgrosso?" I said, remembering the somewhat stocky man who used to stare a little too long at us whenever we walked past his dealership, which happened to be on the way home from our junior high.

"What? He's a good-looking guy."

"Who's the weirdo now, Delgrosso?" Doreen said, eyes narrowing gleefully.

"Thank you for calling Lee and Laurie Catalog…" Michelle chirped into her headset as she flipped Doreen the bird.

These were the people I was turning to in my time of need? I suddenly, painfully, missed Grace. Maybe we could meet up for a drink. "Thank you for calling Lee and Laurie Catalog…" I said, relieved to be taken away from these mad ramblings, if only for a moment. I even managed to sympathize with the 38C-sized woman who was desperate to find out if the dress on page 35 of our summer catalog could accommodate her. And believe me, ordinarily I had a hard time sympathizing with anyone who had "more than a handful," as Nonnie always described the ample-breasted women of the world.

When I finally convinced the woman that $6.95 in shipping was a small price to pay to discover whether this dress would get her through her brother's bar mitzvah, I turned back to the Committee, only to find Michelle and Roberta still engaged in phone calls.

"You realize that once you go to Newton, there's no turning back," Doreen said. "You show up for one family function and you're expected to be at all of them. Suddenly it's this one's seventieth birthday, or that one's anniversary and it's 'Where's Angela, Kirk? Is everything all right with you two?' Soon you can't even go on one little march on Washington without the family getting in an uproar…."

Oh, brother. Suddenly the disaster of Doreen's marriage unfolded before me.

Fortunately, Michelle clicked off just in time. "Look, Doreen, it's not your ex-husband's fault he married a lesbo!"

"Doreen, is it true?" Roberta asked, getting off her call. "I mean, that's okay with us, if you are…."

"I'm a feminist. That doesn't mean I'm a lesbian."

"I'm a feminist, too," Michelle said, "but we got bigger things to worry about right now." Then, turning to me, she asked, "Now, what are you gonna wear?"

★ ★ ★

Though I might be guilty of leaving my love life in Michelle's hands, when it came to fashion, Grace was the girl to call. Thank God, I finally reached her on the way home from work that night. "Come shopping with me?" I pleaded.

As it turned out, I was in luck. Grace was going to Bloomingdale's the very next day during lunch, which really wasn't all that unusual, since she spent so much time there they practically had a fitting room with her name on it. She still hadn't managed to come up with something to wear for her work-dinner thing with Drew and had decided a new purchase was in order. Though I had a whole month and a half to make my own purchase, I saw no reason not to rush to Bloomingdale's as soon as possible—now that I had a reason to shop.

"So that's it?" she probed, as I followed her up the escalator to the second floor of Bloomingdale's. "He asked you to come along and you said yes?"

"Uh-huh," I said somewhat smugly, considering the level of deceit, cajoling and outright threats it had taken to get my relationship with Kirk to this new level. Of course, I hadn't told Grace that. In fact, I had carefully hidden from her that I had embarked on Michelle's handy little three-step plan, because I feared my best friend would never understand. Things just came easier to Grace—like men, marriage proposals (I was sure one was coming any minute from Drew) and great clothes—I thought as we stepped off the escalator onto the second floor. The designer floor.

At that moment, I knew I had made a huge mistake. Tastefully arranged rounders filled with well-cut dresses, tops and pants beckoned, making me realize just how long it had been since I'd allowed myself to set foot in a department store. Not that I have anything against shopping. Quite the contrary. Shopping is my obsession. In fact, I almost shopped my acting career into oblivion in the early days when I had just given up my sales rep job without realizing I would have to give up other things in the name of my art: like my thirst for the perfect pair of jeans, my belief that a forty-five-dollar foundation *will* truly illuminate me from within, and my inability to ever say no in the face of footwear. Over time, I got a better grip, but by then

I still had some pretty hefty debts I was managing. In fact, a year ago, during a particularly vulnerable moment as I was balancing my checkbook and wondering how I was going to pay for the four pairs of shoes I had just purchased (returning them never entered my mind), I confessed my financial woes to Kirk in a plea for help. Kirk, a monument to fiscal responsibility with his healthy 401K and solid budgeting, helped me outline a plan to make myself debt-free. And despite a few random splurges I had made when the season warranted a new pair of shoes or fashion demanded I update my skirt length, I had pretty much stayed on an even keel, financially speaking. Even imagined sometimes that I was free from that desperate craving that caused me to wield my credit card without a care for my financial or emotional well-being.

Now I knew I was wrong to think I had the shopping thing under control at last. Knew that I was still perfectly capable of succumbing to that primal urge that practically made my Visa card ache in my wallet as I followed meekly behind Grace through Bloomingdale's hallowed aisles. The Shopping Urge.

I stoically marched past the denim section, reminding myself that I had allotted myself only a hundred dollars to spend and that I could *only* spend it on a dress suitable for the christening.

But I felt deprived as I watched Grace carefully drape dresses over her arm as if she didn't have a care in the world. I, on the other hand, remained empty-handed, whether out of fear of overspending or sheer frustration, I don't know. "Everything's too expensive," I whined finally, "and too…black."

"What's wrong with black? Everyone looks good in black," Grace replied.

"I can't wear black to a *christening,*" I replied.

"So what are you gonna wear?" she asked.

"I don't know," I said, fingering a butter-yellow sheath on the rack beside me. Yellow seemed like a good color for a baby event. But I looked like a bumble bee in yellow. Pink was too girly. White too virginal. Green—fuhgetaboutit. The truth was, I only looked good in black.

So I followed Grace through the racks rather hopelessly, dutifully picking up a few dresses that didn't seem too appalling or too expensive, and even feeling a bit optimistic about a baby-blue tank dress I discovered in Theory. I might have been free from all temptation to stray from my shopping mission, if I hadn't looked up suddenly and realized we were in Calvin Klein. I sighed.

No one understood my body like Calvin Klein.

Grace beelined for the back wall where the dresses were, and I should have followed—after all, I needed a dress, only a dress, a dress for the christening—but instead I lingered over a chocolate-brown tank on the front rounder. With one touch of the high-tech fabric, I knew I was lost. The neck dipped low enough to just give my practically nonexistent breasts some definition. The straps spanned the back in a crisscross designed to accentuate the shoulders (my best feature, according to Grace; I would have preferred my ass to be my best feature, but there you have it). Pulling the tank off the rack (it just so happened it was a small—my size), I held it against me before the mirror. I would have to try it on, of course. There really were no two ways about it.

Ditto the two pairs of trousers, the funky bias-cut skirt and the four well-cut T-shirts I stumbled upon on my way to the jeans section. Yes, the jeans section. Because in my now-fevered mind, there was simply no point at all in going to the fitting room without sampling this season's denim.

Grace was already standing in line when I got there, her arms laden with five carefully chosen dresses. I saw her eyes widen at the sight of me struggling under the weight of my booty.

"What? I need jeans," I said, as I stepped gingerly on line behind her.

"I didn't say anything," she replied.

And Grace wouldn't say anything, I realized, when we got fitting rooms side by side. She was a strong advocate of "Shop and let shop," never wanting to deprive herself or anyone else of some delectable little item. Which is why it was so dangerous to enter that cavernous fitting room beside hers, my arms filled with every cute little tank, tee or trouser I had only dreamed of during those months of deprivation.

But there was no time for anxiety, I thought, shrugging out of my T-shirt and jeans. Duty before pleasure, I admonished myself, and slipped into the first dress, an off-white sheath Grace insisted would work with my coloring.

No good, I thought, noting with satisfaction the way the dress hung on me like a potato sack. After all, there was something to be said for knowing right away what you didn't look good in.

I slipped into a gray wrap dress next, but realizing I would need implants to make it work, I promptly took it off. I opted finally for the baby-blue tank dress and discovered it not only fit perfectly, but showed off those fabulous shoulders and even provided a tasteful hint of décolleté that normally escaped me. Then I looked at the price. One hundred fifty dollars! Over budget. But it looked so perfect on me….

I pulled off the dress, decided to think about it, then distracted myself from making any sort of decision by focusing on my true desires: the jeans…and that luscious tank top.

Once I had disentangled the straps and slid the soft, stretchy fabric over my narrow frame, I stood before the mirror, the breath I did not know I held whooshing out of me.

Fate. It was fate. Me and this chocolate-brown tank were meant to be, I realized, studying how it fell over my meager breasts in a way that said "small but proud."

Then I looked at the tag: seventy-eight dollars for *this?* There was barely enough material here to put a price tag on. I glanced back at the mirror, seeing once again the way the fabric hugged my shape, putting curves where no curves had been before….

Seventy-eight dollars. Was *that* all?

I moved on to the jeans. Because the truth is, I am a sucker for a good fit in jeans. Can you blame me? I have one of those butts that toes the line between delightfully rounded and borderline blimp-o. The fact is, no matter how many leg lifts or squats I execute, the sexiness of my can depends almost entirely upon the placement of the waistband and pockets on my jeans.

That was another thing about me that Calvin understood, I realized as I stood before the mirror once more, a vision in low-slung jeans and Lycra. With trepidation, I glanced at the ticket that dangled from one of the belt loops. Uh-oh…

I couldn't afford it. Wouldn't afford it. *Every dollar you spend in excess digs away your future,* came the voice of reason. Actually, that was the voice of Kirk, who had explained as he'd helped me work out a budget that allowing myself every "indulgence," as he called my taste for fashion, was a way of keeping myself from having what I truly wanted. That is to say, a life free from financial burdens.

He was right, of course.

But then, so was Grace.

"Those jeans look amazing on you," she said, after summoning me into her dressing room to help her zip up a black, strapless dress that I was sure cost more than everything I had left behind in my fitting room combined. "The top is fantastic, too. You gonna get them?" she asked, as she snugged the dress around her large breasts and then turned to me so I could zip her up.

I didn't answer. Couldn't answer, because I knew what that answer should be. Yet I couldn't seem to voice it to Grace, who didn't have such financial issues and for some reason didn't seem to see mine as all that daunting. "You *need* clothes," she always argued, whenever I was in danger of leaving some item behind in the name of budgetary constraints.

I slid the zipper up over Grace's back, until I came to the inevitable point where her body and the zipper's girth no longer complied with one another.

"Damn!" she said, pushing at her large bustline with frustration.

Grace is the only person I know who actually considers 38C breasts a hindrance.

"Unzip it," she said, calmer. And once I did, she dropped the dress down around her ankles, kicked it away and studied the dwindling pile of clothes still to be tried on with a discerning eye, while I studied her—tall, curvy and so completely the opposite of me in every way. Grace is a living, breathing Marilyn Monroe, albeit taller. And wiser. She would never let a man get the better of her, the way Marilyn did. Or the way I seemed to, I thought.

I sat down on a chair in the corner, probably to avoid the temptation of trying on anything else I had dragged in with me. I needed the dress—I could splurge a little for it. I could *only* afford the dress, I chanted silently as Grace stepped into a gray sheath.

"Could you zip?" Grace asked, snapping me out of my mantra.

"Sure," I said, reaching for the zipper, which I could see was never going to make its way all the way up.

"Damn!" she said, once I had reached the inevitable impasse.

"You have big boobs, Gracie. Live with it."

She sighed, her gaze falling on me in the mirror. "You do, too," she said. "At least in that top you do."

I had to get the top. I'd be crazy not to.

"What the hell am I going to do?" Grace bellowed.

"What's wrong?" I asked, wondering at her dismay.

"I'm going to this…this dinner party at Drew's boss's house this weekend, and I have nothing to wear!"

"Gimme a break, Grace, have you looked in your walk-in closet lately? You have more clothes in there than we offer in the fall catalog at Lee and Laurie!" And that was a big issue— a full 124 pages.

She gave me a look that said I didn't understand, and the truth was I didn't. "Can't you just wear something you already have? I mean, it's not like you've never been out with Drew's boss before."

"But this is different," she said, her eye casting over her discarded choices with a look of pure despair. "We're going to his new house in Westport, and I can't just stand around in some old dress while his skinny little wife, Lorraine, serves up some perfectly beautiful meal in her perfectly beautiful palace and goes on and on about the new living room set they just bought or their plans for the nursery they're building for when they start having kids. I just…" She paused, studying her reflection with dismay. "I just want to look good, and I'm too damn fat to look good in anything lately."

Fat? I thought. *"Fat?"* I said with disbelief. "Grace, maybe you haven't noticed lately, but you're fucking gorgeous."

"Well, I don't feel gorgeous," she said with a frown, taking her last dress from its hanger.

Something was clearly bothering her. And when she slid into her final selection and I stood to zip, she let it out.

"I told him, you know."

"Told him?" I said with a frown, studying the way the dress had flattened Grace's breasts into near-oblivion—not an easy feat, but then, it was Lycra.

"Drew. I told Drew. About my mother. I mean not *my* mother, really."

Now I understood. Grace meant her biological mother. Grace had tracked her down through a search organization two years ago and had discovered she lived nearby in Brooklyn, but had yet to contact her. I never understood why. Her adoptive parents had always been supportive of her choice to look for her biological roots, so I knew she wasn't worried about hurting them. But something about discovering that the woman who'd given her life lived a few neighborhoods away from where Grace herself had grown up had bothered her. So much so that she never got the courage to actually use the address she carried around in her wallet like a talisman. Or a wound.

"Well, what did he say?" I asked.

"Nothing. I mean, not really. He's very closed off that way. You know Drew, never likes to see anything without his rose-colored glasses on. As far as he's concerned, my father is still a retired professor, and my mother, a music teacher," she said, speaking of her adoptive parents. She laughed, but before she glanced away, I saw fear in her eyes.

"Drew loves you, Grace. I can tell by the way he looks at you. He doesn't judge you just because you don't have this cookie-cutter life."

"I know that," she said, but I could see in her eyes she wasn't convinced. Then she sighed as she looked at her silhouette in the mirror and noticed for the first time that the dress she was trying on had taken her down three cup sizes, in a most unflattering way.

"I give up," she said, her face filled with despair as she studied her misshapen form.

"Gracie, you are beautiful. Inside and out. Don't let anyone tell you otherwise."

"Okay, okay," she said, clearly embarrassed now at my sudden flow of affection. "So are you, my dear," she continued, turning her back to me so I could unzip her once more. "Especially in that top."

Okay, I was getting the top. I considered it a feminist gesture at this point. I mean, didn't Grace and I deserve to feel beautiful and loved? Didn't we deserve to have the clothes—the lives—we dreamed of?

I went back to my fitting room and began to undress. And to calculate.

One hundred fifty dollars for the dress. Sixty-four dollars for the jeans. Seventy-eight dollars for the top. Total: $292. Well, that was really only $192 over my monthly spending allowance (see how clever Kirk is? He *knew* I'd still need to shop. He just helped me find some reasonable limits). It really wasn't much, not in the face of my future, I thought, rationalizing that my tank top and jeans might also serve me well on my weekend in Newton. I could brown-bag my lunch for the next week, thus saving a whopping…sixteen dollars.

"You ready?" Grace said through the door.

"Gimme a minute!' I replied, with a little more exasperation than was entirely warranted, as I quickly shrugged on my old jeans, my soft (read: overwashed) tee.

When I stepped out of the stall, clutching the blue dress along with that tank and those jeans, Grace was waiting, with one silky camisole dangling from her arm.

"That's all you're buying?" I said, suddenly realizing that I was alone in my shopping splurge.

"Nothing else fit. Besides, I needed a camisole. And this one is on sale."

Leave it to Grace to find the only sale item on the second floor of Bloomingdale's. It was probably purely an accident, too. It wasn't as if Grace needed to shop the sale rack.

"You getting those?" she said, glancing down at items I still clutched, despite my better judgment.

"Well, I have to get the dress. And I could always use the jeans…." Sudden misgivings filled me.

"You have to get the top. It looked so good on you," Grace said, turning toward the register that beckoned in the distance.

I fell into step beside her. "It's seventy-eight dollars."

She barely batted an eye. "It's Calvin."

"With the jeans and the dress, that's two hundred ninety-two dollars, putting me one hundred ninety-two dollars over budget…."

That got her attention. "You're not still using that crazy budget Kirk worked out for you?"

Uh-oh. Clearly I had said the wrong thing—I knew Grace disapproved of Kirk's frugal nature. "It's working for me, Grace. You know I haven't so much as charged a single pair of shoes in over three months?"

With a glance down at my somewhat scuffed but still serviceable Steve Maddens, she replied, "Yippee."

Before I knew it, we were at the register, and Grace was grabbing that soft, stretchy tank out of my hands, because I hadn't managed to put it back, despite the fact that we had just traipsed through Calvin Klein again. "I'll buy it for you," she said.

"No," I replied quickly, pulling it back into my grasp before Grace gave in once more to her endless bouts of generosity.

"I can afford it. You can't. What's the difference who pays?" she always said, whenever she whipped out her gold card and picked up the tab for dinner, drinks and, on occasion, those fashion indulgences I wasn't allowed to give in to anymore. But I couldn't let her do it this time. I was so tired of being the poor and struggling one, cringing under the table for whatever scraps fell. I felt too much like that kid who used to follow my mother through Alexander's, pleading for some fur-trimmed jacket or fringed shirt I simply had to have at my mother's expense (hey, it was the seventies. I can be forgiven those fashion faux pas).

"*I'll* buy it," I said, reaching for my wallet and digging out my credit card, determined now to do whatever damage to my future I could, all by myself.

What was I worried about, anyway? I thought. Kirk was my future, at least according to Michelle. Wasn't that why I was in Bloomingdale's today in the first place? To assure myself a lifetime of love and fiscal responsibility?

I had nothing to worry about, right?

And neither did Grace, I thought, studying her clean features as she handed the cashier the camisole and her credit card. We were both going to be happy, no matter what the cost.

8

I have seen the future
(and it's gonna cost a bundle).

If you think that I came home elated from my shopping extravaganza, think again. I was even more stressed when I walked through the door, packages in tow and my impending Visa bill weighing on my mind like a migraine. Because on the subway ride home, I suddenly remembered that my little fashion splurge wasn't my only indulgence this month. How the hell was I going to pay for all this stuff?

I went to my room, dropped down my bags in the only unoccupied corner, then went back into the living room and sat down at the Early American desk Justin had pulled from some trash heap or another and placed before the window, because, he claimed, it was better for the creative mind.

All I could see at the moment was that damn azalea.

I pulled out a pad of paper and a pen from the drawer. I needed to know how much damage I had actually done.

Okay: Azalea, $54.95. I could live with that. In fact, I was living with that. The damn thing was thriving on the windowsill, so much so that Justin had taken to pruning it once a week.

One fifty for the dress. *(Cringe.)* A hundred forty-two for the tank top and jeans. *(Big cringe.)*

Then there was dinner with Josh, of course, a few weeks ago: $32.50. (He had to have the wine, didn't he?)

I added it up: $379.45. I was in the hole for $379.45. That was more than one week's pay at Lee and Laurie. And my check from *Rise and Shine*—well, that just about covered my travel and laundering expenses.

Every dollar you spend in excess chips away at your future....

Shut up!

I had a future, right? And it was with Kirk. Kirk, whose lovely family I was meeting in a little over a month. At least I had a great dress, I thought, feeling a moment's satisfaction as I pictured my gracious self, smiling on the sidelines as the baby was baptized, helping Mrs. Stevens serve the cake, expressing delight over each new gift as it was opened....

Each new gift. Gift! I didn't have a gift. Kirk had the gift. Of course he had the gift. He was the *godfather,* dammit. *Oops*—I didn't mean *dammit* in reference to godfather. I automatically made the sign of the cross, feeling incredibly stupid while I did it and, worse, reminding myself of my mother.

My mother would never show up empty-handed. But I wasn't showing up empty-handed. I was showing up with Kirk, who would have a gift and a card with both our names on it. Love, Uncle Kirk and...Angela. Hmm...

Would he sign my name to the card?

I picked up the phone on the desk, hit the speed-dial number labeled Kirk Home. Which could have just as easily been labeled Kirk Work, because he worked from home.

"Yeah?" he answered, sounding annoyed. He knew it was me (caller ID—Kirk always had the latest technology). He knew it was me, and he was annoyed. What was that about?

"Hey, it's me," I said, stating the obvious.

"What's up?" he said, exasperated.

Something in his tone made me suddenly afraid to ask the question that had seemed so simple a moment ago.

"Nothing. What's up with you?" I stalled.

"I'm working, what do you think is up?"

He hated when I bugged him while he was working. Suddenly I felt stupid. I knew he was stressing over this new client he was trying to land, and here I was bothering him with my petty concerns. What petty concerns? It was *his* godchild.

"Um, I was wondering…that is, what are you getting the baby?"

"Baby?" he asked, all recollection of the beloved godchild forgotten in the face of the project he was currently immersed in. And clearly he was still immersed. I heard typing in the background, imagined the scramble of codes moving across the screen before his eyes.

"You know, Kimberly. For the christening."

"Oh, uh—" tap, tap, tap "—I started a mutual fund for her."

"Oh." *Oh.* Well, that was *nice.* Leave it to Kirk to think of his godchild's fiscal future.

"Why?"

"I, uh, I was just curious," I said, wondering now how I was going to broach the subject of the card. Would there even be a card? Of course there would be a card. And a mutual fund. From Uncle Kirk. And Aunt Angela.

There was no Aunt Angela. At least, not yet.

"So, um, we still on for tonight?" I said, quickly changing the subject before it made him as uncomfortable as it was making me.

"Tonight?" he said now, as if suddenly our standing date were an issue. "Look, Ange, there's not gonna be any tonight if I don't finish this program I'm working on…."

"Okay, okay," I replied. Sheesh. Clearly I had called him at the wrong time.

"I'll call you later," he said.

Click.

Yeah, love you, too.

The only thing clear to me after I hung up with Kirk was that I did, in fact, have to buy a present for baby Kimberly. A very inexpensive present, judging by the harrowing little tally I had scratched out on my notepad.

The second thing that became clear to me the next day as

I wandered the aisles of the Enchanted Child, the only toy store I knew of in the East Village (not that I'd ever looked), was that I had no idea what a ten-month-old baby might want.

It wasn't that I had never shopped for a child before. I had hit up the variety store on the way to Brooklyn often enough to provide Tracy and Timmy with a sufficient supply of water guns, noisy drums and Silly String with which to torment Miranda and Joey to last a lifetime. But the fact was, I had never, ever, shopped for a baby.

, Now, as I studied the rows and rows of dolls, trucks, music boxes, books and stuffed animals, I didn't know where to begin. I probably should have waited and asked Roberta, a veritable expert on all things maternal. I mean, it was only July—I had over a month. But I wanted to get this over with as soon as possible.

"Can I help you?" came a soft voice. I turned to find a little gamine of a girl who looked to be no more than fifteen on first inspection, but as she approached I realized she was probably my age. It was the strawberry-blond braids that did it, or maybe the overalls and striped top. She looked like an overgrown Pippi Longstocking.

"Yeah, I'm looking for a gift. For a ten-month-old girl?"

"That's a nice age," she said, her blue eyes twinkling.

I was gonna have to take her word on that, I thought, as I followed her to a row of dolls. "A doll is always a nice choice," she said, picking up a rubber-faced monstrosity in the fluffiest pink dress I had ever seen.

I immediately bristled. I'd always hated the idea of giving girls dolls, maybe because I had had so many foisted on me in my childhood years, being the only girl in my family.

"I'm thinking maybe…not," I said diplomatically to the woman, who stood blinking at me as if she held the answer to my prayers in her tiny, tiny hands. I didn't want to be responsible for molding this baby into the image of her mother. Because isn't that what dolls were supposed to do? I was no feminazi or anything, but I knew that much.

"All kids love blocks," Pippi said, leading me over to a stack of brightly colored blocks, each painted with a letter of the alphabet, "and these have a learning component."

I suddenly remembered how Kirk had bragged to me about how brilliant his niece was. Surely she knew her ABCs, right? Wasn't that like the first thing you taught a kid? I really had no idea…. "Oh, this baby's smart," I said, finally, figuring it would be best to err on the side of caution. I didn't want to insult the Stevenses by underestimating their progeny. "She knows her alphabet by now, I'm sure."

"Really?" She beamed at me. I have to say, I even beamed back.

"How about shapes? Does she know her shapes?" She picked up a puzzle with cutouts of circles and squares.

Who didn't know shapes? Wasn't that something everyone was born with? "Of course," I replied on the defensive, as if Pippi had somehow insulted *my* niece's intelligence.

"She sounds like a remarkable child," Pippi said, smiling up at me.

I smiled back. I was sure Kimberly was brilliant, just like Kirk. I think just about everyone in his family was brilliant. According to Kirk, Kate had graduated from Brown magna cum laude. Kayla was a bit of the black sheep, dropping out of the University of Chicago a few credits shy of a B.A. in fine arts. But she had dropped out in the best way, having landed a key spot in a group show at the Smithsonian for a seminude photo Kirk claimed his parents still wouldn't acknowledge was her. I couldn't wait to meet Kayla.

"I think we might want to go a little more advanced with this kid."

"Well, we do have this children's computer. I would usually say it was more appropriate for an older child, but even so, it's the kind of development item that could grow with a child…."

Now this was cool, I thought, eyeing the shiny plastic monitor and mini-keyboard. It was just perfect for Kirk's niece, I thought, picturing Uncle Kirk introducing little Kimberly to the wonders of Windows. Then I saw the price—$159.99? Were they kidding? The wonders of Windows could wait until those mutual funds matured a bit….

"Do you have anything a little less expensive?"

The woman looked at me then, and I could swear there was a disgust in her eyes. As if I were the grinch about to steal Microsoft.

My eye fell upon a tiny farmhouse set up on a nearby table, complete with cows, chickens and little farm implements. "This is cute," I said.

Pippi popped over. "Yes, it's one of our most popular products." She smiled as I picked up a tiny hoe to examine. "Of course, it's generally advised for children over three because of the choking hazard."

"Choking?"

"Yes, those little ones *love* to put everything in their mouths."

I studied the tiny hoe, imagined it in the tiny hand of a tiny baby being put in an even tinier mouth. God, this kid business was for the birds, I thought, imagining spending hours trailing behind some little tot who seemed determined to off herself the first time Mom wasn't looking. "Yeah, well, we wouldn't want any family tragedies," I replied with a nervous chuckle. Pippi laughed, too, though hers was a bit strained. I think I was starting to get on her nerves.

Well, too bad. This was not just any baby we were talking about. This was Kirk's godchild. I had to find something special. Something that said I had taken great thought and care. Something that said I was the Girlfriend…and I was here to stay.

But as Pippi recommended puzzles (puzzles made me think of old people, not *babies,*) stuffed animals *(borrrring)*, music boxes (did *anyone* like those stupid things?), porcelain tea sets (wasn't this a broken-glass hazard?), I realized there was nothing in this whole store in the under-twenty-five-dollar category that would make Kirk's family realize that I was not only the Girlfriend, but the prudent and perfectly suitable mother of Kirk's future progeny.

"Could you excuse me for a moment?" I said finally, realizing there was one prudent person I could count on to help me make this all-important decision.

My own mother.

Given the opportunity, Pippi practically fled my now angst-ridden presence while I stepped deep into the heart of the stuffed-animal section and pulled out my cell phone.

"Ma, it's me," I said, once she picked up.

"Angela? I can hardly hear you. You're not on that cell phone, are you?"

My mother claimed she could never hear me on my cell phone—I think this was mostly to discourage my using it. "Remember Uncle Gino!" she would warn at every opportunity. Uncle Gino had died of brain cancer two years ago, and my mother attributed his untimely demise to the way he had embraced the cell phone movement so wholeheartedly he'd given up his home line in favor of complete mobile usage. Of course, she never thought about the fact that he'd worked in asbestos removal for most of his adult life.

"Ma, listen to me. I'm at the toy store and—"

"Oh, Angela, don't go buying Timmy and Tracy any more toys. Your brother can barely move in that apartment as it is, with all the stuff they have. If Miranda had half a brain, she'd give some of the older things to the poor, but of course, Miranda doesn't listen to anything *I* have to say—"

"Ma, I'm not buying anything for Timmy and Tracy. I'm shopping for Kimberly. Kirk's niece?"

That stopped her short. "What are you doing that for?" she asked.

"The christening, Ma. Kirk invited me to the christening," I said, as if this were no big deal—as if he might have even done it without her inquisition a few days ago.

But my mother wasn't buying it. "*Now* he invites you? Why didn't he think of it before?"

I sighed. "Ma, please, can't you just help me out here? I don't know what to get for a baby—"

"Shouldn't *he* be buying the gift?"

Now I was the one tongue-tied. I knew Kirk was treading on thin ice in my mother's estimation, and I didn't want him to plunge into the freezing waters just because Ma deemed it important that we give a gift *together*. "Um, he *is* giving a gift. Money, Ma. He's giving money. He just…he just asked if I could pick up something for the baby to open," I lied, trying to make my solo shopping mission sound more like a couple effort.

"Money? What kind of gift is that for a *godfather* to give his *godchild?*"

I sighed. "Ma, that's why I'm at the toy store. I'm picking out another gift…from both of us."

"Well, if Kirk's the godfather, shouldn't he be buying a cross? You did say this was a christening, didn't you? What kind of spiritual nourishment can money or *toys* provide? I don't know about this guy, Angela…."

"It's a mutual fund, Ma. He's opening a mutual fund. You know, for the baby's future?"

"Still, I think *someone's* got to buy a cross. Whoever heard of a christening without a cross? That's the godparent's job, Angela, to get the cross."

I sighed. Up until now, one of the few things my mom had liked about Kirk was that his mother had raised him Roman Catholic like she had been raised, despite the fact that Mr. Stevens was Episcopalian. Now even Kirk's faith was being called into question. "I think Kayla's buying the cross," I said finally.

"Who?"

"Kayla. Kirk's sister? She's the godmother," I replied, knowing that the chances of a woman with a seminude photo of herself hanging in the Smithsonian buying a cross were slim to none.

"Well, I don't know what to tell you then," she said.

"What do you think of a doll?" I asked, that rubber-faced monstrosity suddenly looking good. Besides, it was only $24.95.

"A *what?* I can't hear a damn thing, Angela, with that cell phone. I don't know why you use it. You know, your Uncle Gino, God rest his soul—"

My temper spiked. "A doll, Ma, a *doll!*" I yelled.

An earsplitting yowl rang through the air, and in my state of pure frustration, I thought for a moment it had come from *me*. Until I looked down and saw a toddler had wandered into the aisle where I stood and had inadvertently received the full strength of my wrath in her delicate little ears.

"Ma, I gotta go," I said, as the child wailed louder and a woman (likely the mother, given the angry look she shot at me) came by, crouching low to soothe the little girl. "I'll call you later...."

"What?" my mother said, "I can't hear—"

"I'll call you later!" I yelled, earning myself another dirty look from the mother of the traumatized tot.

I clicked off, smiling apologetically at both mother and child as I stepped carefully around them and headed to the next aisle, which was somewhat quieter.

Spying a plastic cash register, I picked it up almost defiantly. I studied the tiny keys, pushed a few and watched stoically as numbers lit up the window at the top and a series of bells and whirls occurred. Perfect. Mutual funds. Cash register. Now that was a couple effort, I thought, glancing at the price tag: $39.99. I almost groaned, until I saw the angry mother walk by the aisle, carrying the now-screaming child. I had to get out of here. I picked up the cash register. It was only fifteen dollars more than I wanted to spend. What was fifteen dollars in the face of my future? Besides, a cash register might teach this little girl the value of money, which she was going to need if she spent any amount of time around her spendthrift aunt-to-be.

I carried it to the register, where Pippi now stood, a look of expectation on her face. "I'll take this," I said, fishing out my wallet and slapping down my Visa before I could change my mind. Or before Pippi could point out any potential hazards my choice might bring to little Kimberly. I had to get out of here, I thought again, glancing at my watch and realizing it was already two-fifteen and I was going to be seriously late for work.

"Would you like that gift-wrapped?" Pippi asked sweetly.

"Yes, please," I said with relief. Another great failing of mine. I have no gift-wrapping abilities whatsoever.

I waited (somewhat impatiently) while Pippi folded corners, cut ribbons and applied tape with a mastery I grudgingly admired. Then almost choked when she cheerfully tapped on her register and said, "Fifty-six dollars and sixty-nine cents."

"But the price said thirty-nine ninety-nine!" I argued.

"Seven dollars for the batteries inside the register. They aren't included. And five-fifty for the gift wrap."

"Five-fifty for gift wrap?" I grumbled, then felt embarrassed when I looked down at the beautifully wrapped present and realized I had probably hurt poor Pippi's feelings. She was obviously a crafts queen, judging by the way she had twirled the ends of those ribbons. I handed over my card.

Fifty-six dollars and sixty-nine cents. I sighed. Well, it really wasn't that much, right? After all, I was buying it for Kirk's godchild…and, if all went according to plan, my future niece.

As it turned out, my future niece was going to cost me a whole lot more than $56.69 Or I should say, $436.14, which was the new grand total I had arrived at, if the calculations I did when I got to work that day were correct. And I was pretty sure they were, since I had added them up no less than three times, probably out of pure disbelief. Suddenly I became aware that I was investing an awful lot in this relationship, financially speaking. And I was getting very little return on that investment, I realized when I called Kirk before I left Lee and Laurie, to tell him I was on my way over.

"Can we make it another night?" he said.

"Another night?" I asked, eyeing the overflowing overnight bag I had stuffed beneath my desk (yes, I was still overpacking, despite my closet-space gains). I had had this stupid bag packed for two days now, as last night Kirk had decided at the eleventh hour that he couldn't hang out after all.

"I just figured out a better design for this program I'm working on for Norwood and I want to see if I can get it to run."

I sighed. Who was I to argue with my boyfriend's ambition? After all, someone was going to have to make some money in this relationship if we ever hoped to have anything someday, and clearly, I thought, glancing at the gift I had crammed beneath my desk beside my overnight bag, it wasn't going to be me.

"Okay," I replied reluctantly. Then, because I wasn't yet ready to face my co-workers, who were obviously hanging on every word of my conversation despite the magazines they pretended to be buried in, I said, "Hey, I got a gift for Kimberly today."

"Oh yeah? You didn't have to do that," Kirk said casually.

I didn't?

"My family isn't very big on gift giving…."

They weren't? What kind of people didn't give gifts? Especially at a christening. I mean, it wasn't every day a child was recognized in the eyes of God.

Eesh. Now I was starting to sound like my mother.

"I…I wanted to."

"That reminds me," he said, "you need to book your ticket soon if we hope to get on the same flight."

Book my ticket? "I thought you were going to do that…."

"I booked mine weeks ago. Just after my sister called to invite me."

And before he had invited me, I realized with a sinking feeling.

"Hang on, let me get you the flight details."

As I dangled on the line, another realization struck me. I was going to have to pay for this ticket. On my Visa. You know, the one I'd already put a whopping $436.14 on? Now you might be wondering why this never occurred to me before. And that was because Kirk and I had one of those convenient little relationships where he paid for most everything, no questions asked. That was the difference between me and Kirk: He could whip out his Visa (Platinum, by the way) without a worry in the world. And, of course, he wasn't aware that I was already way over budget for this month and that whipping out *my* Visa would have huge implications for me. Somehow this little turn of affairs made me realize how very unmarried we were….

"Okay, got the ticket," he said, coming back on the line. "It's Metro-Air flight to Logan Airport in Boston." He rattled off the flight numbers and times. "If you can't get a seat next to mine, it's not a big deal. It's only an hour flight."

What was he, crazy? I hated to fly at all, much less fly alone. Who was going to assure me that an air pocket was just an air pocket, and not some indication of an impending crash? "Maybe you should book it," I said, realizing this was the best solution all around. Kirk makes the call, Kirk pays the bill. No questions asked.

"Ange, I got enough to worry about right now. As it is, I'll be working all night on this program, and probably most of to-morrow. You, on the other hand, have the whole middle of the day off!"

Leave it to Kirk to remind me how empty my days were.

"Okay, okay. I'll do it!" I said finally.

"Gosh, Ange, if it's too much trouble, you don't *have* to come…."

Don't have to come? Don't *have* to come? What kind of thing was that to say? "I thought you *wanted* me to come…."

He sighed. "Angela, why do you have to make everything such a big deal?"

Big deal? I was meeting his parents! I was going into major debt! Not that that was Kirk's problem. No, it wasn't, was it? I couldn't expect him to solve it. And somehow that thought made me unbearably…lonely.

"Never mind, I'll call you later," I said, hanging up and turn-ing to face the Committee, who no longer tried to disguise their interest in my life.

"Problems?" Doreen asked.

"No, everything's fine."

"You're still going, right?" Michelle said, as if she suspected I had foiled the whole plot with my little phone tantrum.

"Of course I'm going!" I replied. "I just have to book my plane ticket." I said, picking up the notepad where I had jotted down the flight information. "And I have to make sure I can get that Saturday shift off—on Labor Day weekend." Everyone wanted that Saturday off, and full-timers got first choice over us part-timers.

"Talk to Jerry," Michelle said. Then, fishing around in her pocketbook, she pulled out a bright red lipstick and handed it to me. "And don't forget to smile real pretty."

As it turned out, getting the Saturday shift off was easier than I'd expected. Maybe it was the extra lipstick I had dabbed on before going in to see Jerry, or the fact that he had just gotten a new, blond admin and was noticeably distracted by the way she kept crossing and uncrossing her legs at her desk outside his door, but he gave me the day off, no problem.

My real problem came when I called Metro-Air to discover that my ticket was going to cost me $179. I was tempted to hang up and call Amtrak, until I thought about the five or so hours I would have to spend alone, worrying about derailment. But I suppose derailment was not as big an issue as crashing into the ocean from thirty thousand feet. I was irrationally, painfully, angry at Kirk when I hung up the phone. Why couldn't he take the train to Massachusetts, like normal people? Him and his love of air travel, the speed, efficiency of it all. All I could think about was the cost.

And all I could hope for was a return on my investment.

9

Caution: This jar is not a toy!
Please keep out of reach of children.

I discovered that there were other costs. And I wouldn't find them on my monthly statement from Visa.

After a restless night of sleep, during which I dreamed my credit card had sprung arms and legs and was chasing me around with a hatchet, I woke up the next morning feeling even more bleary-eyed than usual. But I got up, of course, and hauled my ass to the studio, of course.

Did my little dance for the camera, of course.

Once the "recording" light blinked off and the parents rushed forward to claim their sweaty and now-rambunctious progeny, I grabbed a towel from the shelf of supplies we kept safely off camera and headed to the small dressing area I was forced to share with Colin, mostly due to the fact that Rena had to have her own office, for reasons never specified. It usually wasn't much of a problem, however, since I was always the first one in the dressing room, eager to be on my way. And while on most days I was quickly slipping into my street clothes and contemplating the carbohydrate-laden breakfast I felt I was owed after taping, Colin always remained out there, chatting with the parents and heaping praise on each and every one of those kids. It was kind of sweet, the way he adored children. I suspected he even got a little emotional at the end of the six-week segment, when the kids were given their "fitness diplomas" complete with an official *Rise and Shine* workout tee, and sent on their merry way, only to be replaced by ten equally eager kids whose parents, more often than not, hoped to make them the child stars of tomorrow, no matter what amount of dysfunction the parents inflicted along the way.

But today I wasn't so lucky. "Angela, Colin," Rena called out as she disentangled herself from a particularly strident mother who felt it necessary to regale our producer with the details of how extraordinarily adept her child was, "Meet me in my office in five."

Damn, I thought as I made my way to the dressing room, slipped out of my leotard and tights and climbed into jeans and a tee. A shower would have to wait until I got home. My stomach rumbled unhappily as I realized that there was a strong chance I wouldn't make it out of the studio for at least another forty-five minutes, maybe even an hour. For on those rare occasions Rena called us into her office after a taping, it was usually because she had some "brilliant" idea for a new workout routine and felt a burning need to not only share it, but possibly even begin choreographing the new steps with Colin and me. Pulling on my sneakers and taking a long chug out of my water bottle in an attempt to quell my hunger, I accepted my fate and made my way to her office.

Colin was already there, still in the baby-blue workout shorts and bright yellow tee designed to complement my own workout duds, one long leg folded casually over the other as he sat comfortably in the chair beside Rena's desk. Rena herself sat in her usual spot, legs folded Indian-style on her office chair, shiny black hair bound in the usual low bun at the base of her neck, harking back to her days as a dancer years ago. My eyes quickly roamed to the desk, seeking out the pad of scribbled notes Rena would more than likely go over with us, but I saw nothing other than the usual mishmash of papers and head shots of impossibly adorable children, along with a can of V8, which seemed to be Rena's only nourishment in life, judging by her bony frame.

At the sight of me in the doorway, she sat up and gestured me hurriedly into the office. "Come in, come in, and sit down," she said, waving toward the only other empty chair in the tiny office, which happened to be a bright orange beanbag Rena kept there to interview prospective candidates for the show.

As I struggled to find a comfortable slump to mold myself into for the duration, she said, "I was just telling Colin our good news."

"Oh?" I said, preparing myself for whatever wondrous new idea she planned to torture us with. As my mind quickly skimmed over the cartwheeling clowns she once added to our show and the Pilates-inspired stretches that I had almost dislocated a shoulder on, I braced myself for the worst. But instead I heard something I might have described as wonderful, if I could wrap my mind around it.

"One of the networks is thinking about picking up the show," Rena said, her thin, pointy features alight with happiness.

They were the words every actor with ambition longed to hear. After all, despite the critical acclaim *Rise and Shine* had garnered from parenting magazines and industry rags, a cable-access show could only garner a marginal audience at most. Suddenly my mind was filled with visions of me and Colin, our blue-and-yellow-clad images gracing everything from print ads for the show to cereal boxes (because, as with any successful network children's show, there were bound to be some advertising tie-ins), all in the name of good health. Overwhelmed by a swell of surprise and—dismay?—I quickly glanced at Colin. I was momentarily steadied by the happy smile exploding across his perfect mouth as he raised his eyebrows at me as if to say, *This is everything we'd ever* dreamed *of.*

And it was, I realized once my insides stopped jumping. I mean, a network affiliation on the résumé was sure to boost my career as well as my paycheck, which right now just about covered the cost of laundering my lovely yellow leotard.

"What network?" I heard Colin ask, and was relieved I was

not in this alone. Colin was asking the right questions, while I was…well, freaking out, to be honest.

Leaning back in her chair, Rena clasped her veiny hands around one knee and said, "Well, I'm not at liberty to say. Nothing is official yet—the network is reviewing its current programming and they've asked to see some tapes…."

Then, as she explained that it would be another month or so before they made their decision and that the decision was dependent on many factors that were out of even Rena's grasping control, I felt a calm settle over me that my future fate wouldn't be decided today at least. Because I wasn't quite sure how I felt about following the career footsteps of…*Big Bird*.

One subway and a bus ride later, I had gotten enough of a grip on myself to call Kirk from my cell phone. At the sound of his cheerful voice on the other end, I felt reassured.

"Hey," I said, feeling something between excitement and dread strum through me as I prepared to tell him my news. For despite all the benefits Colin had cheerfully chattered about as we left the studio together, I still felt an anxious twinge of doubt at this turn of events.

"Hey," he answered, "what's up?"

"One of the networks is considering picking up *Rise and Shine*," I blurted out.

During the silence that ensued as Kirk absorbed this information, I imagined all sorts of responses—a gasp, shocked laughter, a few cutting barbs about the fact that I was destined to spend my life in a yellow leotard—and was surprised at the one I got.

"That is awesome. Oh, Noodles, I'm so happy for you. Wow, this calls for a celebration. Should I make a reservation at the Blue Water Grill?"

Maybe it was the mention of the Blue Water Grill, which was the restaurant Kirk normally reserved for megacelebrations, like the time he landed his first client, that made me realize the magnitude of what was happening to me. Because suddenly I was just as thrilled as he was that my acting career, such as it was, finally had the potential to put me on the map.

Still, I reined in my joy and suggested instead we celebrate at Jimmy Chen's—that Chinese restaurant a few blocks from

Kirk's apartment we often frequented when a hunger for ginger chicken and pork lo mein overtook us. After all, I told Kirk, it wasn't as if there were any contract signed yet. Nothing was definite.

But as I sat over a plate of ginger chicken later that night while Kirk poured me yet another glass of wine—not a usual choice for us at Jimmy's, but we were celebrating—I felt as if my life had taken definition.

And I realized how much definition when Kirk gazed at me happily over our half-finished meal and said, "Everything's coming together. As soon as I get this proposal in to Norwood, I could have the major client I need to get my company off the ground. And if you get this contract, Noodles, that could mean big money."

"Yes," I agreed, thinking of my recent expenditures and realizing big money might be just what I needed.

Then Kirk looked at me, his gaze somewhat shy. "With the regular hours and all, I imagine it's not a bad gig to have while raising a…a family." He blushed at his words, and it suddenly occurred to me that he was not thinking any family, but *our* family. And by the way he was looking at me, it seemed like he was ready to get started on those babies right now.

Oh God. This was serious, I realized, staring at him and attempting to plaster a smile over my stricken features. Suddenly it occurred to me that Kirk's lid had not been properly…childproofed. He was not only thinking marriage, he had already moved ahead to babies.

I should have been ecstatic.

Instead, I felt …scared.

Which was probably why I found myself in Grace's apartment the following night, after the kind of warm couple-y weekend at Kirk's that could convince any woman she'd be happy going down in TV history as the limber, cheerful host of a borderline wacko exercise show and, judging by how much of that couple time Kirk spent bent over his computer, the wife of a leading software entrepreneur.

Almost happy anyway.

Now, as I sat anxiously chewing the ice cubes in the rocks margarita Grace had promptly served me when I arrived (I had sucked down the drink while telling her about my meeting at *Rise and Shine),* my little facade of happiness fell apart. Helped along by Grace, of course. I should have expected it from my best friend. Even Justin had been hesitant to endorse my latest career leap when I'd told him about it yesterday. But then, Justin never did endorse my whole *Rise and Shine* routine anyway.

"You don't have to sign the contract, Ange," she said, studying my now-empty glass as she sat on the sofa across from me. "Maybe this is a sign that you should move on. Weren't you telling me a couple of months ago that you missed auditioning?"

"No one misses auditioning, Grace. That's like missing a toothache. I mean, does any actor like spending hours learning a character's motivations, right down to the smallest gesture, only to stand in front of the casting director and be told that your eyebrows are a quarter inch too thick to carry the character?" (Yes, this really happened to me. I've been waxing ever since.)

"I mean acting, Ange. You told me yourself you were only going to do *Rise and Shine* long enough to make the TV credit matter. It's been over six months now. Maybe you ought to put yourself out there again."

I shivered involuntarily. Because if the thought of spending my life in a yellow leotard was scary, the idea of subjecting myself to the scrutiny of casting agents again was positively frightening.

"Kirk thinks it's a good career move for me," I said. "In fact, when we were talking about it over dinner on Friday night, he started talking about...about how perfect it would be for when we...we started having...kids."

"Wow," she said, her eyes widening. "He made a three-sixty, huh? I didn't think Kirk was even ready to get married."

"Of course he's ready," I replied defensively.

"But the question is," she said, taking my empty glass and standing, "are *you* ready?"

As Grace headed off to the kitchen to refresh our drinks, I felt a new resolve fill me. Of course I was ready to get married. I was thirty-one years old. I was practically living with an adorable, ambitious man, a man who wanted to father my future children.

Oh God. Children. Did I even want to have children? Had I even thought about children? Oh yeah, I thought about them. Thought about them every weekday morning for at least a half an hour. Of course, after half an hour, I was always free to go home and leave said children behind. Whereas if I had children of my own…

Oh God, oh God, oh God…

"Are you okay?" Grace said, returning, drinks in hand, and staring at me in confusion.

"I'm fine!" I said, a little too quickly. I didn't want to examine the fear pervading my system at the moment. I was supposed to be happy. Happy. Happy. Happy. "I'm just…tired," I said finally, averting my eyes. And I realized it was true. It wasn't easy making your whole future happen over the course of a few short weeks.

"I've got something to perk you up," she said, putting our drinks down on the table and disappearing into the bedroom.

She returned with a shopping bag overflowing with clothes and plopped it on the floor in front of me. "I did a little closet cleaning. You can have whatever fits you."

Normally the sight of designer hand-me-downs from Grace did my heart good. But not this time. There were just too many—and it made me suspicious. Because the only time Grace did away with this much clothing was when she was trying to exorcise something…or more specifically, someone.

"What's going on, Grace?" I demanded, suddenly forgetting my own fears in the face of my suspicions.

"Nothing." This time it was she who averted her eyes.

Suddenly it occurred to me how unusual it had been to find Grace home alone tonight. She had been spending so much time with Drew it seemed like he had practically moved in. I glanced quickly at the pretty brass coatrack by the door, where Drew's cashmere coat had hung since he'd left it there during the last warm days of the winter before. The rack was bare.

"Where's Drew?"

She met my gaze head-on. "I haven't a clue. And I couldn't care less."

"Grace!"

"Don't start, Ange—" she warned.

"Don't start?" I replied, exasperated. After all, Drew was the best guy to ever happen to Grace. Not that Grace didn't get great guys all the time, she just never hung on to them as long as she had hung on to Drew. I had thought that maybe this time, Grace had found someone real.

"I thought we were getting married!" I burst out. "You and me both, taking the plunge together."

She snorted at that. Actually *snorted*.

"Why is wanting to spend your life with someone such a foreign concept?" I said. "I mean, Drew is a good guy. Kind. Generous. Financially stable. And hot!" I added, remembering all those ribald tales Grace had told of his prowess in the sack.

She shrugged, then looked me in the eye. "He wasn't the one."

I felt all my insides deflate as that truth hit home. "But how do you *know*?" I asked, my own uncertainties rearing up once more.

"A woman just knows," she said simply.

This statement bothered me all the way home from Grace's, especially since she refused to elaborate on her breakup, focusing instead on those designer hand-me-downs until she had dug out the only items that might fit me: two tops that hadn't been stretched out of shape by her larger bust and a pair of pants that had lost two inches off the length in the wash. But my new wardrobe additions couldn't take my mind off her words, even as she practically shoved me out the door, saying, for the umpteenth time, that there wasn't anything to discuss. Nothing to discuss? How often had I been certain of anyone the way I had thought Grace was certain about Drew?

My mind immediately settled on Vincent. Vincent, to whom I had pledged my undying love at age sixteen. Vincent, who had been so sure, even after I came home from my first semester at college with a new boyfriend in tow, that we were meant to be. "You'll date those other guys," he told me with the same fierce intensity that had once caused me to fall madly in love with him, "but you'll marry me."

A part of me had even believed it. Up until the day my mother called me at school to tell me Vincent Salerno had just gotten engaged.

See what I mean? This was a man I once believed was my soul mate. Whom I once asked, in a moment of newly spent passion, what he would do if I died. (I was seventeen at the time, I could be forgiven the melodramatics.) He had replied, with the solemnity of a young man who had just experienced his first simultaneous orgasm, that he would die, too.

I hadn't asked for logistics. Hadn't needed them. I only needed to know he was it. The man I would go through time with.

I didn't have time to ponder if Kirk was that man. I had to keep things in perspective. After all, as things stood now, he was simply the man I would go to Massachusetts with. And that was all a girl could really expect at thirty-one, right? The party was over.

According to Colin, however, the party had just begun. "Angie, that is fantastic," he said the next morning when I relayed my conversation with Kirk to him after we had both donned our workout clothes and stood waiting for Rena to finish a phone call so we could begin taping.

"Yeah," I replied with a smile, feeling the first rush of excitement since my dinner with Kirk. I couldn't help but get excited, with Colin beaming at me as if I had just been offered a lead opposite Mel Gibson. But, as Colin pointed out, I *had* been offered a lead of sorts—I had, for a change, a starring role in my own life. So why did I feel like William Shatner probably did in the later seasons of *Star Trek*—trapped?

"I guess this means you're not going to be the mother of my children?" Colin joked, referring to the pact we had made over breakfast one morning when he was lamenting that he would never find anyone, in the entire gay community of NYC, who wanted children as much as he did. At the time, it seemed safe enough to offer up my own eggs in the event I didn't marry and have children of my own.

Just then an earsplitting wail shattered the room, and Colin and I looked up to see our tiny tumblers filing into the studio.

And one of them—a diminutive redheaded girl in a purple leotard—was clearly not happy.

Studying that bunched-up little face as the girl yanked herself forcefully out of her mother's grasp, I wondered, exactly, what kind of crazed instinct had driven me to promise Colin such a thing.

Or if I could make such a promise to Kirk.

"I hate you!" the girl declared now, and was just about to throw herself onto the floor in a tantrum, much to her mother's horror, when Rena popped out of her office and, with a clap of her hands, declared, "Positions, everyone!"

I watched with something close to admiration as Rena, zeroing in on the little girl, stepped gracefully yet decisively on her dancer's feet over to the mother in question. Saw the confidence with which she spoke in hushed yet forceful tones to the mother as she gestured to the child, who was now writhing on the floor in what looked like pure agony. I was thoroughly amazed at how swiftly the mother scooped up the still-screaming child and hauled her out of the studio. By the time Rena turned to the remaining children, now lined up in neat little rows before Colin and me, her smile was back in place. "Shall we begin then?"

I decided, right then and there, if I ever did have children, I would need an army of Renas to manage them.

But I didn't have time to contemplate a frightful future of squalling children, because the music had begun....

Wake up, wake up...

My heart sank, right along with my body, as I bent into the opening stretch.

It's time to come alive....

Suddenly my legs were like lead, and I felt a decided tremor in them as I pulled back up again, my arms going mechanically over my head to reach for the sun, which was, in this case, a beaming spotlight that somehow seemed hotter than usual on this fine summer morning.

Wake up, wake up! the Barney clone intoned once more, as I felt sweat begin to pop out, on my forehead, my arms, my legs....

It's time to rise and shine!

By the time we got through the half-hour segment, I was shining everywhere. And it had nothing to do with the workout.

I called Grace from my cell phone on my way home from the studio, whether out of fear for her state of mind post-Drew, or my own, I wasn't sure. But I only got her secretary, who told me Grace was in meetings all day.

"Um, this is her friend, Angela?" I said, hoping this might cause the young woman to realize I was someone who might warrant calling Grace out of her alleged meetings.

"Okay, I'll tell her you called," she said cheerfully before she hung up.

I sighed, though I wasn't surprised. This was the way Grace handled every breakup—alone. I should have been used to it. Only I needed her now. I knew it was selfish, but after my morning at *Rise and Shine* I needed someone to tell me I was doing the right thing by taking my relationship with Kirk to the next level.

Then it occurred to me that Grace would be the last person who would encourage me when it came to marriage and— *gulp*—children. Especially now.

But there *was* someone who I knew would come down solidly in the marriage camp, no matter what doubts I was having.

"This is big, Ange. Big, I tell you," Michelle replied. "His lid is off. I wouldn't be surprised if he buys you a ring the minute you guys get back to New York. Once he sees how much his family adores you, the whole marriage thing will just be a given."

"But his family liked Susan, his last girlfriend," I countered, wondering why it was suddenly so important to argue the other side.

Michelle shook her head, as if I still wasn't getting it. "Susan was the lid loosener. Haven't you been paying attention to me all this time?"

"Lid loosener?" Roberta said, strolling in from the bathroom. "What are we talking about?"

"Yeah, that's what I'd like to know. You lost me there, Delgrosso," Doreen said, turning in her chair to join the conversation.

I cringed. Up until now, I had striven to keep this whole engagement plot a secret from the rest of the Committee, who, I feared, might think of it as the insanity that I had initially seen it as. But now that Michelle had deemed her little scheme a success, she made no bones about letting Doreen and Roberta in on it.

"That's a load of crap," Doreen said, when Michelle had finished her explanation.

"Oh, Angela, I don't know about this," Roberta chimed in, looking at me as if she feared for my future just as much as I did, now that I had apparently forced my way into it like a bulimic forced her way into a size-two dress.

I suddenly felt nauseous. And I wished the call volume weren't so low, so we could end this conversation sooner rather than later. But it was the daily four-o'clock lull, when all the Lee and Laurie shoppers apparently contemplated something else besides the perfect T-shirt or a great fit in trousers.

"I'm sorry," Michelle said, shaking her head, "but a man doesn't bring up having a family with a woman unless he's serious about her."

"Kirk's talking babies? Oh, Angela, this *is* serious," Roberta said, her eyes joyful, as if she thought it was not only serious, but seriously good.

All my doubts resurfaced. "Roberta," I asked, "did you know you wanted to have kids when you got married?"

"Oh, I always wanted to have kids," Roberta said. "Ever since I was a kid, I think."

"Well, I never wanted them," Doreen said, her lip curling at the thought. "In fact, the minute my ex started demanding them, I was outta there."

"Oh, Doreen," Roberta said, her face reproachful, "didn't you two discuss children before you got married?"

"We discussed them all right, and we both agreed that we didn't want them. But after we got married, he suddenly changed his mind. See, that's the problem with the whole institution of marriage," Doreen said, warming to her subject. "It's a trap designed to keep women down. Why do you think everyone from the government to advertisers to society at large perpetuates this myth of happily-ever-after? *Somebody* has to keep the population going. So they set about brainwashing women to accept our biological destiny as our *only* destiny. But the truth is, marriage isn't the fairy tale everyone from your mother to the government with their big family-values toot claims it to be. It's an institution designed to regulate breeding habits."

"Sikorsky, you freak," Michelle said, "I'm married, and you don't see me popping out babies."

Good point, Michelle. But then I wondered why Michelle didn't have kids. She'd been married seven years; she had a three-bedroom house. It wasn't like she had much of a career, I thought, glancing around the cubicle-filled space we lived in four times a week for the sake of steady pay. What was she waiting for?

Doreen snorted. "Well, Delgrosso, first you gotta have sex to have babies."

"Fuck you, Sikorsky," Michelle said. "Look, Ange, you gonna listen to this idiot? You don't *have* to have babies right away."

She was right, I realized. Because, after all, I *did* have a career I was still working on. Kirk knew that. If there was one thing he did understand, it was ambition. So if I decided I didn't want to have kids right away in the hopes of pursuing a new gig, surely he would understand.

"I wouldn't wait too long," Roberta said. "I mean, once you hit thirty-five, your fertility goes down by fifty percent, you know."

"Fifty percent?" I said, new worry filling me. Gosh, that was only four years away. I mean, I didn't want to have kids now, but if I hoped to have them eventually, I needed to make some strides.

"Angie's only thirty-one, Roberta," Michelle said, "which is exactly why she should get married now. This way, she and Kirk could have some time as husband and wife before kids enter the picture."

Gosh, Michelle was smarter than I realized. Maybe I could have everything I wanted someday, if I just put all the pieces in place. And they were falling in place, weren't they? Kirk's lid was off. We were going to get married. He was going to be a leading software entrepreneur, while I…

I didn't know what I was going to be.

"I think it's time you started thinking about what you want," Michelle said now.

"Want?" I replied, still dazed by the thought of the career choices that lay ahead.

"In an engagement ring," she said simply.

Oh, right. Engagement ring. I was getting married. I was going to be a *wife*. And a mother, I thought with a shiver as I remembered Kirk's happy face when he brought up the "F" word (family, that is). Someday. Someday I'd be a mother. But first there was my acting career.

What acting career? a little voice whispered.

"I think you should start dropping hints," Michelle suggested.

"Hints?" God, I could use a few myself. Because it was just becoming apparent that I didn't have a clue…about *anything*.

"About the *ring*," she reminded me, shaking her head as if *I* were the idiot now.

"How the hell do I know what kind of ring to get?" I said, all my fears and frustrations reaching a fevered pitch.

Michelle's eyes widened. "You need more help than I realized," she said. "But don't worry. I got you covered. We'll go see Rudy. He's right in the Diamond District."

"I can't shop for a ring without Kirk," I said, wondering anew at her madness.

She sighed. "We're not gonna *buy*, we're just gonna *look*, Ange. You don't want Kirk dropping a load a cash on a diamond you don't want."

Suddenly I remembered the heart-shaped pendant Kirk had bought me for our first anniversary. I shivered. I hated heart shapes. And it was gold. I never wore gold. Kirk should have known that, having seen my silver-jewelry-clad self often enough. Maybe Michelle was right—Kirk was clearly going to need a little guidance in the jewelry department.

Because if I had no idea what I wanted, Kirk certainly didn't.

In a ring, I thought, with another shiver. Or in life…

If I thought I was overwhelmed yesterday, I was completely bowled over when I met up with Michelle on the corner of

47th Street and Fifth Avenue, the so-called Diamond District. The street was lined with signs that promised fair prices, quality cuts, great selection—everything, that is, short of happily-ever-after. I didn't even know where to begin. And I wasn't even sure I should begin. Because, in truth, now that I had committed to this little pre-Lee and Laurie shopping spree, something felt wrong about it. What was I doing in the Diamond District on a Wednesday afternoon with Michelle? If I was ring shopping, shouldn't I be with my future husband?

"I feel like I'm getting engaged behind Kirk's back," I told Michelle as she led me down the street, taking out her cigarettes and handing me one without even asking if I wanted it (I did).

After she lit us both up with a neon-pink lighter she promptly dropped back into her purse, she said, "Stop worrying. We're just going to get an idea. Rudy will never steer you wrong."

"Is Rudy's where Frankie got your ring?" I asked, puffing furiously on that cigarette as we passed glittering storefront after glittering storefront.

"Of course," she said. "He's got a great selection, too."

We stubbed out our cigarettes in front of a battered steel door halfway down the street, which was half-hidden by a placard that read, Diamonds R Us, then passed through that door and headed down a long, dark hallway that gave me the creeps. "Who is this Rudy guy anyway?" I asked.

"He's my mother's cousin," Michelle replied. I wondered how related they really were. After all, Michelle's mother seemed to be cousins with every Italian from Brooklyn to Manhattan. The real estate agent who had sold Michelle her house. The headhunter who had landed Michelle her job at Lee and Laurie. Even the priest who married Frankie and Michelle was some kind of uncle or cousin.

When the shadowy hallway ended in another door that opened into a brightly lit space lined with glass counters that housed jewelry, I felt a moment of relief.

Then I saw Rudy. Five foot nothing and almost completely bald, he wore a shiny button-down shirt John Travolta might have sported in *Saturday Night Fever* and a pair of pleated trousers that emphasized his somewhat squat stature. Oh, and then there were the chains—thick, gold and dangling deep into the chest hair that was sprouting from the top of his shirt. "Michelle, baby, how are ya?" he said, standing up from the stool where he sat at the back of the store, a cigarette burning in the large marble ashtray that rested on the glass counter before him.

"Hiya, Rudy," Michelle said, rather coquettishly, as Rudy stepped around the glass counter and gave her a hug that swallowed her small frame and a kiss right on the lips.

"God, you get more gorgeous every time I see you!" he exclaimed, releasing her and gazing into her eyes. "How's Frankie? Treating you good?"

"You tell me, Rudy. Has he been in here lately? You know my birthday's coming…."

"You send him right to me, Michelle, I'll take care of him. After all, Rudy knows just what you like, baby," he said with a wink that implied he wasn't just talking about earrings.

Then he turned to me, his dark eyes roaming over me as if he might be able to determine just what *I* liked, and I'm not talking about earrings either.

"Angie DiFranco, meet Rudy Michelangelo," Michelle said.

"Oh, like the sculptor," I said, with a small smile.

"The very one," he said, gesturing to the corner of the store, where a plaster replica of the famous *David* sculpture stood, his neck draped in a what looked like a thick rope chain. "But to tell you the truth," Rudy said, leaning in closer and giving me a solid whiff of the cologne he apparently bathed in, "if I had sculpted that puppy, I woulda given David a little more of the family jewels, you know what I'm saying?" He laughed raucously.

"Rudy, you are *too much*," Michelle said, swatting his arm playfully.

She wasn't kidding.

"So what can I do for you ladies today, huh? Some nice tennis bracelets? I got some great styles in—".

"Actually, Rudy, we're here for Angie," Michelle said, turning toward me with a smile. "She's shopping for an engagement ring."

"Is that right?" he said, looking me over again in light of this information. "Breaks my heart! Another beautiful girl off the market!"

"Rudy!" Michelle said with a tinkling laugh. "What would Vicky say if she heard you talking like that?"

He put a hand to his chest, his eyes wide. "You know that woman is my heart. *My heart,* I tell you!" Then he held up his left hand, which was covered in an assortment of gold rings, one of which looked like a wedding band. "I'm married thirty-two years next week, and I never regretted a minute of it. Not a minute!" he cried. "But I'm a flirt. Can't help myself. My Vicky knew what she was getting into," he continued with another chuckle.

I have to say, I felt a little better now that Rudy had established himself as a harmless married flirt instead of a lecherous old man. Despite the *Saturday Night Fever* attire, he seemed like someone I could trust. In fact, with his dark Italian looks and bushy little mustache, he looked a bit like my late uncle Gino.

Then as if he were some doting uncle, he turned to me, his face serious. "Good guy?"

It took me a moment to realize he was asking about Kirk. "Um, yeah, he's a good guy."

"Kirk is a great guy, Rudy. You think I'd let my friend Angie marry a bad guy?" Michelle said, making me wonder how she could know so much about Kirk, having only met him a few times almost two years ago, when he was installing software at Lee and Laurie.

"Just checking," Rudy said, holding up his hands, palms out. "I wouldn't want to lose a beauty like this to some schmuck, huh?" He barked out another laugh, picked up his cigarette, which had burned down to the filter, and took one last puff before he stubbed it out. "Come on. I'll show you what I got."

He led us to a long case on the left wall, which housed more diamond rings than I had ever seen in my life. I began to feel hopeful.

Until I leaned over it to study the hordes of glittering shapes that stood up from the velvet trays that lined the case. It suddenly occurred to me that I had never, ever, contemplated what kind of ring I would want to grace the ring finger of my left hand...for the rest of my life.

My God, this was big. I was about to make a commitment. To jewelry.

"See anything you like?" Rudy asked.

Well, yeah, a lot of things. But nothing jumped out at me. Nothing I would want to wear…forever.

I looked up to see that Michelle had found something *she* liked. And Rudy had already obligingly opened the case to let her try on what looked like the biggest diamond I had ever seen.

"God, Rudy, I wish I could get married again," Michelle said with a sigh, gazing at her left hand, where she had removed the colossal rock Frankie had given her and replaced it with this newer monstrosity.

"Hey, there's always the ten-year anniversary," Rudy replied. "You're coming up on that soon, aren't you?"

"Bite your tongue," Michelle said reproachfully. "I'm not *that* old. It's just seven years now. You should remember. You came to the wedding."

"Oh, I remember, little girl. You were the most *beautiful* bride! Just as beautiful as my Vicky. And this one," he said, looking at me as I still stared somewhat ponderously into the case, "she's gonna be a knockout! But first we gotta find her the perfect ring."

Now that all attention had turned back to me, I made my first tentative choice—mostly because it wasn't gold and because I had to start somewhere.

Rudy pulled out the tray and handed me the ring. "This is a princess cut," he began, then rambled on some more about the clarity and color. I didn't understand a thing he was saying—I was too caught up in staring at the ring, which I held between my two fingers as if any moment now his words were going to make sense.

"Try it on, sweetheart! It's not gonna bite ya!" Rudy said finally, his eyes twinkling at me as I looked up at him.

I felt a moment's hesitation, then slid it on. At first I was struck by the whiteness of the stone against my skin—I had never worn a diamond on my hand before. And I discovered I liked it. Very much.

But I knew, without knowing why, that this wasn't the ring. So I moved to another. And another. And another. Soon enough, I was hooked but good, suddenly understanding why Michelle had been so eager to go on this little shopping spree.

I think she might have been trying on almost as many rings as I was. There's nothing like the feeling of a diamond on your hand. I realized I could become a Diamond District addict, too. Yet despite all my eagerness, none of the styles stood out as something I could see myself wearing every day. Something I would cherish forever.

Until I moved on to my third tray and my eye fell upon a round stone set in platinum, horizontal baguettes on either side.

"That's it," I breathed, leaning over the ring like a bee drawn to honey. Without hesitation, I pulled it from the tray and slid it on my hand.

"That's a classy ring," Rudy said, eyeing my choice with satisfaction. "And a helluva stone, too. Almost a carat and a half. Tiffany setting," he continued. Then, when he saw the confused look on my face, he explained, "Four prongs, round stone, two baguettes. It's a classic."

A classic. Yes, that was what I wanted to wear for the rest of my days, I thought, gazing at the ring once more.

"You sure you like that one, Ange?" Michelle said, as I held my hand out to relish the splendor of it. "It looks kinda...plain."

"No," I protested, still staring at my hand. "It's...perfect."

"I think it's love!" Rudy said with another chuckle. "Ain't nothing like the sight of a beautiful woman in love," he continued, gazing on me with what looked like genuine fondness, despite the fact that I had known him all of a half an hour.

I decided now might be an ideal moment to get a price quote from good old Rudy. "How much?" I asked.

"For you?" he said without batting an eye. "I'll give it to you for ten thousand." Then he winked. "Nine thousand if he's a good guy."

Well, I thought, that seemed reasonable enough. But then, I realized, as a woman who had once spent two hundred bucks on a pair of strappy sandals I'd only gotten one season out of, I was not the best judge of reasonable. Maybe nine thousand dollars *was* too much to spend for a...a piece of jewelry.

"I'm not sure what Kirk's budget is," I said finally, wondering if Kirk had even budgeted in a ring yet. Because he did budget everything, efficient boyfriend that he was.

"Don't tell me Bill Gates, Junior, has got you on a budget!" Michelle exclaimed.

"He's not Bill Gates, Junior—he's just starting out," I said, glancing quickly at Rudy with embarrassment.

"Sweetheart, *sweetheart*," Rudy said, touching my cheek gently with one chubby hand. "Doesn't matter if he's as poor as Mother Teresa. The man loves you, he's gotta do the right thing."

I smiled uncomfortably, looking down at that ring once more. And I got that feeling again. *Meant-to-be.*

"I tell you what," Rudy said, grabbing a notepad and pen from behind the counter. "I'll put all the information here about the cut, the clarity and the weight," he continued, "and you look around, see if you get a better price. All my diamonds are certified—you won't find a better deal."

I felt better as I took the paper. Maybe I just needed to research it a little. I mean, I didn't even know what those figures he'd scratched out meant. And Kirk always liked to know what he was investing in before he put down his money.

Me, on the other hand, I thought, glancing down at that ring again...I didn't need to know anything more. This was the ring I wanted.

Of course, I had to take it off eventually. And I did, with great reluctance.

Then we moved on to tennis bracelets, and I watched as Michelle began to try them on and Rudy chattered merrily about how he had just gotten one for Vicky to celebrate their first grandchild together. Maybe it was the obvious love in Rudy's voice as he spoke of sharing new grandparenthood with his wife, or maybe it was the cheerful confidence with which Michelle finally settled on the bracelet Rudy might suggest Frankie buy on his next trip in, but suddenly I felt good again. Strong. Satisfied. And I realized I hadn't felt that way since this whole engagement plot began.

"See? Didn't I tell you Rudy was great?" Michelle said after we said our goodbyes and headed out the door.

I smiled as a fresh wave of satisfaction washed over me. Yes, *everything* was great.

I was starting to believe I could have everything I wanted.

10

A nose is a nose is a nose....

What I wanted, more than anything, as I headed home from work that night, was to be with Kirk. To revel in the romance my little ring-shopping expedition had induced.

To feel as loved as a woman should when she was contemplating her life with a man.

But I was not granted this wish. Kirk, it seemed, had other things on his mind. Like his latest software design, which he swore had a glitch that prevented him from seeing me that night. Or the night after that. In fact, the week flew by with barely more than a few brief good-night phone calls.

Now I am not a superstitious person (though Justin will tell you I am), but I am prone to believe in signs. Like the way my father's tomato plants didn't bear any fruit the summer he died (Sonny said it was the new fertilizer he'd used, but I knew otherwise) or how I blew an audition for a pain-reliever commercial right after Justin accidentally put my Nikes on the kitchen table. Okay, okay, so I'm a little superstitious. Can you blame me? I grew up with a mother who honestly believed a pair of shoes on the table could bring bad luck. I suppose her belief might have *some* basis in reality. 'Cause if you think about it, a pair of shoes on the table isn't such a good thing, especially if you've spent half the day wandering around New York City in them. Think about how easily some parasite can find its way into your take-out Chinese. You could be dead before you even unwrapped the fortune cookie.

So forgive me if I got a little worried about the fact that now that Kirk had pledged to make me a real part of his life, he disappeared, quite literally, from mine.

"You think we could take the weekend off?" he said when Friday rolled around. "The CEO of Norwood just told me he's got another designer putting in a proposal. Now that I've got competition, I need to make sure my design is even better."

I had been looking forward to a little TLC (not to mention a little s-e-x). So much for that idea.

"These are the things you have to accept about Kirk if you really want to spend your life with him," Grace said when I called her to complain.

"What, that I'm never going to see him again? We used to hang out three or four times a week, and now suddenly he's working all kinds of crazy hours for this new client he's hoping to land. I just don't get it."

"He's ambitious. That's one of the things you love about him, as I recall," she replied. Leave it to Grace to remind me of all the reasons I should be happy. And I was happy. I think.

"Isn't that what you loved about Drew, too?" I asked, bringing up the forbidden subject of Grace's recently-discarded-but-otherwise-perfect beau.

In typical Grace fashion, she changed the subject. "Look, maybe instead of sitting around waiting for Kirk, you ought to do something for yourself. You know you don't really want to sign that network contract, so you need to start auditioning again. Why don't you call that agent Josh hooked you up with last year? See if she'll take you on now."

She was right, as usual. But that didn't mean I was ready to follow her advice. First of all, that would require a phone call to Josh to get the agent's number, as Ms. Viveca Withers hadn't exactly forked over her business card when Josh introduced me to her almost a year ago. And since I hadn't spoken to Josh ever since I learned I wouldn't be buying a dress to attend the two-hundred-dollar-a-head affair I'm sure Emily Fairbanks was planning, I wasn't so inclined to call. But as luck would have it, Josh called me the following week.

"Hey, Ange, how's it going?" he began, catching me at home (where I seemed to be all the time now that Kirk wasn't around), and acting as if he hadn't thrown me over as a friend at his future wife's request.

"Sorry I haven't been in touch," he continued, taking control of the conversation by not acknowledging that I hadn't exactly called him either. "I've been so busy with the wedding plans and all. You wouldn't believe the number of decisions you gotta make. Tablecloths. Hors d'oeuvres..."

Guest list, I thought to myself but didn't say. I didn't want to give him the satisfaction of knowing how hurt I still was.

I decided to change the subject, because clearly the only reason Josh had called was to let me know how thrillingly his whole life was falling into place. So I let him know where I was at. "Hey, I'm thinking about auditioning again. Maybe even getting an agent. Do you still have Viveca's phone number?"

"Didn't Viveca decide not to take you on?" he asked.

"No," I replied, defensive. "She just thought I should broaden my experience first. You know, get some work in TV on my résumé. And now that I have six months' worth—"

"On that kids' show? Ange, I don't think that's what she meant—"

"Hey, it's work in front of a camera, isn't it? Besides, the show has a network interested in it," I said, somewhat smugly, I'll admit.

"Is that right?" he asked, surprised.

"Uh-huh. But you know, even though they're probably going to offer me a big fat contract, I should keep my options open."

"Well, to be honest, Ange, a contract with a network might just be your best option. You know what it's like out there. And you're not getting any younger...."

"Look, are you gonna give me the number or not?"

"Okay," he said, but his tone implied it was useless. So much for supporting your fellow actor. Oh, that's right. Josh wasn't acting anymore. Or acting much like a friend either. It made me sad. After all, Josh had been the one to help me through my father's death, encouraging me to keep working, to channel my grief into my acting. And he had been right, too. Two months after we had buried my father, I had been a finalist for an Obie award for my portrayal of a grieving widow in *Nightfall*, the hottest off-off-Broadway ticket that season. I don't think I've done any finer work since. Which made me hesitate as I jotted down the phone number Josh rattled off to me a few moments later. Maybe he was right. Maybe I wasn't ready to pursue a big-time agent like Viveca Withers.

But if Josh's phone call had left me discouraged, the call I put in to the Actors' Forum, which was the name of the agency Viveca Withers headed up, made my spirits skyrocket. So much so, I felt stupid for spending the whole day avoiding the phone and angsting over what I would say. But when I finally did make the call—at four forty-five on Monday (I think I was half hoping she would be gone for the day), I was pleasantly surprised to find that she was not only in but eager to talk to me. The moment I told the secretary who answered the phone who I was (that is, Angela DiFranco, co-host of *Rise and Shine*), she put me on hold, to "see if Ms. Withers was available." Not only was Ms. Withers available, but she picked up moments later, chatting me up as if I were some big box-office draw rather than the somewhat disenchanted host of a cable-access kiddie program.

"You should come up to the office," she said, "How's eleven tomorrow?"

"Eleven is perfect," I said, reeling with excitement. I hung up the phone. I had an eleven o'clock! With an agent! And not just any agent, but Viveca Withers of the Actors' Forum!

I immediately hit the speed-dial button for Kirk, figuring this was big enough news to warrant a phone call, no matter how much he hated to be interrupted while he was working.

"Hey, it's me," I said.

"Uh-huh," he replied, clearly distracted. I heard the distinct tap of keys in the background.

"I have big news…." I continued.

Tap, tap, tap.

"I just got off the phone with Viveca Withers, head of the Actors' Forum?"

"Who?" Tap, tap, tap.

"Viveca Withers. You know, she was Suzanne Somers's agent, back when she was doing *Three's Company*. And Robert Blake's…" I said, realizing how dubious these references seemed now, especially since Suzanne Somers was now doing infomercials and Robert Blake had been all but convicted of murdering his ex-wife. "Um, I think she may have worked with Sarah Michelle Gellar, too," I added, trying to remember some of the more recent actors Viveca had signed, according to Josh. I *thought* he mentioned the star of *Buffy*, but I wasn't entirely sure now.

"Uh-huh," Kirk said again, clearly unimpressed. Or uninterested. I couldn't tell which.

Tap, tap, tap.

"So, anyway, I'm meeting her tomorrow. At eleven."

Tap, tap… "That's great, Noodles. You could probably use an agent. Now that you've got that contract on the horizon, you're gonna need someone to negotiate it."

"I guess…"

Tap, tap, tap. "Listen, sweetie, can I call you later? I'm just putting the finishing touches on this program I'm working on."

"Uh, sure," I said, "I'll be here." Where else would I be?

"Okay." Click.

Yeah, love you, too, I thought, feeling a bit deflated. I headed into Justin's room, where he was bent over his guitar, his gaze fixed on the wall opposite him. He was obviously working on new material, though he had yet to take it to the stage.

"Guess what?" I said.

Justin raised his head.

"I have an interview with an agent tomorrow. Viveca Withers. Of the Actors' Forum?"

"Hey, that's fantastic," he said. "Wasn't she Sarah Jessica Parker's agent?"

I knew it was *some* significant Sarah! "I think so…."

"This could be the beginning of the end of your days at *Rise and Shine.*"

I nodded vigorously.

"I'd say this calls for a celebration."

Though I felt a little guilty dragging Justin away from his guitar—after all, it had been quite some time since I'd seen him doing anything remotely creative—he didn't seem to mind. "Ah, don't worry about it. I wasn't getting very far anyway," he said, cheerfully throwing on his shoes and running his hands through his hair, tousling it even further. Not that it mattered. Tousled worked for Justin.

"So where do you want to go? Three of Cups?" he asked, naming our favorite neighborhood bar.

"No," I said, shaking my head firmly, knowing suddenly exactly what would make me happiest.

"Then where?"

"To the movies."

So that's where we spent the night, sunk down low in a comfy two-seater at the Union Square multiplex, watching Woody Allen's latest offering, a heaping bag of popcorn between us that we refilled before we sneaked into a second theater to catch an action-adventure flick that was fortuitously starting just moments after our first feature ended. Justin even suggested going for number three—he was as hopelessly addicted to movies as I was—until the voice of reason reared its ugly head when I glanced at my watch and realized it was closing in on ten-thirty.

"God, it's so late," I said, blinking as the lights went up and feeling a bit dazed. I had to prepare for tomorrow—dig out head shots, think about answers to whatever questions Viveca might have. And then there was the all-important sleep aspect. "I have to get home, get ready and get to bed soon if I hope to look my best tomorrow." After all, the body at thirty-one didn't bounce back as well as it did four years ago, when I first started subjecting myself to the scrutiny of agents and casting directors. A vision of myself, puffy-eyed and bloated (I knew I shouldn't have eaten so much popcorn, but it was soooo good....) rose before my mind's eye. "I haven't even thought about what I'm going to wear!"

"Relax, everything will be fine," Justin said, leading me out of the air-conditioned theater and into the humid night air.

I did start to feel calmer as we walked side by side, passing the rows of tenements that lined 10th Street once we hit the East Side. It was probably Justin's demeanor that soothed me. He always walked around like he had nowhere to go, no place to be, pointing out some unusual street sign or intriguing storefront I often missed as I scurried by, always in a hurry to be somewhere, whether it was the studio or work or Kirk's. Tonight Justin was especially animated, remarking on the unusual facades of the buildings we passed and giving what architectural history he knew. I could tell he was inspired by the movie we'd just seen. Not that he was as big a fan of Woody Allen as I was, but Justin respected anyone who lovingly recorded the buildings and streets of this fine city the way Woody Allen did. Though I always loved listening to Justin as he waxed poetic over whatever pretty brickwork or intricate doorway caught his eye, tonight his meandering discourse made me feel a little sad.

"God, Justin, you should be making a movie about New York!" I said, remembering that film he'd abandoned. That film, too, had demonstrated his great affection for New York City, as it was about street gangs of the Lower East Side. He had modeled it a bit on *Mean Streets* by Scorsese (one of Justin's favorite directors), except with more of a romance.

"Yeah, maybe," he said pensively, that dreamy expression coming over his face.

I had seen that expression before at least a thousand times. The hopefulness, the belief that one day some of this magnificence he was surrounded by would show up somewhere in whatever creative work he chose. But outside of that one critically acclaimed—and now shelved—film and the various production projects he had worked on as a grip, the only creative work I'd seen from Justin was three television commercials and a handful of pretty little songs he'd played for me at our apartment. I wondered what kept him from fulfilling his dreams. Especially tonight, when I felt like I was on the brink of finally seeking my own.

***

Whatever joyful feelings I had were quickly dispelled when I came home to discover a big fat zero on my answering machine. Kirk hadn't even called to say good-night, much less wish me luck on my interview tomorrow. I sighed, knowing that Kirk had likely sat in front of his computer until his hands were practically cramped and his eyes bleary. Whenever he had a hot new client to woo, he was like a madman, working until the wee hours of the morning before crawling into bed in subhuman condition. I glanced at the clock and saw that it was eleven. Considering the fact that he wanted to get his proposal into Norwood by month's end, I knew he was probably still seated at his computer, working his fingers to the bone. I supposed I could call *him* to say good-night, but I was tired of being the pursuer in this relationship. Besides, I had other things to pursue at the moment.

With that in mind, I headed for the file cabinet I kept in my bedroom to dig out the head shots I kept there, and had had no reason to seek for quite some time. When I came across the folder where I'd stored them, I felt a moment's hesitation before I opened it. I had taken these pictures three years ago, when I was closing in on a year of training at HB Studios and realized I had to start putting myself out there if I hoped to make it someday. And though I still had the same shoulder-length hair, I was worried that the thirty-one-year-old me looked vastly different from the twenty-nine-year-old version.

Then I opened the folder and wondered if I had ever really been the woman who stared back at me from the photo.

This woman gazed out at the camera with a confidence I wasn't sure I'd ever felt, her smile knowing, and even somewhat…sexy. And her hair…

I sighed. There was no way I could maintain the studio coif depicted in this photo. I had hired a stylist to blow my hair straight, a makeup artist to even out my skin and make my eyes glow and a photographer who snapped the shot just moments after the finishing touches were applied. Now, if I never had to face a humid New York City day again, I might just have a shot at looking like this.…

I didn't have time to worry about it, I realized, sliding a few of the copies into one of the envelopes I had handily placed next to the folder in the file cabinet, along with my résumé. I had already added my *Rise and Shine* experience one idle morning a few months back when I'd come home from an especially grueling taping and resolved to change my life, then only got as far as updating my résumé. After settling on a simple red tank (to show off my toned arms—there were some side benefits to all those arm lifts I did five days a week) and a pair of black capris, I headed to the bathroom to wash off whatever popcorn grease was endangering my pores, then climbed into bed.

But I didn't sleep. Not right away. Though I knew I had to, or risk bags under my eyes. No matter how I tried to still my mind, however, anxious thoughts crept in. Like how I was going to convince Viveca Withers I was the next big thing when my six months on *Rise and Shine* had only served to show me how insignificant my life really was. I mean, who but a handful of anxious parents and maybe a few pedophiles actually got up at the ungodly hour to watch? Then I remembered that it really *hadn't* been so long ago that I had played Puck in *A Midsummer Night's Dream* in Washington Square Park. And I had been good—people laughed—not that I usually did humorous roles. I had always sought out the serious parts. I was magnificent as Maggie in *Cat on a Hot Tin Roof* and radiant as Nora in *A Doll's House* (okay, the only company that would cast me as this soulful Norwegian housewife was the one doing the Hispanic version, but still, I was damn good for an Italian girl who had lied about her heritage). I even knocked some socks off playing Mrs. Claus in *A Christmas Story* one year (some even said I added a bit of weightiness to the plight of Santa's wife, but I'm not sure that was meant as a compliment).

I sighed as anxiety rolled through me once more. Sleep, *sleep,* I had to sleep. I shut my eyes again, trying to quiet my mind by using a meditation technique I had picked up during my training at HB. And as my mind cleared, an image of my father rose forth, as it often did whenever I stayed up too long and loneliness crept in along with the late hour. I guess it was natural for him to show up tonight, after the way I had gorged myself on movies. After all, a love of movies was the only common ground my father and I ever really had. I couldn't talk to him

about baseball or auto parts or the myriad of things he had in
common with my brothers. But when it came to movies, we
could while a night away in front of the TV or on the stoop,
arguing over whether DeNiro or Pacino was a better actor or
who would be the next Brando. I knew he enjoyed those times,
could see the way his eyes lit up whenever he got on a roll. It
was the only time, I suppose, that he wasn't the guy with a mortgage and a family and a business that had its ups and downs. I
wondered sometimes if he ever wanted to be more than he was,
but being a man, he never talked about what he was feeling.
The only clue I got came too late, when during those last days
he propped his skeletal form up on a lawn chair in our small
backyard, gazing on his fruitless tomato plants and talking about
his past as if he realized he had so little time left to remember
it. In fact, I learned more about my father in the few brief weeks
before his death than I ever knew about him prior to that. He
told me about how his own father had built the business from
the ground up. How as a boy he hated working Saturdays while
all his friends were at the matinee. How he had vowed never,
ever to work so hard for so little, like his father had. And he
hadn't really. Auto Man of Marine Park became the biggest sup-
plier in Brooklyn under his steam.

But it hadn't been enough, I realized one day when he was
so weak he couldn't even drag himself out of bed and just lay
there, his eyes alight in his pale face. "I coulda been a contender,"
he joked, holding up one painfully thin arm and attempting to
curl it into a fist, before he closed his eyes to sleep.

He was long gone before I woke up to myself. Realized he
had been trying to tell me that life was short, and that if I had
a dream, I'd better get on it.

I didn't know if he'd be proud of me now, living like I did
with less money and only a little thread of hope left. I only knew
I had to try. And I sensed, though I would never know for sure,
that he would understand why.

When the piercing sound of my alarm clock shot through
my brain at five the next morning, I wondered if I even understood why I did any of this. My limbs felt like lead, and my
head was fuzzier than usual, since I had drifted off to a fitful

sleep no earlier than one o'clock. When I finally managed to pull my sorry self from the bed, dreading the thought of the day ahead, the smile I would be forced to wield in the face of all those starry-eyed kids, the lull of the middle of the day, which I could never seem to fill with anything useful while I waited for my next sentence—the seven-hour shift at Lee and Laurie. Until my eye fell upon the outfit I had carefully laid out the night before, and I suddenly remembered that this was no ordinary day. I was meeting with an agent today!

I scrubbed my hands over my face, stepping before the mirror, and was filled with another realization, this one a bit more harrowing.

I looked like shit.

My eyes were puffy, the rings beneath them deeper due to lack of sleep, and the worry lines that sometimes showed in my forehead suddenly seemed semipermanent.

It was nothing a good, hot shower couldn't cure, I rationalized. At least I hoped so anyway as I stepped out of my bedroom, creeping past Justin's open door, where I saw, from a quick peek in, he was sleeping, his mouth curved into what looked like a smile. God, he even looked good when he slept. It was probably a guy thing, I thought, remembering how adorable Kirk always looked in the morning, his face flushed with sleep. It was so easy to be a guy....

But then, if I were a guy, I wouldn't have the beauty-enhancing benefits of cosmetics, I thought, packing them into my duffel bag along with the outfit I'd selected and the folder containing my head shots and résumé. My plan was to shower and get ready at the studio after the show, then hopefully coax Colin into having breakfast and dawdling around the neighborhood until the appointed hour. The Actors' Forum was on 36th and Park, which wasn't exactly close to the studio on W. 54th, but there really didn't seem to be any use in heading all the way back down to the East Village only to go uptown again a short while later.

I don't know how I even got through the routine at *Rise and Shine,* though I have to say, the rush of pheromones I always got from such rigorous morning exercise did soothe my nerves somewhat. Not that that lasted very long. I could barely eat a thing at breakfast afterward, my stomach in knots despite the encouraging words Colin heaped on me. "This is just the beginning of it all for you, Ange. For both of us," Colin said happily once he'd cleared his plate of his western omelette. Of course, I hadn't told him I saw Viveca as my ticket out of *Rise and Shine*. I wasn't sure how he would take my news, since he seemed to think our impending contract was a dream come true. And it was—for Colin. Now I watched him uneasily, gulping coffee and nibbling the toast that came with my own omelette, which I could only take two bites of before I was filled with nausea.

"I mean, don't you feel it? Everything is falling into place— your relationship with Kirk, your acting career...."

If that were true, why did I feel like I was falling apart?

Colin bid me goodbye shortly after nine-thirty, having made plans to watch his nephew all afternoon (see what I mean about Colin? He couldn't get *enough* of other people's kids). Since I had no place else to go and no desire even to glance at the windows filled with fall fashions as I walked by, I decided to head to the New York Public Library, which was only two avenues and six short blocks from my ultimate destination. Besides, the reading room was one of my favorite New York City spots to unwind, with its high ceilings, long wooden tables dotted with reading lamps and air of serenity. I arrived there just as the doors opened at ten, headed straight for my mecca and found a comfy chair at the end of one of the tables. Pulling out my actor's scene book—somehow I thought reacquainting myself with some of the monologues I had studied long and hard during my auditioning days might put me in the proper frame of mind for my meeting—I settled in to relax.

And promptly fell asleep.

I'm not even sure how it happened. Well, okay, I kinda know how it happened. I had opened up my book to one of my favorite monologues, and within moments the words blurred on the page before me, causing me to rest my head on my opened book. Only for a moment, I told myself. Just long enough to take the burning sting from my tired eyes.

Unfortunately, I had taken more than a moment. In fact, I

had slept a full forty-five of them, I realized, when I came awake with a start and anxiously glanced at my watch.

I wasn't even sure what had roused me from my sleep, only knew that it was now ten forty-five and I had fifteen minutes to pull myself together and get myself to 36th and Park. Suddenly the six blocks and two avenues I needed to traverse seemed like a marathon.

A cab, I'll take a cab, I thought, mentally batting away the thought of the dwindling funds I had discovered in my wallet after paying for breakfast. Suddenly I wished I had taken up Justin's offer to pay for my movie ticket last night in honor of my latest achievement, which was right now shaping up to be my worse nightmare. Shoving my book in my duffel, I raced out the door into the humidity, trying not to think of what havoc it was inflicting on my hair.

My whole body seemed to shake as I bounded down the broad cement steps to the curb, my eyes roaming up Fifth Avenue for a cab. What was *wrong* with me, I wondered, noticing a tremble in my fingers as I raised my hand to hail a taxi. My stomach gurgled, and I knew exactly what was wrong with me. I was *starving.* And why wouldn't I be? I had only managed to get down two bites of that $5.95 omelette I had treated myself to that morning. Stupid! I was never going to make it through without some sustenance, I realized now, feeling my glucose levels sinking to new and dangerous levels at the thought of facing Viveca Withers in this state. Glancing frantically around, I spotted a hot-dog stand mere steps away. But if the thought of passing out from sheer hunger at the foot of Viveca Withers's desk was alarming, the idea of putting that strange combination of beef byproducts into my roiling stomach almost made me want to heave onto the sidewalk whatever remnants of nutrition might be still lingering in my system from my popcorn binge the night before.

I stalked over to the stand, took one look at the menu items, each more horrifying than the next (what animal *was* that sizzling on those kebab sticks behind the glass?) and made my decision.

"Diet Coke, please."

It was really all I could handle at the moment. Besides, the caffeine jolt might just be enough to get me through. It had to be. "How much?"

"Two dollars," the vendor said, his accent so thick I thought I misunderstood him.

Two dollars? Since when did a can of Diet Coke cost two dollars? Not wanting to take the time to inform him that I was not some stupid tourist he could blatantly overcharge (because I was sure that's what principle this guy was operating on, judging by the gleam in his eye as I practically tossed the money at him), I turned toward the street once more and felt a momentary relief as a cab pulled up, rescuing my now-overheated and (I was sure) sweat-stained self from the curb.

Five bucks later (there was traffic, yes, there was *always* traffic) I was riding the elevator to the fifth floor of the Park Avenue building where Ms. Viveca Withers ran her illustrious agency. At least I had the illusion of a full stomach, I thought, feeling somewhat more human now that I had pumped myself up with that heady mixture of carbonation and caffeine I adored. And I was only three minutes late, which really was an all-time record for me. I only hoped Ms. Withers kept the same kind of schedule I did.

It turned out she did. "Have a seat," the secretary said. "Ms. Withers is with another client."

I spent the next twenty-five minutes in the somewhat spare waiting room, seated across from a tall, willowy blonde who must have been dropped into the waiting area via helicopter, judging by the way her makeup was flawlessly unsmudged, her hair perfectly smooth and her linen dress impossibly unwrinkled, despite the oppressive August humidity outside. Then there was the chiseled-faced guy who came in and immediately began flirting with the secretary, whether because he was trying to get an in or because he needed the attention, I couldn't tell. There was another Adonis to my right, who seemed to have some skin condition judging by the way he kept scratching his arms. Or maybe he was nervous. Who could blame him? He seemed close to my age, and here we were surrounded by a group of beautiful people with a sum total of years among them that probably wouldn't even get them a senior citizen's discount.

And just as I was contemplating the price and possible side effects of a few Botox injections, I heard my name being called. "Angela DiFranco? Ms. Withers will see you now."

I stood, picked up my bag, ran a shaky hand over my hair one last time and headed for the door I'd seen others taller, stronger, prettier than myself emerge from, and went through it to discover what fate, or at least Ms. Viveca Withers, had in store for me.

If I had been surprised by the spareness of the waiting room, I was even more surprised by Viveca Withers herself, who seemed somehow…tinier and a bit younger than the late-forties woman I remembered having met a year before. No, not younger, I realized as she shook my hand and gave me an ingratiating smile—*tighter.* Around the eyes and the chin. It occurred to me that Viveca had had a little nip and tuck since we'd first met.

"Thanks for agreeing to meet with me, Ms. Withers."

"Call me Viveca," she said immediately, studying me with her dark eyes beneath brows obviously dyed a yellow blond to match that short, spiky yellow-blond coif she sported. "I mean, we should be on a first-name basis if we're going to work together."

Well, this was getting off to a fortuitous start, I thought, smiling at her and taking the seat she gestured to. She smiled back, and this time I noticed the way the skin around her mouth seemed to strain with the effort. Clearly she hadn't paid enough for that face-lift. I was a little grossed out, imagining the kind of procedures that had taken place to make her flesh move like that. It was the same way I felt whenever I looked at Michael Jackson nowadays. I couldn't help but think of the scalpel, the blood, the suffering involved….

I shivered.

"Cold?" she asked.

"Oh, no, I'm…fine," I said, hoping she wouldn't realize the real source of my discomfort was her face. I wondered where the scars were. *Stop looking!* a little voice warned, and I focused instead on the little wrinkle that formed between her brows as she spoke. I guess no amount of surgery could get rid of that rebellious little piece of flesh.

"So how're things at *Rise and Shine?* Good?" she started in.

"Good. Great, in fact," I said. Then, realizing I was overstating things a bit, I continued, "Actually, I've been feeling like I need a change. That's why I'm here. I've been performing on *Rise and Shine* for a full six months now. I don't know if you've seen the show…." I began, praying she hadn't and would see it as the solid TV acting experience I knew it wasn't.

"I have seen it, actually. You're quite…agile," she said, flashing me that stretch of skin.

Gazing steadily at that sole wrinkle so as not to grimace, I replied, "Thanks. It has its moments."

"It's not a bad gig at that. I understand it won a children's programming award?"

"Yes, for Best Children's Fitness Program." I neglected to mention that it was the *only* show on TV that could possibly be nominated for that category.

"And I understand there's recently been some interest in it from a couple of networks?"

Gosh, I guess the word had gotten out already. "Yes, there has been some interest, according to my producer."

Her eyebrows lifted now, and I might have even said she looked a bit…perky—if not for the way her forehead seemed to be threatening to pull her nose, chin and upper lip to brow level. "You realize that if a network does pick up the show, there could be quite a nice contract involved. With considerably more money."

Now her words were scaring me more than her face was. "Actually, I was hoping, that is, I was looking to make a change. I'd like to continue to do television. Or even film. But I'm interested in a role that's maybe…more diverse."

Her skin slumped back into place and her mouth moved into what decidedly looked a frown. What was going on here? Did Viveca Withers actually think I wanted to make a *career* out of *Rise and Shine?* Chances were, she was just as tempted to take this contract—and her percentage—and put me on a course I wasn't willing to go on just to make an easy killing. If that was the case, I needed to set the record straight.

"As an actor, I've been feeling a bit…unfulfilled in this role. I'd like to do something…something—" Something where I actually had lines other than *Reach for the sky, hold your head high!* Instead, I said, "Something more personally meaningful."

But Viveca was no longer looking at me. She was fiddling a pen over a pad of paper on her desk. Her expression said, *I've heard this a million times.*

Still, I persevered. I wasn't leaving here until I had some commitment from Viveca that she would guide me toward my next great thing. Or even my next thing, because I knew how few and far between moments of greatness came in this business. "I brought my head shots and my résumé for you to review."

Her head snapped up, and she looked at me once again as if I were suddenly a menace rather than a promising new client. "Yes, yes, you can leave them with me and I'll take a look," she said, her tone annoyed.

With trepidation, I pulled the folder from my bag and handed it to her.

I watched as she opened it, worried as she studied that fresh-faced younger woman I feared I no longer was. Felt a momentary happiness when she said, "You know, you look a bit like Marisa Tomei." Then, looking up at me, she continued, "Of course, that's only useful if you actually *are* Marisa Tomei."

I felt my insides slump.

"Have you considered getting your nose done? Maybe a little thinning at the bridge, perhaps a little tilt up at the tip? It would make you look a little less…ethnic."

I touched my nose in horror, as if she had laid the scalpel to my face. "I…I kinda like my nose the way it is." So did my mother. In fact, she was so damn proud of the fact that I hadn't wound up with my father's hawklike beak, it was as if she'd sculpted it herself.

"Never mind. Okay, look, I'll call you if anything comes up." Now she sounded almost angry at me. Even that happy little wrinkle seemed to frown.

"So, that's it. No…agreements to sign, or…anything?" I asked hopefully, knowing that whenever an agent committed to take on a client, there were papers to sign, commissions to be negotiated.

"Look, let's just see how you fare at whatever auditions I line up for your type and we'll go from there, okay?" Then, as if she realized she was snapping at me for no reason except that I happened to like my nose better than she did, she stretched that skin into one last strained smile and said, "I'll call you if anything comes up."

And as I left that little office, passed the would-be models in the waiting room and the bevy of photos on the wall, I knew the only thing that was likely to come up for me was two bites of a ham and cheese omelette and a Diet Coke.

I headed straight to Kirk's afterward, maybe because his apartment was conveniently located a short walk away or maybe because I needed someone to validate my worthiness in the face of Viveca's apparent rejection. He was there, of course. Working, of course. He seemed a bit disturbed to be interrupted so unexpectedly, but I didn't care. I needed him now.

And maybe it was the look of utter despair he saw on my face when I told him that Viveca had suggested a nose job, but he allowed himself to be pulled from that blinking cursor long enough to provide the comfort I so craved.

"I think you have a beautiful nose," he said, planting a kiss on the tip.

Yes, I felt a bit like a baby, standing there red-faced, sweaty, my eyes burning with tears, whining about how Viveca Withers hadn't jumped for joy at the prospect of signing me. But I didn't care. At the moment, I didn't need Viveca Withers and her wax-faced smile. I needed the feel of Kirk's arms around me, his hands as they gently caressed my back, his eyes as they greedily roamed over my features, telling me that I was wanted. Truly desirable, despite what anyone else said.

And after he had demonstrated that fact, right there on the kitchen floor in a display of passion I had not seen since those days just after I instituted the deprivation tactic, he gave me something else I needed. Food. Lots of it. Sesame chicken. Orange beef. All handily ordered from Jimmy Chen's takeout before I'd barely even snapped my bra back on.

This was what it was all about, I thought, sitting cross-legged on the bed across from Kirk as we dined. This was all I needed.

11

When life gives you
lemons, screw the lemonade.
You need a *real* cocktail.

Apparently it was all I was going to get. Because I hadn't even gotten to my fortune cookie yet when Kirk started glancing anxiously at his laptop, which still sat on the desk where he left it, screen aglow. I knew he needed to get back to work, so I went back to my life, feeling somewhat better about it despite the fact that not much had changed.

But something had changed. My apartment, I discovered, when I came home and found Justin on a ladder, where he'd just hung some kind of netted hammock from the ceiling.

"Hey, Ange," he called out, beaming at me as he stepped down to the floor once more. "How'd it go today?"

All thoughts of Viveca were forgotten now as I studied this latest addition to our happy home. "What is that?"

"It's a tree swing," he said, as if this should have been obvious. "C.J.'s wife gave it to me when I went up to visit them in Westchester a couple of months ago," he explained. "They got it as a housewarming present, but they really didn't have a tree in their yard that could support it."

"Um, Justin? You might not have noticed, but *we* don't have a tree at *all*."

"I know that," he said, giving the swing a tug as he looked up at the hook he'd hung it from on the ceiling, "but it works just as well indoors. I don't know why C.J. didn't think of it."

It was a wonder how even Justin had thought of it. But I suppose he did like to make use of his finds.

"Hey, it works," he said, sitting in the swing and looking at me happily. "And it's comfortable as hell. Try it out, Ange." He got up and gallantly offered me the seat.

I sat down, the netting molding around me as I leaned back into it. It was almost like a hammock, but upright like a seat. "It is pretty…cozy," I admitted.

"Turn around. I hung it from a swivel hook so you can face the window."

I swung around and saw that Justin had moved the desk away from the window to reveal the azalea in all its splendor. God, that thing had gotten big. The branches were even fuller now, probably because Justin took such damn good care of it. But I could still see just above it, out into the courtyard and the pretty brownstones across the way. I felt an easy contentment settle in my bones as I swung gently back and forth.

"So tell me how your meeting at the Actors' Forum went," Justin coaxed.

I felt all my satisfaction drain away as I turned to face him once more. "Not so good."

"What happened?"

"She…she thought I should get a nose job," I said, touching my nose sorrowfully.

"What? You have a great nose!" he said, clearly outraged on my behalf. "That's the DiFranco nose!"

"Actually, it's the Caruso nose," I said. Caruso was my mother's maiden name, and after all, I had inherited this illustrious schnoz from her.

"Whatever," Justin said. "It's your nose. It goes with your face."

"She said it made me look too…ethnic."

"Ethnic? Well, what's so bad about that? That's just the kind of look that launched the career of DeNiro, Pacino, Turturro. It's the face of New York! It's the face that flooded Ellis Island when your ancestors took their first courageous steps into this fine city. It's—"

"Okay, okay, I get your point," I said, smiling tentatively at him. I couldn't help myself. He was so cute when he got on the whole New York thing. Or the Italian thing, I thought, understanding once more why my mother had made Justin an "honorary Italian" from the moment she first met him. I sometimes think Justin wished he *were* Italian, like his beloved director, Martin Scorsese. Or at least a native New Yorker rather than the transplanted Midwesterner with a penchant for red sauce that he was.

"So are you gonna look for another agent?" he asked.

"I don't know," I replied, all my fears rising up again. "She seemed very…encouraging about the *Rise and Shine* contract. Maybe she's right to see that contract as an opportunity. It could mean higher pay. Health insurance."

His brow furrowed. "You already have health insurance through Lee and Laurie."

"I know, but I don't want to work there forever."

"But you won't be working there forever. Just until you get a better acting gig. You have so much experience. You played Fefu. Hell, you almost won an Obie Award," he said, reminding me of my accomplishments on the stage.

"I know, but I haven't really gotten anywhere so far."

He frowned. "You're not actually considering taking that contract if it comes?"

I held my tongue. I knew Justin was going to try to talk me out of it. Try to convince me that pounding the pavement in search of a role I wasn't too ethnic, too short, too…ordinary for was what I needed to do. But I wasn't sure I should be talked out of this contract anymore. I was so tired of wishing for things that seemed like they were never going to happen.

"Kirk thought it was a good gig for me." For *us,* I thought but didn't say. I hadn't told Justin how much of an *us* Kirk and I had become. I think I didn't want him giving that azalea any more credit than it deserved.

"What does he know about what's good for you?" he said, with something that looked like anger. Which was surprising for Justin. He never got this worked up about anything, it seemed. Or anyone.

But rather than examine his sudden wrath, I turned mine on him. "At least he knows you have to work for what you want in life. You can't just sit around, dreaming up stuff and never doing it. I mean, you talk big about putting together some music and starting to perform around town, but I haven't seen you do much more than strum a few chords now and again while sitting on that lovely sofa you've cluttered up our apartment with!"

When I saw the sadness that descended over his features, I immediately regretted my words. Until Justin hit me with his.

"I am going to do it. I just have to get my stuff together. That's all. These things take time, you know. Success doesn't happen overnight. Not in this business."

He was right. Sometimes it never happened. And as things stood now, I doubted it ever would.

Because if I didn't trust Justin to achieve his dreams, with his contacts, his natural charm, his blond good looks and his seeming talent for everything he took up, I certainly didn't trust myself. Despite whatever "star power" Justin thought my nose had.

As it turned out, in the weeks that followed, I had only myself to rely on. Between managing his other clients and working his butt off to finish his design for Norwood, Kirk was so buried in work, I barely saw him. And even on those nights we did get together, I usually spent it watching him sleep, as he seemed to fall into bed exhausted within an hour of my arriving at his apartment.

I was starting to feel I had won the battle…and lost the boyfriend.

And one of my best friends. Because Justin too had discovered a sudden yen for work, accepting a grueling production job that kept him away from the apartment for most of the day—and most of the night, as he had taken to hanging out with the crew until long after I had gone to bed.

I felt almost as lonely as I'd felt just after my father died. But at least then I had had my family. Now I couldn't even go out to Brooklyn, because showing up without Kirk would only prove to my mother that she was right—that Kirk didn't take me seriously enough to make me a real part of his life.

I was starting to wonder if she was right.

"We'll be spending all next weekend together at my parents'," Kirk said, when I called him on Wednesday night, hoping to make him commit to plans for the weekend before he bogged himself down with more work. "Besides, I want to get this design for Norwood done before I go home so we can just relax and have fun while we're away."

Fun? I was seriously doubting how much fun I was going to have while under the scrutiny of the Stevens family.

Not wanting to face the upcoming weekend alone, I found myself dialing up Grace, hoping I might get some quality time with her, since she had been all but avoiding me since her breakup with Drew. Probably because she didn't want to talk about it and I somehow managed to bring it up every time I got her on the phone. I couldn't help myself. I was still mystified about why she had shoved him so completely out of her life.

She picked up on the second ring, sounding somewhat breathless and…exhausted.

"Are you okay?" I blurted out by way of greeting.

"I'm fine. Just…tired."

"What have you been up to?" I asked, ever curious as to how the other half—the Single half—lived, now that I had joined the Hopelessly Coupled. Hopeless? Where did that come from?

"Oh, God. Everything. Claudia and I must have hit every hot spot in Manhattan this week."

"Claudia?"

"My boss. You remember her, right?"

How could I forget her? We had met at a cocktail party Grace had thrown at her apartment shortly after starting at Roxanne Dubrow. Claudia had been freshly divorced, and the sting of her philandering ex's rejection was still working its way through her system, judging by the tart comments she made about every single woman in the room, and not a few of the men. I couldn't help but wonder what she said about me, but Grace assured me that I wasn't even on Claudia's radar. Somehow being ignored by the woman who was the vice president of marketing at one of the most powerful beauty-product companies in the world seemed even worse than being put down by her.

"You're hanging out with *her?*" I asked now. "I thought you didn't like her."

"She's better now than when you first met her. I don't think she's as...bitter. Besides, we're both single, and you know we single girls have to stick together."

I was still single, I wanted to protest but didn't. I might undercut all my claims of newfound commitment with Kirk. Though, in truth, I wasn't feeling the warm, fuzzy security of commitment now that Kirk had all but disappeared from my life.

"In fact, we were down at Lola's last night. On Nineteenth Street? I think you and I might have gone there before."

Yes, we had, I thought, trying not to feel miffed that Grace had come all the way downtown and hadn't even called me. Why would she call me, now that she had *Claudia* to pal around with? I'll admit I was jealous. But I didn't have time to pout when I heard Grace's next words.

"You'll never guess who I ran into."

"Drew?" I asked hopefully.

"No," she replied somewhat irritably. Then she laughed. "I couldn't see Drew at Lola's. It's a little too...downtown for him."

"So who then?" I said, ignoring her little jab at Drew, whom I was still rooting for.

"Billy Caldwell."

"*Bad* Billy Caldwell?"

"Yeah. And he's still just as good...."

Uh-oh. Bad Billy Caldwell was one of the first men Grace had dated when she moved into Manhattan. With his dark hair, cool blue eyes and somewhat rough-around-the-edges good looks, he was one of those guys most women couldn't resist. Which was essentially the problem with Billy. He usually didn't resist either, reaping whatever conquests his killer good looks brought. And they brought a lot of conquests, Grace had discovered within two months of their initial, torrid affair. But rather than give him up completely like she should have, she seemed to gravitate toward him whenever the need for debauchery arose, usually right after she'd given up one of her perfectly great men...like Drew.

"I hope you didn't sleep with him."

"Well, we didn't exactly sleep...."

"Grace, what are you doing? You know you always feel like shit after spending any time with that guy." In fact, it was almost a pattern with Grace. Break up with Mr. Perfect, sleep with Billy, wish Billy *were* Mr. Perfect, break up with Billy.

"Well, I don't feel like shit now."

Of course she didn't feel like shit now. She was probably cruising on the pheromone rush that would always inevitably be followed by crashing disappointment when Billy abruptly disappeared after a few mind-blowing weeks of sex—you know, so mind-blowing that you might actually mistake it for love.

"I hope you used a condom."

"Yeah, yeah," she said. "So how are things with you and Kirk?"

"Fine," I said quickly. Then, feeling as if I should be somewhat honest, I said, "Well, he's been kind of busy lately with work. He's trying to get this big proposal done before we go home for the christening."

"Ah, the big meet-the-parents weekend. When is it—Labor Day weekend?

"Uh-huh," I replied, swallowing around my fear.

Sensing my discomfort, she said, "Don't worry so much. They're going to love you. The question is whether you'll like them."

That made me even more nervous.

"Look, you need to take your mind off this whole thing with Kirk," Grace counseled. "What are you doing this Friday? There's a new salsa club opening in Soho—kind of a swanky lounge with a DJ that spins Latin tunes. And you know what that means...."

Clearly I was out of the loop, because I had no idea. "What?"

"Gorgeous Latin men. Lots of 'em. Wanna come?"

"Okay," I agreed immediately. Not that I was in the market. I just wanted to be with Grace. I missed her laughter, her rowdy embrace of life. It seemed she was back to her old self again. Her old single self, but I would take what I could get.

"Good. I'll call and get us on the list so we don't have any trouble getting in. Let's see, that will be you, me, Claudia…."

Claudia. I almost groaned. I could handle Grace and her new rambunctiousness, but Claudia and Grace together would make a pretty formidable team of Single and Seeking Females. And the last thing I needed was to find myself with two ravenous women in a room full of hot men. I felt like I needed protection…or something. "Can I bring someone?"

"Like who?"

"Michelle?" I said, not even sure why I suggested her. Michelle and I hadn't hung out since the days when we were dating the Salerno cousins back in high school. Besides, I wasn't even sure I *could* drag the Queen of the Brooklyn Marrieds out for a big girls' night out in Manhattan. But I was desperate. If Grace was bringing Claudia, I needed backup.

Now Grace groaned. "Oh, God, Ange. Why her? She's a little…weird."

Grace had had the misfortune of hanging out with me and Michelle when Michelle was just getting over her breakup with Eddie. Grace had come back to Brooklyn for a weekend with a brand-spanking-new boyfriend from Long Island, whom Michelle had proceeded to hang all over. But that was back in high school….

"She's different these days," I argued. "She's more…stable now that she's married. Besides, I've been hanging out with her a bit lately," I hedged, remembering that night we shared drinks, cigarettes and man-snaring plots at the bar. Then there was our little ring-shopping expedition.

"Okay, but don't say I didn't warn you."

Much to my surprise, Michelle leaped at my invitation, which was given somewhat halfheartedly, I'll admit, after Grace's admonitions. "It'll be just like old times!" she said, referring to the brief friendship we'd shared in high school.

Now here we were, comrades again, I thought on Friday night as we waited out front of the Spectrum Lounge on Mercer Street for Grace and Claudia to arrive from uptown. In a shiny black dress that looked scarily like spandex from the way it clung to her curves, Michelle gave the impression that she hadn't recovered from the disco era. I was kind of surprised, as she looked fairly normal at work. I guess she didn't get out much these days. And her hair! Was Aqua Net really still the official hairspray of the Brooklyn Beauty Queen? I was afraid she wouldn't make it through the door with that coif. Or past the velvet rope, I thought, eyeing the big, black-clad bouncer who seemed to be judicious about who he was letting through the dark glass door.

I can't say my hair looked any better. Despite a painstaking twenty-minute blow-dry to make it straight in keeping with the current fashion, the cloying heat was threatening to unravel all my attempts at sleekness. Thank God for my Calvin Klein tank, which I'd paired with a sleek black skirt and strappy heels. At least my boobs looked fabulous.

But fabulous couldn't even begin to describe the sight of Grace as she stepped out of the cab with Claudia a short while later. Her short blond hair had that tousled, just-got-out-of-bed look (which was entirely possible, now that Bad Billy was back in the picture), and her legs were six miles long in the sleek silver-gray halter dress she wore, which made her smoky eyes glow. Hell, *she* glowed, especially next to Claudia, who was draped in black from head to toe. With her long, pin-straight hair and heavily made-up dark eyes, Claudia looked like a Goth-who-just-happened-to-shop-at-Saks. The only thing that saved her from a completely bohemian look was her somewhat strained aristocratic features and the diamonds that glittered on her ears and at her throat.

"Hey, Ange," Grace said, leaning in to hug me. "Hi, Michelle, long time no see," she added, embracing Michelle, too, because no matter what Grace thought of Michelle these days, she'd never be unkind to a fellow Brooklynite.

I tried to follow suit, even leaned in to give Claudia a hug until she lifted one well-manicured hand and waved it in my face. "Hello, Angela. Don't you look darling?"

Darling? Suddenly I felt like a twelve-year-old. Even more so when I found myself huddling with Michelle behind Grace and Claudia as Grace dazzled the doorman, smiling widely at him as she gave him our names to check off the guest list. Even if our names hadn't been there, he would probably have let us in, judging by that smile he was beaming back at Grace as he let us by.

It did feel like old times, I realized as we stepped into the darkly lit lounge. Because as Grace entered the room and heads turned to watch her stroll by, I remembered how difficult it had been over the years to live in her glow. Whenever Grace was in a room, she owned it. Men just fell over her. In fact, I often felt like a bump in the carpet, the way they usually tripped all over me to get to her.

And it appeared nothing had changed, I thought, watching as she wound her way to the bar. What else could I do but follow, noticing how all eyes slid over her, then flitted past the rest of us as we filed by in the shadow she left in her wake.

Thank God I had Kirk, I thought, watching as Grace shimmied up to the bar. "Bacardi O Cosmo?" Grace said, turning to Claudia as if to confirm that this was also her drink of choice. When I saw the wink Claudia gave Grace as she nodded, I said, "I'll have the same."

"Me, too," Michelle said, apparently not wanting to be left out of the loop either. Then, once the bartender had poured our pretty little drinks, Michelle elbowed her way to the front. "I got it!" she said, shoving a fistful of cash at the bartender.

She sure knew how to spend Frankie's money. I was grateful for her generosity, however. My wallet was feeling a little lean after my recent expenditures. But when I saw the uneasy look in Michelle's eyes as she clinked her glass into Grace's while we toasted (at Claudia's suggestion) to good sex, I realized that Michelle was probably feeling more insecure than I was. Maybe she sensed Grace didn't feel all that fondly about her. Or maybe she just wasn't used to being in bars anymore, I thought, as I watched her down half her drink in one fell swoop.

Whatever it was, I didn't have time to contemplate it, because, suddenly, standing before me, was the most beautiful Latino man I had ever seen. Broad-shouldered, with thick dark hair and beautiful dark eyes. "Would you like to dance?" he asked. I looked around, as if uncertain he was talking to me, and caught Grace's eye as she raised her drink to me and mouthed, *Go.*

I turned to look at him, saw those beautiful eyes were still smiling at me and plunked my glass on the bar. "Hold my bag," I said, practically whapping Michelle in the chest with it.

And suddenly, there I was, out in the middle of the dance floor, hip to hip with a man I barely knew but who gazed at me as if he wanted to know me better—a lot better.

It was just an innocent dance, I told myself, though I knew there was nothing really innocent about salsa. For one thing, you really couldn't do it without a man's hand pressed firmly against your back, his groin moving rhythmically with yours. Or against yours, as was often the case with me, at least in those first few steps, as I strove to get my rhythm.

But I got my rhythm all right. Because suddenly we were grooving together like there was no one else on the floor. And I remembered how much I loved to salsa. Why hadn't I done it in so long? I needed to make Kirk take some lessons. Then I remembered Kirk hated to dance.

All thoughts of Kirk dissolved from my mind as the song changed to a faster beat. I rose to the challenge, even managed a few dips and twirls, which were surprisingly easier now that I had some strength and flexibility in my arms and legs from my daily morning workout. I twirled again and again, laughing as our bodies met over and over under the glittering lights. I was having so much fun, I didn't even notice that Grace had joined me on the floor with a hottie of her own, until she grazed up close to my ear and whispered, "Just be careful. You go three dances with these Latin guys and they think you're going home with them."

As she whirled away once more, I almost stumbled over my own feet, leaning somewhat heavily into my now-sweaty dance partner. "Are you okay, beautiful?" he asked, touching the back of one large hand to my cheek. God, those hands were big…could it mean that wasn't his belt buckle I'd been feeling out there?

"Um, I'm going to take a breather," I said, then felt a pang at the sudden dismay that spread over those gorgeous features. "But thanks for the dance. It was…fun."

"Can I buy you a drink?"

"No thank you," I said quickly, and rushed away. If three

dances got me a roll in the hay, God only knows what a drink would garner. Probably a venereal disease.

When I got back to the bar, I found Michelle engrossed in a conversation with yet another gorgeous Latino. God, Grace was right. This place was teeming with good-looking men. And the way this one was looking at Michelle made me queasy. Hello? Did he happen to miss the two carats she was waving around on her left hand?

"Hey, Ange. This is José," Michelle said, as José took my hand and kissed the back of it.

Michelle beamed at him. "Isn't that cute? José is a descendant of the Spanish conquistadores," she announced proudly.

I wondered if Michelle even knew what that meant and realized she had no idea, since the Spanish conquistadores never set up shop in Brooklyn, which is all Michelle really knew anything about. But that was probably what good old José here was counting on, I thought, watching as his eyes flitted down to Michelle's chest for the third time in the thirty seconds I'd been standing there.

"Where's Claudia?" I asked, wondering how Michelle had managed to lose the Ice Princess so she could warm up to Mr. Hot and Spicy. "Over there," she said, gesturing to the lounge area. "Here's your bag," she said, slapping it into my hands as if to say, "Get lost." What had gotten into her? She was married, for chrissakes. And very happily, from the looks of all those photos of her and Frankie she had crammed into her cubicle.

I glanced at the bar, thinking a good swig of my Bacardi O might make this new version of Michelle a little easier to swallow. "Where's my drink?" I asked when I saw my glass was gone.

"Oops. I think this one might have been yours," she said, taking one last sip before she handed it back to me, half-empty. "Sorry!" she said, with a smile that wasn't all that apologetic, then promptly turned her back to me to focus on José.

Since I felt kind of stupid standing there while Michelle flirted like a woman who'd been sprung from a cage, I headed over to one of the sofas where Claudia sat, regally sipping her drink and looking around the room with a kind of disdain.

"Hi," I said, sitting on the chair across from her.

She actually smiled, as if she were glad to see me. But she was probably just glad to have any sort of company, I realized as that frost descended over her features again and she reached for her chic black bag and pulled out a pack of cigarettes.

"Those things will kill you, you know," I joked, trying to make some sort of conversation.

There went that smile again, waxen, patronizing.

"Can I bum one off of you?" I asked somewhat ruefully in light of the comment I had just tossed at her. "I mean, I'd hate to see you fritter away seven minutes of your life alone."

She leaned over, holding out the pack to me, and I took what looked like the thinnest cigarette I had ever seen. "What are these?" I said, studying the pink design on the filter.

"Capris," she answered blandly, dropping the pack back into her bag. "They're much lighter than regular cigarettes. And you don't have to tug so hard on them to get a drag. Protects the face," she added, leaning back in her chair and gesturing carefully to the area around her mouth, which did, in fact, look pretty smooth for a woman who, according to Grace, had been doing a pack a day for at least a couple of decades. But that could have been Botox....

I leaned back in my own chair, grabbing a pack of matches from the table next to me and lighting up. "At least we'll make good corpses."

This gained me another fake smile, followed a forced chuckle. Actually, could you call what came out of her laughter? Sounded more like a cough.

But the moment I had Claudia pegged as some kind of sub-human, unfeeling female, I saw a vulnerable look suddenly come into her eyes. I glanced up to see that a broad-shouldered hunk had stopped just beside the couch where she sat and was smiling down at her. Well, well, well. It seemed darling Claudia *was* human, I realized, seeing the hope that came into her eyes as she smiled up at him.

"Got an extra cigarette?" he asked.

I didn't miss the crushing disappointment that flitted through Claudia's eyes before she bent her head to search jerkily through her bag. By the time she'd located her cigarettes and held out the pack to him, that cool mask was firmly back in place as she met his gaze once more. When he stalked off again with a muttered thanks and I saw her glance down at her low-cut top and smooth a hand somewhat self-consciously over her hair, I realized that maybe Claudia wasn't as secure as she seemed, especially in this environment. I tried to think how I would feel, pushing forty and sitting in a dark club surrounded by men who were half my age and seemingly only wanted me for my nicotine supply.

Fortunately, Grace came back then, preventing me from making any attempts at female camaraderie that would likely have embarrassed Claudia.

"God, that was fun," Grace said, somewhat breathlessly, running a hand through her sweat-damp hair and returning it to its tousled splendor. "I almost went for a third dance and a cab ride back to my place with that guy. Did you get a good look at him? He was amazing."

"So why didn't you?" Claudia asked. "*We* wouldn't have cared." But the tight expression on her face said otherwise as she tugged—yes, *tugged,* I saw the lines bracketing and hardening around her mouth—on her cigarette.

Grace simply shrugged and plopped down on the couch next to Claudia.

"*You're* smoking?" she said, looking at me with a mixture of shock and concern.

"Only when I'm at a bar," I hedged, or when I was with Michelle, or when I was contemplating yet another hit to my Visa or shopping for engagement rings, all in the name of my future with Kirk…God, I had been smoking a lot. But I would stop, I knew I would, just as soon as I got back from Newton. Yeah, that was a perfect plan. After all, I wouldn't be able to smoke while I was there. I was certain that no one in the illustrious Stevens family ever polluted their bodies with nicotine. I could wean myself off in one weekend, I rationalized, stubbing out the cigarette after one last, stimulating puff. But just the thought of my upcoming trip—and that blasted plane ride—made me want to light up another one immediately.

"Where's Michelle?" Grace asked, glancing around.

"Over there, talking to José," I said, gesturing toward the bar.

"What's the matter?" Grace asked. "Is our little married friend not getting any at home?"

"She and Frankie have a great relationship," I argued, somewhat halfheartedly, as I watched Michelle laugh merrily and lean in closer to José.

"How long have they been married?" Claudia asked, turning to study them, too.

"Seven years," I replied.

"Ah, the old seven-year-itch," Claudia said. "I know that one well. Suffered from it myself, but at least *I* had the good grace not to act on it," she continued with a bitter smile, referring to all the philandering Grace told me Claudia's husband did in the last year of their marriage. "Good for her," she said, raising her glass in Michelle's direction. "I wish I had taken my shots when I was still young enough to enjoy them."

"You're still young enough to enjoy them," Grace replied. Now *she* sounded defensive. "I mean, you're only a few years older than I am."

Claudia turned to Grace and gave her a one-raised-eyebrow glance that said she didn't think Grace was any spring chicken herself.

Whether to save Grace from Claudia's killing stare, or protect the now somewhat shadowy fantasy of Michelle's marriage, I blurted out, "It's just innocent flirting. I was out there dancing my heart out with a guy, but I wasn't exactly going to have sex with him. I mean, I have Kirk at home for that…."

Now they were both looking at me, and their expressions said they were curious about just what I was getting at home that was keeping me from partaking of that fine young stud I'd been grazing crotches with.

"Lucky is the woman who can be happy with one man," Grace said philosophically.

"You were happy with Drew," I insisted, remembering how warm and cozy they'd seemed the last time I'd seen them together. Hell, Grace had been talking houses in Westport, I thought, wondering once again what the hell could have turned her 360 degrees from everything she'd been dreaming of, not even a month ago.

"Yeah, I was happy, I guess," she said. "If you call sleeping with a man who wouldn't even take his socks off during sex happiness."

Claudia laughed uproariously at that, as if she shared some secret joke with Grace. And maybe she did. I certainly didn't know about this little quirk of Drew's. And what the hell was the big deal anyway? Kirk sometimes wore his socks during sex, especially in the winter. His feet got cold, dammit.

"Then there was the fact that he hardly ever went downtown," Grace added.

Now she was sounding ridiculous. "Grace, you hardly ever come downtown yourself. I can barely get you to come to my apartment!"

This time it was Grace who was laughing.

"Darling girl," Claudia said, looking at me as if I were some kind of a dimwit. "She means *downtown,*" she finished with a glance down at her lap.

Ohhh. *That* downtown. "Big deal," I blurted. "I mean, Kirk doesn't like to…to do that either. And I don't mind. I mean, I'm not even sure I like it," I finished, though this last part was said a little less forcefully, as a memory of Vincent's—and even Randy's—prowess in this particular area flickered into my mind.

Now neither of them were laughing. No, they were looking at me with a kind of horror.

Finally Claudia sputtered out one of her characteristically superior chuckles. "Oh, it's true, Gracie darling," she said, turning to her with a roll of her well-lined eyes. "Youth *is* wasted on the young…."

Fortunately I was rescued from this merciless little dialogue a short while later by a new dance partner, who called himself Umberto and wasn't quite as stunningly good-looking as my first, but that was fine with me. I'd had two Bacardi O Cosmos at this point and a shot of Herradura at the prodding of Claudia, who had developed a thirst for tequila after we had moved on to our next topic—her divorce. Now, as I strutted and twirled about the dance floor with Umberto, my head was swimming with thoughts of going downtown. And I didn't mean Chinatown.

I quickly changed partners, taking on a man so tall, I felt like I was merengueing with his belly button.

But I had a good time—how could I not, when my best friend joined me on the floor and was laughing beside me as we flew through the steps with our partners. Even Claudia had moved herself to the edge of the dance floor, and if I was seeing correctly through the blur of bodies on the floor, she might have even been shaking her hips to the pulsating beat.

I was having so much fun I didn't even notice the time—or the fact that Michelle had seemed to disappear. But when we finally ventured away from the crowded dance floor and headed to the bar for another round, I suddenly realized that my little married friend, as Grace had referred to her, had gone AWOL.

"Hey, where'd Michelle go?" I asked after the bartender poured our drinks and we'd made yet another toast—this time, to Latin men, whom Grace had just proclaimed the last good men on earth.

I whirled around to the last place I'd seen Michelle, at the other end of the bar where we'd started out the evening. But there was no sign of her or her sexy little charmer.

"She's a big girl," Grace said, seeing my sudden anxiety.

"Indeed," Claudia said. "Especially in that dress."

The thought of Michelle's slinky outfit wasn't very soothing, especially when I remembered how much José had been appreciating the view of the cleavage oozing out of it. And she *had* been sucking down those drinks....

"I'm just gonna take a look around," I said, placing my drink on the bar and making my way through the crowd.

I circled the bar, then skirted by the lounge, before I finally made my way down the steps to the bathroom.

Stepping into one of the stalls to relieve myself of some of that Bacardi O I'd been pouring down all night, I had just settled into a blessed squat when I looked down to see two sets of feet in the stall next to mine. One clad in shiny black loafers that I knew couldn't possibly belong to a woman—at least not any woman *I* knew—and another shiny pair of four-inch stilettos, which I knew could belong only to one person.

"Michelle!" I said, pulling my panties up and my skirt down faster than you could spell relief. Without waiting for an answer, I put the lid down on the seat and climbed, somewhat unsteadily in my own three-inch heels, on top of the toilet.

Looking down into the stall, I saw the top of José's head and felt a shudder of alarm when I realized his face was buried deep in that cleavage Michelle had been flaunting all night.

Michelle herself had her head thrown back against the wall, her half-closed eyes widening at the sight of me peering down.

"Hey, Ange," she said with a giggle, "what are you doing up there?"

"Never mind that. What the hell are *you* doing down there?"

José looked up, a somewhat annoyed expression on his face. "This is a private party."

"Well, the party's over," I said, hopping somewhat ungracefully off the toilet and heading out of the stall.

"Come on, Michelle, open up," I said, pounding on the door of their little love nest.

The door swung open and Michelle stared at me, her eyes glassy and her mouth curved in a mischievous smile, until she opened it and began to slur out merrily, "Every party needs a pooper, that's what we invited you fer, party pooper, party poop—"

I yanked on her arm, pulling her out of José's clutches. Normally I wouldn't be so aggressive, but she was clearly plastered and, from the look of things, might not have left that stall without some show of force. Raising the arm I still held, I waved it in José's face. "Can't you see she's married?"

His gaze flicked over that diamond-clad hand. "And your point is?" he said.

"Point!" Michelle said, thrusting her hips forward drunkenly. "José has a point! So does Frankie," she added somewhat mournfully. "But his is so tiny."

Oh, brother. "C'mon," I said, dragging her out of the bathroom as she waved merrily at José. "Bye, Javier," she called as I pulled her through the door.

As I half carried her up the stairs, she leaned in heavily and slurred, "You used to be so much fun, Ange. Wha' happened to you? Remember how we used to ha' so much fun? Me and Eddie and you and Vincent..." She sighed. "Wha' happened to all those good times?"

"They're gone," I said. And good riddance, I thought, suddenly remembering all the angsting I had done over Vincent, whether he really loved me, whether we would grow old and die together. It was all so pointless, really. Yes, those days were over. Thank God.

Michelle magically regained her footing once we reached the top of the stairs, but since I didn't trust her not to wander off, I grabbed her hand and led her back to the bar, where Grace and Claudia still stood sipping cocktails.

"You found her," Grace said, her gaze moving over Michelle as she leaned heavily against the bar, plunking her oversprayed head right on top of it and closing her eyes.

"And it's a good thing you did," Claudia said, her eyes widening as she brought her glass to her lips once more.

"I'm gonna take her home," I said.

"All the way to Brooklyn?"

"No, just to my place," I said, suddenly exhausted with the thought of having to watch over Michelle all night, making sure she didn't choke on the vomit she was sure to spew the minute she lay down. Yuck.

"Okay," Grace said, with a look that said *I told you so.* "It's too bad you can't stay. We were having so much fun. I mean, it's been a long time since we've had a chance to hang out."

I was grateful, at least, that Grace had noticed how long it had been. It made me feel a little better as I hugged her good-bye. Even Claudia granted me an embrace and air-kiss, though whether it was from some girls'-night-out camaraderie or those three cosmopolitans she had downed, I didn't know.

Once outside in the cool night air, I felt better. Never again, I thought, glancing back at the crowd still clawing to get in the door. There was a reason I didn't go to clubs anymore, I realized, heaving a huge sigh of relief at the thought of Kirk, sleeping peacefully at home, like I should have been, right by his side.

But I had other things to deal with right now.

"Let's get a cab," I said, dragging a sleepy-eyed Michelle to the curb and raising my hand in the air.

Once we had settled into the back seat of the taxi that rolled up moments later, I quickly rattled off my address.

"No, no, no, no, *no!*" Michelle said, "I have to go home."

"Just crash at my place," I said, glancing at the cabbie, who was peering at us somewhat impatiently through the opening in the plastic-glass divider.

"*No!*" she cried. "Frankie would *kill* me."

I sighed. "Okay, but are you gonna be all right going home by yourself?"

"I'll be fine," she said sleepily, waving a hand in my face and slumping down farther in the seat.

"She'll be fine, miss," the cabbie agreed, his eyes roaming greedily over all that flesh falling out of Michelle's dress as she slid still farther down.

Yeah, right. I sighed again, realizing I couldn't leave her at the mercy of this guy, who was leering so much he was making Michelle's little friend, José, look like a Boy Scout.

It looked like we were both going to Brooklyn.

12

Happiness might just be a warm gun.

Thirty-five dollars poorer, I was standing on the doorstep of Michelle's lovely three-bedroom abode in Marine Park, ringing the doorbell at two-thirty in the morning. Apparently, not only had Michelle lost—or spent—whatever money she had stuffed into that minuscule evening bag she carried, she'd lost her keys, too.

Suddenly I saw the lights flick on in the living room and the door swing open to reveal Frankie Delgrosso, in a T-shirt and a pair of gray sweatpants that had seen better days. His hair was considerably thinner and he looked a lot…puffier than I remembered him, though he still had that same handsome face, which was looking none too happy at the moment.

"What the hell are you doing?" he demanded, glaring at Michelle, whose sleep-slackened features snapped to attention at the sight of him. "Don't tell me you lost your keys again."

She averted her eyes, looking a little like a ten-year-old child who'd just been caught with her fingers in the cookie jar. Frankie should only know where those fingers had been tonight.

"She had a little too much to drink," I said by way of explanation.

He looked at me as if suddenly realizing I was there. "Hi, Angie. How are you? Long time no see, huh?"

I smiled. It had been a long time. Probably since the wedding. "How you doing, Frankie?" I asked, leaning in to receive the sloppy kiss he planted on my cheek.

"I'm sorry about this," he said, studying Michelle, who was moaning wearily as she eased herself down into a sitting position. "I hope she didn't ruin your bachelorette party."

Bachelorette party? I thought, realization dawning. So *that's* how Michelle had gotten herself a night out in New York City. God, why couldn't she just tell him the truth?

As I glanced down at her, I realized Michelle probably hadn't uttered an honest word to Frankie since the day she said, "I do." And even the truth in those words was debatable, judging by her little tryst in the bathroom stall tonight.

"Congratulations, by the way," Frankie said, smiling down at me now. "So little Angie DiFranco is finally gonna settle down." He laughed, as if the whole idea amused him. "We didn't think you'd ever get married!"

I laughed, too, somewhat halfheartedly, as I carefully tucked my ringless left hand behind my back. "Yeah, well, we all gotta do it someday, right?"

"Yeah," he said, resignation in his tone as he turned his gaze to Michelle, who had curled herself up in a ball to sleep right there on the brick stoop. Frankie leaned over and picked her up easily, throwing her slack form over one shoulder. Then, ever the host, he turned to me and said, "You wanna come in?"

"Oh, no...I'm just gonna head over to my mom's to sleep."

"You sure?" he said, looking out onto the darkened street. "It's late. I can call you a car."

"Nah, that's okay," I replied, too embarrassed to admit that this little trek to Marine Park had wiped my wallet clean. "It's only three blocks."

I realized, after Frankie had slammed the door shut and left me to my fate, that three blocks was an awfully long way to walk at 2:30 a.m. on a Friday night in Brooklyn. There was no one on the streets.

But this was my old hood, I thought, feeling a little better as I passed the familiar brick houses on the way to my mother's block. I even found myself stopping before a house that used to be as familiar to me as my own. Vincent's.

Funny thing was, it was still his house. After he had gotten married, he had happily moved into the upper level with his wife, having no qualms about spending the rest of his days mere steps away from the parents who had raised him in their image. I looked up to the third floor, saw the flickering blue haze of a television set lighting up the front bedroom and was certain that was Vincent's bedroom I was staring up at. He had been just as much a night owl as I had been back in the days when we were dating. Apparently he still was, I thought, wondering if his wife stayed up with him or if she was simply snoozing comfortably beside him.

I wondered, too, if he was happy. And I decided he was. After all, this was all he ever wanted—to get married, have a houseful of kids and a solid paycheck, I thought, my eye wandering to the Brooklyn Union Gas van that sat at the curb.

I had always yearned for more.

Have you gotten it? a little voice prodded.

"Of course!" I said aloud, my own voice echoing back to me in the quiet night and startling me, reminding that I was on a very empty street, not a soul in sight.

So whom was I trying to convince?

"Angela!" my mother shouted at me when she found me standing on her doorstep.

"Hi, Ma," I said, as if dropping by in the middle of the night were a normal thing.

"What happened?" she cried, grabbing my face between my hands and staring into my eyes. "My God, are you all right?"

"I'm fine!" I insisted, stepping out of her clutches and into the front hall, where I glanced at my reflection in the long mirror that hung there. My eyes were bloodshot, my cheeks pale and my lips drained of whatever color I had dabbed on them hours earlier. No wonder Ma was worried. I looked like hell.

She hugged me fiercely, as if I had just emerged alive from a car wreck. And in truth, I felt like I had. My body ached with exhaustion from too much salsa dancing, and all that alcohol I had drunk was already starting to throb at my temples.

"Have you been in a fire? You smell like smoke!" she said, pulling back and studying me as if looking for third-degree burns.

"No," I said, somewhat guiltily, realizing what she smelled was the stink of cigarette smoke.

Of course, that was the next conclusion she drew. "Oh, Angela, please don't tell me you're smoking again. Think of your father, may he rest in peace. What would he say?"

"Ma, he can't say anything! He's gone, for chrissakes!" I said, then immediately felt bad when I saw the sadness that lit her eyes.

"Say may he rest in peace," she insisted, invoking the old superstition that said you could do the dead eternal damage if you didn't wish them peace every time you uttered their names.

"May he rest in peace," I muttered, hating myself for half-believing her crazy superstitions.

"Now tell me what the hell you're doing here at—" she looked at the clock on the mantel in the living room "—almost three in the morning!"

"I went out with Grace and Michelle and—"

"Michelle?" she said. "Where was Frankie?"

"Home," I replied. "It was girls' night out. We just went out…dancing."

"Oh," she said. "You went out in Brooklyn?"

"No, no," I said, getting tired of this interrogation. "In the city. Downtown. Michelle had a little too much to drink, so I wanted to make sure she got home all right."

"Is that right?" she said, surprised. "That doesn't sound like her. I hope you didn't influence her. You know, her mother always worried about her hanging around with you and Grace. You two were such a handful when you were younger!"

"Me and Grace?" I said, suddenly wanting to let her know just what kind of influence *Michelle* had been acting under tonight.

Fortunately, my mother saved me from disgracing Michelle forever. "You want something to eat? Come into the kitchen, I'll make you some pastina."

Once I was seated at the table, a bowl of steaming pastina before me, I was suddenly very glad to be in Brooklyn. God, I hadn't had pastina in such a long time, I thought, spooning up a mouthful of those buttery noodles with gratitude for my mother's culinary expertise. It really was a simple dish—just tiny noodles, butter, maybe some milk. But it was heaven.

Of course, it was a little hard to enjoy once my mother finished washing out the pot she used and sat down across the table from me, staring hard.

"So where's Kirk tonight?" she asked.

"Home," I replied. "He had some work to finish up before we...before we go away," I finished, not wanting to invoke the name of Newton and all that it implied. My mother had already made clear during a recent phone call how she felt about this little foray to Kirk's parents' house, right down to the plane ride, which scared her even more than it did me, since she'd never stepped on a plane in her life.

Thankfully, she let it slide. "So it was just you and Michelle and Grace?"

"And Grace's boss, Claudia."

"Do I know her?" Ma asked, as if it was still her business to make sure I wasn't hanging out with the wrong crowd.

"No," I said, "But she's...okay. She owns an apartment on the Upper East Side," I added, trying to find Claudia's one redeeming quality. After all, owning real estate in New York City was no small thing, even if you had gotten it because your husband felt guilty about dumping you for someone twenty years your junior.

"How's Gracie?" my mother asked next, her face creasing in a smile.

"She's fine," I replied, remembering how fine Grace had looked, shaking it for all she was worth on that dance floor—as if she had some demons to exorcise.

"She still going with that nice young man she told me about when she was here for dinner last? What was his name?"

"Drew. And no, they broke up," I said, realizing Drew was the demon Grace was probably trying to shake. I still didn't get it, sex with socks notwithstanding.

"That's too bad," my mother said, echoing my thoughts. "But she'll meet someone else. She always does, that one." Then she laughed. "Maybe that's just it—maybe our Gracie has too many options!"

"Maybe." I wondered suddenly if the only reason I was with Kirk was because I truly believed I had run out of options. *No way,* I thought, remembering the myriad men who had asked me to dance. God, I was on fire tonight. I couldn't remember being desired by so many men at once in my life. Maybe I looked like I was almost engaged. Hell, once I got a ring out of Kirk, I'd probably have to beat them off with a stick. Somehow this thought wasn't soothing. Why were men so contrary? They wanted us when we didn't want them, and wanted nothing to do with us the moment we wanted to hold on to them forever. Yeah, I was going to meet Kirk's parents next weekend, but judging from the amount of time we'd spent together since that illustrious decision was made, I barely felt like I had a boyfriend anymore, much less a future husband.

I sighed, shrugging off the thought and pushing away my now-empty bowl of pastina. "Thanks, Ma. That really hit the spot."

She smiled at me, her eyes tired.

"I'm sorry if I woke you up and all...."

"Me? I wasn't sleeping," she said, waving a hand in the air as if sleeping was never an issue with her. That probably wasn't too far from the truth. If I didn't know better, I would have thought she hadn't shut her eyes since that awful night when my father shut his forever.

"Your grandmother and her shenanigans kept me up till all hours. You know that Artie Matarrazzo's car was parked out front until about fifteen minutes before you got here?"

"You're kidding?"

"Oh, yeah. So I go down there to find out what in God's name that man is doing in her apartment at two o'clock in the morning, and she answers the door in a robe and says they're playing cards. Playing cards! And she's looking at me with this smile on her face like she's just won a round of strip poker!"

"Ma, c'mon. What is he, eighty-six years old? He can't—I mean, he probably isn't even in working condition."

"Oh, he's working all right. You know I was doing your grandmother's laundry the other day, and what do you think I found in there? A pair of Fruit of the Looms. And I know they weren't either of your brothers'."

Uh-oh. It looked like Nonnie was getting a little more than those nickels she bet during her friendly little card games. Suddenly I felt like one of us should talk to her. But what would we talk to her about, exactly? Safe sex? She was eighty-four years old. I guess she didn't have much to worry about. Except maybe a heart attack.

"Do you think it's healthy?" I asked, suddenly afraid Nonnie, who'd had an angioplasty not even three years ago, couldn't take whatever she was getting from good old Artie Matarrazzo.

"Healthy! It's downright outrageous!"

But what was even more outrageous, I discovered a short while later, was that my mother had turned my bedroom into a veritable shrine to my father. The closet was filled with all those old clothes of his she'd been advised by everyone to throw away and which she'd only managed to move into another room. And there were photos of him everywhere—at least a half dozen of them tucked into the Sacred Heart she had placed by the door. But then, all of our pictures were tucked into that colorful portrait of Jesus, because my mother believed that she somehow bought us extra protection from God by keeping our images close to the gilt-framed oil she'd gotten at Kings Plaza. I stopped to study it now, as my mother came in to turn down the bed (yes, I could have done it myself, but I decided not to deny my mother the pleasure of treating me like the child she believed I still was). There were pictures of me and Sonny and Joey as kids. Sonny and Vanessa on their wedding day. Joey and, yes, Miranda, too, standing proudly with Timmy and Tracy in front of a Christmas tree. Grace, of course, was there, as Ma had always considered Grace a part of our family. The photo, which was taken back in junior high, featured Grace and me in matching halter tops that Nonnie had bought us at Alexander's (Grace, of course, was already starting to fill hers out), smiling smugly, as if we owned the world. And we did own it then, I thought. My eye strayed next to a photo of Justin, sitting at my mother's kitchen table, a half-eaten dish of pasta before him and a bright smile on his face. My mother had tucked his photo there after he'd fallen off a ladder on the set and broken his leg a few years back.

Kirk, I noticed, was suspiciously absent.

"Hey, Ma, how come you don't have Kirk in here?" I said.

"Huh?" she said, stepping behind me to study the photos there. "It must have fallen out," she said, though her tone implied she'd probably taken it out. I knew exactly when she'd done it, too—just after she had learned that Kirk had gone home to see his parents without me. Apparently, *she* hadn't forgiven him, and I wondered what it would take to make her see that we were meant to be? A wedding? *Maybe not even then,* I realized with a feeling of dread.

"Oh, look at him," my mother said, interrupting my thoughts as she reached out to touch, somewhat reverently, a photo of her and my father, probably taken when they were both mid-twenty-something—I knew because my father was leaning proudly against the brand-new Cadillac he had bought just after Joey was born and his business was taking off. "He was so handsome, your father, may he rest in peace."

"Yeah, he was," I said softly, studying his twinkling dark eyes and Hollywood smile. My father could have been an actor, I thought, studying his face and trying to see him as someone I didn't know—a stranger I just happened to see on the big screen. He'd been gone four years now—it seemed like forever. He felt like a stranger to me. Had I ever really known him? I wondered, thinking of all those conversations we never had.

"I was lucky to love a man like that," my mother said now, bringing her hand to her mouth thoughtfully and then turning to me, her eyes searching mine, almost anxiously. "You gotta love a man like that, Angela. A man who loves you the way your father loved me. You hear me? You don't settle for anything less, you hear me?" she insisted, grabbing my shoulders as if she were about to shake me.

"Ow!" I said, shrugging off her painful grasp. "You're hurting me!"

"All right, all right!" she said, pulling me toward her for a hug that was even more painful before she swept out of the room.

Leaving me standing there before the Sacred Heart, staring

at a yellowed photograph of a man I never really knew holding the only woman he had ever loved, and wondering if love like that really existed, outside of an old photograph or my mother's still-grief-stricken mind.

I came home the next day after a too-long day at Lee and Laurie feeling lower than low. I had been late, of course, having had to trek all the way there from Brooklyn. And hungover, as well. As was Michelle, though she'd never let you know it. She made just as light of her drinking the night before as she did of her drunken antics. "It's not like I slept with the guy!" she'd replied, dismissing the act that could have wrecked her marriage as nothing more than a harmless dalliance. Somehow her lack of a response made me even sadder. Was nothing sacred anymore?

"You're home," Justin said, looking up hopefully from sofa #3, where I found him sitting once I came through the door. He said it as if I were the one who had been spending so much time away from the apartment.

Still, it was a comfort that he missed me. I could see in his eyes a loneliness that mirrored my own.

"No Smirk tonight?"

I smiled. "No Smirk tonight." Then, looking at the digital camera he held in his hands, "No hanging with the guys from the crew tonight?"

"Nah. The gig is over. Besides, those guys were beginning to get on my nerves. All Pete keeps talking about is that feature film he's planning on making. If he can ever find an investor," he added, with a snort that indicated he had little faith in Pete's big dreams.

It sounded to me like a reflection of his lack of faith in his own dreams. "What are you doing?" I asked, watching as he slipped a disk into the camera.

"Oh, I was gonna go take a walk, shoot some film. Wanna come?"

I didn't know whether it was the look on Justin's face—a mixture of hope and something else I couldn't quite place—or a desire to escape the apartment and the phone that I was sure would remain silent while Kirk worked the night away, but I found myself nodding.

Two subways later, I found myself on the Upper West Side, uncertain what mission had led Justin here, but satisfied to walk in companionable silence beside him as we headed down W. 71st Street, except for the odd moment when Justin would remark upon a particularly artful doorway before turning the camera on it to record. I smiled every time he did it, and remembered how many times we had taken this type of stroll together, aimlessly into the night, while Justin simultaneously tried to take in every crevice, every scarred storefront, every stony facade, with his camera.

Finally I spoke, giving voice to all the doubts that had been plaguing me during these many lonely nights without Kirk. "Do you think some people are meant to be together?"

Justin shrugged. Then, easing the camera away from his eye, he looked at me. "I dunno."

"What about you and Lauren?" I persisted. "Do you think you'll wind up together?"

He thought about this for a moment. "Sure. Why not? I mean, who knows what will happen when she gets back from Florida?"

If she gets back, I thought but didn't say. Lauren seemed quite devoted to that repertory company, and I'd never understood why Justin hadn't broken it off when she'd decided to stay on for a second season. Maybe he really was in love with her. Or maybe he was a commitment-phobe. *Like you are,* a little voice whispered in my head. Stop that, you *love* Kirk, I reminded myself. Love, love, love…

"Grace and Drew broke up, you know," I blurted now, dispelling the anxious chatter in my head and replacing it with a whole new set of worries. After all, it was easier to worry about someone else. And I *was* worried about Grace. Especially now that I had finally been forced to accept that she and Drew were really over. Up until last night, I secretly had harbored hopes that they would get back together. So much hope, that until now I hadn't even told Justin they were through.

"Is that right?" he said. Then he laughed. *Laughed.* "Well, I could see that coming."

"What's that supposed to mean?"

"God, the way he hung on her. No woman likes that. Especially a woman like Grace."

Trying not to acknowledge how much it bothered me that Justin had noticed so much about Grace, I asked, "And what kind of woman is Grace, exactly?"

"Difficult," he said. Then, sliding a glance at me, he added, "Kinda like you." Suddenly he trained his camera on me, probably because he sensed I was about to burst out in a tirade over that comment and he knew I'd never do it on film.

"Shut it off, Justin," I said, looking away. "Please."

He sighed, then put the camera down.

"I'm difficult?"

"No, I didn't mean that," he said, studying the camera with new interest.

"So what did you mean?"

He looked up at me, studying my face thoughtfully. "I meant…complex. Kind of like an aged wine."

Great. Now I was old. "So, what—men should only date women under thirty, is that it?" I asked, thinking of Lauren, a ripe old twenty-five. What was Justin doing with a twenty-five-year-old anyway? He was a year older than I was!

"Forget it," he said. Then, with the wisdom of a man who knew better than to go any further in this conversation with a woman—especially the woman he had to live with—he suddenly pointed into the distance and exclaimed, "Now, that, Angie, that is an entryway. See that? C'mon." He rushed ahead, leaving me with nothing to do but follow helplessly along.

"That's gotta be a Stanford White building," he said, naming his favorite architect (also a New Yorker, of course) before he raised his camera once more and began to film what did look to be an extraordinary arch over an elaborate door.

As I stood before the building, studying the grandness of the architecture, I felt the fight die out of me. What were my problems in the face of all this greatness?

So I stood there taking in Justin as he took it all in with his camera. I thought for a moment that he had forgotten I was even there, until he stepped back, put the camera down and turned to me, the look on his face ponderous. And somewhat sad.

"You know what today is?" he said.

"No, Justin, I don't know what today is. And I'm not just being difficult," I replied, still bothered by his comment.

"August twenty-fourth."

"Yeah, so wh——" I began, then I remembered. And was ashamed for not remembering sooner. Justin's parents had died this day, twenty years ago.

"Oh, Justin, I'm sorry, I——"

But he wasn't listening to my lame attempt to make up for the fact that I had been so self-absorbed lately I didn't even remember the day Justin paid reverence to yearly. Usually with me, though I guess I hadn't been much of a friend these days....

"They met here, you know. In New York. Somewhere in this neighborhood, I think. Did I ever tell you that?"

"Yes, you did," I said, peering up at him, trying to see through to the emotion he was clearly struggling with. It was an emotion I knew well, having lost my own father. But I had been luckier than Justin. I had had my father for so much longer, while Justin had lost both his parents at age twelve. He'd been just a boy. Probably not looking very different from the way he did now as he gazed down at me, his eyes a mixture of hopefulness and harrowing sadness.

"I know this is going to sound kinda hokey, but——" he began, then laughed and looked away. "But sometimes I imagine that I'm recording all this for them, you know? It amazes me that they'll never see any of this again. These buildings. That tree. None of it."

And you'll never see them, I thought, remembering well the worst part of losing my father. Knowing I would never get a chance to see his rare smile, to tell him that I loved him, more than I'm sure he ever was able to realize....

When I looked into Justin's eyes once more, I saw it all. The loneliness that would never go away.

Maybe that was just it. Maybe no matter how many people we surrounded ourselves with, or whom we ultimately spent our lives with, that was all we were ever meant to feel.

Alone.

13

Till death
(at 30,000 feet) do us part.

"You're bringing that big thing?" Kirk said when he opened his apartment door the Friday night before our scheduled departure to find me standing there, sweaty and out of sorts after lugging my giant suitcase on and off the Third Avenue bus. "I thought we were carrying on," he said, gesturing to the compact nylon duffel that sat in the foyer awaiting our early-morning flight.

"I...I couldn't fit everything in my other bag," I hedged. Actually, I hadn't even pulled it from the closet when I realized that no weekend bag could possibly hold the clothing options I felt absolutely necessary for my maiden voyage to Newton. There were the two pairs of jeans I couldn't travel without—the boot-cut ones that looked so cool with my wedge espadrilles (and I *had* to take my wedge espadrilles); and the slim-leg style that was perfect with my sneakers (and I couldn't go to the country without sneakers, now could I?). Then there were the four T-shirts—two short sleeved for day, one long sleeved in case we had a cool night and one tank in case the weather heated up. Two pairs of shorts (in case it was too hot for jeans), two pairs of capris (in case it was hot but shorts seemed inappropriate) and a thick cotton sweater (in case it was too cold for anything else). My denim jacket, because it went with everything. My beautiful new dress, of course. My strappy slides (for the dress), my strappy sandals (just in case I wasn't in the mood for the espadrilles). Pajama pants (I was sure Kirk's parents wouldn't appreciate me marching around in Kirk's boxers) and another (softer) tee to sleep in. Underwear (lots of it because I never could decide ahead of time whether I was going to go thong or brief). Bras, toiletries, makeup, brushes and a blow-dryer (because I really couldn't count on the Stevens family to keep styling equipment with the kind of voltage required to keep my frizzy locks tame).

Then there was the gift, which I'd surrounded in bubble wrap that Justin "just so happened" to have around.

Oh, and then there was the required reading material that traveled everywhere with me, due to a fear I would find myself alone, awake and with nothing but my own anxious thoughts to keep me company (which was often the case whenever Kirk and I were together, as he usually fell asleep before me): three magazines, two books of monologues (because despite the fact that I hadn't been auditioning recently, I somehow couldn't help seeking out all those audition scenes I had rehearsed and was quite capable of playing, given the chance) and a somewhat ratty 1986 edition of *Fodor's Boston* (in case we headed into the city) that Justin had bought for fifty cents at a book fair and was happy to loan me.

I mean, really, how could I expect to carry all that on the plane? I thought, watching (somewhat guiltily) as Kirk reluctantly lugged my (heavy) bag into the foyer and set it next to his own. "Jeez, Ange, we're only going for three days," he said, shaking his head as he looked at my bag, which dwarfed his neat little duffel. He sighed. "Never mind. Did you eat anything?"

"No, actually," I said, realizing that in all my packing anxiety, I hadn't had so much as a cracker since lunch.

Kirk glanced up at the kitchen clock, which indicated that it was almost ten (my packing had taken longer than expected) and well past any hour normal people (read: Kirk) would eat dinner. "Well, there's some leftover Indian food in the fridge if you feel like eating now," he offered, his tone implying that ten o'clock was no hour to be ingesting curry.

My stomach gurgled. "Sounds perfect," I said, ignoring his disdain and heading for the fridge.

"I'm just gonna finish up some work I was doing," he said, heading for the bedroom and his beloved laptop.

At the discovery that Kirk had none other than chicken tikka masala tucked away in the take-out bag in his fridge, I could have cared less if he and that laptop of his disappeared into the sunset together. I loved chicken tikka masala. *Lived* on it, which wasn't hard to do, since I lived only a few short blocks from East 6th Street, the infamous Indian Food Row. Of course, Kirk had gotten his chicken tikka masala right in his own neighborhood, and in truth Murray Hill Indian couldn't even come close to the fare on Indian Food Row. But the way my stomach was growling as I filled a plate and popped it into the microwave, I realized Kirk could have bought it next door to a cat farm and I still would have eaten it.

Two minutes later, I had settled on Kirk's sofa to eat and tuned in to the ten o'clock news. Normally I wasn't a news watcher. I got whatever bits I could handle from the headlines I read over people's shoulders on the subway and whatever rambling discourses I happened to catch on NPR, which Justin kept on continuously in his bedroom. But as I had gathered together my clothes for my big weekend away, I had wondered what I would actually talk about with Kirk's family, once I found myself in their presence. Then I had remembered Kirk's father was big into politics, having even held a councilman position for a short while when he was first married. And Kirk's mother had practically been an official member of the board of education in Newton, judging by the number of petitions she had put before them when she was head of the PTA, a position she had given up when Kayla, her youngest, had graduated, but still... These were some smart people I would be spending the weekend with. And was I was going to look pretty dumb in comparison if the only current events I could chat with them about were the effects of El Niño (weather was the only thing I actually did follow, news-wise). I had some catching up to do.

But as soon as the studied seriousness of Belinda Chen, the

bright-eyed and perfectly coiffed anchorwoman of Fox Five News, came on screen, I was filled with foreboding. And as Belinda and her helmet-headed male colleague bantered back and forth about a drive-by shooting on 125th Street, a fire that killed a family of five and a routine back surgery that had left the hapless patient paralyzed, I remembered why I didn't watch the news. It was all about death, and as a person who during most waking moments was all too aware of her own imminent demise, I didn't need any reminders.

And yet, I couldn't look away. Especially when, just moments before the program cut to a commercial break, Belinda faced the camera dead on and announced, "Next up—are airline cutbacks a prescription for disaster? Don't miss our special report on how belt-tightening choices made by major airlines could impact *you* and *your* loved ones this holiday weekend...."

You see? *This* was why I didn't like to fly. I glanced anxiously toward the bedroom, where I saw through the half-opened door that Kirk was still working merrily away, oblivious to the fact that his love of flying was going to get us *killed*. My eyes were glued to the set as Belinda returned and began (somewhat cheerfully, considering the subject matter) to recount incident after incident where major airline after major airline had "overlooked" some seemingly minor mechanical problem in the name of saving money and maintaining flight schedules.

I almost swallowed my tongue when they cut to an interview with a recently fired mechanic, the airline he had reportedly worked for for twenty-two years clearly identified in boldface letters at the bottom of the screen: Metro-Air.

Oh, God. "Kirk! *Kirk!* Come quick!" I shouted, picking up the remote and making the volume louder.

To his credit, Kirk was standing next to the sofa within moments, a bewildered expression on his face. "What's wrong?"

"Look!" I said, gesturing wildly to the screen with the remote as the mechanic explained how he'd advised airline personnel that the fuel gauge was working improperly, only to have his assessment ignored.

"So you risked your job and reported it to the FAA?" the reporter said, his square-jawed face creased with concern.

"Hey, somebody has to protect the American people," the mechanic said, a bit smugly, I have to admit.

"Angela…"

"What, it could happen! Especially on the shuttle. Do you know they run flights every hour on the hour from Boston to New York? Who's to say they wouldn't let one of those planes go up into the air just because some peon in maintenance figured a small splice in the fuel line wouldn't be a big deal?"

"Are you done now?" Kirk inquired. "Can I go back to finishing my work, so I can get some sleep before our flight? I mean, if we *are* going to go down into the ocean, I at least want to be awake enough to figure out how to use my seat as a flotation device!"

I did feel a little dumb, especially when the formerly disgruntled mechanic smiled into the camera and mouthed, "Hi, Mom," the minute the reporter turned to face the camera once more. What could I do but let Kirk go back to his bedroom and his laptop, leaving me to face my own anxieties alone?

And I was still facing them long after Kirk had drifted off to sleep and I lay beside him, eyes wide open against the darkness that blanketed the room, my stomach raw, whether from nerves or the spicy masala sauce I couldn't help but scarf down despite Kirk's warning tone. But I wasn't thinking about spliced fuel lines or ungreased pistons—I was thinking about Grace, whom I'd called the night before only to learn that she was spending her Friday night with her new best friend and consort in singledom, Claudia, at some hot new bar on the Upper East Side.

I sighed, imagining them laughing merrily at the men who would inevitably buy them drinks, probably more due to Grace's magnetic beauty than Claudia's glamorous yet utterly charmless demeanor. And though wild horses couldn't drag me back to the bar scene, I wished I had Grace to talk to. Because with Kirk snoozing peacefully on the pillow beside me, as if he didn't have a care on his mind, I suddenly felt the weight of the world.

I glanced at the clock, which showed just past midnight. I could always call Josh. After all, he never used to make any bones about calling *me* at any hour of day or night when anxiety or loneliness plagued him. Then I remembered that Josh was living with his soon-to-be-wife now, and I was certain Princess Emily would not be happy if I disturbed her beauty sleep. Besides, the rat hadn't been acting much like a friend anyway.

Then I remembered there was someone whom I could always call any time, day or night. Justin. I knew he'd be up. He was just as much of a night creature as I was.

I slipped out of bed, closing the door behind me so as not to wake Kirk, and crept into the living room.

Justin answered on the second ring. "Hello?"

"Hey," I said, suddenly realizing how odd it was to be talking to Justin on the phone in the middle of the night. I mean, I never usually had a reason to call the man I spent a good portion of my waking moments with.

"Hey, Ange, what's up? Where are you?"

"I'm at Kirk's. I just called…" I paused, suddenly not understanding why I *had* called. "I just called to see how you were doing…." This felt like the truth, because I had been worrying about Justin since last weekend, when we had walked all over the Upper West Side. It seemed with all my running around to get ready for this crazy weekend away, I hadn't even had a chance to talk to him and see how he was feeling since that night.

"Me? I'm fine, fine," he replied, as if he hadn't bared his soul to me less than a week ago. "Are you okay?" he asked.

"Me?"

"Yeah, 'cause if you need to talk, I can call you right back. I've got Lauren on the other line, long distance."

Don't ask me why this came as a surprise. Maybe because it seemed Lauren hadn't been calling as much as she used to. "No, that's okay," I said. "I'm going to go to bed soon anyway. I just called…to say goodbye."

"Okay. Have a good trip." He paused. "And don't worry about the flight. Everything's going to be fine."

I smiled. At least maybe he understood why I'd called. But once he hung up, leaving me in the silent darkness once more, I felt lonelier than ever.

You're just tired. It's late! an inner voice chided, sounding suspiciously like my mother's. *Go to bed. You'll be spending the whole weekend around people.*

Not just any people. Kirk's people.

I needed a cigarette.

Before I knew what I was doing, I was slipping my flip-flops on my feet and heading out the front door without a plan in mind, only an urge that I had not felt even during my pack-a-day period back in college. I was on the elevator before it occurred to me that walking down Third Avenue in my boxers and tank top to the deli for a pack of cigarettes was not the brightest thing to do in the middle of the night. I wasn't even wearing a bra, I thought, bending my knees and giving myself a test jiggle. Hmm…

The elevator doors opened, and like a savior in silver-blue security uniform, Henry sat at the front desk, bent over a newspaper.

"Hey, Henry," I said, as if wandering the halls in pajamas were my usual habit.

"Hey, Gorgeous," he said, greeting me as he usually did—one of the reasons I adored Henry. "What are you doing up at this hour?"

"Can't sleep," I said, approaching the desk and spying the tell-tale pack of Marlboros he kept in the cubby beneath the counter. "Can I bum a smoke?"

"Sure thing, sweetie," he said, grabbing the pack and holding it out to me.

I took one. "Thanks. Can I borrow these?" I asked, grabbing the matches there and heading for the door.

"You're not going outside like that?"

"Just on the stoop," I replied.

"I better come with you," he said. Another reason I adored Henry—he was probably pushing seventy and clearly from an era when men were hardwired to keep a protective eye on the fairer sex.

Once I seated myself comfortably on the one of the three steps that constituted the small stoop in front of Kirk's building, Henry took the matches from me, lit my cigarette, then pulled out one for himself.

We puffed in companionable silence for a few moments, until finally Henry asked, "Does Mr. Kirk know you smoke?"

Alarm shot through me with the realization that my little

midnight adventure might unmask my newfound vice to my…future husband. "Um, no actually, he doesn't. I mean, I don't really smoke…."

"I won't say a word," he said, flashing me a conspiratorial grin.

"At least not until after the wedding," I joked.

"Ah, is that how it is? You and Mr. Kirk getting married?"

Oops. There I went again, putting my flip-flop in my un-usually big mouth. But then I realized this was Henry I was talk-ing to. Henry who had once loaned me car fare when Kirk and I got in a fight in the early days of our relationship and in a flare of temper I had stomped out of the apartment without a dime to my name. "I don't know if we'll get married," I said now, and even as I uttered the words, I realized how true they were. I mean, nothing was definite. No vows, exchanges or pledges made. And suddenly I realized, with the clarity that only the late hour and a solid dose of nicotine could bring, that I wasn't sure if I ever wanted to take that step. Not with Kirk. Maybe not with anyone. Because if I couldn't make it with him…

"What do you think of Kirk?" I asked now, looking up into Henry's warm brown eyes as if I might find some answers there to the questions that seemed to now swirl freely through my sleep-deprived mind.

"Mr. Kirk?" He paused, gazing at me speculatively as he rolled his cigarette back and forth between his long brown fin-gers. "Mr. Kirk is a good man."

Yes, I thought, blowing out a last puff of smoke. He was a good man. But the question rose unbidden like a siren's song in the night: Was he a good man for me?

When the alarm buzzed at the ungodly hour of seven-thirty (ungodly for me, who though used to rising at five for the show felt entitled to sleep in a little on Saturday) I didn't have the an-swer. In fact, the question had been put to sleep shortly after I had crept back into the apartment at two in the morning and slid back into bed next to Kirk's sleep-warm body.

There was no time for uncertainty now, I thought, watch-ing groggily as Kirk bounded out of bed with an energy I could never muster at any hour of the morning, my regular *Rise and Shine* routine notwithstanding.

"Wake up, sleepyhead," Kirk said, leaning in to brush my cheek with a kiss.

I opened one eye, smiling when I saw his face so close, his eyes still sleepy and his hair endearingly tousled. "I don't want to go to school," I whined like a recalcitrant child, and pulled Kirk down until he was lying on top of me. "Can't we just stay in bed a little longer?" I whispered, rubbing my hips suggestively against his as I felt his body come to life. He bent his head and touched his mouth to my breast, biting gently through my tee and sending a pleasing ache to my lower body. Mmm-hmm…he *was* a good man, I thought, lifting up my tank to give him better access. The minute his lips closed on my nipple, I knew everything would be all right, just as soon as I got out him out of those damn shorts….

But before I could get that promising bulge free from his boxers, Kirk sprang up once again. "C'mon, c'mon, let's save that for later. We have a flight to catch."

Oh, right. The flight. Suddenly all desire fled from my body, replaced by mind-bending fear.

If Kirk noticed, he certainly didn't acknowledge it. Instead, he walked, somewhat merrily, over to the bathroom. "I'm gonna take a shower, unless you wanna go first…?"

"No, no, you go," I said, nestling farther into the bed and closing my eyes, as if I could go to sleep again and wake up in Newton without even having to pass through the airport security sensor. But my eyes flew open immediately, as a vision of Kirk's parents staring down at me somewhat austerely filled my mind.

Suddenly an emergency exit out the airplane escape hatch seemed infinitely preferable.

"What if they don't like me?" I said when Kirk stepped from the bathroom a short while later, his hair damp and a towel draped around his waist.

"What if who doesn't like you?" he said, stepping in front of the mirror above the dresser and proceeding to comb his hair.

"Your parents. Who else?"

He didn't answer, which wasn't very reassuring.

"Kirk!"

He put the comb down on the dresser, then turned to face

me. "Look, my parents aren't the easiest people to get along with. You should see the rows they get into with my sister Kayla." He studied me for a moment. "My best advice is just to steer clear of any contentious subjects, especially politics or religion."

Well, that was easy enough, I thought. I didn't know enough about either, really, to converse at any length about them.

"And maybe you ought to steer clear of art, too. Including theater. Ever since that whole NEA endowment fiasco, my father has formed pretty strange opinions about government-funded art."

"Kirk! You're not making this easy for me."

He sat down on the bed next to me, brushing my hair from my face. "Look, it'll be fine. I told you my parents were…difficult."

"You said odd, not difficult."

"Same difference. Just stop worrying so much," he said, plopping a kiss on my forehead. But not before I saw the worry simmering in his eyes.

Oh, God. What had I gotten myself into?

What I had gotten myself into, I discovered, once we cleared the security gate at LaGuardia after having every item in my carry-on examined for foreign substances, was a big, fat nightmare. My stomach was a mass of panic as I gazed through the windows at a plane that was leaving the ground. It wasn't like I'd never flown before. But I only did it if I deemed it absolutely necessary.

And as I sat beside Kirk in the terminal, awaiting our flight, I wondered if this trip *was* absolutely necessary.

By the time we'd boarded the plane and I'd taken my aisle seat next to Kirk, I was starting to feel a bit tight in the throat, as if I'd eaten something I was allergic to. Oh, God, maybe I *had* eaten something I was allergic to.

"Kirk, do you think there might have been nuts in my breakfast burrito?"

He turned from the magazine he'd already began to thumb through—one of the twelve I'd grabbed when I'd discovered one of the few benefits of shuttle travel was the free magazine rack. "What kind of nut would be in a breakfast burrito?"

Obviously he was tired of my anxiety. I was tired of it, too, frankly, but what could I do? Well, I remembered, as the plane began to taxi away from the terminal, I could pray.

Now, I am not a religious person, but whenever I found myself, as I did now, strapped to a chair and about to be lifted thirty thousand feet into the air, I suddenly discovered my faith again. And like the good Catholic girl I was raised to be, I remembered my Our Fathers and Hail Marys the minute I found a way to put them to good use. Like right now…

Our Father, who art in heaven, I began, closing my eyes and clutching my hands in my lap in a way that was sort of prayerful, but, to the unwitting viewer (like Kirk), might seem just like a handclasp (because I didn't want him to realize I was so far gone I was actually resorting to prayer).

I was cut off mid-prayer by the sound of a female voice over the intercom. "Ladies and gentleman, please direct your attention to the flight attendants as they explain the safety features of this aircraft."

Oh, right. Safety features. Though I was a bit superstitious about leaving off mid-prayer (like the good Catholic girl I'd been raised to be, I also believed in God's wrath), I was even more afraid to leave myself without survival skills in the event of—God forbid—a crash. I faced forward, watching as a curvy blond flight attendant whose face was so made up she looked like a rubber doll, showed us how to buckle the seat belt.

Got it, I thought, giving mine a reassuring tug and glancing at Kirk, who was now buried in that magazine. I guess it would be up to me to rescue *both* of us in the event of a crash, considering the amount of attention he was giving our little blond friend here. But then, he traveled so much he probably had the whole thing memorized.

Now she was holding up an oxygen mask and advising us to put our mask on first before assisting a child. Well, this seemed kind of selfish, but I supposed it made sense. I looked over at Kirk again, wondering if he'd help me with my mask, should it come to that. These things looked complicated. And how could I trust that the flow of oxygen would start once my mask was in place? Who knew *what* would be working on this plane once it started hurtling toward the ocean?

Still I listened carefully as Blondie explained how the seat cushion would turn into a flotation device and the aisles would light up, leading me to safety. Frankly, I wasn't buying it. So as soon as she was done, I returned to my prayer. And just in time, too—the plane was picking up speed.

Our Father who art in heaven, hallowed be Thy name.
Thy kingdom come, Thy will be done, on earth as it is
In heaven. Give us this day our daily bread. And forgive us
Our press passes...

Forgive us our *press passes?* What the hell was that? Now I had to start all over again. I know, I know. Stupid, right? What can I say? I'm not only Catholic, I'm obsessive-compulsive. And I was scared to death when I felt the ground pull away from us.

We were in the air. *We were in the air! Oh, God,* I thought as my stomach plummeted with our ascent and I closed my eyes to pray once more.

"Hey, Noodles, check it out. You can see the Empire State Building."

"Been there, done that," I said, my eyes still tightly shut. I began again, rushing through the prayer before anyone else could interrupt. I even rattled off a quick Hail Mary, for good measure. Then, as I had done ever since I was five and believed prayer was the equivalent of sending a wish list to Santa Claus, I put in my requests.

Please, God, let us land safely. In Boston. On the tarmac.

(I also believed specificity was important. I mean, technically you could land safely in the water, right? Wasn't that why they gave us these floating seat cushions? Oh, God, how the hell could a fucking airplane land "safely" on the water? Hello? We were being lied to! Lied to by the fucking FAA!)

Please, God, on the fucking tarmac. I mean the tarmac. Sorry!

While I was at it, I figured I'd throw in one last request.

One more thing: Could You make Kirk's parents like me? Even just a little bit?

Amen.

I opened up my eyes to find Kirk staring at me, as if I were some alien creature.

"Are you all right?"

"I'm fine!" I practically shouted, because clearly I wasn't. And when I saw the cool, assessing way he was looking at me, I wondered if I would ever be again.

When the plane touched the ground forty-five minutes later, I realized at least one of my prayers was answered. I took it as a good sign.

I took the sight of the tall, dark-haired woman waving frantically at us from the gate as another.

"Hey, Kayla," Kirk said as we approached, wrapping her in a hug. "How are you, brat?" he said, stepping back to take her in.

She looked a lot like Kirk—same square face and beautiful brows, same dark hair. But she had about fifty pounds on him. She wasn't exactly fat—she carried her weight well, probably due to her height (she was almost as tall as Kirk's six feet), her broad shoulders and her womanly hips. Her eyes were the same silver-gray as Kirk's, though there was a keenness to them, as if she looked fearlessly into the dirty underbelly of things and might even take a perverse pleasure in the view, judging by the way her wide mouth curved into a smile.

"Well, well, well, the girlfriend," she said, once Kirk had made the introductions. "Nice to meet cha." Then, before I knew what was happening, I was wrapped in a bone-crunching hug. "I figured I'd pick you up myself and spare you the parents for the car ride," she said. "Kirk knows how Dad gets when he's in traffic." Then, in a deeper voice, which I assumed was supposed to be the voice of Mr. Stevens, she said, "Intolerable!"

"Don't start, Kayla," Kirk warned.

"Don't start? *They've* already started. I got there this morning and received the full rant about the problems with interracial relationships, of all things. Apparently they'd been listening to Dr. Laura again…." She rolled her eyes, then, turning to me, she said, "Don't worry. They'll be on their best behavior while you're there. They can't wait to meet you. I don't think Kirk's brought anyone home since... *Susan.*"

"Yeah," Kirk said, his expression so grim I wished I could climb back on that plane again.

Because suddenly I was ready to risk a faulty fuel gauge rather than face Kirk's formidable parents.

14

I shoulda packed the ruby slippers....

Whatever fears Kirk had instilled in me Kayla put to rest with her wry commentary as she negotiated her sturdy Volkswagen Jetta through traffic. The car was apparently another point of contention between Kayla and her parents, who always advocated buying American. I also learned that Kayla had ditched her latest boyfriend (you know, the one who had *already* met the family), and was having her portrait painted, this time completely nude, by a male friend of hers. "Wait till Mom and Dad find out I spent that much time with Lars *naked*," she said with a chuckle that I was beginning to find contagious.

I was starting to think everything might go all right this weekend, until we got off the highway and entered the town limits of Newton. Suddenly we were surrounded by white-picket fences, triple-decker Victorians and some of the lushest landscapes I had ever seen. It was like I had been dropped into a Norman Rockwell painting, which made me vaguely nervous. After all, I never saw anyone quite like me in a Norman Rockwell painting.

And I realized, after we had parked the car and stepped inside one of those white-picketed Victorians, neither had Mr. and Mrs. Stevens.

"You must be Angela!" Mrs. Stevens said after she and Mr. Stevens had embraced Kirk and stood looking at me as if trying to decide whether to hug me, too, or shoo me out of the large foyer. They were younger looking than the late sixties I knew them to be, and taller than I'd imagined, towering over me in nylon sweat suits that looked like they'd been pulled out of the Lands' End catalog, circa 1986.

"Who does she look like, Phil?" Mrs. Stevens said, turning to her husband. "That actress, you know who I'm talking about."

"Now how in God's name would I know who you were talking about?" Mr. Stevens said, looking at his wife incredulously.

"The one that played that abused wife who seduces that poor young boy in that movie...."

"Marisa Tomei?" Kirk asked, looking at me as if trying to decide whether I resembled an abused wife and seductress.

"I get that a lot," I said, wondering if that was a good thing.

"Isn't Marisa Tomei Hispanic?" Mr. Stevens said, studying me now with something that looked like suspicion. "I thought you said Angela was Italian!" he practically shouted, turning to his son as if he'd withheld some vital information.

"Marisa Tomei is Italian!" Mrs. Stevens insisted. "You saw *My Cousin Vinny,* Phil...."

"What, just because she plays an Italian doesn't mean she's Italian!" he argued back, somewhat heatedly, considering the subject matter.

Fortunately, I was rescued from the immediate tension that buzzed through air, seemingly since the moment I entered the house, by Kayla, who grabbed my suitcase and shopping bag and said, "C'mon, I'll show you to your room."

"My" room turned out to be a white-paneled rectangle punctuated by a twin bed complete with frothy pink bedspread that was strewn with at least thirty stuffed animals. According to Kayla, it had been Kate's room growing up, though I couldn't imagine that Kate had inhabited this room since the age of seven, judging by the dollhouse that stood in one corner and the white rocking chair occupied by the largest Holly Hobbie doll I had ever seen. Once Kayla had put down my bag and pointed out the bathroom along the hall and the towels that had been laid out on the trunk at the end of the bed, she turned to me and said, "Just a little footnote on the old parents. They were born and bred in Newton—even met at a school dance right in town. In other words, they haven't seen much of the world." She paused, as if trying to find words for her thoughts. "Let's just say that living in their little world has bred in them a certain malignant indifference to anyone who isn't a part of their own private planet. So try not to take any of their ignorance personally. They mean well," she said, then frowned. "At least I like to think they mean well...."

I nodded, though her little speech had filled me with foreboding. I understood what she was saying all too well. Wasn't my own mother guilty of a little small-mindedness? I guess I had just never been on the receiving end.

"C'mon," she said. "I'm sure Kirk's got them under control by now."

Kirk did seem to have them under control by the time we got back downstairs, where we found him sitting across from them in the living room, a pitcher of iced tea and some glasses on the table before him.

"Here they are!" Mrs. Stevens said, jumping up and handing me a glass of iced tea. "Come in, sit. You must be tired from traveling."

"Thanks," I said, sitting down on the love seat next to Kirk, with what I hoped was a smile on my face. But the smile froze when I looked up above the sofa where Mr. and Mrs. Stevens sat and saw a framed, poster-size family portrait, with Mr. Stevens seated front and center, his wife and Kayla on one side, and what must have been Kirk's sister Kate and her husband on the other, along with Kirk and... *Susan*. At least it looked like the same Susan I had stumbled across in an old photo album in Kirk's apartment—same lush blond hair and wide blue eyes. Same proud smile. It *was* her, I realized. What the hell was she doing here?

If Kirk noticed it, he didn't say a word, only sat quietly while his mother said, "So, Angela, Kirk tells us you're an actress."

"Um, yes, yes I am," I said, getting a grip once again. I suddenly felt like I was on an audition for the role of future daughter-in-law. And the competition was pretty fierce, judging by how warm and cozy Susan looked standing in the loving embrace of the Stevens family.

"Actually, Angela is one of the hosts on *Rise and Shine*," Kirk chimed in, as he if he, too, sensed the need to whip out my résumé.

"I don't think I've heard of it." Mrs. Stevens said.

"It's a children's exercise program on Channel Fifty-four," I explained.

"Children's exercise! What a pissa!" Kayla said, slapping one healthy thigh as she chuckled uproarishly. I would have chuckled right along with her, if I didn't see the way Mr. Stevens was frowning at his younger daughter.

"Anyway," Kirk said, carefully steering the conversation back on track, "it looks like a major network might pick up the show."

"Well, that sounds marvelous," Mrs. Stevens said. "I happen to think children's programming is very important. And an exercise program! I imagine that provides a solid discipline. These days children don't learn a thing about discipline. I mean, look at these kids today. Taking drugs. Bringing guns to school."

"Yes, I guess it does help the kids form good…habits," I said, sounding surprisingly like Rena, the Nazi exercise guru of the six-year-old set. And before I knew it, I was waxing poetic about the benefits of exercise, the solid discipline it provided. All under the watchful eye of Susan, who gazed down at me with that indefatigable smile.

In truth, by the time I got through my manifesto on the proper molding of children, I was exhausted. And thoroughly disgusted with myself.

The Stevenses—at least Mr. and Mrs.—were thoroughly pleased, however, as was Kirk, who was beaming at me proudly. The light in his eyes said I'd just passed some great hurdle. So why did I feel I'd fallen into the ditch on the other side?

Worse, I think I might have dragged someone with me.

"You might have benefited from such a program, Kayla," Mr. Stevens replied, turning to her just as she was reaching for the bowl of nuts on the coffee table. "I told you we should have encouraged her to play more sports as a child, Carol. Now look at her!"

Though it was only there for the briefest of moments, I saw the hurt in Kayla's eyes before she belligerently grabbed up a handful of nuts and began tossing them into her mouth one by one, while staring down her father.

"That's probably where you got that nice shape from, Angela," Mrs. Stevens said, ignoring her husband's jab at her parenting skills as she turned to me. "Look at her arms, Phil!"

I glanced apologetically at Kayla, though I wasn't sure what I was apologizing for. Her parents? My painfully toned arms?

Fortunately Kayla didn't hold it against me. "So I understand you live in the East Village," she said, once she'd swallowed another fistful of nuts.

"Yes, yes, I do." Now here was a subject I could get behind. I was proud of my neighborhood, with its cultural diversity and bohemian personality.

"I *adore* the East Village," she said. "I've even done a show at one of my favorite performance venues there—P.S. 122."

"So you're a performance artist as well as a…a photographer?" I said, remembering the photo she'd had in that group show at the Smithsonian.

"I'd say she's an exhibitionist!" Mr. Stevens said.

Apparently Mr. Stevens remembered that show, too.

Kayla ignored him. "Actually, I just did it the one time. Did you ever hear of the 'Bare Your Body, Bare Your Soul' show?"

Not only had I heard of it, I'd seen it. "That was *you?*"

"Oh, dear Lord, don't tell me you patronize that smut, too!" Mrs. Stevens said. Even Susan seemed to have a little gleam in her eye, I thought, glancing up at the picture.

"Um, just the one time…" In truth, I had found the whole show a wee bit embarrassing, though I did admire the courage of the six female performers who'd gotten up on stage, each one of them completely naked, as they narrated tales of suppression and male dominance. The whole thing was a bit…angry for my taste, but then, I *had* shelled out $24.50 for a ticket.

I never seemed to gain my footing again in the conversation after that. And it seemed to go on for hours. Needless to say, I was enormously relieved when Kayla interrupted Mrs. Stevens in the middle of a diatribe about the lack of family values in the unmarried thirty and over set (read: me, Kayla and even Kirk, for that matter) by suggesting we take a ride into town.

"We'll show Angela around," she said to Kirk, who had already leaped up, clearly eager to escape. "Besides," Kayla continued, turning to her mother, "you're gonna need more bread for tomorrow anyway. You *never* buy enough."

"Well, maybe if you kept your own intake down, we'd have enough," Mr. Stevens grumbled, but Kayla had already snatched her keys and was heading out the front door.

"C'mon, Ange," Kirk said, grabbing my hand and taking me with him.

Once we'd settled into the Jetta, I felt like myself again. I was starting to appreciate the sturdy German car, especially as it seemed to be the only place I could relax. "You okay?" Kirk said to me, touching my shoulder from where he sat in the back seat.

I turned and nodded tentatively at him. Sure, I was fine— now.

Though I secretly hoped "town" meant Boston (I knew it was close, but apparently not that close), I found I liked the charming little streets that we strolled down once we'd parked the car, though Newton was vastly different from the neighborhood I grew up in. For one thing, it was cleaner. Plus everyone here looked alike. And like they all shopped at Lands' End. Or maybe Lee and Laurie, I thought, spying a familiar-looking windbreaker on a young woman we passed.

Kayla talked animatedly the whole time, pointing out the library and claiming she still owed them a book she'd taken out back in high school. "They probably have a Wanted sign of me in the lobby," she said with a gleeful little giggle. Later, when we passed the bakery, Kayla picked up three loaves of French bread for tomorrow and a bag of cookies, which she immediately began popping into her mouth. My stomach rumbled, and I was contemplating one of those tempting black-and-white cookies when I heard Kirk exclaim, "Kayla, Mom's cooking dinner. And you know how early they always eat...."

Right, dinner. Couldn't kill my appetite for the first family dinner. I knew my mother regarded anyone who ate meagerly at her table as bizarre. I didn't want to make a bad impression if Mrs. Stevens was the same way.

Still, I watched with longing as Kayla shoved down cookie after cookie while she continued her tour.

"So what do you think?" Kirk said, when we had traveled from one end of town to the other.

"It's...it's nice," I said, gazing up at his happy features. I could tell he was proud.

"Smile!" Kayla said, turning to us with the camera she had taken with her from the car.

I leaned in close to Kirk, smiling like the happy girlfriend I suddenly felt I was.

And hoped that someday my photo would be hanging over the Stevenses' sofa.

But Susan was still there when we came back around four. As was Mrs. Stevens, who was merrily working on dinner while Mr. Stevens sat in a kitchen chair, listening to what sounded like Rush Limbaugh on the radio. "You're back!" Mrs. Stevens said, smiling brightly at us from where she stood over a pot at the stove. "Phil, get the steaks out of the refrigerator."

"Can't you see I'm busy right now?" he said, eyeing her in disbelief as he leaned in closer to the radio, which he'd placed on the table in front of him.

Sparing her father a single cutting glance that he didn't catch, Kayla went to the fridge and pulled out a package of meat from the refrigerator.

"I can help," I said, going to the long counter that separated the dining area from the kitchen.

"Oh, no—you're our guest!" Mrs. Stevens protested. Then, turning to Kayla, she said, "Can you get out the onions, too?"

Kirk had pulled up to the table and was already engrossed in the newspaper that he'd found there. "Damn Red Sox lost again!" he said, then proceeded to read all the gory details. As I joined him, I glanced at the headlines and saw the Red Sox had lost to the Yankees. I smiled to myself, imagining Justin jumping for joy at home.

But my happiness was short-lived as I sat there, twiddling my thumbs, while Kayla and Mrs. Stevens bustled about the kitchen. I took some comfort in the fact that the Stevens household wasn't much different from mine, with the men lounging about while the women ran around like loons getting the meal ready. The arrangement always bothered me, though tonight I would have been happy to chop up a few hundred cloves of garlic rather than sit here like an idiot with nothing to do. And no one to talk to.

Finally Mr. Stevens was roused from his radio long enough to fire up the grill in the backyard and cook the steaks (men did the grilling in my house, too). Dinner was served shortly afterward, in the elegantly appointed dining room just off the kitchen. Though I usually wasn't one to put a morsel of dinner in my mouth before seven o'clock at night, I was starving, having consumed nothing more than a glass of iced tea and a breakfast burrito all day. But when I cut into the steak Kirk had forked onto my plate, I was horrified to discover how red it was inside. Worse, the vegetable du jour was broccoli, and I *hated* broccoli, though I took a few of the funny little trees onto my plate to appear courteous. And potatoes. Lots of 'em. I had to eat something.

"So how is everything?" Mrs. Stevens asked, beaming brightly at me as I cut up the meat into tiny little pieces in an effort to make it look like I'd attempted to eat it.

"Everything's great," I replied, digging my fork into those potatoes with something I hope resembled gusto. I looked down at my plate. "Your china is lovely," I continued, studying the pretty plate. I wished it were edible.

"That's my great-grandmother's china," Mrs. Stevens said proudly. "And the silverware is from Mr. Stevens's family. Do you know my husband has family that harks back to the *Mayflower?*" Then, as if she hoped I had some equally compelling history to tell, she added, "I don't think we've even asked you about your family…."

I put down my fork. Then, without even thinking, said, "So far as I know, my family can be traced all the way back to my great-grandfather, who came here from Naples and started a fruit stand on Delancey Street. Just under the Brooklyn Bridge?"

"Oh," Mrs. Stevens said, as if she found this information...disturbing.

"Angela's dad started up one of the biggest auto-parts chains in Brooklyn," Kirk chimed in proudly, as if feeling a need to make up for my less than impressive paternal roots.

"Is that right?" Mr. Stevens said, his interest piqued. "Humph. Must be a tough business nowadays, what with auto manufacturers making cars that you pretty much replace after a few years of wear and tear. I can't imagine there's as much use for auto-part replacements as there used to be."

I shivered, feeling as if Mr. Stevens had just foreseen the extinction of my whole family line.

"Does your father run the stores himself?" Mrs. Stevens asked, probably trying to find out if my father was more grease monkey or CEO.

"He did. But now my brothers do," I replied. "My father passed away four years ago."

"Oh, dear. He must have been young!" Mrs. Stevens said, raising a hand to her cheek, which bloomed with health, despite her advanced age.

"Uh, he was fifty-nine. He got...cancer," I said, in answer to the question I saw forming in her eyes.

"Oh, that's just awful," Mrs. Stevens said, glancing around the table at her thriving family as if she couldn't imagine any one of them getting so much as a cold. "Cancer is such an...insidious disease. They say it has a strong hereditary component," she added, looking at me now as if malignant cells were multiplying in my body as she spoke. "Did anyone else in your family have it?"

"Um..." I thought of my paternal grandfather, who'd succumbed to the dreaded disease when I was too young to understand how sick he was. Then there was Uncle Gino. Maybe my mother was right to worry about us all so much. Maybe we were all going to die young. And, worse, I thought, glancing over at Kirk, who had stopped eating altogether and was staring at me as if trying to decide whether he could see himself cradling my head through postchemo bouts of nausea, I was probably going to die alone.

★ ★ ★

Alone is exactly how I felt later that night as I lay in that pink ruffled room, cataloging the events of the night and cringing at the memory of all the polite smiles Mrs. Stevens gave me as each new fact of my life was revealed—my CUNY education (Susan went to MIT, which somehow Mrs. Stevens couldn't help mentioning), my Brooklyn upbringing (which caused Mr. Stevens to go into a diatribe about the Crown Heights beating as if I were somehow personally responsible). Then there was my grandmother's love affair. Kirk brought that up, not me—he thought it was cute. Of course, Mr. and Mrs. Stevens were horrified. "A woman that age!" Mrs. Stevens exclaimed, as if my grandmother were prostituting herself rather than sharing a few harmless shopping sprees and hands of poker with a kindly old man who nowadays probably got his biggest excitement when he was dealt a royal flush. I was painfully glad when Mrs. Stevens suggested an early bedtime for us all, saying we had a big day tomorrow. I tried not to notice that Mr. Stevens headed in the opposite direction from Mrs. Stevens as we said our good-nights (apparently they kept separate bedrooms). Kayla had descended to the basement, where her parents had made her a bedroom when she was a rebellious teen and where she was spending the night, since her own apartment was in Boston and, according to Mrs. Stevens, too far for a young woman to drive to alone at night.

Now, as I lay in my own separate bedroom, I longed for Kirk, who was already snoring peacefully in his boyhood room. The clock ticked loudly beside my bed. It was only eleven. I never went to bed this early in New York.

I got up again and rifled around in my bag for my cell, with the hope of catching Justin at home so I could regale him with the events of the day, and even get a laugh out of it all. After all, it was kinda funny the things about me that seemed to appall Mrs. Stevens. So why wasn't I laughing yet?

I looked at the phone and saw I had no signal. Where in God's name *was* I that I had no cell signal? Maybe it was because I was indoors.

I peered out the window, into the darkened backyard where a table and chairs sat on a wood patio. I could probably get a signal out there.

Though I felt like a thief in the night, I tucked the cell phone into the pocket of my pajamas and crept down the stairs, cringing at the creak in every one. I felt a moment of relief when I reached the foyer undetected, then surprise when I found the front door unlocked. What was this, Mayberry? Didn't anyone get their house broken into around here? It somehow seemed...inhuman...not to have to worry about such things.

I stepped out onto the front stoop and felt a bloodcurdling scream rise up in my throat when my foot made contact with a body in the darkness.

"Shh!" Kayla admonished, then smiled guiltily as she waved a glowing cigarette in the air. "I don't want my parents to wake up. I'm sure you can imagine their feelings on this little vice...."

I smiled down at her with relief. "No problem. You just startled me. I guess I didn't expect anyone to be out here."

"Me either," she said, looking up at me curiously.

"I couldn't sleep," I said, hoping she wouldn't notice the bulge in my pajama pants where I'd tucked my cell phone. I mean, I was sure Kayla could accept a lot of things about me, but I wondered how she would feel knowing I had a hankering to call another man in the middle of the night. Though Justin was only a friend, it suddenly seemed like an illicit thing to do at Kirk's family home.

I took a seat beside her on the stoop.

"Want one?" she said, holding out a pack of Marlboro Lights.

I eagerly pulled one from the pack.

She smiled. "I knew you were a smoker."

"I'm not really," I protested immediately. "Only sometimes." Only since I've been thinking about marrying your brother, I thought with a touch of panic.

She lit me up and my panic subsided as I took a deep drag.

We sat in silence for a few moments. And what silence it was. I don't think I'd ever experienced such quiet in my life—and such...darkness, I thought, my eyes seeking out the front yard and barely making out the shrubbery there. It looked kind of spooky. I decided right then and there, I would never live outside of New York City. I needed noise, I need people. I needed...*light,* for chrissakes. Who knew what serial killer could be lurking out there in the darkness? At least in Manhattan, your weirdos were right out there where you could see them, for the most part.

While your New England weirdos, I thought, could be any-where—or anyone. Could even be living behind a white-picket fence and dressed in Lands' End sweat suits, I thought with a shiver, remembering Kirk's parents' attire.

As if she were reading my thoughts, Kayla said, "So how are you holding up against the old parents?"

"Oh, they're not so bad," I said.

She snorted. "Yeah. They're a good argument for not getting married," she said. "Probably why I can't bring myself to do it. Do you see the way he tears at her?"

I wouldn't call it *tearing.* But Mr. Stevens did have a habit of dismissing almost everything Mrs. Stevens said, as if her opin-ions and concerns were nothing to him.

Kind of like Kirk dismissed mine, I thought with another shiver, as I remembered the way Kirk had looked at me when I'd dragged him in to watch that harrowing report on airplane maintenance last night. But I was a bit neurotic. I was lucky he even put up with me. Maybe his calm, organized approach would balance me out once we were married.

Or cancel me out, a little voice whispered.

"So you and Kirk talking about getting married?" Kayla asked, once again picking the thoughts right out of my head.

"Sort of," I said, stubbing out my now-finished cigarette on the stoop.

She laughed. "Yeah, my brother is a tough nut to crack. I think Susan really wanted to marry him. But I don't think he was ready yet. He was working in a job he didn't like, and I don't think he'd figured out what he really wanted. But now he's got his own business, and it sounds like he's doing well from what he was saying over dinner. He's got some big client on the hori-zon."

"Yeah," I said, thinking of that damn Norwood proposal, which was just about destroying our relationship. Thank God Kirk had finished it before we left. Maybe I would get my boyfriend back.

Then, because I didn't want to think anymore about all the doubts that had risen up during these past weeks, I turned the marriage question over to Kayla. "What about you? Do you think you'll ever get married?"

"Me?" she said, picking up our cigarette butts from the stoop. "I don't know. I don't think marriage is for me."

I couldn't help but wonder, as I studied that dark landscape before us, if marriage was for me either.

I awoke to the sound of a shrieking baby. I was slightly horrified, as I had dreamed that Kirk and I were married and had moved into the basement of the Stevens family house. For a moment, in my bleary early-morning state, I thought that was *our* child crying as if its little life depended on it. I was heartily relieved to realize that this little life wasn't dependent on me. It had to be Kirk's niece, I thought, remembering how Mrs. Stevens had mentioned that Kate and Kenneth would be bringing the baby over early so we could all go to the church together for the christening, which was at one-thirty.

I peeked into Kirk's bedroom and discovered that he was up already, the blue plaid bedspread already laid neatly back in place. I decided I needed time to wake up before I faced the Stevens clan in full force, so I grabbed my toiletry bag from my room, as well as a couple of towels, and hit the shower.

The crying had mercifully abated by the time I got out of the bathroom. Once I'd dried my hair, dusted my face with makeup and dressed in a T-shirt and capris, I headed downstairs, where I found Mrs. Stevens, in yet another Lands' End sweat suit, sprawled on the floor with a dark-haired baby girl, playing peekaboo. Mr. Stevens read a newspaper in the wingback while Kirk and Kayla sat on the sofas talking with a tall, slender woman with sparkling blue eyes who I assumed was Kate, and an equally tall and somewhat rugged-looking bearded guy who must have been Kenneth.

"You're up!" Mrs. Stevens said, glancing away from her granddaughter. "We were worried you were going to sleep all day, Angela!"

The thought wasn't unappealing.

Kirk introduced me to Kate and Kenneth as I took a seat beside him on the sofa. Kayla got up to get me a cup of coffee—I guess she could tell without even asking that I wasn't interested

in whatever tepid brew sat in that china teapot on the table—
to go with the rolls and Danishes that were laid out on the table.

As I munched contentedly on my brunch—relieved that I
could at least eat this meal without fear of food poisoning, I realized the arrival of Kirk's niece was a fortuitous event, as it
meant all attention was now drawn away from me and focused
on little Kimberly, who sat center stage on the carpet before us,
babbling incoherently, much to the delight of her doting
grandmother. I found Kate and Kenneth easy enough to talk
to, mostly because we could barely exchange four sentences before Mrs. Stevens shrieked, "Look at Kimberly, look, look!" and
we all turned to watch Kimberly clap her hands or blow a spit
bubble through her tiny bow-shaped lips.

But the enchanting little Kimberly show ended abruptly
when Mr. Stevens looked at his watch and shouted accusingly
at his wife, "Carol, it's almost noon! Don't we have to be at the
church by one-fifteen? We're going to be *late!*"

"Oh, dear," Mrs. Stevens said, looking up from where she was
still sprawled on the floor with her granddaughter. "We need
to dress Kimberly!" Then, looking down at her nylon sweat suit,
she cried, "We *all* have to to get dressed!"

Chaos ensued as Mrs. Stevens grabbed Kimberly off the
floor, shouting, "Where's the baptismal gown?", sending Kenneth running for the car and Kate running for the diaper bag.
Mr. Stevens eased himself up from the chair and lumbered out
of the room, and Kayla continued to munch contentedly on a
Danish. "The church is only five freakin' minutes away," she
muttered, reaching for her coffee mug. Kirk stood up. "Yeah,
but we better get ready. You know how she gets," he said, referring, I was sure, to his mother. "You coming?" he said, turning to me.

Once alone in my room, I pulled my baby-blue dress out of
the suitcase with something like the anticipation I had once felt
on Christmas morning. I couldn't wait to wear it. Had been
dreaming of it ever since I had dragged it home from Bloomingdale's.

Thank God it had a little Lycra, I thought, watching the
wrinkles smooth out as I pulled it on and zipped up the side.

Perfect, I thought, noting how the spaghetti straps showed off my toned arms and the top fit just tight enough across my small chest to make it seem more pronounced than usual. I sighed. There was a reason this dress cost $150.

After smoothing a little pomade over my hair to take out the layer of frizz that had already developed and slipping on my strappy heels, I knocked on Kirk's bedroom door.

"Hey," I said, poking my head in. He was standing in his navy-blue suit trousers, his white shirt still unbuttoned and hanging loose while he ran a clothing steamer over his suit jacket.

"Hey," he said, putting the steamer back on its stand and turning to look at me. "Wow," he said, "you look...hot."

I couldn't tell whether this was a good thing or not, judging by the somewhat frightened expression on his face.

"You're not so bad yourself," I said, stepping close to him and sliding my arms around his waist beneath his shirt.

He immediately pulled away, "Angie, stop! My *parents* are right downstairs."

"You mean *all the way* downstairs," I said teasingly, pulling him close again. Feeling a bit mischievous, I pressed my lips to one bare nipple.

"Ange——" he practically groaned, his body tensing beneath my hands.

"Okay, okay," I said, letting go of him and going to sit on the bed. Sheesh. You'd think his parents had put a ban on sex, the way he was acting. Then I remembered those separate bedrooms of theirs, and the way I'd seen Mrs. Stevens shrug off her husband's hand when he'd offered to help her off the floor, and wondered if maybe they *had* put a ban on any sort of intimacy.

But this thought flew out of my mind as I waited for Kirk to finish dressing, my eyes roaming over his bedroom, taking it all in for the first time since I'd arrived. Like Kate's, it looked like a shrine to the younger Kirk, with football trophies lining one shelf and beer steins collected from the various pubs Kirk had frequented during his college years at Boston University. I even spotted a couple of model cars. It was cute to see all these artifacts from Kirk's early days, I thought, standing up to study a photo collage that hung on one wall.

A photo collage containing six different photos, all of them of Kirk and Susan.

"What the hell?" I said out loud.

"What's wrong?" Kirk said, turning to me as he adjusted his tie around his neck.

"What's with all these pictures of Susan everywhere? You weren't even living here when you dated her! And that family portrait? What the hell is that about?"

"That's my mother. She put all those pictures up. I think she was trying to make Susan…feel at home while she was here. Don't make such a big deal out of it. Those pictures are old, Noodles. She probably just didn't get around to changing them."

I wasn't convinced. And I was even less convinced that I would ever find pictures of myself in that stately old house when I entered the living room with Kirk and his mother's eyes widened at the sight of me.

"Oh, dear, Angela, is that what you're *wearing?*"

I glanced at Kirk, who suddenly turned to look at me as if seeking out the fault in my outfit.

"I mean, it's a lovely dress, but to church? Your arms are all bare! And your *shoulders* are showing," she said, looking at me as if I were exposing my nipples, too.

As I took in her floral, flowing half-sleeved dress, which was buttoned rather primly to the neck, I suddenly felt like one of the strippers at Jimmy's Topless—not that I'd ever even been there or anything.

"What's wrong?" Kate said, entering the room in an ivory skirt and matching blazer that screamed Mother of the Blessed Child. Her husband followed in a navy suit, holding Kimberly, who was swathed in what seemed like miles and miles of flowing white silk.

Even Kayla the exhibitionist had opted for a tasteful tan pantsuit.

"She looks fine, Mom," Kirk said.

"Yeah, the church isn't really that strict anymore," Kate said.

"Well, *I* am," Mrs. Stevens continued, going to the closet in the front foyer and returning with what looked like a giant lace doily. "Here, put this on," she said, draping the shawl around my scandalous shoulders and covering my hundred-fifty-dollar dress with a piece of material that probably went for ninety-nine cents a yard. Worse, it smelled an awful lot like mothballs. I sneezed two times in succession.

"See that? You're getting a cold, Angela. Better you stay warm," Mrs. Stevens said.

Kirk sighed, glancing at me apologetically, then turned to his mom once more and asked, "Where's Dad?"

"In the car," she replied, grabbing her pocketbook from the table. "Let's go, let's go!"

We arrived at the church a full half hour early, which was fine with Mrs. Stevens, as she wanted to take pictures outside the church. Guess who held the camera? And when it came time for the ceremony, the Nikon was taken out of my hands and I was given a digital camcorder by Kenneth, who looked hopefully at me and asked if I would kindly film the baptism. I didn't mind, really, as my new role as videographer earned me a spot I otherwise might not have gotten, right next to Kirk, who stood beside the rest of his family at the baptismal font when we got to that part of the ceremony. Besides, I felt comfortable gazing at the Stevens family on the little screen. It somewhat set me apart from them, and I realized suddenly that was exactly where I wanted to be. Miles and miles away.

Which was why I was surprised at how oddly affected I was once the priest began to utter the sacred words that would initiate little Kimberly into the Roman Catholic faith. In spite of all my muttered prayers on the airplane, I had not really come to terms with the religion I had been brought up in. Hadn't really even thought about it since college, when I'd studied Wallace Stevens's poetry and decided Christianity was all a farce. But that was just me testing out my intellectual wings, I realized now, as I watched with something close to reverence while the baptismal water was poured. I realized, too, all the decisions that went into this child-rearing business. It was a huge responsibility, bringing a life into this world, choosing everything from what she would eat, what she would wear, to what kind of prayers she would mutter on an airplane half out of her mind on the way to meet her future in-laws. I wondered, not for the first time, if I was ready for it. If I would ever be ready for it.

Kirk certainly seemed to be, I thought, as Kate handed him Kimberly to hold once we got back to our seats and he smiled down at the wriggling child with what looked like pure joy in his eyes. Then he gazed up at me, and I saw a look in his eyes that said he hoped I was ready, too.

Oh, my.

Ready or not, I was soon back at Kirk's house, surrounded by a handful of relatives who, I learned, had been lurking among us in the pews and whom I was introduced to as Kirk's girl-friend—and once as his fiancée by Kate, who realized her mistake when I flushed red to the roots of my hair. I cannot explain my reaction to this little slip of the tongue any more than I can explain the reasons I clung to Kirk's side, hoping against hope that somehow it was possible, despite the way his mother had been eyeing me suspiciously ever since I'd ditched that lace doily into the hall closet.

The rest of the evening whirled by in a blur—buffet meal, followed by cake, which I rushed around serving people, probably in some vain hope of earning Mrs. Stevens's respect by being her personal slave. I even attempted to scrub a few pots back in the kitchen, until Mrs. Stevens came in and practically scolded me for not being around to say goodbye to her great-aunt Bertha, who had left early because her rheumatism was acting up.

I wished I could be so lucky.

Then came the opening of the gifts. There weren't many—mostly cards I assumed were stuffed with money, a few dresses, a children's Bible and a plastic Noah's ark, complete with sets of little animals. I didn't even have to bring up the choking hazard, because Mrs. Stevens seemed to swoop away each gift before Kimberly could get her gooey little hands on it. As it turned out, Kayla *had* bought her goddaughter a cross, which surprised me, since she didn't seem like the traditional type. But when I saw the way she beamed beneath her mother's satisfied smile, I realized I wasn't the only one seeking approval by this family.

My gift turned out to be the largest box of all of them. I stood there practically trembling with anticipation as they allowed lit-

tle Kimberly the inaugural tear of the wrap, before her mother
helped by pulling away the rest.

"Why, it's a little cash register! How sweet! Thank you, Angela!" Kate said.

"How very clever," Mrs. Stevens said. She even allowed Kimberly to grasp onto the little plastic lever that sprang the cash
drawer wide open with a whirl of bells, sending oversized plastic coins all over the carpet, one of which Kimberly immediately grabbed and began to shove right into her tiny mouth.

Oh, God, where had those come from? I thought, not realizing the dangers hidden deep within this seemingly harmless
gift. This time I was the one swooping in to gather up all those
little windpipe blockers. Fortunately Mrs. Stevens didn't notice,
because she was suddenly discoursing to her family and the few
remaining guests on the benefits of teaching children the value
of money at a young age.

"There's nothing worse than debt!" she said, looking at me
with satisfaction as I knelt on the floor, hands full of plastic
money. I nodded a little too vigorously, as the thought of the
whopping Visa bill I would be returning home to swept through
my mind.

"I think a high debt burden shows a certain moral laxity, don't
you agree, Phil?"

Even Mr. Stevens managed to agree with his wife on that
one.

Suddenly I felt the brush of Kirk's arm on my shoulder as
he leaned down to whisper playfully in my ear, "I wonder what
my mother would think if she knew that up until a year ago,
you were demonstrating a little moral laxity." Then he chuckled as he met my eyes, as if he were sharing some joke with me
about the life I had led before he had designed that budget for
me. A life I was still leading, apparently. Not that he knew that.

I smiled, averted my eyes and suddenly found myself wishing our plane would go down tomorrow. At least I wouldn't
have to face the future as some newfangled Mrs. Stevens, complete with a well-hidden Visa habit and a certain propensity for
making small children cry, I thought, as little Kimberly burst into
tears the minute I grabbed a final stray plastic coin out of her
tiny clutches.

★ ★ ★

After the last guest had been ushered out, I tried desperately to help with the cleanup, but to no avail. The moment I stepped into the kitchen with a pile of dirty plates, Mrs. Stevens snatched them from me and shooed me into the living room. "There's no need for that," she said, "you're our guest." I realized now this was code for "outsider." Because in my mother's house, the only way you could gain family status was to scrub a few pots with the womenfolk. Or tend to their children. But Kimberly had already been tucked into the crib Mrs. Stevens kept in the spare room upstairs. I decided to follow her cue, as no one seemed to care what I did anyway.

"You're going to bed?" Kirk said with surprise when I told him my plans after he came in from the garage, where he had gone to return the folding chairs he had brought in earlier for the party. "It's only ten o'clock. That's early for you." But he must have seen some of the bone-deep weariness in my eyes, because he kissed me on the forehead, as if I were a small child, and said, "Okay. Sleep tight."

After a quick stop in the living room to bid Mr. Stevens and Kenneth good-night (they barely looked up from the game they were watching), I popped into the kitchen where Kayla, Kate and Mrs. Stevens worked together washing, scrubbing and wiping like a well-oiled machine. "If no one needs me, I'm going to say good-night," I said.

"Good night," they said in unison, with only Kayla looking up from the table she was wiping down to give me a wink.

So I went to that frilly little room, changed into my pajama pants and tee, and after clearing the bed of those myriad stuffed animals, I climbed beneath the cool sheets and lay there, wide-awake, listening to the disgruntled murmurs of Mr. Stevens, Kirk and Kenneth as the Red Sox lost yet another game, and the relentless chatter of Mrs. Stevens as she discoursed to her daughters about the proper storage of china.

And I felt lonelier than I had ever been.

After a restless night of sleep, I woke up the next morning exhausted. So exhausted, in fact, that I no longer felt the need to press on with my Perfect Girlfriend front. Fortunately Kate and Kenneth had packed up little Kimberly first thing, so I didn't have to worry about any more challenging chance encounters with child-rearing. While Mrs. Stevens rushed around the kitchen with Kayla, preparing breakfast, I lounged in the living room reading *Cosmo,* the cleavage-bearing cover model exposed for anyone to see and comment on my choice of reading material (and I knew Mrs. Stevens would, if she weren't too busy whipping up breakfast to notice me perusing a magazine with headlines like "Achieving a Better Orgasm" or "Hot Sex— Now!"). And once we were all seated in what Mrs. Stevens called the "breakfast nook" (it felt more like a cranny), I made no secret of the fact that I had voted for Clinton (because we finally did get to that forbidden subject when Mr. Stevens tried to blame him for the breakdown of the American family. This was brought on, I think, by the runniness of the eggs Mrs. Stevens prepared and I carefully avoiding eating for fear of salmonella).

Suddenly Mrs. Stevens wanted to talk about the weather. "It looks like it's going to be a nice day out there. Why don't you kids go for a bike ride or something?" (Yes, she really called us "kids.") Kayla begged off, saying she was spending the afternoon with her friend Lars, winking at me before she rose from the table. Kirk leaped all over his mother's suggestion, grabbing my hand and dragging me from the table before I could launch into my next incendiary topic.

"What the hell got into you back there?" he said, once we were pedaling down the driveway on two of the five ten-speed bikes we'd found in the garage.

"I don't know what you mean," I replied innocently. Then, once I had negotiated my bike through the front gate, I began pedaling down the street, faster and faster, though I had no idea where I was going. Kirk caught up to me, his expression still perplexed when I turned to smile at him. "Race you to the end of the block," I challenged, and we took off at breakneck speed, with Kirk pulling ahead immediately. I didn't care though. Because I felt amazingly good for the first time all weekend, with the wind in my hair as I whizzed past all those pretty little houses. Kirk stopped at the corner to let me catch up, and I slowed down as I reached him.

"Follow me—I'll give you a little tour of the rest of my hometown."

So I followed at a somewhat more leisurely pace, listening as he pointed out the houses where his childhood friends had lived, the park where he played baseball. We finished at the high school football field, parked our bikes by the bleachers, then climbed up to the top to sit in the sun. But I soon grew restless, and spurred on by God knows what, I slid my body through the slats of the bleacher seats and stood on the metal skeleton beneath, looking up at Kirk. "Did you know I had the highest score in gymnastics in high school?" I said, suddenly remembering this fact myself as I reached for the metal support pole and began to work my way down.

"What are you *doing?*" Kirk said, gazing down at me through the opening I climbed through.

In truth I didn't know what I was doing, especially when I glanced down at the ground beneath me and remembered that I was scared of heights. But I hadn't always been so scared. What had become of the girl they used to call "Monkey" in high school gym class? *She's back,* a little voice cried as I gripped on to that pole and began to scurry down.

When I got to the bottom, I looked up to find Kirk climbing down just above me. Jumping down from the last metal rung, he grabbed me and pulled me down to the grass.

We began to wrestle a bit, until Kirk got the upper hand, pinning me easily on the ground beneath him. I promptly took my advantage and kissed him full on the mouth.

He pressed his groin into me and kissed me back, then leaned up to look at me through half-closed eyes. "You know, I lost my virginity under these bleachers."

"You're kidding," I said. "Let me guess—her name was Peggy, and she was the head cheerleader."

He smiled, kissed my nose. "Nope. It was Chastity. And she was on the twirling team."

"Your first time was with a girl named Chastity?" I said, laughing so hard my face started to hurt.

"Oh, but you should have seen her with a baton," he replied, playfully biting my bottom lip.

I kissed him again, heat flooding through me as I felt the pres-

sure of his erection between my legs. Suddenly I wanted to be
that twirler named Chastity, spreading my legs for the captain
of the football team.

My hands roamed under Kirk's shirt, touching his sweat-
damp chest. He stopped me, looking at me as if I had issued
him a challenge, then lifted my shirt up, pushed aside my cotton bra and put his mouth on first one breast and then the other.

"Let's do it," I said, "right here." I rolled out from underneath
him, sat up and slid my shorts and underwear off before he could
mouth the protest I saw forming on his face.

Finally he sat up, too, looked around nervously, then seeing
the field was still desolate, unzipped his shorts, slid them and his
briefs down just far enough to free himself and was about to
pull me on top of him when a new panic settled on his features.

"We don't have a condom."

My face must have sagged with disappointment, because
suddenly Kirk was advocating what we had never, ever chanced
before. "Never mind. I'll…I'll just pull out."

And before I could even protest—because in truth, the pull-
out method worried me—he had drawn me down on top of
him, thrusting deep.

Maybe it was the lack of condom, but everything felt different this time. Dangerous. Like I really was sixteen, except we
didn't have outdoor bleachers at my high school. Or a football
field. We had bridges, we had tunnels and we even had bedrooms
when our parents were out of town. Except my parents never
went anywhere. But Vincent's parents did. Vincent, I thought,
closing my eyes as his image filled my head. God, would I ever
be in love like that again? But I was in love like that, I thought
suddenly. Wasn't I?

Fuck love, I thought, closing my eyes and imagining I was
that cheerleader, seducing the captain of the football team.

But Kirk was clearly on another plane, judging by the way
he was gazing up at me almost…tenderly. I moved faster, shut
my eyes, seeking something, but I didn't know what. The image
of Vincent flashed through my mind, telling me he loved me,
but I no longer believed it. Then a new image rose up, a dark-
haired man who seemed familiar, but I couldn't quite place…

Oh, my God! It was my first sexy salsa partner I was picturing beneath me now! And the image was very…arousing. I opened my eyes, and there it was again, love shining in Kirk's eyes. I closed mine tight against the view and along came a vivid picture of Umberto, dance partner number two, who was looking even better than he did that night…. Oh my, oh my, oh my…

I don't know whether it was disappointment or relief I felt when suddenly Kirk lifted me up, balancing me over him as he turned to the side, spilling everything he had onto the ground.

Then he pulled me close again. "God, that was amazing. *You're* amazing," he said, kissing my mouth, my brow, caressing my back.

I wanted to say the same, but I wasn't sure who it was I had been having sex with just then.

Or even who I was, for that matter.

We took a different route back, pedaling leisurely, as if we were in a dream in slow motion. I nodded stoically at the various points of interest Kirk pointed out. And wondered at the sudden emptiness I felt inside until Kirk stopped in front of a large triple-decker. I stopped beside him, looking up at the house and wondering what piece of Kirk's history had played out here.

Gazing up at the house, with its neat lawn and wide front porch lined with potted plants, he said, "This is the house I always dreamed I would live in someday."

Now I felt something. Fear. And with good reason. Kirk was giving me that look again. "You know—when I settled down with the right person." From the way he was gazing at me, it was clear *I* was that person. Which was what I had been waiting for, right? So why did I want to jump on my bike and pedal myself furiously all the way back to New York City?

"Um, you sure you want to live so close to your parents?"

"Why not?" he said with a bright smile. Then his face grew more serious. "Besides, they're getting older. They might need me around."

Now I was really scared, imagining myself feeding food-processed beef to a toothless, decrepit Mrs. Stevens, who, despite her advanced state, still managed to hold forth on the proper management of everything from finances to…daughters–in–law.

"But what about your plans for your business? Isn't New York the best place for you to be while you're building contacts?"

"I'm talking about later. When I have a steady client base. By that time, you should be finished with your contract with *Rise and Shine.* Maybe ready to rise and shine with a few kids of your own?" he said, looking at me almost shyly now.

I swallowed hard against my mounting panic. *I don't love him enough,* some demon voice whispered, sending a coldness through my limbs. *Did* I love him enough? I wondered. Enough to leave my beloved New York City? Enough to give up my dreams?

It was almost a relief to board the plane later that day, after a farewell dinner with the Stevenses in which Mr. Stevens held forth on the benefits of solid investing and debt management while Mrs. Stevens served lamb stew with a fervor that suggested she was trying to shovel into Kirk all the nutritional value she feared he wasn't getting. I had a feeling she laid the blame on me, judging by the way she practically shivered as she hugged me somewhat primly at the door. "You're all skin and bones!" she said, shaking her head in admonishment.

She was right. I did feel like a skeleton. A shadow of my former self.

I even felt a bit sad for Kayla, whom I hugged fiercely goodbye. I hoped she would be okay. Hoped she would get everything she wanted out of life. Just like I hoped I would, too.

Now, as I sat buckled in on the plane, bracing myself for the attack of anxiety that would inevitably set in as soon as we began to taxi, I was surprised to discover that I still felt nothing.

Nothing at all.

Of course, I still said my prayers, just in case. But they felt more like a mind–numbing chant. And when I was done, I put in my requests.

Please, God, let us land safely. At LaGuardia. On the tarmac.

But as I glanced at Kirk, who was engrossed in a software magazine, I suddenly didn't care where I landed.

Just kidding. I care, God, I care. Yes, I wanted to live and I wanted...

I closed my eyes, putting in another request.

I just want to be happy.

As a request, it was bit vague for me. What was happiness, anyway? I wondered now, watching as Kirk put down the magazine and pulled out his laptop, probably with the intent of diving right back into his work.

Now *that* was happiness, I thought, watching as the screen lit up before him and he typed in his password. He was so focused. I mean, any minute now he would be asked to shut down his computer for takeoff, yet there he was, using whatever time he had available to him to grab all he could get.

That was exactly what I loved about him. And it was also what I wanted for myself.

I reached over, ran the back of my palm over the stubble on his cheek, as if I could somehow capture some of that glow. He glanced up at me and smiled. "You okay?"

"I'm fine," I said, my voice strangled with a strange emotion I didn't understand.

Or didn't want to understand.

15

I'm in a
New York state of...mania.

When we stepped off the plane at LaGuardia, I could have kissed the ground. And I would have, if it weren't a dirty breeding ground for disease. Still, I would take the dirty varnished floor of LaGuardia any day over the clean sterility of Logan Airport. I even felt a tickle of joy when, after we had gathered my suitcase from the baggage claim and headed for the taxi stand, I saw two businessmen fighting for a cab. "Listen, nimrod, I was waiting here first," said the taller, clearly stronger of the two. *That's it,* I thought. *Tell him like it is.* Now that's a New Yorker for you—no pussyfooting around with that passive-aggressive politeness New Englanders prided themselves on.

These are my people, I thought, gazing around happily as we stepped into the taxi line.

I'll admit I felt a twinge of guilt when I remembered that Kirk was New England born and bred.

Well, he was a New Yorker now. Just like me and Grace and even Justin, I thought happily, linking my arm in Kirk's. Hell, Justin might even be more of a New Yorker than any of us, based on the purity of his love for this fine city.

Justin. I couldn't wait to get home and see him. Or even Grace, for that matter, despite the newfangled version of my best friend I'd so recently been treated to. I missed my friends desperately. Which was probably why, when we finally did step into a cab, I found myself interrupting Kirk as he rattled off his address to the driver.

"Make that two stops. The second being Ninth Street and Avenue A."

"You're going home?" he said with surprise.

"Um, yeah. I have…stuff to do, and then there's my big bag to lug home…."

Maybe it was the thought of that bag cluttering up his pristine apartment, but Kirk seemed satisfied to get out of the cab alone when we pulled up in front of his building. "I'll call you tomorrow," he said, grabbing his duffel and kissing my cheek clumsily as he scrambled out of the back seat.

As the cab rolled down Second Avenue toward the East Village, I felt reborn. Everything was possible here, I thought, as we turned down 10th Street and passed the Theatre for the New City, where I'd had one of my finer theatrical moments as Fefu, in *Fefu and Her Friends.*

This was New York Fucking City, after all.

Once I'd dragged my suitcase up the three flights, with assistance from David in three-B, whom I ran into in the lobby and who was more than happy to help a neighbor in need, I slipped my key into the lock. I couldn't wait to tell Justin about my freaky weekend with the New England*ahs,* as they called themselves.

But when I got through the door, the apartment was surprisingly quiet. No NPR murmuring in the background. No clatter in the kitchen as Justin whipped together some new culinary delight. No Justin, I realized with keen disappointment.

Just me, three sofas, four TVs, six lamps, a tree swing…

And the azalea.

I sighed, pulled my bag into the middle of the living room and found a note on the coffee table in Justin's loopy scrawl.

Welcome home, Angie! Off to Florida to surprise Lauren. Back next week. Don't forget to water Bernadette!

Bernadette must be the azalea, I realized. Apparently our little tree had a name now.

I crumpled the note in a ball, aimed for the wastebasket in the kitchen and missed, my disappointment deepening. Must be nice to be Justin, able to run off to Florida whenever the mood struck.

Must be even nicer to be Lauren, was my next thought, and have a guy like Justin flying off at the drop of a hat, just to see you.

Ah well, I thought, grabbing the watering can and going to the kitchen to fill it. At least I had good old Bernadette.

And Grace, I remembered, once I'd watered the azalea.

I settled into sofa #3, which was swiftly becoming my favorite, probably due to its proximity to all technology of any importance in our apartment. Like the remote control. And the telephone. I picked up the receiver and was about to dial Grace, when I remembered there was someone I needed to inform right away that I was home (before she started calling all the hospitals in search of crash victims).

"Angela!" my mother cried with relief after I said hello. "Thank God, you're home safe."

I smiled. It was a relief to know that *someone* didn't find my fears unfounded.

"Yes, I'm home."

"So how was it?" she said, moving on to my emotional well-being now that she'd established I was in no physical danger.

"It was…fine," I said. "Kirk's family is…is nice." I couldn't tell her otherwise. Couldn't allow her to try to force me to any conclusions about Kirk based on my weekend with his family. I wasn't ready to draw any conclusions. I wasn't even sure I had to. After all, I wasn't engaged yet, right?

"Did they feed you good?" she asked now. My mother's way of ascertaining goodness in other families is based solely on their ability to overfeed you.

"Yes." Well, they had made an attempt, right? How did they know I didn't like my steaks to moo back at me? Besides, the catered buffet at the christening had been good…if you liked that fresh from the aluminum tray, prefab taste.

"How's Nonnie?" I asked.

"She's fine. When I see her. Do you know that Artie Matar-razzo took her to the Labor Day dance at the Senior Citizens club on Avenue U tonight? Can you believe it? Your grand-mother isn't even a member!" she exclaimed, as if the fact that Nonnie hadn't paid the yearly dues to join the senior club, yet still reaped the benefits, was what outraged her.

I had a feeling what was really bothering my mother was loneliness, as she went on to explain how Joey and Miranda had taken the kids and gone to Long Island for the holiday week-end and Sonny and Vanessa had gone to Vanessa's parents' house. My mother was used to spending Labor Day with her family. But her family had grown up and we were going on with our lives. Something Ma needed to do herself.

"So what did you do today?" I asked.

"Oh, I went to see your father," she said. What she meant was she went to see his grave, which was probably the most well-groomed plot in all of St. John's Cemetery, judging by how often she went there to plant flowers or tend to the ones currently there.

"Ma, you need a hobby," I said. Or a man. Though that thought scared me. I couldn't see anyone but my father with my mother. But my father was gone and my mother was only fifty-nine. She was going to be alone a long, long time.

"I don't need anything," she said, then sensing my sympa-thies, she immediately played on them. "So when are you com-ing here for dinner?"

"Soon," I replied, but refrained from making definite plans. I didn't want to risk going there right now. Not with Kirk. When suddenly things felt so…indefinite.

And maybe because my love life seemed indefinite, I found myself confessing to the definition my professional life had been taking on ever since Rena had announced the network was interested in *Rise and Shine.* I don't know why I decided to share this bit of news with my mother tonight of all nights. Maybe I wanted to show her that my life was secure in some ways. That I might move on from this struggling actor role I'd been playing for so long to something that might have a future.

"Oh, Angela," she said, clearly excited for me. "Your father would have been so proud."

"Would he?" I blurted out.

"Well, why wouldn't he be?" she responded. "He always wanted you to be happy, Angela." Then she paused. "You are happy, aren't you?"

"Yes," I replied meekly, and then, because I didn't want to explore the curl of unhappiness that had begun working its way through my system the moment I made this claim, I quickly wrapped up the call, saying I had to get to bed soon if I wanted to be my best for the happy little show that was to round out my happy little life.

Once I hung up with my mother, I immediately speed-dialed Grace, looking forward to what I hoped would be a more relaxing conversation.

"Hey," I said when she picked up.

"Hey, Angie," she said, "hang on a sec." I heard her speak to someone else—a male someone else—followed by the sound of a door shutting.

"Who was that?" I said, afraid to hope it might have been Drew. Maybe they'd had a big reconciliation over the weekend!

"That was Billy."

"Oh," I said, deflated. "I'll let you go then, if you have company...." Far be it from me to keep Grace from great sex.

"No, I can talk," she said. "He was on his way out the door when you called. You know he spent both Saturday and Sunday night here? At least he's being a little more consistent this time," she finished with a contented chuckle.

Consistent? Is that what Grace was hoping for nowadays? She'd had what looked to me like love, and now she was settling for a regular roll in the hay. But I didn't have time to contemplate Grace's new approach to men, because suddenly she had moved on to another man—mine.

"So how was the big weekend with Kirk's family?" she asked.

"Fine," I said quickly. I don't know why I lied. Especially to my best friend. Maybe I just wanted to prove to Grace—or to myself—that monogamy could work. "The christening was nice. Cute kid." Loud kid, I thought, remembering Kimberly's semifrequent outbursts. "We talked about...things. It was very...stimulating." To say the least.

"Well, that's good," she said, as if she were surprised. "You've gotten over a big hurdle then. Because you never really know someone until you meet their parents."

"What's that supposed to mean?" I said, horrified at the idea of Kirk somehow morphing into his parents after we were married.

"Sheesh, someone's a bit touchy. Are you sure you're all right?"

"I'm fine!" I said.

But I wasn't fine, I realized when I woke up the next morning and headed off to the studio. I could barely make it through the routine, my body and mind were so weighted down with unhappiness. An unhappiness that grew into abject fear when Rena called me and Colin into her office afterward and told us that the interested network was Fox and that she was meeting with two of the executives next week to discuss a contract. Colin was ecstatic. So was Kirk when I called him on my way home. Even more so because he himself had just had a call from Norwood—they had reviewed his designs and wanted him to fly in to their head office in Chicago to discuss terms. "This is it, Ange. If we come to an agreement on the terms, I'll have landed my biggest client yet. They have offices from coast to coast. My software will be all over the country!"

I congratulated him. How could I not? His dreams were about to come true, while mine...mine were about to disappear into the wide blue yonder. As blue as my thick blue tights.

I headed to Lee and Laurie that afternoon with a feeling of doom. Not even the new fall catalogs that had just come in could cheer me up. At least I wouldn't have to talk with the Committee about my impending contract. I certainly couldn't let anyone at my day job know that I soon might not be among their ranks. Because if I got this contract with *Rise and Shine,* I could probably give up Lee and Laurie. That should have made me happy, but it didn't.

Fortunately, I didn't have to worry about blurting out my news about *Rise and Shine.* Because the only thing the Committee cared about was my impending wedding.

"How'd the big weekend at Kirk's parents go?" Michelle said the moment I stepped into our cubicle area. Doreen and Roberta swung around, eager to hear all the details.

And so I told them that the Stevens family had found me as charming as I had found them. Not a lie, right?

But if it wasn't a lie, I realized, my life was one. Especially when I found myself shrugging off Kirk's invitation to his apartment after work. He didn't mind. He was leaving for Chicago in two days and had lots to do to prepare. So he hung up and, I imagined, immediately went back to his laptop and his happy little life without giving me a second thought.

I guess it was a comfort to realize that at least some things hadn't changed.

When I entered my dark apartment that night, my feeling of desolation was complete. Especially after I stumbled into the hall, fumbling for the light switch, only to discover that the bulb was out, and without my tall roommate around, I didn't have a hope of changing it. So I headed into the living room, negotiating around the bag of recyclables and the hordes of newspapers I kept there, hoping to reach one of those six lamps before I fell over something and killed myself, when I saw a shadowy figure standing by the window. I immediately stopped, fear snaking through me as I watched the intruder lean close to the window, as if he were about to steal…Bernadette?

"Ahhh!" I yelled, knowing I should have run instead. Suddenly a light clicked on, and I saw, much to my relief, that it was Justin fondling that damned azalea.

"What is wrong with you?" he said, breathing hard. Apparently I'd scared him, too.

"*Me?* What the hell are you doing here in the dark?"

"I dunno. It was kinda…soothing."

Soothing? What was he, crazy? I thought, feeling my heart starting to return to a normal beat. "Why are you home? I thought you weren't coming back until next week."

He shrugged, turning his gaze to the window once more. "I came home early."

"You went all the way to Florida for…two days?"

"I didn't want to be there anymore."

"Justin, what happened?" I asked, stepping closer and trying to peer into his face, which he had averted.

"Lauren and I…we kinda broke up."

"What do you mean? You either broke up or you didn't—"

"She was there with another guy," he blurted out. "Bob or Rob or something like that. I showed up at her place, you know, thinking I'd surprise her and all." He laughed without humor. "Man, was I surprised."

"Oh, Justin." I reached for his hand.

"It's no big deal," he said. But when he finally looked at me, I saw that it *was* a big deal. I had never seen those sunny green eyes of his look so sad.

"Come on, sit down," I said, tugging him toward the couch. "Tell me everything."

When we were finally sitting on the sofa, me cross-legged and facing his profile as he stared without seeing at the blank TV screen, he said, "There's nothing to tell. I mean, it's not like we said we couldn't see other people…I just thought—" he blew out a breath "—I just thought she wouldn't want to. I guess I thought things were more…more serious than they were between us, you know?"

I wondered, briefly, how serious they really could have been, when Lauren had spent eighty percent of their relationship living twelve hundred miles away. But since I didn't want to undermine whatever sadness Justin was feeling over the loss, I kept silent.

"Stupid me. Thinking I could tell someone I loved her and that would be enough."

It should have been enough, I realized, my heart feeling suddenly heavy in my chest. Wasn't love the reason why we did crazy things—like order azaleas we didn't want or take expensive, scary plane rides—to get closer to that someone we had pledged our hearts to? But then, the thought crept in, why did we have to try so damn *hard* to get closer?

I sighed. "Justin, you know these long-distance relationships are…are difficult."

"Yeah," he said, staring off into space once more. Then he looked up at me as a new thought hit. "Hey, how did your weekend with Kirk's folks go?"

This time I was the one averting my eyes. "It was…it was fine."

"What happened? You hated them. They fed you raw steaks

and told you horrible stories about how Kirk used to run in his sister's dresses when he was a kid?"

"No," I said, almost laughing at how he'd gotten the meat right at least. "I didn't hate them...." I didn't *like* them either, but I supposed I could live with them...if I *had* to. Gulp. Thank God they lived five hours away. "I'm not so sure they liked me."

Justin narrowed his eyes at me. "Of course they liked you. Everybody likes you, Ange. You're smart, funny. Cute as hell," he continued, ruffling my hair playfully. "Hey, did anyone ever tell you that you look just like Marisa Tomei?" he said, smiling at me as if this was our own private little joke.

I bit my lip. That was starting to sound like a curse. But it didn't have to be, I realized now as I looked at Justin, those intelligent eyes that always saw into the heart of things, that beautiful face that could sell long-distance services and just about anything else, those strong hands that could find their way around a guitar with grace or handle a camera with skill. He could be anything he wanted.

"Justin, maybe now that Lauren's out of the picture, you need to get back into your own life. Choose what you want to do next and start working on it. You're so happy when you have your camera in hand. Or your guitar. I mean, maybe you should finally do that open-mike show you've been talking about for so long," I continued, though in truth, I felt Justin had more of a fighting chance with the film. Still, I knew that he needed to grab on to something to dig himself out of his gloom. And since music was his most current pursuit, I tried to encourage him in it.

"I know, I know," he said. Then, smiling, he slapped my knee. "I'm gonna do it, Ange. I feel inspired...."

I smiled back at him, but I was worried. I'd heard that phrase one too many times. What, I wondered, would it take to truly lead Justin back to his dreams?

What led me back to mine was the realization that everything I had said to Justin could apply to me as well. Which was probably why I awoke the next morning filled with a sense of purpose. As if I suddenly understood what it was all about. I needed to find my own bliss. And even that realization filled me with a kind of bliss.

I practically skipped all the way to the studio. Not even the stultifying heat as I headed down the subway stairs could get me down. And the lone guitar player pouring out his heart on the platform for the few measly dollars strewn in his case didn't depress me as it normally would. He was *happy,* I realized, watching as he strummed and smiled and sang as if his soul depended on it. *These are my people,* I thought for the second time in two days. What did I need with the Stevenses and their warped view of the world, or even Viveca, with her warped view of me?

I *was* on the road to happily-ever-after—except *I* was in the driver's seat now.

Once I got to the studio, I bounded through the routine like I was on fire. I roared like a lion, sang like a bird (okay, so we *were* doing the jungle segment, but, still, I was radiant). Even Rena commented that she saw a new energy in me. "Keep it up and those network executives will be banging on our door tomorrow with that contract," she said.

Ha, I thought as I headed to the dressing area to change into my street clothes. They'll be banging on my door all right. But I'll be the one negotiating the terms. And you can be sure they wouldn't include a yellow leotard or an insurance rider that covered my beleaguered joints.

I bid Colin a cheerful goodbye on my way out. "No breakfast today?" he said.

"Not today, sweetie," I replied. Today I had things to do. Like pursue my dreams.

I picked up a copy of *Backstage* on my way home. Then, like I did in the old days when I was pounding the pavement in search of my next great gig, I went to a little Internet café I used to frequent back a few blocks from my house on Avenue A. After purchasing the largest café latte I could, I settled into one of the worn, overstuffed chairs by the window and began to scan the casting calls.

I'll admit I grew a bit despondent when I saw ad after ad I could not even reply to, either because it was for a role I was too old for (what was with this glorification of the twenty-year-old, anyway?) or non-union. That was the problem when you joined SAG and AFTRA—you put yourself in a smaller pool of actors that included people like my pal Jennifer Aniston, or even her pal Gwyneth. And I was no Gwyneth. Or Jennifer, for that matter, I thought with a shiver, wondering if I'd tightened that lid right up again with my antics over the weekend.

But wasn't that why I had joined the unions? Because I thought I was ready to go for those roles that might bring me the successful sitcom or film I dreamed of landing? The ones that actually paid the actors something and, even better, provided health insurance? The ones even Jennifer or Gwyneth might consider.

I continued to scan the lists, sipping my latte for courage. And suddenly my eye caught and held on an ad that seemed as if it had been placed there just for me:

All For Love, *award-winning director seeks actress, 25–32* [that's me!], *ethnic okay* [I go both ways] *for a feature-length film about a woman who sacrifices all for the man she loves* [well, I knew a thing or two about that, didn't I?], *to be shot in Maine in October.* [Not Massachusetts, but close enough to fill me with a sense of irony].

Auditions were taking place at the end of the week!

It was a sign. A definite sign. This part had Angela DiFranco, Third-Degree Girlfriend, written all over it. I circled it, and, while I was at it, went through the list of casting directors and agents and picked out a dozen or so that were willing to receive head shots and audition tapes by mail, and circled those, too. After all, I couldn't put all my hopes on one audition. Just like I couldn't put all my hopes on one man....

Once I had compiled a considerable list, I headed to the stationery store to pick up my envelopes and résumé paper, then went home to get to work. By the time I headed off to Lee and Laurie that afternoon, I had no fewer than ten envelopes to drop into the mail. I'll admit that I had a touch of fear as I opened the mailbox, worrying over just what fresh rejection this little mailing might result in, but that didn't stop me. I felt like nothing could stop me now.

I have to say, I was relieved when Kirk left for Chicago, because I somehow didn't want to share my newfound acting ambition with him. Maybe I was afraid I might jinx myself by saying too much about all the possibilities I saw before me now. Or maybe I was afraid he wouldn't see them as possibilities, especially when he called me the night before he left to say goodbye and said, "Hey, call me if you hear anything about that contract while I'm gone."

Uh-huh, I thought. Opening up my book of monologues the moment I got off the phone and settling on a scene that I knew I could do well, I began again, working day and night to make sure I was ready for Friday. In fact, the week flew by so fast, I barely even noticed Kirk was gone. Even Justin shared my enthusiasm, filming me with his digital camera once I felt I'd mastered the monologue, and then sitting down with me to go over it and to see where I could improve. I'll admit I was still worried about Justin, as he had yet to pick up the reins of his own life. But I realized he might still be in post-Lauren recovery, though he'd barely uttered her name since the night he came home. I guessed that was just how men dealt with things—by not talking about them. I could only hope that maybe my renewed ambition might inspire Justin when he was ready to pursue his own dreams.

I certainly felt inspired. I realized I was finally living again. I knew it from the moment I started practicing monologues, *felt* it the first time I stepped in front of the casting director for *All For Love*. I'll admit I felt that familiar tremble of fear that had built the whole time I had waited outside the studio for my turn, surrounded by at least sixty other women, each more beautiful than the next. But I swallowed down my fear, breathed deep and spoke my lines, felt the character come alive inside me. The casting agent must have felt it, too, because he even allowed me a cold reading of the script, which he wouldn't have asked for unless he saw potential. And I was suddenly all potential. I had never felt more alive in all my life.

I felt even more alive the following week when the phone rang from that very same casting director, who confirmed that he *had* seen something in me, but that something wasn't right for the part in *All For Love*. "I may have a part for you in the future, however. I'll call you if anything comes up." Though it was true that his phone call boded well (usually they didn't call at *all* if you didn't get the part), I couldn't help but feel deflated.

And I began to despair that he would never call again, especially since no one else did that week—none of the casting directors or agents I'd mailed my tapes, résumé, head shot and all my hopes to. Oh yes, my phone did ring again that week, I discovered, when I came home from Lee and Laurie and found a message blinking there from none other than Viveca Withers, who apparently had learned through the grapevine that Fox was almost ready to talk contracts. She invited me to call her back in case I wanted to discuss anything with her (I didn't).

And it rang, of course, when Kirk came home from Chicago jubilant. The Norwood contract would be in the mail to him next week. All it needed was signing. "Let's have dinner on Friday to celebrate," he said, telling me that he had already taken the liberty of making a reservation at the Blue Water Grill.

"He's gonna pop the question," Michelle said as we stood outside Lee and Laurie smoking cigarettes while I informed her of my plans with Kirk Friday night. Not that I was looking for her advice anymore. I had just needed a cigarette and was making idle chat.

"No he's *not,*" I protested, a bit heatedly, I'll admit. "We're going there to celebrate his new client."

She raised an eyebrow at me. "Don't you understand how men work by now? There is nothing like the prospect of a secure income to pop a man's lid right off. They got that whole provider thing going on. Once they know they're able to take care of a wife and family, suddenly getting a wife and family is all they want to do."

"But he hasn't even shopped for the ring! *We* haven't shopped for the ring."

She shrugged. "He probably took matters into his own hands."

"You're wrong," I said. "Kirk wouldn't spend all that money without knowing what I wanted. He's too...practical for that."

But I had a feeling she wasn't wrong when Kirk called me Friday afternoon to tell me our reservation was at eight and that I should meet him at the restaurant, since it was between our two apartments. "And don't be late," he admonished with a chuckle. "I have a very special evening planned for us."

I did the only thing I could do. I bought a pack of cigarettes. And since Justin miraculously was not home on Friday night, I smoked three of them locked in my bedroom while getting ready, waving the smoke out the window in between puffs and mad attempts to put on my makeup, pick out an outfit and take the crazy frizz out of my hair that seemed to creep up the minute I got too close to the window (and I was practically hanging out of it every time I lit a cigarette).

Of course I was late, since I felt an urge for yet another ciga-rette on the way there and discovered I had no matches. I was so wound up I almost got into a screaming match at the newsstand where I stopped to pick some up, because the guy wanted to charge me a nickel for a pack, probably because I hadn't purchased my little cancer sticks at his fine establishment. Then he had the nerve to sneer at me when I handed him a twenty dollar bill (what, it was all I had). I placated him by buying a box of Altoids (I feared I would need them anyway—there was the breath fac-tor) and there would probably be the hello kiss (usually closed lip, but still) and, if Michelle was right—the postproposal embrace. Oh, God. Please let her be wrong. Because I was sure, absolutely sure, that as much as I loved Kirk, the ring he had purchased for me would not be anything I would want to wear. Would it be wrong to bring this up? How long does a girl have to wait be-fore she suggests a new setting without spoiling the romance of the moment? Surely there must be some precedent. I mean, not every bride wound up with her dream ring on the first shot, right?

Or her dream man, a little voice whispered. Oh, wait, that sounded like the voice of Claudia. I wasn't Claudia, though. I was happy, dammit. Or I was going to be.

Even if it killed me.

"One for dinner?" the maître d' said when I walked into the restaurant. Who went to dinner alone at Blue Water Grill? Clau-dia, probably. I was not Claudia! "No, two actually. Um, but my date might be here already."

"Ah, yes," he said. "Follow me."

Uh-oh, he knew exactly who I was talking about. Which meant the ever-punctual Kirk was probably taking out his an-noyance at me on the staff.

But when I saw Kirk seated alone, a beatific smile on his face,

I realized he wasn't annoyed. No, he was pretty damn happy to see me.

And that scared me even more.

"Hey, sweetheart," he said, standing up as I chewed furiously on my mint before he pressed his lips to mine. "You look great."

"Thanks," I said, looking down at my tank top and skirt as if suddenly remembering I had dressed for this occasion. In black. It seemed...appropriate.

"I already took the liberty of ordering us a bottle of champagne."

Champagne? I must have looked confused.

"To celebrate."

Oh, right. Norwood.

But when I looked up at Kirk, the warmth sparkling in his eyes, I realized he might be wanting to celebrate something else.

Oh God, oh God, oh God.

"So I was looking at the menu—they've got some great seafood here."

"Right," I said, remembering that we were here to eat. That's right. Food. What exactly was in all those savory sauces so many of the entrées seemed to be doused in? I was definitely going to die tonight. I was going to die, and Kirk was going to put that engagement ring in a safe-deposit box and go on with his life. Well, he would grieve of course. For a little while. I imagined him telling his parents, his mother nodding sympathetically while secretly gleeful that her grandchildren wouldn't inherit all my maladies. Kayla would miss me. I was sure of that. She might even put together a performance piece in my honor. At P.S. 122. I'd be famous.

See that? Everything would be fine. If I did die, that is.

"Are you ready to order?"

Kirk looked up hopefully at me. "Grilled salmon," I said automatically. It was what I ordered when there was nothing else. I was too mentally exhausted to have the waiter catalog the ingredients in the fancier entrées. And I had decided, as the waiter stared down at me, waiting for my order, that I did want to live. Come what may.

"I'll have the lobster, steamed," Kirk said.

Look at this, I was going to marry a man who ate things that resembled living creatures. How was I going to enjoy this night with that horrible-looking thing staring at me?

Fortunately, the champagne arrived. I was so relieved or so…*something,* I downed my first glass before the waiter had finished pouring Kirk's.

"Angie!" Kirk said, lifting his glass and looking at me as the waiter dropped the bottle into the ice bucket he'd placed tableside and disappeared.

"What?" I said, plopping my glass down on the table with satisfaction.

"I thought we were going to make a toast," he said.

Oops. "I'm sorry, I…"

"Never mind, there's more where that came from," he replied, picking up the bottle from the bucket and refilling my glass. Boy, he was in a good mood. Nothing I did seemed to bother him tonight. He was positively docile. And I didn't like it. Where was that brooding man who had made my life hell all these months? Suddenly I wanted him back.

But instead I picked up my glass.

"To us," Kirk said, touching his glass to mine.

I gulped down half the glass. Then, because I wanted to keep things properly focused this evening, I said, "Shouldn't we be toasting you, darling? As the hot new software designer for Norwood?"

He smiled, reached across the table and took my hand. "But don't you see?" he said. "This is just the beginning of everything. For us."

I studied his eyes, the candlelight casting a glow over his handsome features. Or was that love casting the glow? The way he was looking at me, I thought he might have a ring tucked in that blazer he was sporting.

Oh, God. He wouldn't spend all that money without any idea of what I wanted, would he? No, as I'd told Michelle, he was too practical for that. But what if in the rush of love—or the rush of testosterone that deprivation seems to set flowing—he'd run to his nearest Zales and bought me a rock? That would be terrible, just terrible. Not that I didn't love him. I did.

It was just that I was sure, so sure, that he would have no idea what I wanted in a ring.

Or in life, for that matter.

Maybe that's because you haven't told him what you want, a little voice said. Yes, I thought, maybe I should tell him. It was probably the champagne in my system, or a desire to put off a proposal scene (if that's what he had in mind) that urged me on, but suddenly I found myself confessing to my sudden frantic urge to find a new gig, which had begun just moments after Rena had told us our contract was in the works. I told him about the mailing that had resulted in no calls, the audition that I had worked so hard on, only to hear I hadn't got the part. Not even the sight of the lobster the waiter served during my heartfelt speech could stop me.

And while Kirk sipped his wine and tore that little beast from limb to limb, I saw him nod sympathetically, and when he finally did speak, I was amazed at the insightfulness in his words.

"Maybe it doesn't have to be such a struggle, Ange. I know you're used to working hard for what you want, maybe so much so that you're addicted to the struggle. Why not take this contract, make some money, enjoy life for a change? It doesn't mean you have to stay there forever. Just for a little while. To make your life a little easier…"

It could have been that the champagne warmed my system, but I realized he was right. I did need things easier. Everything I did was always so hard. Why not take that contract? I could probably even keep auditioning. Hell, I'd have more time to audition, since I'd be able to give up Lee and Laurie.

He was so smart, I thought. I almost felt a disappointment when we finished our meal and I realized he wasn't going to propose tonight. Well, not exactly. Because if these past two weeks had taught me anything, it was that if I was going to make a real go of acting, I needed time. But I wondered how much time I had, especially when Kirk reached across the table, grabbed my hand and told me how he'd spoken to his parents. How much they liked me and looked forward to seeing me again.

I would have been shocked at that, if I hadn't been even more frightened of that look on his face—like he wanted to plan a trip real soon, like he might have some other big news to tell them about his future. *Our* future.

Michelle was right. He was pretty much popped—now that

he had Norwood under wraps, it seemed like he wanted me under wraps, too.

Oh, God.

I needed a cigarette.

But of course I couldn't have one while strolling arm in arm with Kirk back to his apartment.

"Hey, Henry," he said cheerfully to the doorman as we strode into his building. Henry smiled and waved and, when I caught his eye, even winked, as if we shared some secret.

I felt an almost Pavlovian urge for a cigarette.

When the elevator stopped at Kirk's floor, I stepped toward his door, only to be pulled back into his arms for a kiss that I felt all the way down to my toes. Then he gestured toward the Exit sign down the hall. "Hey, remember our little rendezvous under the bleachers? What do you say to a little replay in the stairwell?" he said, tugging me toward it. "No one ever uses it...."

I looked at that bright red sign as if at some omen of my future. Remembered that veritable orgy—in my mind, anyway— that had occurred under the bleachers, and immediately backed away.

"I, uh...I don't know, Kirk."

He pulled me close again, his arms roaming over my back. "C'mon, Ange, it'll be wild."

Not knowing what else to do, I leaned up and planted a soft kiss on his lips. "I...I just want to be alone...with you. In bed." That was true, right?

"Well, you'll get no arguments from me on that," he said, taking my hand and leading me to the apartment.

The minute we stepped through the door, he was all over me. His hands searching frantically under my shirt, his mouth on my neck. I felt a wave of desire rush over me, so strong that it almost frightened me. So much so that I pulled away again.

"Angie, you're driving me crazy."

Him? I was driving *myself* crazy. "I just need..." I paused, not sure what I needed. "I need to use the bathroom."

He gestured toward the door. "Anything you want, baby. I'll be right here when you get back."

I went into the bathroom, shutting the door soundly behind me. I even relieved myself, just to keep it honest. But I didn't really have to go. What I needed most was to think. Except my brain was now muddled by wine and desire....

I stood before the mirror and slowly washed my hands, staring at my reflection. What is wrong with you, Angela DiFranco? I asked the woman I saw there, who looked pretty good, in spite of all the angsting she'd been doing. That man loves you, and you love him. Just live for a change. Forget about the future. Just enjoy the moment.

Sound advice, I realized, especially when I heard a knock at the door. "You okay in there?"

I cracked it open and gave Kirk a small smile. "Fine." Then, when I saw he had stripped down to his boxers, I realized I was more than fine as my eyes grazed over that flat, hard stomach, that beautiful chest. Yes, I was in the moment again, I thought. And clearly Kirk saw it, because suddenly he was backing me up on the sink, his hands moving under my skirt and his mouth on mine.

Ah, yes…this was what it was all about, I thought, yanking up my tank and pressing myself against that perfect chest.

Before I knew what was happening, Kirk had my skirt up around my waist, my panties on the floor and my ass on the edge of the sink. He paused, only to pull off his boxers, then suddenly he was inside of me, thrusting like a madman.

And making me feel like a madwoman. I curled my legs around him, closing my eyes as the first waves of pleasure rode through me. This was hot. Why hadn't we thought of it before? I wondered, but soon I stopped wondering about everything as a haze of heat drove my mind blank.

Well, not blank exactly. Because suddenly, behind my closed eyes, another Latino man appeared. Not one of my salsa partners, but José, the happy little adulterer, of all people. And it wasn't Michelle's cleavage he had his face plunged into, it was mine.

"Stop," I whispered, opening my eyes. "Stop!" I said, alarmed at the sight of Kirk's flushed features.

He stopped, looking pretty alarmed himself. "Are you okay?"

"No…"

"Did I hurt you?" he said, staring into my eyes, which I quickly averted. When I saw him hard and hovering there between us, I jumped on the first excuse I could find. "You're not—uh, that is, we forgot the condom."

"Oh. Right. No wonder it felt so good. God, I could get used to this...."

Get used to what? Impregnating me? "Maybe you ought to get one." Then, remembering the illicit thought this somewhat illicit position had invoked, I added, "And maybe we should finish this...in the bed."

Of course, he didn't argue—no man as rock hard as Kirk was in that moment ever puts up a fight with a half-naked woman who has her legs wrapped around him. He stepped back, helped me off the sink and we padded into the bedroom as I tossed off my top, which was starting to cut into me because of the haphazard way it was twisted up over my breasts.

"That better?" he said, once I was lying comfortably on my back, Kirk hovering over me like he was ready to press himself into me once more. But he didn't press into me—not right away. Maybe he saw some of the hesitation in my eyes, because suddenly he was back to foreplay again.

Not that I minded, I thought with a sigh as his mouth moved over my breasts, down my stomach, across my hips, then lower.

And the first touch of his tongue on Avenue A, my eyes flew open again.

"What are you *doing?*" I asked, leaning up on my elbows.

"I thought you liked that," he said.

"I did. I mean, I *do.*" When he continued to stare at me, I said, "But you don't, or *do* you?" I asked, hopefully.

"I can deal with it."

Oh, brother.

"Besides, I think you...you might need it tonight. To relax," he said.

What girl could argue with that?

I fell back against the pillows, carefully keeping my eyes wide-open this time, as he began again. His touch was so tentative at first, I worried over it. He hates it, he hates it, he hates it, I thought, until I felt the first long stroke, then another and another.

"That's it," I said encouragingly, glancing down at his head. Which was the wrong thing to say, apparently. Because he started going at it in earnest. A little too earnest. I felt like I was in car wash with the windows down.

"Kirk, sweetie, I need you up here," I said, gazing down at him.

I could tell he was relieved, judging by the way he scrambled up my body once more. And he was about to make contact again—this time with his most prized possession—when I gently clamped my legs shut. "Condom?"

"Right, right," he said, as if annoyed. Kirk annoyed with condoms? Up until now, he'd been such a strong advocate, I thought he'd owned stock in Trojan.

But he suited up as I requested, and soon enough he was back between my legs, taking me, finally, to the place I needed to go.

He was so beautiful, I thought, leaning up to kiss his closed lids before touching my lips to that well-shaped mouth. He even kissed me back, tangling his tongue in mine so gently I thought my heart would break from the rush of pure feeling that suddenly flooded me. But it wasn't joy I was feeling, or even desire—rather, a sadness so powerful it clogged my throat and filled my eyes. So I closed them, this time against the pain that surged through, and found my mind suspiciously blank, my body going numb. I opened them again to find Kirk's clear gray gaze on mine, and I realized it was just us in bed this time. Just us. So I focused on the feel of him, reveled in the smell of him, even brought my mouth to his once more as I felt his fervor rise. And though I did not quite reach the heights of pleasure that he did, I realized it was enough.

It had to be.

There's something soothing about sex. Or maybe numbing. Because all my former anxieties fled in the face of Kirk's and my newly reinvigorated sex life. Suddenly he wanted to do it everywhere—public bathrooms, Lee and Laurie (in the supply room—no one *saw*). And I was okay with it—all my crazy fantasies had fled now that Kirk seemed to be enacting every one of his at every opportunity. He even sidled his hands up my skirt at the Quad Cinema one Saturday night, when we found ourselves in a half-empty theater watching a French movie. Talk about a dramatic climax. I was surprised at myself, really. I mean,

I hated missing any part of a movie (and clearly I missed something, because the credits were rolling up before I even understood what was happening). Movies were the only thing I was ever on time for. I even found myself rushing Kirk to the theater whenever we went, for fear of missing the previews.

If I was numb during that period, I needed to be. The numbness helped when the phone never rang with agents and casting directors dying to make my acquaintance. No one but Viveca Withers, who was my new best friend, now that I had given Rena her name and number to contact once my contract was ready, and when she informed that the contract had arrived, I found myself agreeing to meet with her the following Monday to discuss it. Even this bit of news turned Kirk on, because when I solemnly informed him of my big meeting with Viveca while we were lying in bed that night, he proceeded to make love to me as if I were in training for an upcoming role in a porn flick. And I might as well have been, as I found myself relying on my actor's training when it came to expressing my pleasure. I was starting to think that maybe that's what monogamy was all about. A commitment to carry on, no matter how you were feeling inside. After all, the show must go on, right?

But if I was ready to pursue a monogamous—and, I feared, a monotonous—life full force, Justin seemed suddenly ready to pursue anything in a skirt. Or rather, the skirts were pursuing him, from the look of things. First, there were the huskily spoken phone messages on our answering machine. Then I came home from Lee and Laurie one night to find a cute little blonde, sitting cheerfully on my sofa (yes, I had by now completely come to see sofa #3 as my own). I can't explain to you the rush of anger the sight of this perky little stranger in my apartment brought out. An anger I quickly squashed when Justin stepped out of the bedroom (fully dressed, thank *God*), guitar in hand.

"Hey, Ange, you remember Jenna from the Back Fence?"

"Hey, Angela," Jenna said, waving merrily at me. I think I may have bared my teeth at her, in some vague attempt at a smile. Jenna was the somewhat buxom bartender at the Back

Fence. Apparently Justin had gotten to know her on all those nights he'd spent there contemplating getting up onstage.

"I was just gonna play her a few of the songs I worked into my act," he said, sitting beside Jenna and laying the guitar across his legs.

Songs he'd worked into his act? *I* hadn't even heard them yet.

But suddenly I didn't want to hear them, especially since Jenna had leaned back on the couch to listen in a way that left her shirt gaping and her tight little midriff bare.

"I gotta work on a monologue," I said, marching straight to my bedroom and closing the door with a little more force than was absolutely necessary.

Of course, I didn't even crack my scene book, once I had thrown myself down on the bed, arms folded like a recalcitrant child. Show Jenna his songs. Yeah, right. I was sure the bartender at the Back Fence was going to open some big doors for Justin on the road to superstardom. Oh, she was going to open *something* for him all right, but I didn't think it would get him more than a…a venereal disease.

I shivered at the thought. Then wondered why I cared so much about Justin's little conquests. Maybe because I had never, ever seen Justin on the make before. For as long as I'd known him, he'd always had some girlfriend or other kept at some careful distance.

Now I was faced with Justin single, up close and personal. And it bothered me. More than I wanted to admit.

So when I climbed the stairs to our apartment a few days later to find him in a cozy little conversation with Tanya Burke from four-B, in the doorway of her apartment, which was conveniently located opposite ours, I found myself inexplicably annoyed. Especially since I couldn't tell, from the way Tanya had practically draped herself over Justin, whether he was coming or going.

I decided to help him with that little decision. "Um, Justin, when you get a minute, I could use a hand changing that lightbulb in the hall?"

"Sure thing, Ange," he said, stepping away from Tanya, who

was suddenly looking a bit miffed herself. "Hey, thanks for everything, Tanya. I mean it."

"No problem, Justin," Tanya said, her smile wide as she looked up at him once again. "Come by anytime. Day or night…"

Slut, I thought, unlocking the door, stomping down the hall and tossing my bag on the couch with barely contained fury.

I whirled around to find Justin right behind me, grabbing a chair from the dining area and testing it for sturdiness.

"What the hell are you doing?" I asked.

He looked up at me, bewildered. "I'm getting a chair to stand on so I can change the bulb."

"No, no, no," I said, irritated. "I mean, with *her,*" I continued, gesturing with violence toward the door. "Tanya is, like, the building slut, Justin. You and I used to make fun of her. Remember? Not a month ago you were joking how she should install a revolving door on her apartment because all those locks and chains were slowing down her man intake."

His eyes widened. "You think Tanya and I—" Then he laughed. "Come on, Ange, you know me better than that."

"Do I?" I asked, looking into those green eyes and trying to find something of the Justin I once knew and adored.

He sighed. "I ran into her in the hall and she asked me about Lauren, and next thing you know, I'm telling her the whole damn story over a glass of wine in her apartment. You know, she's got quite a few good vintages on her wine rack. I was impressed…."

"I'll bet you were."

"Ange, she was just being a friend. She knew Lauren and I were together a long time, she just wanted to make sure I was okay…."

"Yeah, you looked brokenhearted out there in the hall with her."

"What do you know about it?" he said with sudden anger. "You haven't exactly been around to talk to. Always running over to Smirk's apartment every chance you can get. How the hell would you know what I'm going through?"

I felt a twinge of guilt. Until I remembered I had avoided coming home the past couple of nights so as not to find Jenna— or any other woman for that matter, I conceded—on my sofa.

"I didn't think you wanted me around now that you had your…your harem to come home to!"

"Harem?" He laughed. "What the hell are you talking about?"

"Jenna? Hello? Was she not sprawled all over our sofa the other night, looking like she wanted to do a lap dance the minute you put that guitar down?"

"Jenna's just a friend. She's helping me with my act…."

"She's a fucking bartender, Justin! I don't know, somehow I don't think cozying up to a woman known for her ability to keep the head off a beer is going to help you on the road to superstardom you allegedly crave."

"Oh, you don't think so, huh?" he said, "Well, I'll have you know that bartender you think so highly of has gotten me a solo gig at the Back Fence!"

"Really?" I said hopefully. "Justin, that's fantastic. Oh, my God, when is it?"

"Friday night," he said smugly.

"*This* Friday?"

"You got it."

"Justin, that's two days from now! Have you gotten all your material together?"

"Of course. I've been working on it every night since I got back from Florida. Not that you would know that."

"But what about getting the word out? Justin, two days is not enough time to do a mailing to agents or even round up your friends!" I said, quickly going through a mental list of people I could rally to support Justin and coming up short of a healthy crowd.

"I'll send an e-mail," he said with a shrug.

"Last I checked, you can't e-mail agents at the last minute."

"I'll invite C.J. to come," he said, naming his record-industry friend who lived all the way up in Westchester. "Besides, talent scouts drop in at the Back Fence all the time."

"Aren't you leaving a little too much up to chance? I mean, when is the next time you're going to be able to get a solo gig like this? You need to be prepared, you need to get the right people there—"

"God, Ange, you worry too much. It'll be fine."

★ ★ ★

But since it is in my nature to worry, I worried. Why would I stop now that my roommate and best friend was hurling himself further and further toward a life of obscurity and, judging by the breathy female voice I was treated to later that night when I picked up the phone, promiscuity? I did the only thing I could do: sent an e-mail to everyone I could think of, pleading with them to come to Justin's show on Friday. Then, so as not to watch Justin as he lounged on the couch chatting merrily to whatever new female he had somehow unwittingly managed to entice (because it was becoming apparent that Justin really did seem to be unaware of how charming he was, despite all the females flocking after him ever since Lauren had left the picture), I went to Kirk's.

And, as usual, partook in some mind-numbing sex. This time, on the kitchen table. And the living room carpet. And, finally, the desk in his bedroom. And just when I thought I had managed to bang out (literally) whatever anxieties I had where Justin was concerned, I discovered I had someone else to worry about. Myself.

Because as I rested my head on Kirk's shoulder to catch my breath, my eye caught sight of one of the downloads that had scattered to the floor from where they had been neatly stacked on the desk, before our little ink blotter encounter....

From where I sat on the desk, it looked to me some sort of diagram of a...diamond.

"Kirk," I said, lifting my head, my eyes narrowing as I realized it was, in fact, a photo of a diamond, with all sorts of lines drawn to it that led to some sort of explanatory text.

"Hmm?" he muttered into my neck, where he had half gone to sleep out of sheer exhaustion.

"What...what is that?"

He turned and looked down to where I was pointing at the floor somewhat frantically.

"Oh, that." He looked up at me with a smile that was somewhat rueful before he disentangled himself from me and leaned over to pick it up. "Well, I guess it's no big secret, but I did have some idea of surprising you."

My heart started beating so fast, I thought it would rip right out of my chest.

"I figured since we were talking marriage and everything, I ought to do a little research before I, you know, went…shopping. Turns out there's a lot more to this diamond business than I realized. I mean, look at this," he said, pointing to the photo, which had arrows arching down to it with text indicating the various aspects of cut, clarity and weight that determined a stone's value. "There's a lot you gotta know before you invest that kind of money."

"Yes, there is," I said, looking up from that paper and into those gray eyes. There *was* a lot you needed to know before you made that kind of investment in a diamond. Or a person…

While I sat quietly listening as he regaled me with all he'd learned so far about cut, clarity and weight, I realized I did know Kirk, probably better now than I ever had before. I mean, this was so like him, to act prudently and get all the facts, even before making the most romantic gesture he'd probably ever make. Though I took comfort in this strong sense of knowing another human being, I was suddenly failing to see the romance of it all. And that scared me.

"So I was thinking, you know, that maybe we should go shopping together—just to look around. Get an idea of what you wanted before, you know…" He broke off, smiled. "Maybe Friday? I have to meet with a client until five, but we could go afterward…."

"*This* Friday?" I said, panic taking hold. "But Justin's show is this weekend," I continued, latching on to any excuse I could come up with.

"Justin's show?"

"Oh, I didn't tell you yet—Justin's doing a solo show Friday night at the Back Fence."

"Ange, you know how I hate sitting around in a smoky bar," he hedged.

"C'mon, Kirk, you *have* to come. Justin needs the support. I mean, we don't want the club owner to think he can't attract a crowd. And who knows, there may be some talent scouts in the audience we need to impress with loud cheers," I finished, though I highly doubted Justin would get that lucky at this late date.

"Well, my flight's not leaving until nine o'clock on Saturday.

Maybe we can meet up when you get off from work and go then?"

"I don't understand what the big hurry is," I said, looking into his eager eyes.

He smiled. "Now my girl's not in a hurry?" He chuckled. "The truth is, I'm gonna be pretty busy over the coming weeks if Norwood assigns me the rest of their offices. I'd like to get this over with before I go to Chicago."

Get it over with? I thought, suddenly realizing that yes, I did know this man I was marrying a little too well. Even something as big as getting engaged was just an item on his to-do list. The thought made me feel sad.

But still I found myself agreeing, somewhat sullenly, to this little spree. Even told him I knew a place we could go that was open till seven Saturday, saying that I had gone shopping there with Michelle, who had been looking for tennis bracelets. He didn't question this, only seemed happy that we had a destination in mind, that our little venture to the Diamond District would be quick and efficient.

I felt a moment of relief. Even managed a small smile when I remembered Rudy. And that ring.

God, it seemed so easy. Almost too easy...

16

And you thought it was just a common house plant.

Friday night came, and I managed to drag a reluctant Kirk to the Back Fence, along with whomever else I could get there at last minute's notice. Of course, I hadn't been able to invite Josh, because of the Kirk factor, and Michelle was off-limits due to the man factor. There were just too many temptations in this room for her.

Colin, of course, was there, dressed in a crisp blue button-down that made his blue eyes positively sparkle. He had a bit of a crush on Justin, not that his intended target would ever notice, swamped as Justin had been from the moment we'd arrived by the horde of twenty-somethings Jenna had managed to dredge up for the big event and who took up the two front tables. I was desperately glad when Grace arrived, managing to look stunning even in jeans and a black halter that showed off her shoulders and always-fabulous décolleté. Of course in her wake came Claudia, who stepped through the door just behind Grace, draped in her usual black garb and looking around the dark, smoky room, which was decorated in Miller Lite signs and littered with a mostly college-age crowd, as if she'd stepped into the Twilight Zone. I have to say, I was even grateful to see her, as our cheering section was looking a bit meager.

After I introduced Claudia to everyone at the table and Grace had greeted both Colin and Kirk, they took seats to my right and immediately began trolling the crowd, ogling the more manly specimens sprinkled among the twenty-some-things. Didn't these two ever give it a rest? I thought, turning my attention to Colin, who was babbling merrily to Kirk about the impending contract. Colin had already met with his agent this morning, and though he had taken the weekend to think about it, I knew he was more than ready to sign on the dotted line. I made a mental note to call him tomorrow to get as many details as I could before my own meeting.

"I know Angie's excited," Kirk said, reaching around my shoulders and giving me a squeeze that almost made me spit half the margarita I was attempting to gulp down.

But I was distracted from this conversation by the sound of Claudia's voice as she said to Grace, "Is that him?" and gestured to Justin, who had just disentangled himself from the brat pack to climb up on stage and set up.

"That's Justin," Grace replied.

"He's de*lish*," Claudia said, her eyes raking over the oblivious Justin as if she were mentally undressing him. "Where, on God's earth, have you been hiding him?"

A stab of heat went through my gut, which I feared had little to do with the tequila I'd just swallowed. Grace eyed my discomfort speculatively and said, "I haven't been hiding him. Angie has. He's *her* roommate."

"Angela, darling, how greedy of you. Not only have you got one gorgeous man by your side," she said, waving the cigarette she held toward Kirk, who was—thank God—still engrossed in a conversation with Colin, "but you've got another waiting at home? Didn't your mother teach you to share and share alike?"

I was fortunately saved from the biting response I wanted to make when Justin himself finally showed up at our table. "Hey, everyone. I'm so glad you all could make it on such short notice," he said, beaming that beautiful set of teeth at us.

"Hell, I'd get myself a pager for this guy," I heard Claudia whisper gleefully to Grace. "Beep me anytime, baby. Harder,

harder." Grace slid a glance at me, as if looking for some kind of reaction.

I, of course, was trying hard not to react, so I simply watched as Colin stood and threw his arms around Justin in greeting. "How you doing, buddy?" Justin said, patting Colin on the back in his usual friendly manner and probably sending Colin into near cardiac arrest.

"Captain Kirk," Justin said, rounding to the back of Kirk's chair and grasping his hand. "Thanks for coming, man."

"I wouldn't have missed it," Kirk said. I tried not to glare at him (it wasn't easy).

"Hey, Gracie!" Justin said then, completely bypassing me as Grace stood to give him a hug. "You look great," he said, leaning away from the hug and taking her in. "God, when was the last time I saw you? You gotta get downtown more often."

"It really is surprising she doesn't, considering how much Grace loves getting downtown," I said, gazing pointedly up at her.

Grace ignored me, turning to Claudia. "Justin, this is Claudia, my boss at Roxanne Dubrow."

"How do you do?" Claudia gushed. Then she actually held out a hand to be kissed, like some sort of countess. Where did she think we were, Spectrum Lounge?

Justin, of course, missed the cue, and awkwardly shook the hand she held out, palm down.

As I watched him lope over to a nearby table where he greeted a couple of other people he knew—I recognized at least one of them, a voluptuous redhead whom he'd done a few production gigs with—I remembered how I felt the first time I had met Justin. Scared. Then he was the good-looking stranger who, I was so sure, could charm a woman's heart just as easily as he could break it. The kind of man I would have avoided like the plague, if our improv teacher hadn't paired us together. It was almost comical to think of it now that I knew Justin to be the goofy sofa-hoarding roommate that he was. But as I watched him charm the room, he was that stranger again. And though it didn't scare me this time, it bothered me somehow.

Bothered me even more when it looked like he was about to bound up on that stage without even saying hello to me. I turned to Grace, hoping to start a conversation to show I didn't care what he did or didn't do, when suddenly I felt a hand on my shoulder and turned, to find not the charming stranger but the man I knew better than I even knew myself sometimes crouched down beside my chair, those green eyes turned full force on mine.

"Thanks, Angie."

"For what?"

"For getting everyone down here. I know I didn't give you much notice and all…."

"Hey, what are friends for?" I said, looking into his eyes and seeing something else there—something indefinable. Something that looked like it might have been…fear. "You gonna be okay up there?" I asked, suddenly worried for him.

"Ah, I'll be fine," he said. "Besides, it doesn't look like any big music industry execs are sitting out in the audience anyway," he continued, glancing around at the tattered-T-shirt-and-jeans crowd that surrounded us.

Then, before I could come up with an encouraging word to give him before he went on stage, he gave a quick glance over at Kirk, who was chatting with Colin again, and pressed his lips to mine in a quick kiss. "For luck," he explained, giving me a heart-stopping grin before he bounded away from the table once more.

I turned to Grace, whose raised eyebrow said, *What was that all about?*

What indeed? I thought, touching my lips, which were, much to my surprise, *tingling.*

But whatever crazy thoughts spun dizzily through my head in that moment were quickly replaced by the quivering mass of fear that overtook my stomach as soon as Justin stepped onstage. *Please, God, let him do all right tonight,* I prayed, as he grabbed the mike.

"How's everybody out there doing tonight?"

A heartening roar of cheers rose up from the crowd. Grace, God bless her, even gave him a two-fingered whistle.

"How many New Yorkers we have out there tonight?" Justin asked.

Another roar rose up (I banged on the table, spilling Kirk's beer and earning me a somewhat disgusted look, which I ignored).

"God, I love this town," Justin continued, putting the mike on the stand and sitting down. He placed the guitar across his knees. "I wasn't born here, you know," he said. "I figure you might hold that against me, but by God I'm gonna die here—that's for sure." He laughed nervously.

The room went silent, as if those black-clad ranks *were* holding his Midwestern smile against him. My heart went out to him. He looked suddenly afraid he might keel over on the spot, and I glimpsed fear in his eyes before he looked down at his guitar. I worried now that I had pushed Justin to do something he wasn't ready for. I worried even more when he started strumming a chord only to stop, chuckle ruefully and start tuning up. "Sorry about that."

Except for the sound of the unharmonious strings he plucked as he turned the tuning pegs to adjust them, the room was so still I could feel a palpable…aggression. Glancing around, I studied the crowd again, the impatient expressions, the belligerent looks. It was as if they expected—*wanted*—him to fail. Or something. Whatever it was, the room felt decidedly tense.

I wondered if Justin sensed it, too. Especially when he finished tuning, then lifted his head and stared out into the distance, his hand frozen over the strings as if he had forgotten where to begin. I held my breath.

Finally he started to strum, hesitantly at first, then with a growing confidence. The song was fast-paced, a jumble of catchy, bluesy chords. I began to feel hopeful, until Justin opened his mouth to sing. It wasn't his voice—that was as beautiful as his looks. But the words—the words that finally came out of his mouth—were a bit…strange.

> *Said the leaf to the tree*
> *Do you see what I see?*
> *A beam of fresh hot sunlight*
> *Coming down to shine on me.*

Phooo—toooo—synthesis!
Phooo—toooo—synthesis!

I couldn't help but laugh in amazement. Leave it to Justin to write a song about something that most people hadn't thought about since eighth-grade science class. Where did he come up with this stuff? I looked around at the crowd, who seemed to think his happy little tune was as bizarre as I did. I saw heads lean together, heard sputtered laughter. But as Justin strummed away in a rhythm you couldn't help but tap a foot to, I noticed something else. I wasn't the only one tapping a foot. The room seemed to visibly sway to Justin's strange little song.

Said the pistil to the stamen
Where would I be
Without you dropping some of that
Dewy pollen on me!
Phooo—tooo—synthesis!
Phooo—tooo—synthesis!
Pho-pho-pho-pho-pho-pho-pho-pho
Photosynthesis!
That's where it begins....

By the second chorus, everyone had given in to the madness. Everyone, that is, except Kirk, who leaned close to my ear and said, "What *is* this nonsense?" I turned to look at him—actually, I think I glared—before turning back to Justin, who finished out the song to a heartening round of applause. Grace turned to me and winked as we clapped our hands vigorously. Colin was beaming, and Claudia had her eyebrows raised as if she couldn't believe she was enjoying Justin's little tribute to plant life. Kirk rolled his eyes and sipped his beer. I ignored him—it was easy enough—because Justin was leaning into the mike again. "We're gonna take it down a notch," he murmured, then began to strum a melody filled with a soul-searing sadness. A sadness I almost didn't expect from Justin, with his perpetual happy-go-lucky demeanor. The melody was pure blues, and the words...were heartbreaking.

Sharing a windowsill with you
Is all I want to do,
Looking at the world so wide and lonely,
I can't forget,
I love her yet,
And now she's gone I'm lost and lonely.

The room was positively still. Except for the clear, true sound of Justin's voice as it rang out over the room, singing of the sadness only a man who'd loved and lost could feel. I was mesmerized, as was the rest of the female population in the room, considering the dreamy-eyed expressions I saw as Justin purred into the mike.

And once he strummed that last melancholy chord, the room broke out in thundering applause. Grace and I stood up, along with Colin and Claudia. Hell, from the look on Claudia's face, I thought she was going to throw her underwear up there.

He had them eating out of the palm of his hand, and suddenly I wondered why I'd ever doubted him. This was the Justin who had disarmed me from the first moment I met him in improv class, the man who could sweep a room off its feet with a smile—and now a song. He had everyone in the room under his spell except Kirk, who shook his head incredulously the minute I sat down again.

"He's so beautiful," Colin said to me, leaning across Kirk, who eyed him with a kind of disgust. But I didn't have time to contemplate this as Justin, looking clearly encouraged by the audience's response, began strumming again, still in a bluesy vein, but this time with a more upbeat tempo.

Well, I know a gal, she ain't so fine,
She prefers her water to her wine.
She likes a sunny day,
Come what may,
She was built for living the natural way.
Mmm, hmm, my Bernadette...
Mmm, hmm, my Bernadette.

I burst into joyful laughter. "He's singing about the azalea!" I explained when everyone at the table turned to look at me.

No one knew what the hell I was talking about, but it didn't seem to matter. The rhythm was so catchy the whole room had begun to sway again, hands clapping to the rhythm. By the time Justin got to the second chorus, everyone was singing, *"Mmm, hmm, my Bernadette…"*

When Justin was done with that song, he immediately rolled into another one, again with a catchy rhythm and strange lyrics. Something about reaching for the sky from a bed of soil. I was starting to see a theme here. And I found out what it was when Justin finally came offstage, exuberant as the crowd cheered on.

"What'd you think?" he asked, pulling out a chair and sitting down.

"Fantastic!" we all shouted. Well, all of us except Kirk, who stared at Justin as if he'd grown a horn.

"Yeah, it's a little thing I'm working on called 'Ten Songs for Bernadette,'" Justin said, winking at me.

"Who's Bernadette?" Claudia asked, leaning in close. "She must be a very lucky girl."

"Oh, she is. She changed my life," Justin said, still looking at me. "And the best thing about her is, she's always there for me, no matter what."

I have to say, it was a bit disappointing to learn all those songs were for the azalea, but I couldn't help getting excited for Justin. He seemed so happy, so alive, for the first time in a long time. I didn't want to miss a minute of it.

Kirk, on the other hand, had had enough. "Can we *go* now?" he whispered fiercely in my ear once Jenna had bounced over to the table to plant a big kiss on Justin's cheek and offer a round of drinks to the table, on the house.

"Go? Kirk, it's so early."

With a sigh, he leaned back in his chair. "I'm tired, I got a lot of work to do in the morning. And this damn cigarette smoke," he said, waving a hand in the air in Claudia's direction as another cloud rose up. "Besides," he added, leaning in close enough for only me to hear, "I've had enough of basking in that…that idiot's glow."

My eyes widened. "You're jealous," I whispered back.

"Jealous?" Kirk laughed. "Of him? Gimme a break, Angela. Now, are you coming, or what?"

I didn't know what to do, so I stared after him as he headed for the door then stopped, as if waiting for me to make up my mind. I stood up. "I...I gotta go."

"Now?" Justin said. "Jenna just ordered us a round of drinks!"

"Yeah, Ange, hang out with us—we're having a good time," Grace said.

"Kirk is tired and I have to work in the morning," I hedged, and before anyone could change my mind, I quickly bid them all good-night and walked outside, where Kirk was already hailing a cab.

"That was very rude," I said to him.

He dropped his hand, stared at me. "What?"

"You didn't even say goodbye!"

"Look, Ange, I came, didn't I? And you know I have a lot to do to get ready for my trip...."

"But we were celebrating Justin's success. We should be supporting him now—"

"Supporting *what,* exactly?" Kirk said, staring at me with what looked like anger in his eyes. "Did you hear those lyrics? They didn't even make sense!"

"He was singing about the azalea. You know, the one that was delivered that night...by accident," I hedged, realizing Kirk, of all people, would never see the humor if he knew the real story behind that azalea.

"Yeah, that's beautiful, Ange. Just perfect. I think we can go now, seeing as your roommate seems to have a big enough fan club without us."

"You *are* jealous!" I accused.

"I'm not jealous!" he insisted. "I just don't feel a need to sit around making that guy feel good about himself. Do you really think no matter how much we slap him on the back, no matter how many rounds of drinks that bimbo buys him, he's gonna get somewhere? He's got nothing going on, that guy."

"He's very talented, he just hasn't made the most of his opportunities."

Kirk snorted, lifting his hand again to hail a cab. "Opportunities. That guy wouldn't know an opportunity if it kicked him in the head. When was the last time you saw him even make an effort?"

His words stopped me for a moment, echoing, as they did, all the doubts I had had about Justin over the past months.

"I mean, I know the entertainment industry isn't easy to break into," Kirk went on, "but look at you—you're doing it. At least you're getting somewhere."

I stared at him. Was I getting somewhere? Because my prospect of a contract at *Rise and Shine* suddenly seemed like...nowhere.

And maybe it was that thought that made me pause when a cab pulled up and Kirk opened the door, gesturing for me to get inside.

"C'mon, Ange, let's go!" he said, staring at me as if I were some alien creature.

I felt like some alien creature—maybe a little like Bernadette, digging my roots in no matter what the cost. "No, I'm gonna stay."

His jaw hardened. "Fine." And he got in the cab, slamming the door behind him, and drove away.

Leaving me to march back inside and face my friends alone.

"What happened?" Grace said.

"Nothing," I said lightly. "Kirk was just tired, and I...I felt like staying after all." I glanced at Justin, who was just downing a shot with Claudia and Colin when he looked up and saw me. "Hey I knew she'd be back," he said merrily, pulling out the chair next to him as I sat down, feeling a bit uneasy because of the look on Grace's face. She had observed the way Kirk had acted. And she clearly hadn't liked it either.

Fortunately, I was saved from making any further excuses for Kirk by the sight of C.J. and his wife, Danielle, approaching our table.

"C.J., my man! You made it!" Justin said, jumping up to embrace his best friend and his wife.

"Yeah, well, Danielle and I came in to the city to see a new band we have on the label, but I was hoping we'd make your set...."

"Aw, you missed it, man," Justin said, but he was smiling ear to ear, as if it didn't matter that his only hope in the music industry had missed his successful gig.

Suddenly I found myself piping up, "But he was fantastic. In fact, I wouldn't be surprised if they invited him back next week!"

Everyone at the table agreed, heaping praise on Justin.

"Well, this calls for a round of drinks," C.J. said, as he and Danielle sat down at the table. Introductions were made, and soon enough everyone was merrily conversing and pouring back more alcohol. I felt myself relax for the first time since my heated exchange with Kirk. I even began to revel in the excitement of Justin's moment, so much so that C.J. leaned close to me and said, "So he was good tonight, huh?"

"Yes," I said, nodding my head vigorously. "I mean, I've heard him play before, but never before an audience. It was…wild."

C.J. shook his head, sipped his drink. "Yeah, he's always had good presence onstage. We used to jam together in college, but back then Justin was playing bass. I was the guitarist—and the singer, I might add," he said, clearly remembering those times with fondness. "But after college we never did anything with the band. I stuck with music, but the film bug bit Justin. Did you ever see that film he made? Pretty amazing, huh? I'm surprised he's even doing music again. I thought he'd stick with film…."

"So did I," I admitted. But Justin hadn't stuck with anything since he'd made that film. Still, after seeing his performance tonight, I wondered if maybe I was wrong about him. Maybe he wasn't a frustrated filmmaker, but a musician who hadn't had a chance to shine. And he could have a chance, I thought, watching the way he chatted jovially with C.J., who slapped him on the back and ordered him another beer. Hell, C.J. would give him a chance. Justin's life was full of chances, it seemed. He only had to choose what he wanted.

"Hey, maybe we should start jamming again," C.J. was telling him now, "or now that you're a big singer-songwriter, maybe you should try recording a demo instead," he continued.

"Yeah, sure, man. Right after I finish this beer," Justin said, lifting his glass and laughing as if he didn't have a care in the world. Suddenly I wondered if Kirk was right—maybe Justin wouldn't know an opportunity if it kicked him in the head. Or maybe he would—only he ran from life's golden chances as far as he could. Like when he'd dropped the film after it won the award, or fell in love with Lauren the minute she'd stepped on the plane for Florida.

Suddenly everything fell into relief. *All* of my friends were commitment-phobes. Colin, smiling hopefully into Justin's face, as if he had a chance—if there was one thing I was sure about Justin, it was that he was heterosexual. Grace, who bent close to Claudia, probably to avoid the gaze of the guy who had been staring at her from across the bar for the past twenty minutes.

And Justin, I thought, watching as Jenna bounded over to our table with another drink for him. He was the worst offender. Because he not only kept his love at a distance, he kept his dreams there, too.

And if there was one thing I had learned over these past few weeks of auditioning, that was the biggest crime of all.

One by one, everyone left the bar. C.J. and Danielle first, as they had to get back to Westchester. Grace left with Claudia so they could share a cab uptown, and I thought Colin might stay all night, hanging on Justin's every word, but even he eventually felt the heaviness of the late hour and called it a night.

Leaving me and Justin to share the walk across town alone.

"So it looks like this night turned out to be pretty good after all, huh?" I said.

"Yeah." He smiled at me, then gazed pensively down at the sidewalk.

"So why don't you pursue it? Put together another show. Maybe you can even record a demo, like C.J. suggested."

He laughed. "Yeah, maybe. But I was just kinda doing this on a goof, you know? I'm not sure it's really what I want to do—"

"Justin!" I said, stopping in my tracks and turning to look at him. "Don't you see what you're doing?"

"What?" he said, staring at me, perplexed.

"You jump from one thing to the next, never making anything of the opportunities you have. The crowd loved you tonight. You have a good friend in the recording industry who might be able to help you—"

"I know. I know. You're right...." he said, his voice trailing off. Then, as if he wanted to change the subject, he said, "So I heard Colin going on about that contract for *Rise and Shine*. Sounds like he's going to take it." He glanced at me. "Are you?"

I sighed, all the doubts I'd been having rushing to the forefront of my mind. "I don't know. It could be an opportunity...."

"Or the death of opportunity."

"Sometimes you have to make decisions, Justin—commitments—in order to be able to move forward in life."

"Do you really think that show is going to move you forward?"

"No," I admitted. "But it could give me some level of...of security. I was thinking I might just take it. I could still keep auditioning."

"But what if you get another gig? What if something comes along that requires you to relocate to L.A.? Like a movie. Hey, did you ever hear anything back about that audition for that independent movie? What was it called?"

"*All for Love*. And no, I didn't get a callback," I said, then amended myself. "Well, I did get a call from the casting director. He thought I had potential, but that I wasn't right for the part."

"Ange, that is amazing!" Justin exclaimed, stopping to look at me. "Casting directors never call you unless they really think you have something going on. That bodes well."

I looked up at him hesitantly. "He did say he had something else in mind. That he'd call me if it came up. But then he never called...."

Justin shook his head. "You talk about me not seizing my opportunities, Ange, but look at you—this guy saw something in you. The very same something that I see and others saw when you were acting on the stage. *You* have to see that something—you have to *believe* in it."

"But what good is believing in your talent if you never get a chance to use it?"

He laughed. "Oh, so you're going to sign a contract that pretty much guarantees you won't have a chance to use it? You know, there are other ways of blowing your opportunities, Ange. Like taking the wrong opportunity."

He was right, I realized now. If I did get another gig that conflicted with *Rise and Shine,* it would be a big mess to get out of my contract. "But how do I even know I'll ever get another gig?" I asked, suddenly knowing the real reason why it hadn't occurred to me this might happen. I didn't see any impending conflict coming because I didn't believe any other opportunities were coming my way. "This might just be my last chance to make something of myself."

"Angie, you're crazy to think that. You're beautiful, talented. You have a casting director calling you back just to tell you he saw something in you. That doesn't happen to everyone, you know." Justin smiled. "And don't forget, you do live in the best city in the world. Anything is possible here. I mean, look at me—I was up there singing about a fucking azalea, and the crowd loved it. You never know when you're gonna hit that right chord. You just have to be ready to jump on it and ride with it when the moment comes."

He was making a lot of sense. Maybe it wasn't about making commitments. Maybe it was about making the *right* commitment.

I looked up, realizing we were already at our building. Justin pulled out the key and let us in, and I bounded up the stairs ahead of him, feeling lighter than I had felt in a long, long time.

"Man, I'm beat," Justin said, letting us into the apartment. "You gonna hit the hay?"

I nodded, smiling up at him. "Thanks, Justin."

"For what?" he said, turning to look at me.

"For reminding me that I still have a chance."

He smiled. "Angie, if anyone has a chance, it's you," he replied putting his arms around me and pulling me toward him in a hug.

That's when I felt it—the same zing that had sprung up when he'd given me that good-luck kiss. And clearly Justin felt it, too, because suddenly he was practically tripping over sofa #3 to get away from me.

"Well, I'm going to bed," he said, eyes averted as he darted into his bedroom, closing the door firmly behind him.

What the hell was that? I thought, still feeling the warmth from where he'd pressed his body to mine.

I knew exactly what that was. Which was probably why I went into my bedroom, closed the door and locked it—in some vain attempt to shut out whatever madness had just crossed both our minds.

Because it was mad, really. Clearly we'd both had too much to drink. Or something.

And with that thought, I got ready to go to bed.

Though I would swear I didn't sleep a wink.

17

I'll take a carat
and a half—hold the husband.

Kirk did call me the next day to confirm that we were, in fact, still moving ahead with our plan for that evening. He didn't even mention his grand exit the previous night, which I found odd, since I was still stewing over his attitude problem as far as Justin was concerned. I guessed things like people's feelings didn't matter to Kirk—though I was still irritated at him. But of course I didn't have time to voice my irritation. "If you meet me on the corner of Forty-seventh and Fifth by four-thirty, we should have plenty of time to shop before I have to catch my plane. Just don't be late, Angie," he warned.

"Are you sure you can squeeze me in?" I said sarcastically, probably in reaction to his implication that I was often less than punctual.

"I can if you're not late."

Yeah. Sure.

I hung up the line and found Michelle gawking at me. Apparently she had overheard my whole conversation.

"Why didn't you *tell* me you were fucking going to Rudy's?" Michelle said, her face a mixture of indignation and glee.

Why *hadn't* I? Probably because I had so much on my mind, between auditioning, Justin's show, that damn contract....

Oh, right, the contract. I still needed to call Colin and see what he had found out from his agent about what we could expect. Because I certainly couldn't give it up without knowing exactly what I was giving up.

"Um, I'll be right back," I said to Michelle, who was clearly going to launch into some pre-ring-shopping advice, judging by the way her jaw snapped shut as I leaped from my chair and rushed to an available phone in one of the back offices. I had to have this conversation in complete private.

But my conversation with Colin only confirmed my decision that I couldn't possibly sign the contract. At first, as he babbled excitedly about the money, the health benefits, I almost lost heart. Until he told me that the term of the contract was three years. And that it included a no-compete clause. Apparently the network was hoping to cash in on some advertising tie-ins if the show took off as expected. And they didn't want me or Colin tainting the wholesome *Rise and Shine* image by appearing in anything that might even remotely endanger that. Any other gig we considered would require the network's approval, and I wasn't likely to get that for anything stronger than *Rebecca of Sunnybrook Farm*. Fuhgetaboutit. When I hung up the phone, I felt a tidal wave of relief. So my *Rise and Shine* days were almost over. I was glad to be certain about something in my future for a change.

But my happiness was short-lived when I returned to my cubicle and found Michelle waiting to deluge me with all sorts of advice about the next big commitment I was about to make. Of course, she went on and on about the ring. All I could think about was the man....

I was in a tangle of nerves as I scrambled out the door at the end of my shift. Of course, it was already four-fifteen. Not that that was my fault—the delay was due to a last-minute customer who was torn between two aquamarine T-shirts, one V-neck the other a boat-neck. I should have such problems.

Once I hit the sidewalk out front of the building, I immediately craved a cigarette. Fortunately I was so used to puffing one on my way out of work nowadays, I had popped my recently purchased pack into my bag that morning.

I lit up immediately and almost choked on the thick smoke that rolled down my throat on the first drag. But still I carried on, puffing madly as I raced uptown, my nerves not feeling very soothed by nicotine. Especially when I realized I didn't have any mints for the smoky breath factor. After all, it wasn't necessary for Kirk to know about this little transgression. I was going to quit, just as soon as—just as soon as I got through this…stuff.

I stopped at the first deli I came across, grabbed a box of Altoids, then stood impatiently behind a little old lady who appeared to be cleaning out her wallet judging by all the coins she was plopping onto the counter to pay for two rolls of toilet paper. Finally she was closing her wallet with a happy little snap and idling away slowly. I practically plowed her down as I slapped a five-dollar bill on the counter and grabbed the change the clerk quickly made.

Once out on the street again, I glanced at my watch, saw it was four-twenty and I still had eight blocks and four avenues to go. I briefly considered a cab, then, gazing at the traffic-clogged avenue, realized it might be faster on foot. When I got to Times Square, I found myself stuck behind some sort of walking tour. I dodged through the crowd of knapsack-clad, photo-shooting tourists (it wasn't easy and it earned me more than one dirty look), then glanced at my watch again. Shit, I was going to be late. Kirk was going to kill me. Oh, God, now I sounded like Michelle.

I tossed down my cigarette. Then, feeling regretful that I hadn't gotten the necessary dosage of nicotine, I pulled out another. I lit up, briefly considering the insanity of what I was doing. But I was getting fucking married. These things were supposed to be nerve-racking. I mean, I was getting involved in a life. You know, husband, kids, mortgage, combined bank accounts. Oh God, oh God, oh God. I dragged deep, almost stepping into traffic until I realized the light had turned green and the traffic was fully prepared to roll right over me. I stepped back onto the curb and took another fretful puff, as if in thanksgiving that I still had my life. My wits, on the other hand…

I took a deep breath, gazed up at the glittering billboards of

Times Square as I waited for the light to change and felt some measure of comfort at the sight. Tourists aside, this was still one of the most amazing places in New York City. I could remember countless walks through Times Square, alone or with Justin, who was a veritable scholar on this little corner of the city and would often drag me up here to shoot some footage, all the while narrating the story of how this glittering landscape had come into being. I smiled up at the place where the ball dropped on New Year's Eve, remembering the year I had ventured here for that holiday with Justin; how we stood, crushed among the throngs, holding hands to keep from being separated in the crowd. I remember I had held my breath, too. Dreaming, as that ball fell toward the shrieking crowd that I would one day, like Frank Sinatra sang, make it here. And I would, I realized, now that I had given up the crutch of false security I knew *Rise and Shine* had been to me. Now I had a real chance to pursue my dreams. Now I had the power to make myself truly happy.

Of course, I also had the power to make Kirk incredibly *unhappy,* I realized when I reached the corner of Forty-seventh and Fifth and found him glancing around angrily.

But rather than feel bad, I felt just as annoyed as I had last night, when he'd bolted out of the bar, claiming he had better things to do. Clearly he had better things to do right now, I thought, noticing the way he was glancing at his watch as I approached.

I couldn't even bring myself to kiss Kirk hello, but he didn't seem to notice, grabbing my hand and leading me down the street until he realized he didn't know where we were going. So I took the lead, stopping before Rudy's steel door, the first feeling of excitement—or was that anxiety?—fluttering through my stomach.

"What *is* this place?" Kirk said when I led him through the door and down the darkened hall.

"Rudy's," I said.

"It looks like a crack den," he replied.

I was starting to wish it were. I could have used a solid dose of *something* to escape the heat that curled through me.

But once we opened the door to the store itself and I saw Rudy—this time in a purple pinstripe shirt that bared even more of that hairy chest and gold chains and an even louder pair of electric-blue trousers—I felt better.

"Hey, Rudy," I said, smiling at him once he looked up from the newspaper he had been leaning over a glass case to read, a cigarette perched between his thick, ring-clad fingers.

"Sweetheart, how are you?" he said, his merry face breaking into a smile as he slammed the newspaper shut, dropped the cigarette into the ashtray and approached us.

"You're looking even more beautiful today," he went on, grabbing me in his short arms for a hug. In truth, I welcomed that embrace—throat-gagging cologne and all. It was nice that *someone* was glad to see me today, I thought, flicking a glance at Kirk, who stood beside me eyeing the whole exchange with what looked like suspicion.

"Is this the guy?" Rudy said, still holding my hand and pulling my ear close to his, as if Kirk couldn't hear what he was saying.

"Yes. Rudy Michelangelo, meet Kirk Stevens," I said, turning toward Kirk and waving him closer.

Kirk held out a hand, which Rudy pumped vigorously. "Michelangelo, huh? Is that your real name?"

Rudy's eyes widened as he released Kirk's hand and glanced at me. "Just like the sculpta," he said, waving a hand in the direction of that infamous David, who, I noticed, now sported a thick gold bracelet in addition to the rope chain.

"Kirk came with me to look at rings," I announced. Then, no longer feeling any need to hide the fact that I had all but put a down payment on one the last time I was here, I continued, "You remember that ring you showed me when I came with Michelle? The Tiffany cut? Four prongs, two baguettes?"

"Sweetheart, you don't need to tell *me*. Rudy remembers what you want," he said, tapping a finger to his temple. "I got a mind like a trap."

He turned, picked up his cigarette, then headed straight for the case that held the ring.

Kirk didn't seem to mind that I had all but made my selection without him. Instead, as we followed behind Rudy, he took the opportunity to lean over and whisper, "Where the hell did you find this guy?"

"He's Michelle's mother's cousin," I whispered back.

"Are you sure he's legit?"

"Oh, he's the real thing, all right," I said, a bit testily. As if he'd insulted a member of *my* family.

As we approached the case, Rudy dropped his cigarette into the ashtray he kept there before he unlocked the case and unerringly reached for the ring I had fallen in love with.

I slid it on my finger and held it out. It was every bit as beautiful as I remembered.

Kirk leaned in close, studying the ring from all angles. "Are you sure this is the one you like?"

"Of course!" I said. Hell, at the moment I was surer of this ring than I was of *him*.

He looked at it again, then glanced up at Rudy. "Do you have one of those loupes so I can get a better look?"

"Sure, guy, anything you want," Rudy said, with a glance at me. He turned to a drawer behind him, pulled out a loupe and handed it to Kirk. Then he grabbed his cigarette and began to puff, watching as I handed Kirk the ring. Kirk leaned over it, the loupe placed up to his eye as a whirl of smoke drifted in front of his face.

"Do you *mind?*" he said, waving the hand with the ring at the smoke, which I realized I had been savoring, probably hoping to get some of that soothing nicotine secondhand.

"Hey, I'm sorry, guy," Rudy said, taking another tug on the cigarette before he stubbed it out in the tray. He blew out the last puff of smoke, then winked at me as Kirk bent over the ring again.

"What are those black specks I see?" Kirk asked, looking up at Rudy again.

"Specks? What are you talking—?" Rudy took the ring and loupe from Kirk and looked. "Oh, jeez," he said, pulling the loupe away and blowing on it. "Ashes. Sorry about that, guy," he said handing the loupe and ring back to Kirk, who leaned over them once again as Rudy rattled off the facts about the cut and clarity. "The diamond in there is almost flawless," he continued. "No diamond is completely perfect, of course."

"How much does something like this go for?" Kirk asked.

"This ring right here?" Rudy studied Kirk's face as if he

wasn't sure he was going to part with it at any price. "Ten thousand dollars," he said, looking Kirk right in the eye.

"But, Rudy, I thought—" I began, but Rudy silenced me with a glance that said he knew what he was doing. *I* didn't know what he was doing, frankly, except making me very nervous.

"That's a bit more than I wanted to spend," Kirk said, gazing right back at him.

"Well, you got yourself a beautiful girl there. Don't you think she deserves a beautiful ring? I mean, come on, guy, we're talking about your future wife here."

That's right, I thought, realizing once again what a big step we were taking. This was the ring I was going to wear forever. But when I looked up and saw how uncomfortable Kirk looked, I cringed. I thought about his solid budgeting, his careful approach to everything, and realized that maybe he was right to be that way. Maybe it was ridiculous to go into debt over a piece of jewelry. Suddenly I found myself saying, "Perhaps you could show us a few other things."

Rudy looked at me as if I had betrayed him. But rather than express the questions that formed in his eyes as he glanced first at me and then at Kirk, he said, "Okay, if that's what you wanna do...."

He started pulling out rings, keeping to round stones, as he knew that was my preference. But no matter how many rings I slipped on my finger, none of them made me feel like that first one did. After a while, I could feel Kirk getting restless beside me, and I think even Rudy was started to feel a little disgusted, though whether at me or Kirk, I couldn't tell. Finally, I slipped on a plain platinum band with a single solitaire that was just under a carat and just within the price range Rudy had finally gotten out of Kirk.

"This one's kinda nice...." I said, looking up hopefully at Kirk, who was already eyeing his watch.

I turned to Rudy, seeking some counsel there, because in truth I no longer knew what I wanted.

Rudy picked up the ring and eyed it through the loupe. "Yeah, it's not a bad stone for the price. A few flaws, but nothing too serious. Not the caliber of the first ring, of course, but, hey, no diamond is perfect, right?"

And no man, I thought, looking up at Kirk, who was now frowning at his watch with displeasure. "Look, we should get moving soon if I'm gonna make my flight. Is that the one you like?"

I hesitated, my mind in a whirl again. When I felt Rudy's hand on mine, I looked up, startled. "Hey, this ring will be here—or another one like it. Why don't you think about it?" He stared hard into my eyes as if trying to send me some message. "After all, it's a big decision," he said, his gaze drifting briefly to Kirk.

I knew then that Rudy wasn't just talking about the ring....

When we stepped out on to the street again, I had to practically run to keep up with Kirk's stride. "I don't understand what your big hurry is," I said, when I finally met his pace. "It's only six—your flight doesn't leave until nine o'clock."

"Unlike you, I don't like to be late. If I miss this plane, the next one isn't until eleven, and I've got to be on the green tomorrow with Ken Norwood by nine. I didn't think this was going to take so long."

"Sorry to be such an inconvenience," I said tartly. "Maybe I should schedule our wedding between your next two trips. I'm sure Michelle knows a good drive-thru church. All we'd need to do is rent a car...."

That stopped him. "Look, Ange, I'm sorry if this was a little rushed. I'll make it up to you when I get back. Besides, we'll probably have some celebrating to do. Aren't you meeting with that agent on Monday about the contract?" he asked, raising his hand to hail a cab.

"Oh! That's another thing I need to talk to you about. I've decided not take the contract."

He dropped his hand and frowned. "Why?"

"Well, I spoke to Colin—you know he went into his negotiation on Friday, and according to Rena, we'd be getting pretty much the same contract. Anyway, he told me there's a no-compete clause in there. Meaning I can't perform in any other roles without the network's prior approval."

"And?" he asked, as if he still didn't understand.

"Well, that's certainly going to limit my other options, don't you think? I mean, I can't sign a three-year contract that limits my ability to accept other roles!"

He stared at me like I was a crazy woman. "You mean to tell me you would give up that money just on the *vague* hope that maybe someone else will want to cast you?"

"Vague hope?" I said, my anger rising. It suddenly occurred to me that the man I was going to marry, the man whom I'd put all my faith in, had no faith whatsoever in me. "I've been auditioning. I've sent out head shots. I want to do something else besides leap around with a bunch of kids!"

His eyes narrowed on me. "So you're not gonna sign."

"Don't you think I shouldn't?"

He snorted. "What are you gonna do instead? Spend your life waiting in line at auditions? Screaming at bodies falling from windows for a two-second minute of film in a DeNiro flick? Oh, wait, maybe you can get a theater role again. That way you can breathe in dust mites five nights a week while playing a role only two percent of the population will ever see!"

His words brought out all my fears. Until I remembered that I couldn't allow fear to stop me anymore. Besides, things were different now. *I* was different now. I understood better what it took to make it in this business—a commitment to the right opportunities. I saw something in myself now—something I wanted to believe in. And I wasn't the only one. There was that casting director who'd called me. And Justin. "Things are changing for me, Kirk. I had a casting director interested in me recently. I have an agent now—" At least, I hoped I had an agent, after I told Viveca my decision on Monday. But no matter what happened on Monday, I knew I had to try. I also knew I was going to need a lot of support—support I'd hoped the man I'd marry would give me. "I'm going to make it this time out. I know it," I said forcefully, the very words bringing me strength. "But I need someone who believes in me, who will stand by me. That's what getting married is about, Kirk. Being there for the person you love, no matter what."

He shook his head. "Oh, I get it. You run around playing at acting while I break my ass making money, so that when you realize you're never gonna get anywhere, you have someone to fall back on. That's a great gig, Ange. Where do I sign? Oh, and by the way, who is going to raise our children while you're running around tilting at windmills? Because one of us is going to have to work for a living if we hope to have anything."

My eyes widened at his words. "So that's how it works? I'm supposed to be there waiting at home for you to be a big success while I raise your children!" Suddenly I was so sure I didn't want to have those children he professed to want. At least, not with *him*. And with that thought came another—I didn't love him enough. And he didn't love me. Not enough.

That thought hurt the most. So much so that the pain began to flow through me, and I was crying. Crying! Because I knew that if I married Kirk, I would never get anything I wanted out of life. That thought made me so, so sad.

And my tears, apparently, made Kirk so, so mad. "C'mon, Ange. Does everything have to be a big fucking drama?"

"Drama?" I asked, my sorrow turning to anger.

He sighed, shook his head. "Look, let's just forget about this for now. We'll talk when I get back. I have a plane to catch. I don't have time for this bullshit."

"This *bullshit* is my life! And I don't think I should settle for less. In life. In a ring—"

"Oh, so that's what this is about? You're just mad at me right now because I don't want to drop ten grand on a ring?"

"It's not about the ring, you idiot!"

"Now I'm an idiot, that's great. You know, I feel like an idiot. I don't even know what I'm doing here. You're the one who was so hyped up about getting married. Now all of a sudden you have all these conditions."

"The only condition I ever asked was that you love me."

He sighed. "You know I love you, Angie."

I shook my head. "Not enough. And I don't love you enough to settle for less than everything."

"Look, can't we just talk about this when I get back? I have a plane to catch—"

"There's nothing to talk about, Kirk," I said, a new resolve filling me despite the intensity of my pain. "It's over."

"So that's how you want to play it?" he said, anger lighting his eyes. He shook his head. "You're a fool, Angie." Then, raising his hand in the air again, he said, "I gotta go. I have a real life I need to be getting on with."

And with that, he jumped into the first cab that rolled up, slamming the door behind him as the cab darted quickly away.

Leaving me standing in the midst of all those glittering lights as the last flicker of every feeling I'd ever had for Kirk died away.

At least I thought every feeling had died. But apparently not. Because as I rode home in a taxi to my apartment, I began to cry even harder. It was over, I thought. Really over. Things would never be the same. I was no longer the same. But whether I was better was debatable at the moment, judging by the fountain pouring out of my eyes.

By the time the cab rolled up in front of my apartment, I was a mess. So much so that even the cab driver passed a box of Kleenex through the partition. His unexpected kindness made me cry even more. I reached out to grab a tissue, thanking him profusely. "Oh, it's my pleasure," he said, beaming a crooked smile at me. "It's not every day I get to drive around a big celebrity like you, Ms. Tomei."

I started to bawl even harder, which made the cabbie so nervous, he handed me the whole box of Kleenex. I, of course, handed it back, once I'd pulled myself together, paid my fare, and autographed "Marisa Tomei" in my best forgery on the receipt paper he handed me. At least I could feed someone's illusions, I rationalized. Because mine were completely gone.

When I finally made my way up to the apartment, Justin was there. On sofa #3. But rather than holding the remote in his hand, he held his guitar, looking every bit as happy as the night before. Until he saw me walk through the door.

"What happened?" he asked, immediately putting down the guitar and looking at me in alarm.

"I…Kirk…we…we broke up!" I said, throwing myself into Justin's arms as I erupted in a new avalanche of tears, which I promptly soaked Justin's T-shirt with while I sobbed out my tale of woe. How we had been shopping for rings (this caused his eyes to widen—I guess Justin didn't think things had gotten that far), how I told Kirk why I didn't want to sign the contract.

How he had, in a few short sentences, reduced my every hope and dream into a hopeless waste of time.

By the time I was done, I felt a calm descend over me that I had not felt for a long, long time. But like every calm I ever felt, it was immediately followed by an anxious flicker of doubt.

"Please tell me I did the right thing, Justin. That I didn't just throw away my whole...future."

"Of course you did the right thing," he said, taking my hands in his and looking into my eyes. "You don't want a guy like that, Ange." Then he smiled. "Besides, you could never marry a Red Sox fan." He peered at me to see if he had provoked the smile he had hoped for.

I didn't disappoint him, but my grin was halfhearted. Even though I felt lighter now that I had unleashed my burden, I was still scared.

"What am I going to do now?" I asked, realizing that in the course of a weekend, I had decided to wipe my life clean of both a boyfriend and a career.

"What are you going to do?" he asked, taking my face in his two big hands. "You're going to go out there and be the star you were meant to be."

I knew he was trying to comfort me, but the thought of going out there and suffering more rejection only filled me with more sadness.

"But am I going to be happy?" I asked him, gazing into those green, green eyes as if I could find the answer there.

"I would never let you be otherwise," he said, gazing back at me steadily.

I believed him in that moment. He seemed so sure. I guess he had reason to be sure. I mean, in his own life everything came so easily to Justin. He wanted to make a film, he made a film— and gets an award. He wanted to be an actor, so he landed a commercial spot that heaps residuals on him and buys him all the time in the world to be anything he wants. He wants to be a musician; he gets up on stage and wows the crowd. Things were just...easier for Justin. Did he realize how *not* easy they were for me?

As if he read my mind, he said, "You can be anything you want, Ange. You're smart. Talented. And beautiful."

I was sure "beautiful" was not a word that could possibly describe how I must have looked in that moment—puffy-eyed, mascara-streaked. But the way Justin was looking at me, I believed it. I would have believed anything in that moment. Except what happened next.

Because suddenly Justin's mouth was on mine, kissing me like I *was* the most beautiful woman on earth.

And I discovered something I didn't know about my roommate. He had the softest lips I had ever tasted. So I kept on tasting them. Until he parted them, and his tongue was tangling with mine so tenderly I felt a fresh wave of emotion wash over me.

Opening my eyes, I found myself staring into Justin's. "What are we doing?" I asked.

"I have no idea," he whispered, eyes wide. But in typical Justin fashion, he gave in to the chaos of the moment. And suddenly I was pulling off clothes even faster than he was. It was like a challenge. Or a revelation. For as long as I had lived with Justin, I had never seen him quite like this. I mean, bare chested he was always amazing. But naked, he was…glorious. And he clearly thought *I* was pretty glorious, too, once he had helped me off with my bra and panties (I had gotten a little shy at that point) and he lay on the sofa beside me, leaning away from me just to look at me.

"Ange, I always knew you were pretty hot, but damn," he said, his eyes roaming over my stomach, my breasts, as if he were seeing them for the first time. And I guess, technically, he was. Then, as if *he* had suddenly gotten shy, he looked up at my face, seemingly asking permission to touch. I think I must have nodded frantically, because suddenly his hands were caressing my breasts, my hips, my thighs as his lips came down on mine.

It was almost painful when he started to move down my body, as if he was trying to record every curve, every beauty mark (and I had quite a few), with mouth and hands. By the time he reached my lower abs, I almost cried out. And when he reached Avenue A, I did.

How did I ever think I could live without *this?* I thought, as his tongue moved on me in a pleasurable rhythm. Then I wasn't thinking anything anymore. I was just…living.

And the living was good. So good it was almost scary. Even more scary when he moved up my body again, then finally—finally!—slid inside. The feel of him surprised me at first. I realized that, in this regard at least, Justin was a stranger to me. But once those green eyes were locked on mine as our bodies moved in time to each other, it felt like...coming home.

18

Love happens. (And there really is nothing you can do about it.)

Whenever I thought about the fact that I had (nearly) pledged my life to a man who understood me less than his doorman probably did, I had to ask myself the question: What was I *thinking?* But over the wildly euphoric weeks that followed, I only asked myself the question twice. First, of course, was when Justin gave me a refresher course on the glory of downtown loving (was there *anything* he wasn't good at?). The second time was when I was having dinner with Grace, during which I confessed that not only had I passed Go and *not* collected my engagement ring from Kirk, but that I was having a torrid affair with the man who had been living right under my nose for two years. And it *was* torrid. I think in the few weeks since that fateful night, we had made love on every piece of furniture that could sustain us, and even a few that didn't (I never did like that Early American desk anyway). And I do not use the words "made love" loosely. Because having sex was what I'd been doing with Kirk. I knew now that while all that premeditated button-pushing that he passed off as lovemaking could certainly make me come (I had no problems in this area), it could never get me where I really needed to go.

"You're in love with Justin," Grace said, smiling at me over her glass of wine as if she'd just revealed a secret.

"Love?" I echoed. I wanted to protest, but I couldn't. I was, in fact, completely and wholeheartedly in love with my sofa-hoarding, career-jumping, green-eyed roommate.

And there was nothing I could do about it. Trust me, if there was, I would have. Because I was scared shitless. I felt like I had been swallowed whole by a tornado—because that's the only way I can describe the way Justin loved—fully, completely, recklessly.

During those terrifying weeks, I found myself reduced to a shivering mess when he came home late—believing he had been killed in some random mugging (the way he was always cheerfully opening his wallet midstreet to give some homeless guy some money, he was a veritable robbed-at-knifepoint waiting to happen), or worse, seduced by one of those endless females who admired him wherever we went. I know, I know—killed at knifepoint should have seemed worse, but somehow I was in this kind of crazy state of mind where his demise seemed preferable to his abduction by some random leggy blonde.

I was, in short, a mess. So much so that I flew into a fury one night while we were lying in bed and one of those infamous husky-voiced females purred into our answering machine (we had resorted to chronic screening—we didn't want to be disturbed). When Justin saw the state that phone call put me in, he must have called every woman he knew the very next day and told them to stay away, because suddenly the phone hardly even rang.

Oh, wait, it did ring, but it was usually my mother, whom I had promptly told that I had broken up with Kirk (as you can imagine, she was delighted). But she was suspicious of my new-found cheerfulness, as I was afraid to reveal the cause. Afraid to admit the truth for fear it might somehow make it…untrue.

Yes, you could say I was in love. And it was terrible.

And wonderful.

Because I suddenly had a new energy in me that sent me pounding the pavement with an awesome fervor, especially now that my *Rise and Shine* days were over. In fact, I had already been replaced by an even more limber and somewhat perkier version of myself. Or Marisa Tomei. Because this girl looked just like me, except she was Hispanic. According to Rena, who was none too happy when I bowed out at the last moment, the only thing the network had liked about me was the ethnic component I added to the show. I'll give her ethnic. Right up her skinny little gluteus maximus.

At least someone noticed my new energy—Viveca Withers, who took my rejection of the *Rise and Shine* contract a bit better than I expected. In fact, my newfound vigor might have reinvigorated her. I think I even saw those sewn-up features move into a genuine smile when I told her (with much greater force this time) that I couldn't do *Rise and Shine* if it meant I never got the chance to shine again as an actor. And so, with little argument, she added me to her considerable roster of actors. I realized then that people will believe whatever you project to them. When I had first met Viveca, I was likely looking for someone to tell me to give up before it was too late. But it wasn't too late. In fact, I immediately impressed Viveca after I went to an audition she sent me on for a daytime soap. I hadn't gotten the role, but I had gotten great feedback. I impressed her even further when she had been contacted by none other than Robert Foley, who happened to be the casting director for whom I auditioned for *All for Love*. I had taken the liberty of sending him my résumé, updated with my agent info, along with a note saying that I hoped he'd keep me in mind for future opportunities. He not only kept me in mind, he called Viveca almost immediately, saying he had just heard from a producer he'd been waiting on. Seems the show Robert Foley thought I had potential for was a pilot being proposed for next fall on *Lifetime.* Get this—Robert Foley thought I had expressed what he called an "edgy mixture of desperation and vulnerability" during my audition (he should only know). So much edgy desperation and vulnerability that he wanted me to try out for a new nighttime drama series featuring a tough-talking single mother of two who joins the NYPD after her husband is mysteriously killed in the line of duty. Me, tough! (I think it was my muscular arms that made *that* convincing) And a mother! If you think that's amazing, what was even more amazing was how I aced the audition, with the help of Justin, who was a taskmaster when it came to helping me prepare. I was still waiting to hear a week later, but I felt hopeful.

"Hey, sweetie," Justin said when I came home from my seven-hour shift at Lee and Laurie. I found him in the kitchen, where he was making a marinara sauce. You know how I said he was a killer in the kitchen? Now I got a fresh, hot meal when I came home, followed by a fresh, hot man. What was I *thinking?*

Okay, that's three times I asked myself that question.

Justin leaned away from the pot he was stirring, then kissed me as though he hadn't seen me in seven weeks rather than seven hours.

"So how was work?" he asked, replacing the lid on the pot.

"The usual drudgery. But at least Michelle is speaking to me again." Oh yeah, get this—Michelle had been giving me the silent treatment ever since I returned from my little shopping spree with Kirk sans engagement ring—and boyfriend. But she was over it now. Probably because Justin had stopped by the office on the way home from a production gig he'd been working on, to say hello. Michelle took one look at him and reset her sights. Or, rather, my sights. "You know what you gotta do, Ange," she said, once he left. Yeah, sure. There was no room for games in my relationship with Justin. I didn't need them. All I needed was him. And I had him, night after night after night.

In fact, I had him again after a candlelit Italian dinner, Justin-style. Afterward, I lay beside him in his bed, feeling utterly satisfied. So secure…so *loved*. And I knew Justin was feeling the same way. I could see it in the way he looked at me. The way he was looking at me right now.

"So I talked to my friend, Sammy, today," he said, smoothing the hair away from my cheek as he spoke softly in the flickering candlelight. "You remember, Sammy, right? He was taking classes at HB Studios with us. He came to see me at the Back Fence that night, but he had to leave right after the set, so I didn't really get a chance to catch up with him."

"Oh yeah, I think I do remember him," I said. "Little guy, right? And funny as hell. Whatever happened to him?"

"Well, he just got back about a month ago from Vegas, where he's been doing the stand-up comedy circuit for the past year—

you know, casinos, night clubs, that type of thing. He thought the Bernadette stuff was hilarious. He thinks I could be the next Adam Sandler. So I'm thinking about working up some more material and giving it a try."

"Giving what a try?" I asked, baffled as to what new course Justin was about to set his life on.

"Well, stand-up comedy."

"Stand-up comedy?" I said with disbelief. I mean, yeah, some of those Bernadette songs were pretty funny, but I didn't think the humor was *intentional*.

"But what about music? You were just getting somewhere with that," I said, exasperated at this latest career maneuver.

"Yeah, well, you know music was never my first love anyway."

Now we were getting to the heart of the matter. "And what, may I ask, is your first love?"

He sighed. "Well, film, of course."

It was a relief to realize that I had, at least, been right all along about where Justin's true happiness lay. Maybe that was why he hadn't been pursuing much of anything since his success at the Back Fence. But I was even more baffled now that he had confirmed it. Because it seemed to me that ever since I'd known him, Justin had been doing everything *but* following that dream. "So why aren't you making a film?" I asked.

"I *made* a film, Angie," he said, an underlying anger in his tone that I had never heard before. "I gave everything I had to it, and look where it got me."

"It got you an award. It got the industry interested in you. It might have gotten even further if you hadn't jumped ship and gone into acting."

"If I hadn't jumped ship," he said, "I wouldn't have met you."

A warmth curled inside me at his words. Followed by a new determination. I couldn't let the man I loved lead an unfulfilled life. "Justin, you can't leave your life to chance. If you want something, you have to make a commitment to it."

"I made a commitment once, to the movie. Of time, of money—"

"If it's money you're worried about, then you can get investors. All you have to do is show your reel to the right people—"

"It's not *money,*" he insisted, then laughed mirthlessly. "I have more damn money than I know what to do with. Between all the residuals on those crazy commercials I did, and my trust fund—"

"Trust fund?" I asked, confused.

"From my parents," he explained, his voice softer. "They had considerable assets when they…when they died. A couple of properties, life insurance. My uncle put it all in trust for when I turned twenty-one. Though I haven't really touched it yet. It's really all I…all I have left of them."

Suddenly I understood Justin in a way I never had. The trust fund he hoarded. All that French provincial furniture that cluttered up our apartment from his aunt and uncle, along with the new acquisitions he brought in on a regular basis. It was as if all that…stuff was some kind of crazy security blanket. It was like he attached himself to things rather than people. Maybe because he had lost so many of the people he loved the most.

"Justin, what are you afraid—"

"I'm *not* afraid, Angie. I'm just trying to be happy."

"But you have to make choices if you want to be happy! And if film is what you truly want, then that's what you should pursue."

"I can't go through that again, Ange. Seeing that film get shelved after all that work was heartbreaking. I gotta move on. And I have a good feeling about this comedy thing. Once I get to Vegas—"

"*Vegas?*"

"Yeah. I'm gonna fly out there with Sammy when he goes back in a month. He says I can even stay with him while he shows me the ropes."

"I don't understand—New York has comedy clubs. Why can't you pursue it here?"

"Sammy's got contacts. Besides, you know how tough the New York crowds are. I'm gonna try and make a name for myself out there and then I'll come back."

"But what about your…job?"

"Pete's got plenty of grips he can use while I'm out of town. He only offers jobs to me first because we're friends."

"But what about me?" I asked now, the question that had been clawing at my gut finally rising up.

He looked at me then. "We can still be together. There's the telephone. E-mail. And I'll be back eventually. I figure it'll only take me six months, maybe a year...."

A year! "Justin!"

"What?"

"Don't you see what you're doing?"

"What am I doing?" he asked, bewildered.

"You're running. From your dreams. From...from me!"

"Angie, I'm not running from you. We'll still be together...."

"Together like you were with Lauren? Or Denise?" I said. "Let me ask you something, Justin, when exactly did you fall in love with either one of those women, huh? Right after you found yourself hundreds of miles away from them?"

"This isn't the same as that, Angie——"

"Why isn't it?" I said, sitting up and looking fiercely into his eyes. "Because if you stay in this apartment with me another month, another year, you might just—God forbid—really start to care for me?"

"Oh, I see what this is about," he said, shaking his head. "You think if I stay here and...and *marry* you, that will make us happy?" He shook his head. "I don't understand why women think marriage is the answer to everything."

"You think this is about me wanting to get married?" I asked, incredulous. "I'm in love with you, you idiot! And you know what, if you proposed, I'd probably be stupid enough to say yes, that's how much I want to be with you. But do you think I *want* to spend my life with a man with a larger sofa collection than Levitz warehouse? No, I don't. You scare the shit out of me, Justin. You have ever since I met you. But as soon as this——" I gestured to the tangle of sheets at the end of the bed "——started happening, I couldn't control what I felt for you anymore. I couldn't stop myself from loving you, sofas and all!"

"Well I love you, too, dammit!" he yelled, as if the very admission made him...angry. "I love you more than I've ever loved anyone in my life, Angie. Nothing can change that. Just like my going to Vegas won't change what we feel. That's why I *know* we can make this work."

"It can't work, Justin. It can't." I was so sure of that now. *We* couldn't work, not as long as Justin kept running from everything he professed to love.

So I did the only thing I could do. *I* ran. And no amount of arguing could stop me (and we did a lot of that). I packed whatever I could grab during the sad, mystifying squabble that followed, and left.

I finally understood why I had kept myself a safe distance for so long from the one man I could truly love.

Because I had known, probably from the very beginning, he was the only man who had the power to break my heart.

I hailed a cab, not even sure where I was going. But the moment the driver asked me for an address, I gave him Grace's. I only prayed she was home. And alone.

Thankfully, she was both. "Angie, what's wrong?" she said when she answered the door and saw what must have been pure grief in my eyes.

"It's over, Grace. Me and Justin. He's going to Vegas. To be a fucking stand-up comic. Isn't that a laugh?"

"Come in, let me make you a drink."

Once we were seated on the couch, Bacardi O Cosmos in hand, I told her the whole story. And when I was done, Grace said, "To tell you the truth, Ange, I'm surprised. This doesn't sound like Justin. I mean, the career-jumping thing, yeah. But I thought if nothing else, Justin was pretty devoted to you. He always had been as a friend."

"That's just it, Grace. The minute we went beyond that, he got scared. I mean, I was scared, too, but at least I was willing to take a chance on it."

"Yeah, well. That's men for you," she said, a weariness coming into her eyes. "When it comes down to it, you really can't count on them for anything."

Her words made me even sadder. "But there must be some men out there you can count on." Suddenly Drew entered my mind, and though I knew Grace would be none too happy to hear me invoke his name, I had to know why she had given up the one man who seemed like someone she *could* count on.

"What about Drew, Grace? I know you haven't wanted to

talk about him, but I need to understand why you gave him up when he seemed so devoted to you?"

"Yeah, he was devoted. But not devoted to *me*—only to the *idea* of me."

"What does that mean?"

"It means he didn't want to deal with who I really am, Ange."

"How do you know that, Grace? If I know you, you probably didn't let him in."

"Oh, I let him in, all right. I told you about it—how I let Drew know about my biological mother."

"But you said he didn't care."

"He did care, Ange. More than I realized." She sighed, and I saw she was ready to give in and tell me everything she had been holding back about her breakup. "I know I didn't want to admit it—even to you—but things *were* getting serious with Drew. Right after we went to see his boss's new house in Westport, he started talking about marriage and…and babies. And I started thinking that's what I wanted, too, you know? But I couldn't commit to it—couldn't have *children*—without knowing about my own mother."

My heart started to beat faster. Grace had finally contacted her mother! I felt a fleeting sadness that she hadn't turned to me during what was probably the scariest thing she'd ever done, but that was so Grace. "What was she like?" I asked now. "I mean, did you meet with her? Talk with her on the phone?"

"Well, *no*," she replied. "I mean, I was going to, but I was scared, you know? So I talked to Drew about it one night, and if you think *I* was freaked, *he* was even more. He thought I should just forget about her. He was…afraid, Angie. Afraid she might be someone he didn't want to know. A gold digger. Or a tramp. And then he starts looking at me like maybe *I'm* someone he might not want to know—"

Her voice broke, and I saw that her eyes were glassy with unshed tears. "I think after I first told him about her, he thought we could just sweep it under the carpet and carry on. He only wanted to know what he saw on the surface: Grace Noonan, daughter of a retired professor and a music teacher. He didn't want to go…deeper. He didn't want to know *me*. But I had to know."

"So did you contact her?"

She looked at me then, and I saw a paralyzing fear in her eyes. "Well, no. I mean, I couldn't after…after that. I mean, what if he's right, Ange, what if she's someone I don't want to know? Or what if she doesn't want to know me?"

It was then that she broke, tears streaming down her face uncontrollably, which was something for Grace. I had never, in all my life, seen her cry the way she was sobbing now. It scared me. And filled me with a sadness so deep I wanted to cry myself. I wish I had known she was in such pain. I wish I could have done something.

I could do something now, I thought, taking Grace in my arms and holding her until she had cried out everything she had in her. I'm not sure how long we sat there that way, but when she finally looked up again, she smiled. "Well, what a pair we are. I think it's going to take a case of Roxanne Dubrow eye cream to get the puffiness out of our eyes."

I smiled back. "Lucky for us, you probably have a case of it in that medicine cabinet of yours."

"Yeah, that I do," she said, then she sighed, staring around her pretty apartment as if nothing in that room could ever make her happy again.

"Gracie, I know you don't want to hear it right now. But I think you need to contact your mother for yourself. You need to know. *Don't,*" I said, raising a hand as she opened her mouth to argue. "Just listen to me—it's the only way you're going to get past this pain. It's the only way you're going to heal."

The fight drained out of her, and she looked down at her hands, which she'd clasped in her lap. "I'll think about it, okay? But that's all I'm promising."

"That's all I'm asking," I said. "For now." Then I smiled at her again. "Well, that and another cocktail. Now where are you hiding the Bacardi O? I think we both could use another drink…."

So we drank cosmopolitans and talked late into the night, just as we had done when we were teenagers—only then we were without the Bacardi O. I even prodded Grace into telling me about her escapades with Bad Billy, who, she told me, had disappeared again from her life, as expected.

"That's one thing good about Billy. At least I know going in I can't count on him," she said with a weary smile as we pulled her convertible sofa into a bed for me to sleep on.

"You always have me, Gracie," I said, looking at her once the last sheet had been laid on the bed. "You know that, right?"

"I know, I know," she said, standing up from where she had been smoothing the sheet and meeting my gaze. "Best buds, right?"

"Always."

In the days that followed, I was there for Grace. Literally. I had taken up residence on her sofa bed, and we spent a lot of late nights just sitting up and talking like we used to. Going shopping. (Yes, I shopped. What? A girl needs a few splurges to get herself through, right?) We even did a day of beauty at a spa near Grace's apartment. Well, I only got a facial—Grace went for the full package, and would have bought it for me, too, if I'd let her. Between her treatments, we lounged about in the (complimentary) whirlpool, talking about everything from high school boyfriends to first New York apartments (yes, Grace had had to suffer through roommates at one time, too, but of course none of *hers* had managed to break her heart). Getting Grace to talk about her heartbreaks—or her fears about taking that next step and contacting her mother—was a bit more difficult. In fact, all this togetherness was getting to her, I think. She was so fiercely independent, it was hard for her to be around someone who forced her to probe her inner psyche on a daily basis.

But I wasn't going to let up. I knew she needed someone. Maybe even someone other than me. "Grace, maybe you should go see your parents," I said, when we found ourselves up late again one night and Grace, in her usual fashion, had just brushed off my careful suggestion that she needed to get herself out of the emotional rut she was in. I knew her adoptive parents had always supported her decision to find her mother. They'd supported Grace in everything she did, even during those rebellious teenage years. They loved her, and I knew she needed to be around them, if only to be reminded of that fact.

"My parents aren't living nearby on Long Island anymore.

They moved to New Mexico—remember? The big retirement? The dream house in the desert?"

"So take some vacation—go visit them," I urged. "You must have some time coming to you."

Finally she gave in, whether because she was trying to get away from me, with my menacing questions about her emotional life, or because she finally understood that she did need to be in the soothing embrace of the people who loved and raised her. She booked a flight a few days later.

"What are you going to do?" she asked me, the night before she left, her bag packed and waiting by the door.

"I'm going to go back to my life."

Before Grace did finally leave, she assured me that I could stay with her as long as I wanted to. But I knew I couldn't stay there much longer. I had to do something to move myself forward.

And I had a few sofas—and a roommate—to face.

Because I had decided, in that week I had spent at Grace's, that if I couldn't be there for Justin as a lover, I still had to support him no matter what insane choices he made. Maybe it was all those voice mails he had left me on my cell phone, telling me my mother had called or that he'd read about a casting call in *Backstage* that he thought would be perfect for me.

I knew he was trying hard to be what he had always been to me. A friend.

So I had to try, too.

The moment I stepped through the apartment door, I knew he wasn't there. It was too…quiet. And the feeling that pervaded the place was that same loneliness I felt whenever Justin wasn't filling the rooms with his presence. But when I entered the living room, I realized he *had* filled that space with something. A tattered but pretty wingback chair now sat beside sofa #3. And what looked like a bird cage (sans bird, of course) sat on one of the end tables. Then there was the microwave I saw when I peeked into the kitchen (still hopeful that Justin might be in the apartment *somewhere*) stacked right on top of the one we already owned. I almost laughed. Clearly he had missed me, judging by the number of acquisitions he had made while I was gone, maybe in some vain attempt to fill up the emptiness I had left in my wake.

Suddenly I was looking forward to his coming home from wherever he had roamed. I needed to see him, to reaffirm that he was still the same Justin I knew and loved. That we could go back, somehow, to the friends we once were. I dropped my bag on sofa #3 and was just about to head into my bedroom when I noticed the windowsill was bare. Bernadette was gone.

And I knew that could only mean one thing: Justin was gone, too.

19

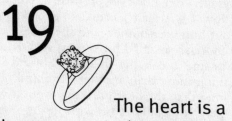

The heart is a hearty muscle (Thank God).

Knowing I couldn't possibly stay in that familiar space alone, I grabbed the rest of my head shots, my résumé and some more clothes, and went back to Grace's. For as empty as her apartment felt without her in it, it wasn't quite as unbearable as mine without Justin. Clearly he had gone on to start his new life without me—and even earlier than planned. And I knew I had to start mine.

I had a lot to do, too. Look for an apartment—because I knew now, there was no way I could live with Justin when he finally did come home from Vegas. Just the sight of the jeans he'd left tossed over a chair, his film collection overflowing the entertainment center, had brought me to tears as I gathered my things together. It was clear to me now that I had only myself to count on. That if I was going to make a commitment, it had to be to me.

So I called Viveca to check in, and she said she had some positive feedback on my audition for *Lifetime,* but no decision had been made yet. I figured that meant they had decided to audition a few hundred more actresses, each more talented and beautiful than the next. Still, the news that my audition had been well received lifted my spirits somewhat. Enough so I could call back my mother, whom I didn't share my news with (I was, as usual, afraid to jinx myself). I did, however, promise to come to dinner that Sunday. Now I was glad I hadn't told her about Justin. If she asked about him over dinner (and she usually did ask about him—even more so since I'd broken up with Kirk), I could just say he was fine and living in Las Vegas and she wouldn't see it as anything more than another delightful new adventure for Justin, rather than the heartbreaking event it was for me. But that was okay. If I couldn't be with Justin, I certainly didn't need him to fall out of my mother's good graces. I didn't want to ever go home to Brooklyn and find his picture missing from the Sacred Heart. Since he had moved himself so far from all that he knew, all that he loved, he would need all the protection he could get.

I don't know how I got through those first few days without Grace, now that Justin was as far from me as he had been in the four years I had known him. But I managed. It wasn't easy, especially when, during a vulnerable moment on Saturday at Lee and Laurie, I had spilled the news of my second heartbreak in as many months.

"Oh, Angie," Roberta said, her face creasing in sorrow. Then, after a moment, she continued, "Well, there's still time. If you meet someone in the next year, you could still possibly have kids before thirty-five...."

This was supposed to comfort me?

Michelle shook her head in disgust as she fingered the tennis bracelet Frankie had just gotten her for her birthday. Clearly she thought I was a lost cause.

"You're better off alone anyway," Doreen said with a somewhat righteous sniff.

Whether I was better off was debatable. But alone I was when I headed home to Grace's that night, a bag of Chinese takeout in hand, along with an early edition of the Sunday *Times,* which I knew I had to start reading if I hoped to find a new apartment before Justin got back. Whenever that might be.

But even after I had stuffed myself full of chicken lo mein, I couldn't bring myself to open up the real estate section. Instead, I found myself watching, of all things, the Miss America Pageant. I was surprised it was even on—I thought they had done away with this nonsense. But I realized why they hadn't when I found myself watching the whole ridiculous thing, swimsuit competition and all, and even found myself smiling stupidly when the current Miss America handed over her crown to Miss New York, who could barely contain her excitement as she did that runway walk, then returned to the host who held out the microphone as she pledged to spend her reign speaking on behalf of breast cancer survivors, tutoring disadvantaged children in the fight against illiteracy, and working with the Landmarks Preservation Society to make sure all that was great about New York City survived.

At least Justin would be happy....

Justin. I sighed, glancing at the newspaper, which still sat untouched on the coffee table. I was going to have to move to New Jersey—or maybe even farther—to escape this city, filled as it was with reminders of him.

As if in answer to an unspoken prayer, my cell phone started to ring. I leaped up from the couch, scrambling for my pocketbook and digging through. Maybe it was Justin, calling to tell me he was coming home, that he hated Las Vegas, that he needed to be in New York, close to all he held dear, close to me—

But when I finally located the phone at the bottom of the bag and looked at the call display, I saw that it was my mother.

"Why aren't you home? It's almost midnight!" she shrieked the moment I pushed the talk button.

My mother still became paralyzed with fear at the thought that I might venture past the three locks that bolted my apartment door and into my alleged dangerous neighborhood after dark. Now do you see why I don't ever tell her about my life? But I realized she must have been in some kind of panic to call me on my cell phone.

I sighed. "Ma, I'm at Grace's. And I already told you, I'll be there early tomorrow to help you cook. I'll even bring the sausage," I said, knowing my mother had stopped asking Nonnie to supply anything for her Sunday dinners because Nonnie would likely disappear on some illicit shopping spree—or God knows what else—with Artie.

"I'm not calling about sausage!" she cried. "I'm calling about your grandmother. Nonnie—my mama!—her heart is giving out, Angela! She had such pains!"

"Where are you?" I said, already pulling my jeans on over the boxers I wore and grabbing my sneakers.

"Kings County Hospital. And, please, Angela, take a cab—I don't want you on that subway at this hour—"

"All right! All right!" I said. "I'll be there as soon as I can."

It was the longest cab ride I've ever taken in my life. Not only because I was all the way uptown. But because I was scared out of my wits. Nonnie—my Nonnie! What if I didn't make it in time? What if—

I pulled out my cell phone. My first instinct was to call Justin. And I could have—I had his cell number programmed into my phone. I knew he could talk me down from the paralyzing heights of anxiety I had reached as the cab rolled over the Brooklyn Bridge.

But I didn't call him. I feared the very sound of his voice might put me in even more emotional turmoil. Instead, I called Grace, knowing it was three hours earlier in New Mexico and praying she'd left her cell phone on.

Thankfully, she had. "Hey, Angie, what's up?"

Maybe it was the sound of her warm, familiar voice, but suddenly I began to cry. "It's Nonnie, Grace. She's in the hospital. I think she may have had a…a heart attack."

"Oh, God, Angie. Have you seen her? Is she okay?"

"I'm on my way to Kings County Hospital right now. But I'm scared, Gracie. What if she's…she's gone by the time I get there? My mother sounded a bit…hysterical."

"Well, you know your mother does overreact, Ange. Besides, Nonnie's strong. She's a fighter. You remember how she used to arm-wrestle us when we were kids?"

"But that was a long time ago, Grace. She hasn't been taking care of herself. She eats whatever she wants. Does whatever she wants. You know she even has a…a boyfriend," I said, wondering if some late night "poker game" had been the cause of this little attack.

"Oh yeah?" She laughed. "You see that, she's gonna be fine. A woman randy enough to take on a boyfriend at her age has got spirit, Ange. Who's the lucky guy, anyway?"

"Artie Matarrazzo."

"Mr. Matarrazzo? That is so cute, Angie. I bet they make an adorable couple. See, she's gonna stick around. She's got a lot more living to do."

"But what if she's been doing a little...a little too much living? You know she did have an angioplasty a few years ago. Her heart can't take *too* much."

Grace was silent for a few moments, then said, "I wish I could be there with you. I'm coming home Monday night. I can see if I could get an earlier flight—"

"No, no—you don't have to do that. I'll be fine," I replied, gazing out the window at the empty streets we rolled down. "If I ever get there."

"Where's Justin? Maybe you should call him, Ange. You know he'd be there for you if you needed him...."

"I went to the apartment today—he wasn't there. He's probably in Vegas, but I don't know. I don't know anything about him anymore."

"Well, you have me, you know that?"

"I know," I said, seeing the lights of Kings County Hospital up in the distance. "It looks like we're almost there, Grace. I...I gotta go."

"Call me if you need me, okay?"

"Okay."

I hated hospitals in general, and this one in particular, as it was the one my father had frequented during his last days. And maybe it was the memory of that loss that scared me even more as I rode the elevator to the Intensive Care Unit, which was where, the receptionist at the information desk told me, my grandmother was.

I was reminded even more of my father when I came off the elevator and saw almost my entire family—and a somewhat woeful-looking Artie Matarrazzo—taking up the small waiting area. Sonny paced the hall, coffee cup in hand. He almost smiled when he saw me. Then, probably remembering why I was here, simply hugged me as I approached. After asking after Vanessa, whom I learned Sonny had forced to stay home because he didn't want her to have so much stress so close to her due date, I went over and hugged Joey and Miranda, before turning to Artie, who practically sobbed as he embraced me and said, "We were just playing cards, honest!"

Finally I headed to my grandmother's room, and I took a certain comfort in the sight of my mother, rosary beads in hand, leaning over the bed.

"Ma," I whispered as I approached and she whirled around, her eyes tired, almost resigned to the scene before her. Still she hugged me fiercely, then held my hand as I turned to look at Nonnie.

Nonnie looked like she was asleep and, I might have thought, peacefully, if not for the tubes that came out of her nose and the patch of wires hooked to her body.

"How is she?" I asked my mother, but she only shook her head.

"Not good," she said, gazing at me with worry in her eyes. "Not good, Angela."

Fortunately, I had lived long enough with my mother not to rely on her gloom-and-doom reports. So when the on-duty doctor came by to make his rounds, I pulled him aside to get what I hoped would be a more accurate report on my grandmother's condition.

"Well, preliminary tests show congestive heart failure," he told me with a reassuring smile. "Of course, she's not out of the woods yet. That's why we've got her in ICU. We'll monitor her through the night, and then run a few more tests in the morning." Then, glancing down the hall and catching sight of my mother—who had just left my grandmother's room—one hand crushing a handkerchief to her eyes, the other still grasping the rosary beads, he continued, "Your grandmother is under good care. It's your mother I'm worried about. Maybe you should take her home, see that she gets some rest."

I was so relieved, I could have kissed him. In fact, he was

pretty good-looking, and I'm sure my Nonnie would have condoned it. But, instead, I went back to my grandmother's room, and after kissing her cool forehead and saying a quick prayer, with the assistance of my brothers and Miranda, I dragged my mother out of the hospital, where she otherwise might have stayed all night.

Sonny drove me and my mother home. Artie had his own car, though I was worried that an eighty-six-year-old man shouldn't be driving at all, much less at night. But Joey and Miranda promised to follow Artie to his house, to make sure he made it all right. And after finally convincing my mother to go to bed—she tried desperately to feed me, but I couldn't bear to eat a morsel—I spent a restless night of sleep in my old bedroom, surrounded by photos of my father, the Sacred Heart looming over me from the far wall.

When I awoke, I called the hospital first thing. Happily, I learned that the electrocardiogram and chest X rays revealed normal heart function and no permanent damage. In fact, my grandmother was being moved to a private room that afternoon and would probably be released in a few days.

My mother, of course, was not convinced, and insisted on stopping at church on the way to the hospital, to light a candle.

Ma must have asked for a miracle—and gotten it—because when we got to the hospital, my grandmother was not only sitting up in bed in her new room, but had a hand of cards in her well-manicured fingers and a handsome young man in blue scrubs sitting bedside, holding a hand of cards himself.

"Nonnie!" I said, relieved to see her awake, alert and, judging from the four aces she laid down on the small table before her, up to her old tricks again.

"Angela!" she called out, forgetting her cards for the moment and reaching out her arms to me.

I moved quickly into her embrace, relishing the feel of her in my arms.

My mother moved in next, quickly planting a kiss on Nonnie's cheek and then grabbing up the cards from the table. "What is this, Ma? C'mon! You're in no condition!" But I could see from the soft look in her eyes as she shoved the cards back into the box that she was relieved to see my grandmother was practically back to normal.

Nonnie sighed. "Okay, Oscar, we'll have to pick this game up later," she said, turning to the young man. "But, remember, that's two Jell-Os you owe me now." Her eyelashes were fluttering in what looked suspiciously like a batting motion.

Oscar stood, laughing. "Okay, Mrs. Caruso, you win. But that's all the hands I can play today. Besides, I don't even know if you're allowed Jell-O on your meal plan."

"I'd trade it all for one frozen Snickers," she said with a heartfelt sigh.

"Never mind, Mrs. C. Never mind," he said with another chuckle, and with a nod to us, he disappeared.

"How you feeling?" my mother demanded.

"I'm fine! I don't know what everybody's getting so excited about."

My mother shook her head. "I'm gonna find the doctor. We'll see how fine you are."

Once she left the room, Nonnie turned to me. "Angela, it's so good to see you. You haven't been around much lately…."

I felt a stab of guilt. "I'm sorry, Nonnie, I—"

"Don't worry about it! You're young. You need to be going out and having a good time. And you are having a good time, aren't you? Now that that Kirk's out of the picture? Not that I didn't like him, but I think he might have been too much of a stick-in-the-mud for you."

"I'm doing okay. But how are you doing, Nonnie? Ma says you haven't been taking care of yourself. Not eating right. Staying up late with…with Artie."

She rolled her eyes. "Your mother's a worrywart. Besides, it was a good thing Artie was over. It was him that called the ambulance. Your mother was too busy having one of her panic attacks."

"She loves you, Nonnie. She worries—"

"I know, I know. I love her, too. I just wish she'd get outta my hair. I'm a grown woman, and she treats me like a child. And Artie—she isn't very nice to him either. But he's working on her. You know, he helped her with the tomato plants this summer. In fact, you just missed him. But he's coming back. I sent him on a little errand."

I smiled. God, I wished I could be Nonnie. It seemed even at her age, she had men at her beck and call. I didn't even have a man to call at all.

Or so I thought. Because just as I sat talking with Nonnie, I suddenly saw her eyes go round. I was just about to push the emergency button for fear she was having another attack, when her lips broke into a wide smile—a flirtatious smile, which, when it came to Nonnie, could only mean one thing.

"Hello, you handsome devil, you!"

I turned around to see what man had piqued her interest now, and *I* almost had a heart attack. None other than Justin was standing in the doorway, in a pair of faded jeans, a Yankees T-shirt and a smile from ear to ear. "Nonnie!" he said. "Look at you in the hospital! Has there been some mistake? You look fantastic!" He bounded into the room and gave her the hug she was waiting for.

"God, Justin, we haven't seen you in a dog's age. Where've you been?"

"Oh, that granddaughter of yours. She's been making me nuts, you know?" he said, turning to me finally and crouching beside the chair where I sat.

He pressed a kiss to my lips, which I saw over his shoulder made Nonnie's eyes go wide with delight. "How are you, Ange?"

"I'm…I'm good. How are *you?*" I asked, questions filling my mind. "I thought you were…you were gone."

"Well, I'm back. Grace called me last night, told me what was going on. I took the first flight I could get. I went to the house, but no one was there. So I came straight here. I was worried about Nonnie—about you…."

"How could you get back from Vegas so fast?" I asked, still in shock, though it was beginning to be replaced by the warmest feeling as I gazed into those green eyes I adored.

"Oh, I wasn't in Vegas—I was in Chicago," he said, as if that explained everything, then stood to look at Nonnie again.

"So how is my best girl?" he said, giving her the grin that had won Nonnie's heart from the moment she had first laid eyes on Justin, when I had dragged him home for family dinner two years ago.

"Better now," she said. "All these good-looking men around. You should see my doctor. What a hunk!"

And as if on cue, said doctor strolled into the room, my mother in tow. "You tell her, Dr. Williamson. Because she won't listen to me—oh, Justin! What are you doing here?" Ma said, her eyes wide as Justin stepped forward and wrapped her in a hug.

"Why wouldn't I be here?" he said, smiling down at her as he released her.

Even Dr. Williamson seemed happy to see Justin, but I think this might have been because Nonnie's hunky M.D. was likely of Colin's persuasion. But he contained himself, of course, and once everyone had settled down, Dr. Williamson explained to Nonnie—to all of us—that her heart was still in good shape and would stay that way, but only with a proper diet and exercise. "And, um, your daughter mentioned something about late-night poker games, Mrs. Caruso. I don't know how to put this, but maybe you might want to start them a little earlier in the evening. And perhaps, uh, lower the stakes?"

"Oh, Dr. Williamson, she worries too much!"

"Well, someone's gotta worry about you," Dr. Williamson said with a wink. "You're lucky you have so many people to care about you," he added seriously, before he made his good-byes.

And it was clear Nonnie had plenty of people to worry over her, because within the next hour, practically my whole crazy family had filed into that tiny room, with Sonny keeping an eye on the nurse's station to make sure we didn't get thrown out for having too many visitors. Everyone was relieved to see Nonnie in such good spirits. And the rest of my family had been just as surprised and happy to see Justin as Nonnie and my mother had been.

Sonny and Vanessa showed up first. Vanessa had refused to stay away, despite the arguments Sonny gave her. In truth, she was so big with child, I thought they should have just given her a bed so she could wait it out. Joey and Miranda came, too. Miranda had dropped the kids off with her mom, and now, as she stood talking quietly with my mother in one corner of the room, I realized she was making big headway as far as my mother was concerned. I guess if nothing else, this family drama may just have gotten Miranda into my mother's heart.

And Artie might have found his way in, too, I realized, when he came back to the room breathless from his mission for Nonnie and carrying a brown paper bag, which my grandmother snatched from him and promptly stuffed in her drawer.

But not before my mother saw. "Ma! What was that? Artie, what are you up to?"

Then, marching over to the drawer, she grabbed the bag and opened it, her eyes widening. "I demand an explanation for this," she said, pulling out what looked like a chocolate éclair.

"It's fat- and sugar-free!" Artie insisted, earning a shocked glare from Nonnie.

"I know you wanted the Snickers bar, sweetheart, but I just couldn't get it for you. We want you around for a long, long time." Then he smiled down at her, taking her hand in between his two. "*I* want you around for a long, long time."

"Oh, Artie, you old rascal," Nonnie said, smiling as she rested her hand over his.

Finally we were ordered out of the room and I was glad. Not only because Nonnie had begun to look a bit tired, but because I couldn't wait to get Justin alone. I wanted to talk to him. To know what had taken him to Chicago and if he would be leaving for Vegas soon. But my mother insisted we all go back to the house for dinner. I could barely eat the lasagna she had tossed into the oven the moment we arrived, but Justin was eating enough for both of us, yukking it up with my brothers, gazing in wonder at Vanessa, even pressing his hand to her stomach to experience the baby's now-furious kicks. Next he was trading baseball stats with Artie, who, as it turned out, was a Yankee fan, too. By the time my mother whipped out the tiramisu, I scarfed down two slices just to get dessert over with. I think Ma knew something was up, because she kept glancing at me every time my eyes strayed to Justin's handsome face, which was often.

And just when I thought Justin and I would make a safe escape to the Avenue U bus together and alone—well, at least surrounded by strangers who could make what they would of the conversation I planned to have with him—Joey gallantly offered to drive us back to Manhattan in his '67 Cadillac, which he couldn't resist giving Justin a ride in once he discovered Justin's appreciation for Joey's careful salvaging and restoration of the old car. Justin, of course, joyously agreed. So while I sat in the back seat with Miranda, listening to her babble on about Timmy and Tracy, I watched Justin examine the dash with gusto and listen avidly as Joey painstakingly described every piston he'd replaced, every dent he'd knocked out. Guys…sheesh!

We did get home—eventually (there was traffic—there's *always* traffic)—and by the time Justin and I stepped into the apartment together, I was burning up inside—and with more than just questions.

"Justin what—" I began, once we were safely inside the living room.

He stopped me, trapping my face between his big hands and kissing me so deeply, I found my knees buckling beneath me until he swept me up, dropped me right down on sofa #3 and pressed that beautiful body into mine.

"I missed you so much," he said once he came up for air. "Why didn't you return my calls?"

"Why didn't I—Justin! I thought you were leaving me. I came home and you weren't here. Even…even Bernadette was gone!" I said, glancing over at the windowsill in confusion and seeing it was still bare. "Where's Bernadette?"

He smiled. "I took her over to Pete's while I was gone. I would've let Tanya take care of her, except I noticed she had this half-dead ficus the last time I was over there. But Bernadette's in good hands with Pete. Did you know he used to work in a nursery during college?"

"Never mind Pete!" I replied, "Where did you *go?*"

"I went to Chicago—actually Oak Park, just outside of Chicago. You know, my hometown?"

"But why?" I asked.

"I had to do some thinking. Besides, I hadn't seen my parents' grave in a long time. So I paid them a visit. Then I went to see some friends from college. My uncle Luigi."

"Uncle Luigi? I didn't know you had an uncle Luigi."

"Uh-huh. He owns a chain of Italian restaurants in Chicago.

You didn't think I learned how to make that marinara from you, did you?" he said, smiling down at me.

"But you're not even Italian! How do you have an uncle Luigi?"

"My mother's sister married him, Ange. I am Italian—by marriage, anyway. And I could get a little more Italian right now," he said, reaching between us for the button on my jeans.

"Wait!" I cried, despite the heat that immediately snaked through me. "I thought you were going to Vegas?"

He sighed, realizing he was going to get nowhere fast unless he disclosed to me whatever revelations he had had in Chicago. "I'm not going to Vegas. I don't know what I'd do without New York City. Without you…" He looked down at me, then blew out a breath. "You were right, okay? Even Uncle Luigi said you were—and that was before I told him you were Italian. He thinks I should go back to filmmaking. He even confessed to being pretty pissed off at me for not taking it any further, since he was one of my big investors in the first film I made. So I thought that if I was going to make a movie, I needed it to be about New York. I even had some ideas for the screenplay while I was there. Kind of like *The Godfather* meets *Moonstruck*. You know, a mob flick and a romantic comedy. Except I don't know where I'm going to find a lead actress. I'm thinking about approaching Marisa Tomei."

"Justin!" I said, pushing at his chest while I felt my own bursting with sheer joy.

He smiled. "I love you, you know that? Every anxiety-ridden, insane bit of you."

"*I'm* insane? You're the insane one, buster," I said, pulling him close and kissing him until I felt insane. Insane with desire for him.

And then we did get crazy. All over sofa #3. Then #2 and #1…

Epilogue

Welcome to Manhattan.
Population: Thriving

It was Sunday night, and Justin, Grace and I were in a taxi heading home to Manhattan, which I could already see glittering in the distance. We were coming home from the Villa Napoli in Brooklyn, a glitzy little hall right on Avenue U, where we celebrated the christening of guess who?—Sonny and Vanessa's baby, a little girl, who came into the world not three weeks earlier. I think baby Carmella (named for my Nonnie, much to her delight) was a big surprise to Sonny, who really did think he was getting a son out of the deal. Not that it mattered—Carmella was the apple of her daddy's eye. And my mother's—you often had to battle her for the right to hold the baby, as Carmella spent ninety percent of the time in my mother's arms. Of course, I got to hold her today—at least while the priest baptized her. You see, I was the godmother. And I was pretty good at it, too. Carmella didn't cry once when I held her, but that may have been because Justin was standing by my side the whole time, making funny faces at her over my shoulder.

My mother had practically moved in with Vanessa and Sonny since Carmella had been born, not that Vanessa minded. She liked to have the help, and between my mother and her own mom, she was getting plenty of it. Nonnie, of course, came, too, when she wasn't dragging Artie through Kings Plaza shopping for baby clothes. She claimed this was her way of getting the doctor-recommended exercise, and in truth I think she was wearing her Cobby Cuddlers thin at the soles.

It was warm for a November night, and I'd cracked open a window to let in some air. Besides, the conversation was getting a bit heated for a while there in the cab. We had been conducting the Furniture Negotiations, which I had taken up with Justin once we got in the car, having learned that Joey and Miranda had bought me a giant-screen TV for my apartment (yes, even bigger than the one we had now) and it was being delivered next week. And no, this was not some random act of generosity on my brother's part. It was a congratulations. Because I had just learned that I had landed the part of Lisa Petrelli on *New York Beat,* Lifetime network's newest dramatic series!

Okay, okay—don't get too excited, it's only a pilot. And the part is smallish. I'm nervous about how I'll do—surprise, surprise. But I'm excited to have a real chance to test my actor's wings on the small screen—and I don't mean by flapping them to tone the upper arms.

Speaking of upper arms, Colin's are still looking fabulous. I had lunch with him the other day, and I thought maybe the new *Rise and Shine* studio he was working out of had a spa, since he was positively glowing. But as it turned out, Colin was in love—with none other than Mark Resnick, network executive at Fox and the guy who had been behind the whole push to add *Rise and Shine* to the network's programming. Apparently, Mark was equally smitten, as he and Colin were spending practically every weekend together. And not always alone—because Mark, who was divorced, shared custody of four-year-old Ryan with his ex-wife. It seemed Colin had gotten the kid he longed for— and the love he'd craved—all in one shot. Not to mention a cool Tribeca loft. Well, that was Mark's. But they spent a lot of time there, playing Candyland with Ryan and, get this, teaching him how to skateboard (yes, it was that big a loft).

"You know, you could always donate sofa number three to charity," Grace was saying now, lifting her head from where she had rested it on the back seat and resuming the negotiation once more.

"Not sofa number three!" Justin and I said in unison. It was amazing how attached to that sofa I'd become. Besides, it was wide enough to hold both Justin and me in the horizontal— which you really can't find in too many couches nowadays. I was thinking of having it reupholstered—a little surprise I had in store for Justin.

"We just need to get rid of a couple of the TVs we have," I said. "And maybe the china closet."

"Not the china closet!" Justin protested, eyes wide. "That was Aunt Eleanor's!"

I sighed. Okay, so maybe not the china closet. "I guess we're just gonna have to move to a bigger place. Maybe we can get more space in New Jersey."

"Not New Jersey!" Justin and Grace said together.

I laughed. God, I was *only* kidding.

I looked over at Grace, as she made an argument next for the removal of sofa #2. She was holding her ground pretty well against Justin, who could be formidable when it came to furniture preservation. I could tell Grace was having fun with it. She seemed happier. Maybe because she had finally decided, with the encouragement of her adoptive parents, that she was going to contact her biological mother. "After the holidays," she told me today. "I mean, it might be a bit much to deal with during Christmas."

In truth, I thought it would have been a wonderful Christmas gift for her birth mother to see what kind of beautiful, special person Grace had turned out to be. But I wasn't going to push Grace. I was satisfied to know that she would do it when she was ready. Besides, my mother had already invited her to spend Christmas with us if Grace decided not to go to New Mexico. And you know my mother—it isn't easy saying no to her.

As the conversation quieted again, I rested my head on Justin's shoulder while the cab rolled over the bridge into Manhattan. I was tired. It had been a long day, after all. And I had eaten way too much, judging by the way my new dress (yes, from Bloom-ingdale's—it's not every day you become a godmother, after all) was snugging against me. I also had a load of leftovers my mother had foisted on us as we left, now packed in my Lee and Laurie tote bag, which had been given to me as a going-away present by the Committee. Yes, they even threw me a little party in the office, which turned into—I found out later from Roberta—the office scandal. Apparently Michelle had been found in the supply closet with none other than Jerry Landry! The worst thing about it was that Frankie found out—Doreen couldn't help but do Michelle in when Frankie called that night to find out when (and if) his wife was coming home. But as always happened with Michelle, she somehow managed to benefit from the whole ordeal. For one thing, Frankie made her quit Lee and Laurie. Which was probably the best thing for her, since she was only doing it to support a shopping habit that grew larger every hour she sat there, circling items in the catalog for purchase. But she hadn't gotten off totally scot-free. According to my mother, who had run into Michelle's mother at the supermarket, Michelle and Frankie were seeing a marriage counselor, who just so happened, of course, to be some sort of cousin of Michelle's mom.

And speaking of Michelle's infamous relatives, you'll never guess who Justin and I went to see last week. My dear pal Rudy Michelangelo. No, no, no, silly—we weren't getting the ring. There's plenty of time for that. Besides, Justin and I have other things to pursue right now. We were shopping for little Carmella's cross. Of course, Rudy adored Justin from the moment I came through the door with him. And when we left the shop, Rudy hugged me tight and whispered in my ear, "Now him—him, I'd give a good price."

"Hey, it looks like we're here already," Justin said, blinking sleepily as the cab rolled up before our building. Grace was half-asleep, too, I saw, as I leaned across Justin to kiss her good-night while he forced some money into her hand to cover the fare. Of course Grace started to argue, but we got out and closed the door, waving at her through the glass as the cab pulled away from the curb.

Then Justin and I climbed the stairs, like the old married couple we had been from the start, I guess, our stomachs full, our minds filled with memories of the day—memories I'm sure

Justin had carefully cataloged for that screenplay he's been working on like a madman ever since he came home from Chicago. I had already read the first draft and it was funny, warm, a little hard-edged (I mean, he *was* still a guy and this *was* a mob movie—you had to have a *few* people die brutally, at least in the first few frames). But there was a juicy little part in it that had Angie DiFranco written all over it. I told Justin I would see if I could fit it into my schedule. But I was pretty sure I would do it—no actress in her right mind would turn down a role this good. Justin was already querying investors—many of whom were glad to see that the man behind all that film-festival buzz years ago was back doing what he was best at again.

As was I. And once we entered the apartment, I kissed Justin, hoping to inspire him to that other thing he was oh sooo good at. I wasn't disappointed.

As I drifted off to sleep, curled in Justin's arms, I realized that I had gotten the life I wanted, though with a little more furniture than I'd bargained for.

But it didn't matter. I was really living for the first time in my life. And I had never felt so pleasantly…engaged.

★★★★★

Don't miss Lynda Curnyn's next novel,
BOMBSHELL—
the story of Angie's friend Grace Noonan—
on sale May 2004 from Red Dress Ink